The ARTFUL MATCH

Books by Jennifer Delamere

LONDON BEGINNINGS

The Captain's Daughter
The Heart's Appeal
The Artful Match

LONDON BEGINNINGS · BOOK 3

The
ARTFUL
MATCH

JENNIFER DELAMERE

BETHANYHOUSE
a division of Baker Publishing Group
Minneapolis, Minnesota

© 2019 by Jennifer Harrington

Published by Bethany House Publishers
11400 Hampshire Avenue South
Bloomington, Minnesota 55438
www.bethanyhouse.com

Bethany House Publishers is a division of
Baker Publishing Group, Grand Rapids, Michigan

Printed in the United States of America

Library of Congress Cataloging-in-Publication Data
Names: Delamere, Jennifer, author.
Title: The artful match / Jennifer Delamere.
Description: Minneapolis, Minnesota : Bethany House, a division of Baker
    Publishing Group, [2019] | Series: London beginnings ; Book 3
Identifiers: LCCN 2018042262| ISBN 9780764219221 (trade paper) | ISBN
    9781493417230 (e-book) | ISBN 9780764233210 (hardcover)
Subjects: | GSAFD: Love stories. | Christian fiction.
Classification: LCC PS3604.E4225 A88 2019 | DDC 813/.6—dc23
LC record available at https://lccn.loc.gov/2018042262

Scripture quotations are from the King James Version of the Bible.

This is a work of historical reconstruction; the appearances of certain historical figures are therefore inevitable. All other characters, however, are products of the author's imagination, and any resemblance to actual persons, living or dead, is coincidental.

Cover design by Koechel Peterson & Associates, Inc., Minneapolis, Minnesota/
Jon Godfredson

Author is represented by BookEnds, LLC.

19 20 21 22 23 24 25   7 6 5 4 3 2 1

He maketh the storm a calm, so that
the waves thereof are still.
Then are they glad because they be
quiet; so he bringeth them unto
their desired haven.

—Psalm 107:29–30

Prologue

La Guaira, Venezuela
August 1881

Julia Bernay Stephenson watched as her father carefully stirred honey into his coffee. For years she had thought he was dead, and now, even though it had been a week since she'd found him alive, she still looked at him with wondering eyes.

Paul Bernay didn't exactly match her memory. He was older now, of course, and not as robust, for traumatic events had aged him. There was a tremor in his hands as he set down the spoon and raised the mug to his lips. His speech had been scattered in the beginning, reflecting a frail and troubled mind, but Julia's presence had begun to set him on the mend.

When Julia and her husband, Michael, first walked into this little pub and saw him, the moment had been electric. Julia had known instantly that he was her father.

Paul had taken longer to recognize her. It wasn't until she had thrown her arms around him that he began to respond. Julia couldn't blame him. He hadn't seen her since she was a child, and now she was all grown up and appearing out of the blue.

But then his arms had tightened as he returned her embrace, and he murmured, "Daughter." He had even gleaned which of his daughters was holding him. When he'd said, "My Julia," her heart had swelled with happiness.

Every bitter thought she'd nurtured for years regarding him had vanished in an instant. "Yes, Papa," she had said, clinging to him tightly. "It's your Julia."

It seemed like such a fantastical dream that just a few short months ago, Julia would never have believed it. She was newly married to a man whose love she cherished, and soon she would return to England to begin her medical studies. Best of all, she would bring her father back with her—if she could get him to agree.

That had been a sticking point, because her father was terrified of the idea of returning to England.

The coffee had been brought out by Diego, a young man who filled a variety of positions at this humble oasis in the port town of La Guaira, Venezuela. He spoke good rudimentary English, picked up over the years through his interactions with Paul and with the English and American sailors who spent time here while their ships were in port. Because Paul had not spoken coherently at first, Diego had told them what was known of his story.

Eighteen years ago, Diego's brother was a sailor aboard a merchant ship that visited a small Caribbean island shortly after a hurricane had left it in shambles. The residents who had survived were attempting to piece together their homes and businesses. Under a pile of rubble, they had found Julia's father.

He'd been unconscious after weathering the storm outdoors, clinging to a stubby tree while being pelted with flying debris. No one had seen him before, nor did they have any idea how he'd come to the island. The few hundred residents all knew each other, so this had been a great mystery. Nobody knew what to do with him, for his mind was too scattered to enable him to care for himself.

Diego's brother took pity on the man and persuaded him to come to Venezuela. Diego had been a mere lad of five at the time, but he and Paul—now christened Pablo—had hit it off from the beginning.

"It took months of my mother's gentle care before he would speak more than two words at a time," Diego had explained.

In the years that followed, Paul Bernay had lived with Diego's family much like a kindly but doddering uncle. He was popular with the sailors because he helped them while away idle hours playing checkers and listening to their stories. He took up carving small figurines in wood and made a bit of money now and then selling them.

Pablo never spoke about his past or what had landed him on that island, although many people, including Diego's family, had tried to prod the information from him. They could not tell whether he was being intentionally secretive or whether he was so battered by the storm that he had lost his memory.

Over this past week, Julia had shared with her father all that had happened to the family while he had been away. He still spoke very little, but every day he seemed to grow more able and willing to speak, his words coming out more clearly.

Julia had been trying to coax him into revealing the information he'd kept silent about all these years, and today they finally seemed to be getting somewhere. With careful, gentle questioning, they had been able to take Paul's mind back to the moment he'd realized his ship was heading directly toward a hurricane.

"It was the barometer," her father said. "It was falling—down, down. There was trouble brewing. I could feel it in my bones. After fifteen years at sea, I could feel the weather, as though the winds were talking to me."

"But what happened to the ship, Papa?" Julia asked. Her father had been the ship's second officer and in charge of navigation. Knowing trouble was coming, he surely would have taken the ship to safety.

His hands began to shake again, and he set down his cup, flattening his palms on the table in an effort to stop their involuntary movement.

Julia grasped her father's fingers. They were as cold and rough as sandpaper. She prayed her touch would calm his heart as well as the nervous movement of his hands. "I've told you, Papa. There is nothing for you to fear. The ship was written off as a loss due to the storm. No one in England knows what really happened. There is no one who can harm you now."

Her father shook his head. "The authorities . . ." He looked into her eyes. His own were lined with worry. "If they discover I am alive, there will be questions. There will be trouble."

"I will be there to aid you with any legal issues," Michael assured him. They had already told Paul that Michael was a seasoned barrister.

"If there are secrets we must keep, we will keep them," Julia agreed. A great burden on her heart had been lifted when she'd learned that her father had never planned to abandon them. "Whatever you were caught up in, I know you were innocent—or at the very least, that you were participating against your will."

His hands grasped hers tighter. "How do you know that?"

"It was that conversation I overheard the last night I saw you, when I came to the pub to fetch you for dinner. You were speaking to another man as the two of you came outside. Do you remember? You noticed me standing just on the other side of some crates."

He nodded. "That was one of my captain's henchmen."

Due to misunderstandings fostered by their mother, Julia and her sisters had grown up thinking their father was the captain of a merchant ship. They'd learned only recently that he'd in fact been a second officer.

"You insisted you hadn't heard anything," Paul continued. "I didn't believe you. I told myself it didn't matter. You could not have understood what we were talking about."

"I heard enough to get the wrong idea about why you never came back. I thought you were planning to abandon us."

His hands jerked in surprise. "What did you hear?"

Julia was able to recite it word for word because she'd turned over the sentences so often in her mind. "'I wish to heaven I could be free from the whole lot of them. I had such plans for my life, you know. And it was nothing like this.'" Julia paused, closing her eyes briefly, experiencing the old, familiar wash of pain. "I thought you were speaking about us—your family."

"No," he protested. "I regret every day without you. And Marie—"

He broke down in earnest, tears flowing. No one moved or spoke, allowing him time to grieve. His joy at seeing his daughter again had been tempered by the news that his beloved wife was dead, and his heartache was still fresh, overwhelming him at times.

After a while, Michael quietly pulled a handkerchief from his coat pocket and pushed it in Paul's direction. Paul picked it up and used it to dry his eyes. He examined the high-quality linen for a moment, then gave Michael a look of approval. "You have done well, daughter," he said to Julia.

Julia smiled. Yes, she had. But it was Michael's goodness and honorable character that she was most grateful for, not his ability to buy fine things.

"What did that conversation mean?" she pressed gently.

She and Michael had heard one theory from Charlie Stains, the old sailor who helped them locate her father. Charlie thought Paul might have been caught up in illegal activities related to the American Civil War. If this was true, it could explain why he'd been afraid to return to England.

Paul studied everyone at the table with him, as though weighing whether to speak. Michael had been gradually earning his trust over these days, but Paul seemed to gauge him one last time.

He then looked to Diego, who'd been listening intently. Diego placed a hand over his heart. "I will tell no one, Pablo."

Finally, after surveying the pub and assuring himself that no one else was within earshot, Paul said softly, "Gunrunning."

Julia and Michael exchanged glances. Charlie's guess had been correct.

"We were taking goods to Barbados," her father continued. Now that he'd shared the heart of it, he seemed ready to tell his tale. "We also had a secret stash of munitions to be delivered at a port in the Bahamas. From there, they would go to blockade runners and be smuggled to the Confederates. I said I wanted no part of a scheme that would prolong the evils of war. They told me I had no choice. They threatened my family. My beautiful wife and my precious girls."

His voice cracked on the last phrase. Perhaps he was remembering how young and vulnerable his wife and children had been at the time.

"I had a premonition things weren't going to turn out right. I could feel it as surely as if someone had laid a cold hand on my arm. I tried to jump ship in Barbados, but the captain's ruffians caught me. They beat me unconscious and hauled me back to the ship."

He paused to take a breath and sip more coffee. His voice had picked up strength as he'd gone along. "Now they knew they couldn't trust me. They didn't believe my warnings about the storm, either. No one spoke to me more than was absolutely necessary. There were whispered conversations that stopped when I approached. So I became stealthier in my movements. I overheard enough to piece together their plans. I was going to fall overboard before we got to the Bahamas."

Julia gasped. Michael said, "They were going to murder you?"

Her father's hands shook as he wiped his forehead with the handkerchief. "The next night, I let down a dinghy and escaped. I decided it would be better to die on the open seas than to let those dogs kill me."

"God was with you," Diego said. "You made it to land. They did not."

"When was this? What day?" Julia asked.

"My brother said the hurricane hit that island on the third Sunday in September," Diego supplied. With a tiny smile, he added, "You can believe there was more prayer going on that day than usual."

A memory sparked in Julia's mind of a Sunday shortly after she'd seen her father for the last time. It had been a beautiful, cloudless day in Plymouth, but Julia had been in a funk. Sorrowful thoughts had plagued her ever since her father had left. She had begun to nurture the fear that he would not return.

That afternoon after church, while Cara had been napping and their mother dozing in a chair, Rosalyn had persuaded Julia to go for a walk. They'd climbed their favorite cliff, where they had a view of the sparkling sea. Julia had confided her fears to Rosalyn, and Rosalyn had suggested they pray for their father. Perhaps those simple prayers of two children had helped save him.

Yes, people had been praying that day. And even if they didn't know exactly what they were praying for, God had answered them nonetheless.

Moonlight shimmered on the water, making a silver trail for the ship to follow as it sailed eastward across the Atlantic Ocean.

At last, they were going home.

Julia said a prayer for her father, now asleep in a cabin below. Despite relatively calm seas, sleep had not come easily for him. Michael had managed to allay his concerns about the legal difficulties of returning to England, but the terrors he'd endured during the hurricane remained embedded in his soul. In the end, only his love for his daughters and his powerful desire to be reunited with them had induced him to board this ship.

As Julia gazed at the sea, she envisioned her sisters' joy when she presented them with their father. It was as if he were raised from the dead, given that for nearly twenty years they had believed him gone.

Except for Cara. She had never once stopped believing their father was alive. She had clung to that hope like an anchor through the storms of life. Julia felt more than a little chagrin at all the times she'd berated her sister for building castles in the air. Cara had been right all along. Julia, with her supposedly clear-eyed view of the world, had learned that sometimes the "sensible" path wasn't the right one after all.

She heard a familiar tread behind her. Smiling to herself, she closed her eyes, waiting in anticipation.

Michael's arm slipped around her waist. "What are you pondering, my love?"

Julia leaned against his chest and said dreamily, "I'm thinking how nice it is sometimes to leave common sense by the wayside."

She felt his chest move as he chuckled. "That's quite a statement coming from you, soon-to-be Dr. Julia."

She didn't bother to explain. Instead, she took a moment to savor being in his arms. They'd been married such a short time, and yet she could not remember, in any tangible way, how she'd lived her life before him. "To be honest, I was thinking of how overjoyed Cara will be. I hope it will make up for my leaving England with no warning."

Julia still felt remorse over not sharing her plans with her sisters. Only after the fact had she written them letters revealing that she and Michael had been quietly married on a Monday morning and were going to Venezuela on their honeymoon. She had not explained why they were making such an unusual journey, lest she raise hopes that would turn out to be false.

The letters had gone into the red postbox at the railway station just minutes before Julia and Michael boarded the train for Southampton. By presenting her sisters with a *fait accompli*, she had hoped to lessen their worry. If they knew her plans ahead of time, they would have fretted endlessly over how to dissuade her. It would have been a terrible strain on them all. The logic was sound, but it hadn't alleviated her feelings of guilt.

Michael stroked the back of her neck, a gesture that soothed and relaxed her. "Any anger she feels will disappear as soon as she lays eyes on your father."

Julia could hardly wait. It was a homecoming that was the stuff of dreams.

CHAPTER
1

IT WAS GOING TO BE A FINE DAY—no matter what anyone else might say about it.

This was Caroline Bernay's firm resolution as she packed up the drawing supplies for her and four-year-old Robbie. After a week of nearly relentless rain, the morning had finally dawned dry, although the sun was filtered by dark clouds that looked delightfully ominous. Cara couldn't wait to try her hand at capturing them on paper.

Filled with anticipation for the day, she went down the back stairs to the servants' hall. There, she found the butler sitting at the long table, drinking tea while reading yesterday's newspaper.

"Shame on you for dilly-dallying, Mr. Lowe," Cara teased, although in truth she was happy to see him sitting there. He never took the luxury of a morning break unless Sir John and Lady Needenham were both gone from the house.

"And may I ask what mischief *you* are up to?" he returned. His voice was curt, but there was humor in it. He was used to Cara's teasing by now.

"Mrs. James promised to make a picnic lunch for Robbie and me. Robbie is desperate to play outside."

He frowned. "You know the entire kitchen staff have their hands full preparing for the dinner party."

"All the more reason why it is good that we shall be out of your hair all day."

The butler turned his eyes heavenward. "Small favors."

Cara smiled and went off to find the cook.

"This is the perfect spot," Cara announced as she and Robbie reached the crest of the rise. "Great views all around."

"It's windy up here," Robbie observed, grabbing his hat before the wind could snatch it away.

"Yes, but see what interesting things it is doing to the clouds." She pointed at the clouds being whisked across the sky, forming beautiful patterns as they went.

Robbie didn't even look up. His gaze was focused on a stream that ran along a stand of trees at the bottom of the hill. "Can't we go and play down there?"

"We'll do that after you've had your lunch." *And a nap*, she silently added to herself. But she knew better than to say it aloud. Robbie was far easier to get down for a nap if he didn't see it coming. She spread out the blanket she'd brought and set the picnic basket on top to keep it anchored against the breeze. "See, I even got the cook to pack some buttermilk for us to have with our sandwiches."

"Hooray!" Robbie immediately turned his attention to the picnic basket. He loved buttermilk and had not yet figured out the connection between consuming it and becoming drowsy. Cara was not usually so ruthless about getting him to nap, but today she was under strict orders from Lady Needenham that Robbie should be rested so he could stay up past his usual bedtime for a brief presentation to their dinner guests tonight. Cara would benefit from this plan, too: while Robbie was sleeping, she could sketch. She'd brought along a pad and some drawing wax. It was all she could manage to bring, since she was also carrying the blanket and food.

After they'd enjoyed chicken sandwiches, fruit, and biscuits washed down with buttermilk, Robbie said, "Can we go for a walk now? I saw a rabbit down by the brook."

"We'll go in a bit." Cara knew the delay would give time for the digesting food to bring on sleepiness. "Look, is that a ladybug?" She pointed toward the grass at the edge of the blanket.

Robbie stretched out on his stomach with his chin propped on one hand to study the ladybug. He watched as it crawled along on a stem of grass. After a while he tired of that and began to riffle through the clovers, looking for any with four leaves. He wasn't yet sleeping, but the yawn he gave was an indication he would be soon. Cara knew the signs. His hand movements became less frequent and eventually stopped altogether as he fell into a doze.

Cara pulled out her pad and drawing implements, happy the clouds were still presenting a dramatic tension to the idyllic fields below. In her sketch, she included Robbie, too. He looked charming with his head on one arm and a few clovers in his hand. Although she loved painting landscapes, she found special joy in drawing portraits. It was so satisfying to capture a person's look or attitude in just the right way.

Soon Cara found herself yawning, too. She'd stayed up far too late finishing a gothic novel. Once she'd found the corner shelf in the library that held Lady Needenham's favorite books, Cara had begun devouring them all. Why hadn't anyone told her, when forcing her to plod through dry tomes for school, that some books could actually be *fun*?

Setting aside her drawing wax, she stretched out on her back and looked up at the clouds moving at a solemn pace across the murky sky. White and gray in a multitude of shades—more than she could find a name for. How fascinating, she thought idly, that God could make a rainbow out of hues of gray. . . .

The breeze rustled the trees below, adding a gentle hum to the murmur of the brook. A perfectly imperfect day.

"Miss Bernay?" Robbie's voice was soft, seemingly coming from a long way away.

"Hmm?"

But she didn't hear anything else. His voice faded into the landscape of her dreams.

Cara only realized she had drifted off when a fluttering movement sent a breath of air across her face and startled her awake. She sat up, blinking, trying to gauge the time. The sun's position seemed far advanced, although it was difficult to tell because the cloud cover had gotten heavier, obscuring the sun. She felt stiff and a little cold. They must have both slept longer than they'd intended. Far from being cranky tonight, Robbie might be too energized to sleep. She'd have to ensure they took a brisk walk before returning home, if they had time.

She turned to wake the boy, but the blanket next to her was empty. She looked around, her gaze widening from the immediate area to the larger meadow and then down toward the brook with worry. There was no sign of him.

"Robbie!" she shouted. "Where are you?"

There was no answer.

"Robbie!" Cara repeated the call louder this time, trying to quell the urge to panic. How could she have fallen into such a deep sleep? It wasn't like her to sleep so soundly during daylight hours.

She hurried down the hill. Robbie was bound to be somewhere along the water's edge or in the trees beyond. Slipping on a patch of mud caused by yesterday's rain, Cara murmured, "Robbie, if you've soiled your clothes, I won't take you outside for a month." But her threats were useless if she couldn't find him first.

To her growing alarm, Robbie seemed to be nowhere. Over the next hour she covered every inch of ground he might reasonably have traveled, reprimanding herself the entire time for having been so negligent.

At last she returned to the foot of the hill where they'd picnicked. She paused, wiping sweat from her brow. The sun was definitely low on the horizon. The clouds, which had seemed appealing earlier today, now only threatened. She would have to return to the house and get help. She would have to admit to Sir John that she had lost his son. She was terrified at the thought of Robbie being out in the dark. How in the world could he have traveled so far?

Tears began trickling down her cheeks, matched by the newly falling rain.

It was raining on a lost child.

Leaving behind everything she had brought with her, Cara took off at a run toward the manor house.

The hours that followed were perhaps the worst Cara had endured since her mother died. The disruption of the Needenhams' orderly household, the ruin of their elegant soiree, and most of all, the fear in Lady Needenham's eyes—these added more fuel to the guilt already consuming her.

Sir John hastily organized a search party comprised of four servants, several dogs, and two of the gentlemen from the dinner party who volunteered to come along. Starting at the picnic area, the dogs eagerly followed Robbie's scent.

Dusk became night, and they continued the search by lantern light. The dogs drew them onward, all the way to the hedges lining the fence at the far edge of the estate. All at once they clustered around one of the bushes, wriggling and wagging their tails. They were too well-trained to bark but emitted enthusiastic high-pitched growls. One of the footmen held his lantern high to light the area. Cara let out a cry of thanksgiving. Robbie was asleep under the bush.

The boy opened his eyes when one of the hounds began to sniff his face. "Jack?" He murmured the dog's name, his voice raspy and his expression dazed. Even by the wavering light of the lantern, Cara could see his cheeks were pale and he was shivering.

"Robbie!" She lunged forward to pick him up.

The steely arm of Sir John stopped her. *"Don't go near him."*

His words carried the force of a threat. He had barely kept his anger at bay these past few hours, only tolerating Cara's presence because he needed her to show them where to begin the search. Now that they had found his son, Sir John only seemed doubly furious.

Cara obeyed, watching as Sir John scooped the child into his arms. Robbie turned instinctively into his father's chest, nestling there. Cara's heart pinched at the tenderness of it. Sir John's first words to his son, however, held reprimand. "Robbie, why did you wander so far away from Miss Bernay?"

Robbie rubbed his eyes, still not entirely awake. "I was following the bunny. I wanted to see where he lived. Miss Bernay didn't want to come. She was sleeping."

"Yes. I know." Sir John shot Cara a look. She shrank back, feeling the weight of his justified rage.

"Are you angry, Papa?" Robbie's voice was plaintive.

Sir John pressed the boy close to his chest. "You must promise never to do that again."

Cara had often thought Sir John lukewarm in his affection for the boy. Watching him now, she understood how wrong she'd been to judge him so unfairly.

Robbie began to shiver violently.

"Where's that blanket?" Sir John barked.

A footman stepped forward, pulling a blanket from an oilcloth pouch. In no time, the boy was bundled up and securely in his father's arms again. Sir John turned without another word and began walking with long, swift strides toward home.

Cara and the others followed in his wake. The footman gave her a sympathetic glance, but she was so crushed by remorse that she could not bring herself to acknowledge his attempt to make her feel better. This child now looked terribly ill, and it was her fault. And if the worst should happen . . . She gasped, needing air, and began to pray fervently as they trudged along the muddy track. Even if Robbie fully recovered, everything had changed. Sir John would soon give full vent to his anger, and it would be directed squarely at her.

It was, she thought miserably, no less than she deserved.

Dawn arrived feeble and wet, the sun barely piercing through heavy gray clouds. Cara sat by the window in her room, as she'd done for the past four days, staring out at the sodden landscape and praying.

The day after their nighttime search for Robbie, fever had set in, and he appeared to be getting worse.

Her back and neck ached, but she kept her vigil. With her door adjoining the nursery left open, she could see the door to Robbie's bedroom on the other side. It was closed. Those coming and going from the sick child's room used another door that opened onto the main hallway.

Cara's room was located near the top of the stairs, and she could easily hear all who went by: the servants, the doctor, Sir John. She did not think Lady Needenham ever left her son's bedside. Cara had been instructed in no uncertain terms to remain in her room. Only once did she dare break this command, and that was to tiptoe through the nursery late one night. She'd put her ear to the door of Robbie's room and heard her ladyship crying, imploring her son to be strong and get better.

Heartsick, Cara had slumped back to her chair and resumed her own feverish prayers. She had kept praying through the long days that had followed. As she faced yet another dismal dawn, helplessness welled up within her. Why should God listen to her prayers? What were they but desperate pleas to be saved from the consequences after her own negligence had endangered the life of a child?

She ought to have known a catastrophe like this would happen. Her life with the Needenhams had been going well, but that could not negate the truth that Cara had never been able to keep anything for too long without ruining it. She ought never to have been entrusted with a child's care. Even though she'd spent two years overseeing the little ones at the orphanage where she had grown up, there had always been an adult present—especially after one of the toddlers had climbed on a chair to look out an open window and nearly fallen out. Although it was never stated aloud, the staff must have known that Cara was too inept to keep the children safe.

Shivering as the morning chill permeated the window, Cara

wiped back a tear. It had been a bleak, overcast day just like this when Mama had died. The kind of day her mother, who flourished on sunny days, had hated. Cara was the only other person in the room when her mother had finally slipped away after a long illness. *"Watch over her,"* Rosalyn had said. *"Julia and I are just going to make tea."*

Cara had tried her best. But she'd wanted only to snuggle up to her mother as she'd often done before Mama became too weak to hold her. Craving the comfort of her mother's arms, Cara had climbed into the bed. Mama had placed a feeble hand on her head, murmuring a few weak and unintelligible phrases. At that moment, it had been enough for Cara. She had not realized that whatever her mother had said, they were her final words. Cara had dozed off, and the next thing she knew, she was awakened by the sound of Rosalyn crying out in distress. Mama had died, and Cara had not prevented it.

No matter how often her sisters told her it was a foolish notion—that Cara was only six and that Mama would have died even if Cara had been awake—Cara knew in the depths of her heart that it was her fault. She had not kept watch, and the consequences had been terrible.

Propped up on the windowsill in front of Cara was the drawing she'd made of Robbie the day he'd gotten lost. It was smeared from the rain, and his face was barely recognizable. But in her mind's eye, she saw him with crystal clarity, running across the field, vibrant with life.

Please, God, don't let him die. I promise I will never, ever do anything so foolish again. I will change. I will be different.

She had been praying this for days to no avail. Did the Almighty think they were empty words? Perhaps He knew she could not be trusted to carry out her promise. She would always fall short, no matter how sincere she was. Exhausted from sleeplessness and worry, Cara decided she must change her prayer.

Dear God, please allow Robbie to live, and I promise I will not watch over children ever again. I will find a different occupation—one where I cannot endanger an innocent life.

With this prayer, Cara was offering up everything she had. She loved Robbie. The prospect of leaving him was crushing her heart. It was sorrowful enough, without adding the fact that she would once more be without work or a place to live. But wasn't the life of this boy worth it?

Yes. Yes, it was.

Cara allowed the tears to fall unabated as she repeated her new prayer.

Later, when the sun was higher and endeavoring to gather strength to break through the clouds, Cara heard a commotion coming from Robbie's room. Lady Needenham cried out, and there was rapid talking from the men. Cara heard a fervency in their words that ratcheted up every one of her fears. She bolted from her seat, wringing her hands and wishing for the millionth time that she could see for herself how her beloved little boy was faring.

Someone left Robbie's room and scurried down the hallway. Cara cracked open her door and saw a maid rapidly descending the stairs. Something had most definitely changed. She dared to cross the nursery and place an ear to Robbie's door. She heard Sir John and the doctor in earnest conversation. Cara no longer heard her ladyship's voice, but she had a vision of her seated in a chair, crying. What was the cause?

Hearing the door to her adjoining bedroom open and someone entering, Cara raced back to it, alarmed at being caught. To her relief, it was Esther, one of the kitchen maids. She was carrying a tray of food for Cara's luncheon. Esther had been bringing her meals ever since Cara had been consigned to her room. Each time, the maid offered condolences and comfort, a kindness that Cara had received from no one else since the bedraggled search party had returned with the sick child.

Cara knew that Esther was a trusted servant who was always privy to what was going on in the family. "Esther, what is happening in Robbie's room? Do you know?"

The maid set down the tray and turned to face Cara. She was smiling. "Yes, miss. Master Robbie's fever has broken."

CHAPTER

2

LONDON

HENRY KNEW, just by the way his mother entered his study, why she was here. Viola Burke, the Countess of Morestowe, never failed to telegraph her feelings through her actions—especially when she was furious at one person in particular.

He sighed and stood up, throwing his pen on the desk and splattering ink across the papers he'd been reading. Not that it mattered. Marring the documents couldn't make their content any worse. He already had a headache from dealing with it, and his mother wasn't going to make things any better.

He said, with grim resignation, "What's she done now?"

The countess crossed her arms and drew herself up to her full height, which was considerable. At nearly six feet tall, she made a daunting figure, even with her slender frame. "If you are referring to Amelia, she has gone tearing out of the house. For all I know, she's halfway across London by now. We'll probably have to send out the dogs to find her. If you are referring to *Miss Leahy*"—she paused, allowing all her disapproval for the governess to fill the void—"she had the temerity to tell me I wasn't disciplining the girl properly."

"Well, she *is* supposed to be an expert in these matters."

"That doesn't give her the right to address me as though I were also under her authority."

It wasn't the first time she had lodged this complaint. Henry understood why the governess irked her so. Miss Leahy's manner was too brusque when a more circumspect approach would yield better results with the countess. His mother had deeply entrenched ideas about how servants—including governesses—should keep to their station.

Henry held up an appeasing hand. "I'll speak with her. In the meantime, shouldn't we send out that search party for Amelia?" If she truly was running loose in the streets, that was by far the greater concern.

"That won't be necessary, sir." Miss Leahy appeared at the study door, looking disheveled but triumphant. She pushed her wire-rimmed glasses up her nose and wiped a loose strand of hair from her forehead. "I found her just outside, in the shrubbery edging the house."

Miss Leahy was as wiry as the countess, although much shorter. She couldn't be more than forty years old, but her hair was already showing streaks of gray. Henry thought her choice of occupation—a governess who specialized in difficult children—might have something to do with that.

"And where is the girl now?" the countess demanded.

"I sent her upstairs with the nursery maid. She is to sit quietly and think over how she ought better to behave."

"A lot of good that will do!" his mother returned. "She ought to be here, apologizing to me for her wretched behavior. And furthermore, she is not to be given her tea until she does so."

Miss Leahy frowned. "I do not think a child can be coerced into proper behavior."

"Of course she can!" the countess shot back in exasperation. "It's called *discipline*. It's the hallmark of any well-bred person. It's no use making excuses for why Amelia is out of control. She is so because you allow her to be."

Miss Leahy drew herself up. "With all due respect, your ladyship,

25

I believe she acts badly because you push her too hard. Some children respond better to a light touch."

This comment didn't even penetrate his mother's steely resolve. "I demand you do your job and get that child down here right now."

Miss Leahy turned her gaze to Henry, appealing to him to take her side. She had no recourse against his mother except when Henry intervened. He wanted to but refrained. After all, what did he know about raising children? His mother was better qualified on that front, even if she had been a less-than-perfect parent.

On the other hand, Miss Leahy's years of experience with troubled children could not be discounted. In the six months she'd been here, she had proven herself right in many situations regarding Amelia. Unfortunately, he could not risk pushing his mother's ire too far, or there would be worse things to contend with than whether Amelia got her tea.

Suppressing a sigh, he said, "Miss Leahy, please do as Lady More-stowe requests."

"Very well." A flash of anger in the governess's eyes punctuated her response. She turned on her heel and left the room.

Immediately Henry had second thoughts. Should he have taken her side after all? Was it possible that if she were continually forced to go against her better judgment, she would resign? He didn't want to search for another governess. It had taken months to find Miss Leahy. He could not have foreseen that she and his mother would develop such animosity toward one another.

The countess pointed an angry finger toward the door Miss Leahy had just exited. "You see how I am treated. Furthermore, Amelia is going from bad to worse. Miss Leahy's condescension only makes her bolder. Today is a prime example."

Henry thought she was overstating things. Although Amelia still had her bad days—such as today—he thought that overall they were making headway.

He also thought Miss Leahy was a vast improvement over the previous governess. Miss Gunther had managed, through use of an iron hand, to keep Amelia in line. But Henry had let her go when it was discovered her punishments veered into unacceptable territory. He was not averse to gentler forms of corporal discipline, but he could not countenance abuse. By contrast, Miss Leahy had infused kindness and understanding into her discipline of Amelia. At times, it seemed to have the desired effect. But this past week had devolved into a series of endless battles. Amelia was in full-scale rebellion, and Henry was at a loss to explain why.

Wiping his forehead, he went to the window in a vain effort to find a breeze. He thought of Amelia being found under a bush. It was probably cooler there than anywhere in the house. It was early August, and the real heat had set in. It put everyone's tempers on edge.

The weather in London was hot and dry, but Essex had been deluged with rain, delaying the completion of critical repairs needed to make his estate habitable again after the fire. Henry and the others had been stuck in town far past the time when everyone else had left for the countryside. As he looked out at the traffic, it occurred to him that perhaps the answer was to get out of the city anyway. Amelia's favorite toy was a brightly painted wooden boat. She loved the water and had been begging to go to the seaside.

He turned back to his mother. "You shouldn't stay in London. It isn't fair to you or the child. She longs to run and play outside, and who can blame her? Perhaps you should spend a few weeks at the seaside."

Her face brightened at the thought but was quickly soured by a frown. "You would *reward* the child for misbehaving?"

It was astounding how quickly she could turn a negative outlook to anything. "Think of it as relief for you. It will be cooler there, and Amelia is not as testy when she isn't cooped up."

"That's true." She thought this over. "It doesn't make me any more approving of Miss Leahy's methods."

"At least she's willing to do the job. Such people haven't been easy to come by." *Or to keep.* Miss Leahy was the third governess in almost as many years. He wasn't going to lose her if he could help it.

Although not entirely mollified, his mother gave a sigh of acceptance. "I shall make plans for us to leave for Brighton as soon as possible. I

27

might have preferred someplace more fashionable, but there's no point in advertising to the world what sort of child you are keeping for a ward."

"Thank you." Henry was hard-pressed to keep the sarcasm out of his voice.

"I am sorry to say, that child is turning out to be more badly behaved than her father was at that age. I hadn't thought such a thing was possible, but there it is."

The mention of Amelia's father made Henry grimace. He hadn't yet told his mother about Langham's disappearance from the sanitarium. Given her current mood, he certainly wasn't going to raise the subject now.

A heavy *thump-thump* on the stairs signaled that Amelia was coming down as directed. Ever since the countess had reprimanded her overly energetic way of moving, telling her that "the step of a lady must always be light and graceful," the girl had taken to deliberately sounding like an elephant on the stairs.

The countess gave a shudder of annoyance. "I warn you, Henry, my patience is growing thin."

Patience isn't all that is growing thin, Henry thought morosely. Money was, too. Amelia and Langham were both wasting time and precious resources. Henry always had to be the one who kept things on track. He knew it was childish to harbor the feeling that this wasn't *fair*. After all, as the eldest son, it was up to him to shoulder the family burdens. But he resented that his unstable younger brother was making those burdens far heavier than they ought to be. Henry could only hope to locate Langham before he caused any irreparable damage.

Miss Leahy entered the room, her right hand firmly gripping the seven-year-old who was the cause of this strife. Amelia's face and white pinafore were smudged with dirt, and she was glowering in the countess's general direction without actually looking at her.

"Amelia, what have you to say to her ladyship?" Miss Leahy prompted.

"I'm sorry that I was rude and disrespectful to you earlier, ma'am." Amelia's words were mechanical, like a recitation in a badly acted play. The flat look in her eyes as she met the countess's gaze confirmed that she was speaking by compulsion and not from any sincere regret.

"And how will you behave toward me at all times in the future?" the countess demanded.

"With respect, ma'am."

"And why must you treat me with respect?"

"Because you are my elder."

If his mother noticed the slightly peculiar emphasis Amelia had placed on *elder*, she thankfully chose to ignore it. "I forgive you this time, but mind you don't forget this lesson in the future."

Everything was officially solved, but the air still crackled with discontent. Henry clapped his hands and said with false brightness, "Well, that's that. I believe it's time for tea."

"Yes, that will be all."

Having given Amelia and Miss Leahy this dismissal, the countess looked at them expectantly, waiting for them to go. They looked more than ready to do so, but Henry stopped them.

"I'd like to speak with Amelia for just another minute, if you please." He spoke with the same brusqueness as his mother, because if she thought Henry intended to further reprimand the girl, she would be happy to leave and not feel as though *she'd* been the one dismissed. Sure enough, she lifted her chin with the air of a victor and sailed from the room.

Amelia stared daggers at her back, frowning at the door even after the countess was out of sight.

Henry walked over to her and crouched down so he would be at eye level with her, drawing her attention back to him. She regarded him with wide hazel eyes.

He said, "Thank you for apologizing to Lady Morestowe."

Her expression didn't change. "Miss Leahy said there would be currant tarts for tea."

"I see," Henry replied gravely.

He felt an urge to laugh, even though finding humor in this situation was as wrong as Amelia expecting payment for good behavior. He ought to be supporting the reproof his mother had given her. After all, Langham's incorrigible behavior probably stemmed from the way he had been overindulged as a child. Maybe this knowledge was lodged in his mother's heart as well. Maybe her drive to discipline Amelia was a misguided attempt to make up for Langham. Amelia was her grandchild, after all—even though no one except the countess and Henry knew it.

Looking at Amelia now, Henry felt sorry for her despite her bad behavior. He knew how hard it must be for a child to be restrained by such ruthless boundaries. Amelia had so much energy and no good outlet for it.

"I do not in any way condone your behavior today toward Lady Morestowe." He paused to allow his words to sink in. She continued to watch him, waiting warily for whatever would come next. He gave her a little smile. "However, I do sympathize with the fact that we've had to stay in London longer than anticipated. I know you're anxious to leave this hot and crowded city and return home."

Her eyes lit with a tiny ray of hope. "Is the house ready?"

"I'm sorry to say we still have several more weeks to wait. However, in the meantime, we're going to arrange for you to take a trip to the seaside. What do you think of that?"

Amelia's mouth widened in happy surprise. "Oh yes!"

Her response was not surprising, but Henry found it surprisingly gratifying.

"That's very kind of you, sir," Miss Leahy said.

"Perhaps the two of you can continue your nature studies. I'm sure the area will afford plenty of opportunities for that—in addition to recreation and sea bathing, of course."

"Will it be just me and Miss Leahy?" Amelia said hopefully.

Henry straightened. "No, Lady Morestowe will accompany you." As he expected, Amelia pouted at this. "You will have plenty of time to play outside and explore the beach," he reminded her. "I expect you probably won't even see her for most of the day. She will have her own pursuits. But when you are with her, you must always be on your best behavior. That doesn't sound too onerous, does it?"

"It sounds quite pleasant," Miss Leahy put in. "Amelia, after tea you can decide which books and toys you want to take."

Amelia started nodding at the word *tea*, and visions of currant tarts probably kept her from hearing the rest. "Can I go now?" she said to Henry.

"May I please be excused," Miss Leahy corrected.

"May I please be excused?" Amelia parroted.

"You may," he said.

Henry could tell Amelia was happy because the noise as she took the stairs, while still too loud, sounded more like excitement than a mere desire to irritate his mother.

Was he doing the right thing? Or was he rewarding a child for misbehavior? He couldn't say. He could only pray that his decisions would help the child and were not foolish indulgences that would harm her character in the long run. But seeing her joy over the trip to the seaside, he understood why his mother had at times chosen to be lenient. There was something about making a child happy that did good to one's soul.

He had a moment of disappointment that Amelia had not asked whether Henry was coming with them. But that was foolish. He was not her father, and he had never encouraged her to think of him that way. He was her guardian only, doing his best to handle a daunting task that had been committed to him through no fault of his own. But really, he was Amelia's uncle, too, even if he could never publicly admit this. Maybe that gave him license to grant her a few wishes from time to time and the right to feel satisfaction in doing so.

Henry returned to his desk. With the current crisis averted, it was time to turn his worries back to his brother. The letter from the sanitarium's director could provide only one clue to Langham's possible whereabouts. Another patient recalled Langham talking excessively about how he wanted to join some friends in St. Ives. He desired to *study the spectacular light that is to be found there.* Not only was Langham still obsessed with this foolish idea of becoming an artist, now he'd devised a new way to waste time and money. He was bound to find plenty of excuses to drink heavily in addition to painting, which would be a big setback to his recovery. So to save his brother from himself, Henry would have to trek all the way across southwest England in order to bring him home.

The irony was that Langham was ultimately responsible for the other problem Henry had just handled. Henry wanted desperately to disclose to his brother all they had done to protect him. But now was not the right time. It never seemed the right time. Each passing year only made the truth harder to reveal.

For now, Henry must concentrate on finding Langham and figuring out how to get him to act like a responsible adult.

It was far more difficult than dealing with a recalcitrant seven-year-old. Even if it seemed, in many ways, remarkably similar.

CHAPTER

3

CARA WALKED SLOWLY down the staircase, her feet dragging on every step. She shouldn't keep the Needenhams waiting, yet she was reluctant to face what was to come. God had heard her prayers, and now she must keep the vow she'd made to Him.

Sir John had sent word for her to meet them in the parlor. Lady Needenham habitually spent her mornings here, because the sunlight pouring through the large window was excellent for reading and needlework. As Cara entered, she saw that although the lady was seated in her favorite chair, her hands were idle in her lap. Sir John stood at her side, one hand resting lightly on her shoulder. It was the first time Cara had been in their presence since the night they'd brought Robbie home. Lady Needenham looked tired. She offered Cara a tiny smile, but her lips wavered and there was a dullness in her eyes that hinted she'd not entirely overcome this ordeal.

By contrast, Sir John's displeasure radiated from him despite his composed bearing. When he spoke, it was with icy formality. "I assume you are aware that Robbie's fever has broken and that he is on the mend."

"Yes, sir," Cara replied. "It is wonderful news."

Sir John's frown only deepened. "You are lucky no serious harm came to him."

"Yes, sir." She did not dare contradict him by stating what she knew to be the truth: that God, not luck, had saved the boy.

Lady Needenham, however, murmured, "God be thanked."

Sir John did not even seem to notice it. His attention was fixed on Cara. "Although this event has reached a happy outcome, it does not change the fact that your irresponsible actions nearly caused our son's death."

The words pierced her soul, but they were true. Cara offered a sorrowful nod.

"Furthermore, you must understand that we cannot allow such gross negligence on the part of one of our staff to go unpunished. Your employment with us is hereby terminated. You will leave this house immediately."

Immediately? Cara felt a jolt of worried surprise. For all the time she'd spent alone with her worries and prayers, she'd not spared a single thought to where she would go.

Perhaps noticing her dismay, Sir John added, "We will give you the rest of this day to get your things together, but you will be gone before luncheon tomorrow."

This was the outcome Cara had anticipated, and yet now that it was here, she found her heart could not fully accept it. She looked to Lady Needenham. Her ladyship had always been fond of Cara, praising her for the way she was able to keep up with such an active child and generally ensure he was where he was supposed to be at the appointed times. The lady's eyes were misty, but she nodded in affirmation of her husband's words.

"That will be all." Sir John dismissed Cara crisply, expecting her to leave with no other words passing between them.

But she couldn't leave before she'd apologized. Not that she hadn't given countless apologies as they spent hours looking for Robbie. Still, she had to make one final attempt. "If I may say, sir and madam, how deeply sorry I am for what has happened. I have been chastising myself continually."

34

Something flickered in Sir John's eyes, but it wasn't warmth. "No doubt you were worried about losing your position. Meanwhile, we have spent these days worrying we'd lose our only son."

Lady Needenham visibly winced at her husband's harsh words. She said quietly, "Thank you, Miss Bernay. We have no doubt that you care for Robbie. The circumstances are regrettable, but you can see why the actions we are taking are necessary."

"Yes, ma'am." Cara wished she could tell them of the penance she planned to pay. But Sir John looked pointedly at the door, reminding her she'd already been dismissed.

Cara gave them a small curtsy and turned away, blinking back tears. In the main hall she paused at the foot of the wide staircase, placing a steadying hand on the railing and trying to regain her breath, as though preparing to climb a mountain and not simply a staircase.

Hearing steps behind her, she turned to see the butler approaching.

In the past, Mr. Lowe's attitude toward Cara had generally been good-natured condescension. He had a lighthearted streak, despite his dignified role. Now, however, his manner was grave and unsmiling. "His lordship has directed me to oversee the details of getting you to the railway station tomorrow."

Given the circumstances, his words were kindly phrased. He might have said, *"My job is to ensure you get out in a timely manner."*

Her throat tightened. "Thank you."

Mr. Lowe motioned for her to walk up the stairs with him. As they went, he said, "I also need to know where to ship your trunk. I don't imagine you'll be able to carry everything away with you tomorrow."

"I hadn't thought of that," she admitted. "I haven't given much thought to anything. Except Robbie."

"It has been a difficult week for everyone," Mr. Lowe pointed out. "His lordship was absolutely beside himself. And milady—"

"She never left his side." Cara recalled the haunted look in her ladyship's eyes and knew she was responsible for putting it there. She gave a despondent sigh.

"This was the first time their child has been in such serious jeopardy. We cannot be surprised if they need time to recover."

Mr. Lowe's observation was thoughtful. Cara realized with gratitude that he seemed to direct no malice toward her.

"I love that boy!" Cara exclaimed, desperate to share her sorrow with anyone who would spare her some empathy. "I would never wish any harm on him."

"I have no doubt of it."

They reached Cara's door. Mr. Lowe glanced up and down the hallway. "If I may speak to you a moment in private?" They stepped into Cara's room, and the butler pulled a purse from his pocket and placed it in her hands. "Some members of the staff took up a collection. We hope it will help ease the transition."

The purse was small, but the weight of it felt like a lifeline. Cara had never been good at saving money, despite Julia's constant harping that she ought to prepare for a rainy day. "I-I'm overwhelmed."

This display of kindness was more than she had expected. Finances were tight for everyone, and Cara was humbled that the staff had been willing to share their hard-earned money with her.

Impulsively, she gave Mr. Lowe a hug, then pulled away, embarrassed at herself for such a breach of protocol. "Oh! I beg your pardon—"

He gave her a kindly smile that held a touch of his former teasing. "Things certainly will not be the same without you, Miss Bernay."

"Small favors," she said, repeating his quip on the morning of the picnic. She found herself smiling despite her tears.

"Do you have any idea where you will go?"

Cara hated to admit that she did not. After nearly two years with the Needenhams, she didn't even know where to look for work.

Then it occurred to her that the answer was obvious. Unlike the last time she'd been out of work, her sisters were in a position to offer aid. Rosalyn was married, and Julia was engaged to a wealthy barrister.

Rosalyn and her husband, Nate, were touring northern England with a traveling production of *The Pirates of Penzance*. But Julia was in London, and Cara had to admit she was the best person to turn to for advice. Her sister's admonitions were invariably difficult medicine to swallow, but she was always annoyingly right.

Mr. Lowe was looking at her expectantly, waiting for an answer.

"I'm going to London," Cara said.

Perhaps things would not be so bad after all. Perhaps, after doing it so many times, starting over was the one thing Cara was good at.

Henry had the driver stop at the top of the hill. When the carriage he'd hired at the railway station came to a halt, he got down and walked to the edge of the road, looking out over the valley below. Just as he did every time he came here.

He stared down at the foundry, which was alive with activity. The name *Reese Cast-Iron Products* was proudly painted in bold white letters on the largest of the red-brick buildings that clustered around an open yard filled with wagons. Smoke belched from tall chimney stacks, sending out a smell that was not unpleasant to Henry. It spoke to him of men at work, of products that would improve people's lives. This was a world so different from the one he usually inhabited, and it always invigorated him.

In the main yard, workers were loading wagons with crates of various sizes. Some cargo was so large it required a pulley lift. Four men were operating one now, while two others guided the crate into place on a sturdy wagon. Soon a team of draft horses would be brought out from the stable that stood a comfortable distance away from the buildings that housed the massive blast furnaces. They would haul the goods to the train station located ten miles away at Shrewsbury.

As much as Henry admired the outstanding example of industry on display here, it wasn't why he always stopped to take in this view. He had a far more personal reason. This was the exact spot where he'd been standing the first time he saw Olivia.

She had been in the yard, overseeing the workers unloading supplies. She was checking items off a list and directing the dispersal of goods to various buildings. The incongruity of a woman at work in a place like this, and so clearly in a position of authority, had struck Henry immediately. As did her beauty. She was a statuesque blonde, and even from a distance Henry could see she moved with graceful confidence. Then had come the most wonderful moment of all: she had looked up. Seeing him standing there, she had cheerfully waved a greeting.

In truth, she had not been waving at Henry, but at the man who'd been standing next to him. Jacob Reese was Henry's only real friend from university. At some point during their first year at Oxford, they'd met through mutual acquaintances on the squash courts. They'd played a fierce but friendly match, which Jacob had barely won—despite the fact that Henry was the acknowledged champion of their college. From there on out, they'd been inseparable.

Jacob had been able to attend university because of his father's success making cast-iron products. On that bright summer day when Henry had first seen Jacob's sister, Olivia, he'd been accompanying his friend to do some hiking in the nearby mountains. They had just completed their second year at university. It had been Henry's first visit here, but when he saw Olivia, he knew immediately that it would not be his last.

Today, as he stood in the heat of the August sun, Henry allowed free rein to all the pleasures and pain of those memories. Olivia had been in his life only a few short months, but they were among the happiest he'd ever known. He was aware it was foolish to linger here with the hope that somehow he would see her again. No matter how vividly she appeared in his mind's eye, she was gone forever. Living only in his memory. And his heart.

He did see Jacob, though. His friend came out of the business offices. This foundry was now run by Jacob, and it was still impacting Henry's life in vitally important ways. As a silent partner in this operation, Henry had no official duties, but his trust in Jacob's ability to run the business never faltered.

Jacob was headed for one of the neighboring buildings, but he paused as a worker came up to speak to him. While they talked, Jacob happened to look up the hill, just as Olivia had done on that day eight years ago. He caught sight of Henry and immediately waved a greeting.

Henry returned the gesture, then returned to his carriage. It was time to bring his thoughts back to the present. There were a lot of pressing issues on his mind, as he'd just wasted three days on an unsuccessful search for his brother. He hoped his friend could offer some sound advice.

An hour later, after they'd reviewed the prospectus Henry had brought with him, Jacob leaned back in his chair and regarded Henry from across his desk. "This is a good plan. I'm sorry you're being forced to do this, though. I know reopening the copper mine wasn't your first ambition."

It was true. Henry had been on the verge of partnering with three other men to form a company to expand the steelworks and flax mills in Cumbria. It was a venture critical to rescuing his family's finances, which were in a precarious state after several years of bad harvests. Like many large landowners, Henry was looking for ways to diversify his income.

He had even pushed to get Langham a position on the board, which would have netted the family even more money. Unfortunately, Henry had been forced out of the deal when the Duke of Crandall had come aboard. The duke didn't like Henry's politics or his brother. Now Henry had to resurrect a copper mine in Cornwall that had been in the family for over a century. He'd been using it as collateral for other investments, but he was going to see if it could be made profitable again in its own right.

"There are still some unknowns, of course," he pointed out. "One is whether we can retain enough quality men to run the mine. Many of the experienced miners are being drawn away to work in other countries, where the career is more lucrative and their knowledge is in demand."

"I'm guessing plenty of men would welcome the opportunity to remain at home. But it does seem critical that the sooner the project can get underway, the better."

"That's another problem," Henry said. "Now that the long vacation is upon us, everyone has scattered to their country estates. I may have to wait several months to get anyone to meet with me."

"What about Lord Nigel Hayward?" Jacob suggested. "I understand his father has given him Roxwell Abbey. That's near Morestowe, I believe."

"I hadn't thought of that." Hayward had been a friend of theirs at Oxford. He was also the son of a wealthy marquess. "Though I wonder whether his connections will prove an asset or a stumbling block."

Jacob nodded. "It's possible that the Duke of Crandall's comments regarding your stance on South Africa—and questioning your loyalty to the Crown—will cause some of the aristocracy to avoid doing business with you."

"Not to mention Langham's growing bad reputation." Henry had already told Jacob about his brother's disappearance from the sanitarium and his own fruitless efforts to find him. The duke had trotted out stories of Langham's bad behavior while a student at Lincoln's Inn as yet another reason to keep Henry out of the Cumbrian business venture. The house fire at Morestowe and the rumors that Langham had caused it had only provided more fodder.

"Nevertheless, it couldn't hurt to pay Lord Nigel a friendly visit," Jacob insisted. "Perhaps feel him out on the idea. In the meantime, I can send out a few queries among businessmen of my acquaintance who are not so highly placed in society."

It was a good plan, although Henry wondered if even those men might also be swayed by the duke. It seemed most of them were trying to buy their way into the upper classes, either through marriage or even at times acquiring a title. They were not likely to risk getting on the wrong side of such a powerful man.

Jacob pulled a watch from his waistcoat pocket. "There's still an hour yet before dinner. Would you care to see what's new?"

This had become a routine over the years, one which Henry enjoyed immensely. Glad to set aside his concerns for a while, he said, "Absolutely. What new designs have you come up with?"

"You'll be interested in an improvement we've made to the heating conduction in our radiators, including the ones we're constructing for you."

They went to the warehouse and walked down a long aisle, passing a variety of cast-iron merchandise from stoves to umbrella stands. They reached the storage area for the radiators being built for Henry's house. Jacob explained the changes in their construction, and it wasn't long before Henry was pleasantly engrossed in the technical details.

The radiators were not only functional, but beautiful, too. They had fine patterns along the columns and feet that would lend a touch of beauty to their surroundings.

"These are outstanding," Henry agreed. "I hope they won't have to sit here much longer."

Jacob gave him a sympathetic glance. "Things going slowly with the renovation?"

Renovation was too kind a word, considering the circumstances. "Rain has plagued us all summer, setting back the work."

His friend's eyebrows rose. "Too much rain in Essex, the driest county in England? Seems ironic."

"More like a continuation of everything else that has happened this year," Henry replied gloomily. "Bad crops, the house fire . . ."

"Cheer up, friend." Jacob gave him an encouraging pat on the back. "Once it's all done, the setbacks you've had along the way won't seem so bad. Sometimes what we make of bad situations leaves us better off than we ever expected."

That was Jacob, always looking on the bright side. Henry gave a noncommittal shrug, even though he'd come here today precisely to hear that encouragement. Jacob had a way of making otherwise banal words seem entirely believable. Perhaps this was because he'd been a divinity student at Oxford. He'd planned to dedicate his life to the church, but everything had changed after Olivia's death. Jacob was honor-bound to continue the family business. In truth, he'd become such an excellent businessman that Henry couldn't imagine what his life would have been like as a clergyman.

"Look at it this way," Jacob continued. "The fire, although it was terrible, caused no loss of human life. That is the most important thing, wouldn't you say? And now the mansion will be vastly improved and modernized, making it better for your family and your posterity."

"Yes," Henry agreed, although he didn't like Jacob's use of the word *posterity*. The need for an heir, someone to carry on the Burke lineage and the earldom, was real. At one time it had been Henry's dream, too, but now it was too painful to contemplate. "Jacob, do you ever regret how your life changed? How you had to give up your original plans in order to work here?"

"No," Jacob replied without hesitation. "I wanted most of all to help people. Here, I can provide a good living for many workers and quality goods that will benefit countless more. I'll admit it was hard at first, but perhaps Olivia's passion for this business found its way to me. I'm grateful for that, even though I miss her every day."

Henry nodded as the familiar grip of sorrow wrapped around his heart.

Jacob placed a hand on Henry's shoulder. "We don't always know why terrible things happen. We can only search for any good that can come from the bad. Whatever the situation, we can always seek the Lord's help. I know you still grieve for Olivia, but I also pray you will be able to find a way forward, as we all have done. Will you pray this also?"

"I'll try." Henry couldn't promise more.

Later that night, as Henry rode the train back to London, he turned over in his mind everything he and Jacob had discussed. He even offered up a quiet prayer. What was he to do about Langham? And what, ultimately, would he do with Amelia, to see that she found a place in the world that was best for her?

The one thing he couldn't do, however, was ask for a wife, despite the way his heart ached with longing at what he'd lost every time he saw Jacob and Lila together. They were immensely happy. Who wouldn't want that? And yet, how could anyone possibly replace Olivia in his heart? But if Henry didn't get married, there could be no heir to carry on the title. Langham was next in line, and given his dangerously irresponsible nature, that would surely bring the family to ruin. It was a quandary he couldn't even begin to untangle. So he prayed that somehow God would find a way to solve that problem, too.

It was perhaps the most sincere prayer he'd offered up in many years. He only wished it could give his heart more ease.

CHAPTER

4

EVERYONE IN PADDINGTON STATION seemed to be in a hurry—running to catch a train, dashing outside to the cab-stand, pressing forward impatiently at the ticket counters.

It was exactly as it had been when Cara had stood on this very spot only a few weeks ago. She had accompanied the Needenhams on one of their rare trips to the city. At that time, Sir John commandeered three porters to take their mountain of baggage to the waiting carriages, while Cara kept Robbie out of harm's way, pulling him from the path of people and baggage carts.

Out of harm's way.

Cara gripped her carpetbag and took a deep breath. She must not dwell on the past. She must concentrate on what to do next. Admitting her present circumstances to Julia wasn't going to be easy. Cara deserved all the reproof her sister would undoubtedly level at her. But what choice did she have? She pushed her way forward through the crowd.

In the busy carriage yard, Cara walked to the cab that had the friendliest-looking driver. He was tall, and his face was weather-beaten, but he wore a pleasant expression as he absently patted his horse's neck. He tipped his cloth cap at Cara as she approached. "Where to, miss?"

"How much is the fare to 11 Harley Street?"

The cabbie looked her over before answering. Cara wore her nicest and yet most practical walking skirt with a matching jacket. This, plus the few items she'd been able to fit in her carpetbag, was all she had. The rest of her belongings were in a trunk at the Needenhams', waiting for her to send word as to where they should be shipped. Now, as the cabbie eyed her, she got the impression he was calculating more than mileage.

"Two shillings."

"Oh." That was more than she'd expected. Then she remembered that Sir John always complained that the London cabbies overcharged if they thought they could get away with it. This was one of many reasons he disliked the city. Cara furrowed her brow. "Last time I was here, I paid less than a shilling."

This was a complete fabrication, but it seemed to work—especially as she accompanied the words with a little shrug and a movement indicating she was about to seek another driver.

The cabbie's smile broadened. Maybe he thought of bartering as a game. "Tell you what. I'll drop the price to one and threepence. Can't go no lower, or I won't make enough to feed Elvira."

He gave the mare a scratch behind one ear. The creature whinnied and stamped a front hoof, as if she agreed that getting fed was a critical consideration.

Cara allowed herself to laugh—ostensibly at the horse's antics, but really from elation. She had just saved nearly a shilling! "Done," she said jovially.

As the cab made its way down the busy streets, Cara imagined how she might draw the scenes unfolding before her. London was loud and crowded, and the air today was filled with a hazy fog. Particles of soot hung in the air, and several had already besmirched her clothes and bag. Costermongers hawked everything from mussels to fresh milk. Handsomely dressed men and women rode by in fine carriages. Men who might be clerks or business owners strode along the pavement and filled the knifeboard seats on the roofs of omnibuses.

There were even some streets that seemed familiar. Perhaps they were ones she and Julia had taken when they walked through London together during Cara's visit. Cara savored the lift it gave her heart whenever some building or street corner sparked a memory.

London can be my home.

She leaned back and sighed at the thought. Cara deeply regretted the mistakes that had brought her here, and yet here she was. She had not forgotten her promise to God, made during those dark hours. Perhaps He was telling her now that her life could turn out all right after all.

When they arrived at the lodgings for students at the Queen's College for Women, the driver helped Cara down from the cab and placed the carpetbag at her feet. She paid him and included another two pence for the tip. It was the best she could afford. "My thanks to you—and Elvira," she told him.

He grinned, tipped his hat, and pocketed the money. "Good day to you, miss."

Cara walked up the steps to the large front door and knocked. Although she had been dreading this encounter, now she found she was anxious to unburden herself to her sister.

Mrs. Holloway, the house matron, whom Cara had met on her last visit, answered the door. Cara reintroduced herself and asked whether Julia was at home.

Mrs. Holloway looked perplexed. "Your sister moved out several days ago. She's married now."

"But she can't be married!" Cara protested.

Mrs. Holloway's eyebrows rose. "She didn't tell you?"

"I knew she was engaged, but they hadn't set the date. Are you quite sure?"

"Oh yes. There was a notice in the paper. They were married at All Saints Church before leaving for their honeymoon. They are on their way to South America."

"No," murmured Cara in horror. Julia could not have gotten married without telling her *and* gone overseas. The thought made Cara nauseous, as though she were the one being tossed about on a rough ocean. She felt her cheeks growing hot under Mrs. Holloway's quizzical gaze. Perhaps the matron was wondering why Julia had kept this information from her own sister. Cara knew full well why Julia hadn't told her. She knew Cara would do anything in her power to persuade her not to leave the country.

"I'm sorry to surprise you with this news," said Mrs. Holloway. She opened the door wider. "Would you like to come inside for a bit—perhaps have a cup of tea?"

"No, thank you," Cara said, too mortified to stay here any longer. She'd just admitted that her own sister thought so little of her that she'd decided to cut her out of the most important day of her life.

Somehow she managed a polite good-bye before hurrying away. She had to find someplace where she could sit and think. Although her vision was blurred by tears of anger and confusion, she spotted a green oasis ahead. It was a small park lined with benches and shaded by leafy trees.

Settling on a bench, Cara took several deep breaths to calm herself. Perhaps there had been some mistake. Perhaps Mrs. Holloway had been wrong, or the newspaper had printed incorrect information. But the more she thought about it, the more Cara realized it probably wasn't a mistake. It would be just like Julia to do this. From the time they were children, Julia had always been stubborn and unreasonable. Whenever there was any kind of disagreement among them, she would insist she was right and bully the others into going along, no matter the consequences.

Did Rosalyn know that Julia was married and traveling overseas? Did the Morans, Rosalyn's in-laws, know? Was Cara the only one who'd been left in the dark? Humiliation flooded through her at the thought.

No. Surely Rosalyn didn't know. Like Cara, she would have been vehemently opposed to Julia's leaving the country. Julia might never listen to Cara, but there were times when Rosalyn's common sense could prevail. Being the oldest of the three sisters—and in Cara's view the most sensible—Rosalyn was the only person who might have averted this. Surely once Rosalyn discovered how Julia had betrayed them, she would finally understand what Cara had been telling her for years about how self-serving and heartless their sister was.

As Cara saw it, the only way to get to the bottom of things was to go to the Morans' home. Rosalyn and Nate were still traveling up north with the opera company, but perhaps the others would be able to tell Cara what had happened.

Despite her desire for answers, she was not eager to go to the Morans'. She would have to explain to them the circumstances that had brought her to London before she'd had a chance to discuss the matter with her own sisters. But she needed to stay somewhere, and she had no money to pay for lodging. The Morans would take her in without hesitation. They had treated Cara kindly the few times she'd met them. She ought to think of them as her family, too, but she had yet to bring her heart around to the idea. For nearly as long as she could remember, her family had consisted only of three sisters, fiercely dependent on one another even while growing up in a large orphanage. It had been hard for Cara to warm up to her brother-in-law's family.

Except for Nate's brother Patrick, perhaps. He was always so easygoing, especially in contrast to the others, who were much more . . . Cara couldn't think of the right word. *Intense*, maybe. Even when they were enjoying themselves, there seemed to be some underlying sense of purpose to it. Cara loved Patrick's ready laugh. He could find humor in any situation. She could imagine the disapproval the others would direct at Cara for making such a mess of her life. Patrick was bound to treat her more gently. He worked backstage at a theatre called the Opera Comique. Cara knew it was on a street called the Strand. Perhaps if it wasn't too far from here, she could go there and talk to him first.

It was a good plan.

She stood up, taking stock of her surroundings with clear eyes. The far side of the square led to a busy road lined with shops. Asking directions at any of them should be simple.

As she joined the other pedestrians along the crowded thoroughfare, it occurred to her there might be no reason to rush. Patrick worked nights. He might not even be at the theatre yet.

The day was overcast, so judging the exact time was difficult. Cara paused in front of a shop that advertised the sale and repair of jewelry, watches, and clocks. What better place to find out the time? She stepped through the doorway and was immediately surrounded by an array of timepieces, ranging from tall grandfather clocks to small clocks set on tables. According to every one of them, it was nearly half past one.

Having settled that question, Cara wandered over to a glass case filled with jewelry. Oh, such lovely jewelry. Bracelets and chains of fine gold and silver. Rings of many designs, some set with precious stones. Pendant earrings of finely wrought gold. Cara gave a little sigh of pleasure as she drank in the sight.

A man with thick jeweler's spectacles perched on his forehead sat at a work desk on the other side of the case. He came over to her. "Looking for something special, miss?"

She didn't want to admit that she couldn't buy anything. "Everything is so lovely," she murmured, as if unable to decide.

"Let me know if there's something you'd like to look at more closely," he offered.

Cara nodded, and he turned his attention to a woman just entering the shop. The lady had come to retrieve a watch she'd left for repair. The jeweler brought out the watch, and the two stood together at another counter while the jeweler described what he'd done and the lady inspected it.

Free to browse, Cara took her time, picturing how each ring or bracelet or pair of earrings would look on her. After her recent troubles, it felt good to indulge in this bit of fancy, to imagine owning such fine things. The *tick-tock* of dozens of timepieces echoed through the shop, providing a comforting backdrop to her daydreams.

She moved on to the next case, which contained pocket watches. Not finding these as interesting as the jewelry, she was about to turn away when one of the watches caught her eye. It was a ladies' gold watch with a heart-shaped button clasp. Cara let out a little gasp. The only other time she'd seen a clasp like that was on the watch her mother had owned. It couldn't be the same one, of course, for that had been in Rosalyn's possession since their mother died. Still, the design etched into the gold casing looked astoundingly similar.

The other customer left the shop, and the jeweler returned to Cara. "Something caught your eye?"

"May I look at this one, please?" She pointed to the watch.

He pulled it out of the case. "This is a secondhand watch, but I've fully refurbished it. It's in excellent condition and runs beautifully."

He set it in her hand. It fit naturally in her palm, reminding her of the many times she'd played with her mother's watch. Holding her breath, she pressed the latch to open it. For several long seconds she stared at the inside cover, unable to believe what she was seeing even though the inscription was plainly visible on the brightly polished gold.

To Marie. Oceans can never separate us. Love always, Paul.

Feeling her hands shaking, Cara rested them on the counter, although she did not let go of the watch.

"It's a lovely sentiment, don't you think?" the jeweler said.

"Where did you get this?"

"From a pawnbroker's auction, I believe. I get many watches that way."

Cara's astonishment turned to anger. Her mother's watch—a precious gift from her father—was lying here for sale to any stranger who might come by. Why had Rosalyn pawned it? She was working for the most successful impresario in England! Did the watch mean nothing to her? Frowning, Cara stared intently at the watch, as though it could somehow answer these questions.

"The engraving can be polished out if you don't like it," the jeweler offered. "Or I can craft a new cover. That would add to the price, but I'd be happy to—"

"How much is it?" Cara said brusquely. Whatever the cost, she had to buy it.

"It's written right there." He pointed to a small paper tag attached to it by a string.

Cara's heart nearly stopped when she read the price. It was more than she had. She remembered how she'd haggled for her cab ride. "Might you be willing to take five shillings?" It was all the money she possessed.

The jeweler shook his head. "I might take ten percent off the price, but that's all. This is a fine piece, as you can see, and I've put a lot of work into the refurbishment."

"Would you accept a barter?" She couldn't leave the shop without this watch. She couldn't risk that someone else might buy it before she could find more money and return for it.

"That depends," he countered. "What are you offering?"

Cara owned only one thing of any value: a thin gold bracelet that Miss Sarah Needenham, Sir John's nineteen-year-old daughter, had given her as a thank-you gift for helping her complete a painting to give to Lady Needenham for Christmas. Cara pushed back her sleeve to uncover the bracelet, which she'd kept hidden as a precaution against theft while she traveled. She removed it and laid it on the countertop.

Placing his magnifying glasses over his eyes, the jeweler picked up the bracelet and scrutinized it. "It's a nice enough piece, but only gold-plated."

Cara's heart sank. Sarah had given her something not so fine after all. Nor was it enough for the watch.

"However, this bracelet plus four shillings would be acceptable."

It would take her down to her last shilling. Cara would have to throw herself on the mercy of the Morans now, no matter how much it hurt her pride. But she was bolstered by her anger that Rosalyn had let this precious family heirloom out of her possession. Cara's mistakes had been terrible, but she had not committed a deliberate act of treachery. In her mind, that gave her the high ground.

"I'll take it."

The transaction was quickly completed. Cara left the shop and stood close to a wall, where she was out of the flow of pedestrians. She opened the watch and stared at the engraving, reading and rereading the inscription. Words of love from her father to her mother. *Oceans can never separate us.*

Cara squeezed her eyes shut against the tears. Their father *had* loved them. She was sure of it, even though Julia had at times implied otherwise. Cara prayed once more, as she had countless times over the years, that her father might be out there somewhere, and that God would bring him home.

CHAPTER
5

CARA TUCKED THE WATCH into a secret pocket in her waistband, where she also kept what scant money she had left. She was the guardian of this precious timepiece now, and unlike Rosalyn, she was never going to let it go.

Realizing she'd forgotten to ask the shopkeeper for directions, Cara looked around for someone who might help her. Most of the passersby looked so intent on getting to their destinations that Cara hesitated to interrupt them.

The one exception was a man leaning against a nearby lamppost. He tapped a cigarette against one palm but looked in no hurry to smoke it. He wore checked pants and a light brown jacket unbuttoned over his red silk waistcoat. His bowler hat was pushed back to reveal sandy-colored hair, and a walking stick was hooked over one wrist. Catching Cara's eye, he tipped his hat. "Why are *T* and *V* the luckiest letters in the alphabet?"

She stared at him in surprise. "I beg your pardon?"

He winked. "Because they are next to *U*!" Disconnecting himself from the lamppost, he sidled toward her, smiling at his own joke. "Why is a pawnshop one of the most paradoxical places in existence?"

Cara shook her head, unable to suppress a smile. "I don't know. Why?"

"Because although it is full of people, it is a *loan*-some place."

This time she laughed out loud, which left the man beaming with gratification.

"The name's Langham Burke," he said. "You can call me Langham. Everybody does. They have no choice, really, for I won't answer to anything else." Tucking the unsmoked cigarette back into his pocket, he held out a hand. "My brother says it's bad form to offer a handshake to a lady instead of waiting for her to initiate it. However, you have such an excellent sense of humor that I think you will excuse my breach of etiquette."

Cara accepted his handshake. "My name is Caroline Bernay." She added impulsively, "But I usually go by Cara." It was incautious to offer her Christian name to a stranger, but there was something so genial about this fellow that she liked him on the spot.

His handshake was cool and brief. He seemed more interested in scrutinizing her face. "I feel sure I've seen you before. You are a stunner, aren't you?"

"I beg your pardon?" This had to be a compliment, if a brash one. Had she misjudged him?

Langham smiled, and his blue eyes seemed to be smiling, too. Surely he didn't mean any harm; he was too well-dressed. His accent sounded very proper, too. Not like most of the others she'd heard today. In fact, the upper-crust way he spoke reminded her of the marquess's son who was courting Miss Sarah Needenham.

Langham absently stroked his mustache as he looked at her. Then he snapped his fingers. "I have it! I always told Hughes he has the prettiest models for his paintings. Some say brunettes make the best stunners, but I go my own way in these things."

"You don't mean Mr. Arthur Hughes, by chance?" Cara could not believe he was making such a casual mention of a famous painter.

He grinned. "You *are* one of his models. Where has he been hiding you? Why hasn't he brought you to any of our parties? Surely his wife doesn't object. She's too sensible to think he'd cheat on her. He's a family man, through and through. But I'm sure you know that. Especially if you've been out to his home in Kew Green."

It was dizzying to keep up with the shifts in conversation. He thought she was a model. That was incorrect, but if he really was a friend of Arthur Hughes . . .

Cara found her heart racing with excitement. Arthur Hughes was at the forefront of the art world. "I've never met Mr. Hughes. Do you know him?"

"You're not the model in *Memories?* I can't believe it. But you *are* a model, aren't you? Seeking immortality by being painted by one of the greats?"

"I'm not a model." Cara had never even considered that possibility. She added impulsively, "I am an artist, though. That is, I'd like to be."

"There is no *like to be* when it comes to being an artist. Either you are, or you aren't." He was still looking her over. "You can't have been to the Grosvenor. I go there all the time, and I'm sure I'd have noticed you."

The Grosvenor Gallery was the most forward-thinking art gallery in London. It was a place Cara longed to see. Now that she was in London, she would ensure she got there someday. But for now . . .

"I haven't been anywhere. I've only just arrived in London." As she said this, Cara's thoughts were yanked uncomfortably back to her present situation. "In fact, I wonder if you might give me directions to the Opera Comique? I hope it isn't too far—I need to walk, for I cannot afford a cab."

"It's a fair distance away, but an omnibus will get you there for threepence. I don't think the theatre will be open, though. It's not even teatime yet."

"I'm not going to see a show. I need to speak to a man who works there."

"Aha! You're an actress. Another promising occupation for a stunner such as yourself."

Cara had never heard the word *stunner* before today. She couldn't help but feel proud at this compliment even as she shook her head. "I need to speak to one of the stagehands. He's my brother-in-law . . . sort of, I think. Is the brother of one's brother-in-law also a brother-in-law?"

"I see you like conundrums as much as I do. What are you going to talk to him about?"

"Well, I . . ." Cara was taken aback by his forthright question. Yet she found it hard to take offense. He had a slight tick in his eye and a certain nervous movement that made him seem different from most people. And he'd already proven that he didn't like to follow rigid social conventions. Maybe he didn't even realize he was overstepping polite rules of conduct. Still, Cara wasn't going to explain herself.

Langham didn't seem to notice her lack of an answer. He was looking down at her carpetbag. "Have you brought samples of your work? I'm always curious to see what other painters are doing."

"Are you also a painter?"

"Yes, indeed. I'm having a showing at the Grosvenor in a few months. I feel I am a mere dilettante, but Sir Coutts assures me my work is equal to the professionals."

That explained not only why he knew Arthur Hughes, but everything else about his manner. Painters, like many others in the arts, were notorious for flouting the rules of society. Cara knew this because she'd often purloined the society journals after Lady Needenham had read and discarded them. They were filled with stories of how artists, authors, and even actors rubbed elbows with royals and aristocrats at the Grosvenor Gallery's special events. The owner of the gallery was Sir Coutts Lindsay. Some of the artists whose work was displayed in the gallery were aristocrats, too! And here she was, after being in London for only a few hours, talking with someone who was friends with such people. She could hardly believe her good fortune.

Langham's name wasn't familiar to Cara. Not that she knew the names of every artist in London—how could she? But if he wasn't famous yet, he soon would be. Being invited to show his work at the Grosvenor Gallery guaranteed that.

"So, have you brought your work with you?" he asked again.

Cara did have two of her favorite drawings in her carpetbag. She couldn't bear to leave them behind, even though the butler had assured her he would forward her things as soon as she sent him an address.

If Langham's work was good enough for the Grosvenor, his skill would be far superior to hers. Yet Cara believed the drawings in her bag represented her best work. To get an assessment from a master would be an invaluable piece of good luck. How could she pass up the opportunity?

She reached down to open the clasp. "I did bring a few items." She tried to sound offhand about it and not at all nervous. She pulled out the first, which was a drawing in charcoal of her sister Rosalyn. It was a modest-sized picture, about fifteen inches square. It showed a smiling Rosalyn from the waist up, in three-quarters profile, one hand up to brush a strand of hair from her face.

Langham held the drawing at an angle to catch the light as he studied it. Cara began to feel self-conscious as some of the other pedestrians sent curious glances their way. She grew more uneasy as the moments passed and Langham said nothing.

"It's my sister Rosalyn," she said, and then felt even more foolish. What did it matter who the subject was? Langham would judge the work on its artistic merits.

She was becoming so convinced he didn't like it that she was stunned when he murmured, "This is very good."

Those few words were enough to make her forget her discomfort. "You think so?"

He nodded. "Your sister is an earnest person. Innately quiet, perhaps, yet she has an energy that can burst forth when she allows it."

"That's amazing! But you can't have gotten all that from my drawing. You must be a fortune-teller of some kind."

"Reading a painting the way a gypsy reads tea leaves?" Langham waggled his eyebrows. "I've often said I have a drop of gypsy blood in me, although I confess that's figurative, not literal. But yes, I did glean that information from your portrait. What's more, I see your love for her as well. I can always tell when someone paints out of love. There's something magical about catching that spark in a person's soul, isn't there?"

After the horrible things that had happened this week, to suddenly have an accomplished artist complimenting her and *understanding* her art brought tears to Cara's eyes. "I think that's the nicest thing anyone's ever said to me."

"Then you can't know many nice people."

She didn't reply, but in her mind the answer rang crystal clear. Considering what she'd learned today about her sisters, neither was very nice in her eyes. They had betrayed her. If she were to paint Rosalyn's portrait today, it would come out a lot differently.

Langham's gaze returned to the portrait. "I feel as though I know this woman already."

These words caused Cara's ballooning pride to deflate a little. "Perhaps you have seen her. She's touring with *The Pirates of Penzance*." If he had seen the production, he might have gleaned those things about Rosalyn from her performance rather than this portrait.

He shook his head. "Opera is not my cup of tea. Not even the works of Messrs. Gilbert and Sullivan, though they are wildly popular. I did, however, see their newest show, *Patience*, because it is a satire on the Aesthetics. I expected it to be dreadful, but in fact it is terribly funny. I thought it brilliant that the main character is named Grosvenor!"

Most of what Cara knew about the Aesthetic Movement was that its adherents were interested in "art for art's sake" rather than creating works for edification or to illustrate some important lesson. The Grosvenor Gallery was filled with such paintings, and Cara was eager to see them. What would she think of them? How would they make her feel? What could she learn to make her own work better? "Are you an Aesthetic?"

"I don't tie myself down to one school. There are infinite ways to view the world, and therefore infinite ways to capture it on canvas. Wouldn't you agree?"

"Yes!" Cara replied heartily. "I've never put it into words before, but that is exactly what I think."

His eyes twinkled as he handed back the drawing. "I knew the moment I saw you that you were an exceptional soul. Let's see your other one."

Cara rolled up the drawing and put it away. She reached for the second, which was a watercolor she'd made of Robbie last spring.

"Oh, hang on," Langham said. "Here comes the omnibus. I'm on my way to the Grosvenor now. Why don't you come along? Lady Lindsay

56

is still in town. If she's there, I'll introduce you. You know there is an entire room set aside just for showing the works of ladies, don't you?"

She was hardly able to believe her ears. "You would introduce me to Lady Lindsay?"

To be introduced to the famous Lady Lindsay, who co-owned the Grosvenor with her husband, and who was an accomplished painter in her own right, was too good to be true.

"I'm itching to show you that painting of Hughes's," Langham continued. "You'll be astonished at the likeness!"

It was tempting, to be sure. So tempting that she could already hear Julia's reproof about how easily she could be led astray from her purposes. And *that* made up her mind for her. She hadn't forgotten her predicament, but neither was she going to pass up this opportunity. Something this good might never come around again. Perhaps it was God Himself who was making this possible! She'd always sensed His presence with her, even if she had not been a model Christian. There was no reason why Cara couldn't go to the gallery now; she would have plenty of time to get to the theatre afterward.

As the omnibus came to a halt, Cara pulled out her remaining coins. "Threepence, did you say?"

"Don't worry—I'll pay," Langham said, motioning her toward the door. "Come quickly! Omnibuses are like time and tides—they wait for no one." He helped Cara aboard, taking hold of her bag and stepping on after her. "There are seats inside. What luck. Otherwise I'd have to sit on the knifeboard seats up top, and I detest that." He dropped some coins into the waiting hand of the conductor.

The seats were composed of two long benches that ran the length of the omnibus. Cara and Langham had not gotten fully settled before the omnibus lurched forward. The sudden momentum tossed Cara sideways, toward the rear of the vehicle. She nearly fell into Langham's lap.

"Careful!" he said with a laugh. "It takes some work to keep your balance in these things. Have you ever ridden an omnibus before?"

"Never," she confessed. "Thank you for paying my fare. That's very generous."

He waved a dismissive hand. "Think nothing of it. I've plenty of money. The truth is, I could take a cab if I wanted to."

"Why don't you?" Cara asked in surprise. Surely it would be more comfortable than this cramped omnibus. It had an odd smell, and the straw lining the floor was filthy.

"This is much more interesting. You never know what kind of people you'll see."

Given that the woman seated opposite her was wearing a massive hat decorated with flowers and fruit and what appeared to be a stuffed bird, Cara had to agree.

"Besides," Langham said in an elaborate stage whisper, "I like the anonymity. Many of the cab drivers know me, and they are bound to report my whereabouts to my brother. *Again.*"

This seemed an odd statement, like so many he'd made today. "Don't you want your brother to know where you are?"

"No. He's a good man, but he's too inclined to direct every aspect of my life. As though I could not take care of myself. It is tedious to have a domineering sibling."

"It sure is," Cara agreed with feeling.

Langham's eyebrows lifted. "*Domineering* is not a trait I spotted in your sister's portrait. Or do you have an overbearing brother like I do?"

"It's my other sister, Julia. Rosalyn worries about me, but Julia only badgers me."

"I should hate to see what sort of portrait you'd paint of her!" he replied with a laugh.

"Every time she thinks she's being helpful, all she does is make me feel worse."

Langham nodded. "I understand completely."

It felt good to be with someone who, although his life was obviously so different from hers, seemed to be going through similar troubles. Cara was glad she'd accepted his offer.

She was on her way to the Grosvenor Gallery! This day had turned into an adventure better than anything she could have imagined.

CHAPTER

6

ALTHOUGH HE KEPT UP a stream of conversation, Langham looked out the window a lot, keeping tabs on the progress of the omnibus. It made many stops, slowing their pace.

"Here we are at last," he said, interrupting a story he'd been relating about a scandal at the Royal Academy's spring show. They swiftly disembarked. It was clear he was as anxious as she was to visit the gallery.

As they approached the entrance, Cara paused, staring up at it in wonder. The Grosvenor was grander and more ornate than she'd imagined. Two giant marble columns, several stories high, stood on either side of a massive door. It looked like a Greek temple.

"Lovely, isn't it?" Langham said. "The building itself is a work of art, and the interior is just as magnificent." He opened the door for her. "Come on."

Stepping through the doorway, Cara thought she'd walked into a palatial mansion. The spacious foyer was edged with plants and statues, and a wide marble staircase rose majestically to the next floor.

This wasn't a home, though. An attendant standing at a tall desk next to a sign stating the entrance fee made it clear this was a place of business. Cara stopped in alarm. She hadn't even considered the entrance fee.

Langham greeted the guard like an old friend. "Lester, how are you? How is business today?"

"Very slow."

"Have the Kinnard sisters been through here today?"

The guard scratched his chin. "No, sir, don't believe they have. Most of our best patrons have left the city to get away from the heat."

Langham appeared disappointed at this answer. Cara wondered who the Misses Kinnard could be, aside from some of the gallery's "best" patrons. But he seemed to shake it off. "I hope Lady Lindsay has not yet fled town."

"No, sir. She's upstairs in the watercolors gallery."

"Excellent." Langham took Cara's elbow to lead her upstairs.

The attendant held out a hand to stop them. "Excuse me, sir, but . . . well . . . rules are rules." He motioned toward Cara.

"This is a rising artist Lady Lindsay will want to meet."

Lester looked unconvinced. His gaze traveled over Cara, taking in her dress, wilted from the heat and hem brown with dust from the streets, and her well-worn carpetbag.

"I couldn't expect you to pay my way," Cara protested.

"All this angst over a mere two shillings," Langham said with a dramatic sigh. Two shillings wasn't exactly a pittance to Cara, but Langham's world was evidently much richer. "You know Sir Coutts has commissioned two paintings from me for the autumn showing. My bill will be paid in full once they sell." He gave Cara's arm a tug. "Come along."

The attendant frowned but did not stop them. He did, however, make a note in a large ledger. Cara determined that at some point she would pay Langham back. How or when that would be, she had no idea. But she would find a way.

When they reached the top of the stairs, Langham sent a quick glance back toward the entrance. Cara wondered if perhaps he was still looking for the Kinnard sisters. Someone was coming through the main doors, but it was an older gentleman and his wife. Langham turned back to Cara and led her through a wide entryway on their left. "This is the watercolor gallery."

At the far end of the long room, a woman was surveying a newly hung painting while a worker descended a ladder. "Yes, I knew it would be better here," she said, nodding in satisfaction.

The lady had a light falsetto voice that seemed at odds with her appearance; although she was not tall, she tended toward stoutness.

She turned as Langham and Cara entered. "Langham!" she said warmly, walking toward them. "What are you up to today?"

"No good, naturally, my lady," he joked, giving her a peck on both cheeks.

"Will there be anything else, ma'am?" the worker asked.

"No, that will be all. Tell Mr. Warren I'll be down shortly."

"Very good, ma'am," he said, tipping his chin deferentially before picking up the ladder and leaving the room.

Cara guessed the woman was in her late thirties. She had bright, piercing blue eyes, a pretty contrast to her dark brown hair.

"I'm so pleased to meet you!" Cara gushed when Langham introduced her to Lady Lindsay. "I've wanted to come here for ages."

"It's always nice to meet a fellow art enthusiast," the lady replied with a smile.

"She's more than an enthusiast—she's an artist, too," Langham said. "I believe she has real potential. She has the drawing here, if you'd like to see it." He motioned toward Cara's carpetbag.

Cara froze in mortification. They were surrounded by true works of art. It didn't feel right to press Lady Lindsay to look at her amateurish artwork.

Lady Lindsay must have thought so, too. A look of annoyance crossed her face. She glanced down at a watch attached by a chain to her dress. "I suppose I have a moment."

"I don't want to be any trouble—" Cara began.

"She just said she has time," Langham interrupted. "Show it to her."

Only a desire not to keep Lady Lindsay waiting prodded Cara past any further hesitation. She pulled out the portrait of Rosalyn and handed it over, holding her breath as Lady Lindsay studied it.

"This is reasonably good. Your instructor has given you a good grounding in the basics."

"Oh, I haven't had any lessons. I suppose you could say I'm self-taught."

Upon hearing this, Lady Lindsay looked at Cara with new interest. "In that case I revise my estimate. You have a natural eye for framing and perspective. You could go far with proper instruction."

Cara was nearly beside herself at receiving this praise from an expert. "Thank you!"

Lady Lindsay handed the portrait back to Cara. "It was lovely to meet you, Miss Bernay. However, if the two of you will excuse me, I have to solve some issues down in the restaurant before I leave. Sir Coutts and I are catching the train for Scotland in the morning."

"Do give him my greetings," Langham said. "I'm already looking forward to your return in October."

"While you are waiting so earnestly for us, be sure to keep working. Remember, your pieces must be ready by the end of September. I don't want you to take up Mr. Burne-Jones's bad habit of taking years to complete a painting."

"I will be an absolute slave to my brush."

Lady Lindsay's response was a lift of her brow and an ironic smile.

"Your ladyship, might I ask before you go . . . I hope you will pardon me, but is there a retiring room here?" Cara's cheeks burned, but she had to ask.

Lady Lindsay looked sympathetic. "Of course. They are down by the restaurant. You can follow me."

"Just take the stairs all the way to the top floor when you are done," Langham said. "I'll wait for you in the main gallery."

"Have you known Langham very long?" Lady Lindsay asked as she and Cara walked downstairs.

"I met him just today," Cara admitted. "He's very nice, isn't he?"

"Most people find him likable, although he hasn't much respect for the rules of polite society. At times I feel he is too lax. As a member of the aristocracy, he has a reputation to uphold."

"Aristocracy!" Cara exclaimed.

Lady Lindsay pulled up short. "He didn't tell you? No, I don't suppose he would. He's too enamored with the idea of being a bohemian painter. His brother is the Earl of Morestowe."

Cara stared at her, dazed.

"You mustn't go after him expecting piles of money," Lady Lindsay warned. "His brother controls the purse strings, and very tightly, too. My husband and I hoped Lord Morestowe might become a patron of our gallery, but he has shown no inclination to do so. In fact, I don't think he cares about art at all."

"That's too bad," Cara agreed. "He must not have much imagination."

Lady Lindsay shrugged but didn't answer. She led Cara down a hallway and pointed her toward the ladies' retiring room. "Good-bye, then. I look forward to seeing you in the fall."

When Cara had finished, she made her way once more up the wide staircase, still thinking over the startling information Lady Lindsay had given her about Langham. The brother of an earl! It seemed too fantastic to believe.

She found Langham in the main gallery. He immediately led her to a painting midway along one wall. "This is the one I was telling you about."

Cara saw right away why he thought she had been the model for it. The focal point of the painting was a young woman kneeling on the floor. There was a resemblance, although the model's eyes were brown, not blue like Cara's. The girl in the painting also had reddish tones in her hair that Cara did not have. But the roundness of the face, her large eyes, small mouth, and soulful expression—these were all things Cara had seen in her mirror countless times. The girl knelt next to an open violin case. A small white cloth and a square of rosin lay where they had fallen onto the floor. Cara recognized the rosin because her brother-in-law Nate owned a fiddle.

"What do you think?" Langham said. "Now that I see the two of you together, the likeness is perhaps not so great. And yet there is something in the expression . . ."

Cara didn't hear the rest. Her attention had focused on an older man in the background of the painting. He was seated at a window, playing the fiddle. The girl's father, perhaps? A brass plate proclaimed the painting was titled *Memories*. What story was being conveyed? Was the father dead? Was he living only in the girl's memories? Cara's eyes misted at the thought. She had no real memories of her father, only a tintype photograph taken in the prime of his life. What would he look like now? Most importantly, where was he? Cara refused to believe he was dead, but she could not account for his staying away from his family all these years.

"Are you all right?" Langham drew near her.

She nodded, although she couldn't help giving a little sigh. "It's just that the painting reminds me of my father."

"Is your father still living?"

"Yes!" The answer blurted from her lips immediately. Her shoulders sagged. "In truth, I don't know." She gave him an apologetic smile. "It's a rather long story."

"You needn't tell me if you don't want to. I'm sorry I showed the painting to you if it makes you sad."

She wiped back a tear. "I'm moved, that's all. Isn't that what great art is supposed to do?"

Langham gave an appreciative nod. "Come and have a look at these by Frederic Leighton. If you aren't transported with delight, I will eat my hat."

Cara smiled as his quip lightened her mood.

They made their way through the gallery. Many paintings were inspired by Greek myths or old legends. Cara studied each work in detail: the drape of the gowns, the flow of a woman's hair, the emotion on the faces. They were beautiful and powerful and captivating. Langham discussed the merits of each one, as well as what he considered its shortcomings. To Cara, they were all perfect.

Throughout this time, she sensed that Langham's mind was partly on something else. There were other visitors, though the crowd was sparse, and he kept turning to look whenever someone new came into the main gallery. At one point he pulled out his pocket watch to check the time.

Cara sighed. There were too many paintings to view all in one day. "I could live here, I think."

"So could I, if they didn't charge a king's ransom for a cup of tea." He grinned as he snapped his watch shut, but Cara saw he was not merely smiling at his own joke. He'd caught sight of two young ladies just entering the main gallery.

They easily stood out from the other patrons. Their gowns were brightly colored silk so loosely gathered at the bodice that Cara suspected they weren't wearing corsets. Neither was there evidence of crinolines or bustles, for the gowns fell in a smooth line down to their feet. Instead of hats, they wore garlands and scarves in their hair, which wasn't even pinned up but worn loose around their shoulders. The effect was odd, yet Cara thought them beautiful.

Seeing Langham, they rushed forward, calling his name. He met them halfway, giving them each a kiss on both cheeks. "I thought you might not be able to come."

"It required some subterfuge," admitted the taller of the two women. "Papa thinks we are shopping for parasols."

The other woman was still holding Langham's hands. "I missed you at the Grosvenor's open house on Sunday afternoon. Where were you?"

"I'm afraid I was . . . indisposed."

She frowned. "I'm concerned about these recurring illnesses. Has the doctor not identified the issue?"

"I'm afraid not." A shadow passed over his face that seemed out of character with everything Cara had seen of him so far. She couldn't imagine what kind of illness could be troubling him. Langham tweaked his mustache. "Nevertheless, I soldier on. I am so glad you made it here today."

When the woman caught sight of Cara, her expression changed to surprise—and, Cara thought, consternation.

"Let me introduce you all," Langham said. "Miss Cara Bernay, these are the Misses Kinnard—Mariana and Louise."

"Lovely to meet you," Mariana, the taller one, said, taking Cara's hands and speaking in deep, resonant tones. Cara thought she sounded like an actress in a play.

"Your gowns are beautiful. I've never seen anything like them— except in these paintings." Cara indicated the artwork all around them.

"It's the clothing of the Aesthetics. We purchased these from Monsieur Liberty's shop on Regent Street. Do you also wish to cast off the yoke of ordinariness and the social strictures that have smothered appreciation of all that is truly beautiful and good?"

Cara blinked, not understanding the question.

"Cara is an artist," Langham informed the sisters.

"I don't recall meeting you before," Louise said. She eyed Cara with suspicion.

"I just met her today myself," Langham said. "How about we go for tea, and everyone can get better acquainted?"

"We haven't time. Papa insists we be home early today."

"This is our last day in London," Mariana explained to Cara. "The *pater* is taking us to the country tomorrow. He's arranged for us all to stay in some drafty old mansion in Gloucestershire."

"He's still trying to get you engaged to that rich industrialist from Birmingham?" Langham asked.

Mariana heaved a dramatic sigh. "He's trying. Not that I mind *so* much, for Mr. Everson is rich. It's just that in the meantime, we shall be forced to act proper—wear corsets and attend garden parties and play croquet and talk about the weather."

"I feel sure you'll be able to stand strong against such banalities," Langham assured them, although to Cara it sounded like an idyllic summer—except for the corsets. No one enjoyed wearing them, but Cara had never even considered doing otherwise.

"Be sure to take a copy of Swinburne's poems," Langham continued. "Perhaps you can win them over to deep contemplations of art and beauty."

Louise drew closer to Langham, fanning her long lashes at him. "I do wish you could be there."

"I would ruin that party, I'm afraid, when your father pitched me out of it like a cricket ball." Despite his joking tone, he looked down at Louise with an expression that Cara interpreted as tender regard.

Mariana took Cara's arm in a friendly gesture. "Have you seen that painting by Albert Moore? It's *fascinating*."

Cara allowed Mariana to lead her away, ostensibly to view the painting located at the opposite end of the gallery. She understood this was really to allow Louise and Langham some private time together.

"They are fond of one another," Cara said.

"They are, although our father forbids her to see him, so we have to resort to these secret meetings whenever we can. Once I am married to Mr. Everson, I shall have money and freedom to do as I like, and perhaps I can help those two get together."

"I really did just meet Langham today," Cara said, worried Louise might perceive her as a romantic rival. "I don't . . . that is, I wouldn't . . ."

"I believe you. My sister has a jealous streak, that's all. But I don't think Langham would be swayed. He fell hard the first moment he saw her. Heaven knows why."

"Why doesn't your father like him? I would think that being a member of the aristocracy would be a strong selling point."

"Yes, well . . ." Mariana looked at Cara as though trying to judge how much to say. "Langham is still trying to make something of himself in his own right, I think."

"Do you mean his goal of being a painter?"

"Yes, that's it." But something in her expression made Cara think more was being left unsaid.

They spent several minutes discussing the Albert Moore painting before Mariana turned to look at the couple, who were now seated on the viewing couches at the center of the gallery. "I hate to break them up, but we really must be going."

Langham insisted on escorting the sisters to their waiting carriage. The four of them walked downstairs and out into the hot sunshine.

Just before handing Louise into the carriage, Langham said, "Remember our little code: 'Everyone here sends kind regards.' When you read that in Georgiana's letters, you'll know it's from me."

She beamed at him. "I'll remember."

"They are very nice," Cara said after the sisters had gone. She didn't know what else to say, lest it sound like prying.

"Louise thinks she'll marry me one day."

His directness took her by surprise. "Don't you want to?"

"There are other problems to sort out first."

The Artful Match
Cara thought of Mr. Kinnard's objection to the match. She was
about to mention it, but before she could, Langham said, "It's nearly
time for tea. Why don't you come to the studio with me? I'll introduce
you to Adrian and Georgiana, the two artists I live with. I know they'd
love to meet you. Georgiana sold a painting this week, and she always
lays out an excellent spread when we're in the money."

"Is it far from here?"

"It's in Holland Park, a few miles west. It's a pleasant walk if you go
through Hyde Park, although today we should probably opt for a cab."

"But isn't the Opera Comique to the south?" Despite how she felt
about her sisters right now, Cara needed to ask the Morans for help.

"I've been thinking about that. There may be someplace else you
can stay. I've got an idea up my sleeve."

"An *idea* up your *sleeve?*" Cara repeated in amusement.

He grinned. "I'll explain after we get there."

After spending the afternoon with him and knowing he came from
one of England's best families, Cara was willing to trust him. And why
shouldn't she follow her own path, even if it veered from what others
thought was *normal?* From now on, she was going to make her own
decisions and live life her own way.

68

CHAPTER
7

THEY WALKED to a nearby cabstand. While they were still perhaps twenty yards off, Langham paused to get a look at the cabbie before stepping closer. This must have been one Langham didn't know, because he nodded to himself and led Cara to the cab.

Once they were underway, she said, "Why don't you like your brother?"

"I already explained why."

"But maybe he has his reasons for being so dictatorial?" she ventured.

Langham frowned. "Lady Lindsay told you about him, didn't she?"

"Yes," Cara admitted.

"I should have known. Although Lady Lindsay comes from a wealthy family, she had no title until she married a baronet. Now she is obsessed with the social hierarchy. Still, I wish she hadn't said anything."

"Don't you like being a member of a titled family? Forgive me for sounding so inquisitive. I can't imagine enjoying such a privileged status and not wanting to talk about it."

"*Privileged*," Langham said with disdain. "You don't understand how terribly stifling it is. It's always 'do this' and 'don't do that' and 'you must *absolutely* behave in such-and-such a way' at this event or that. There's never any freedom to do what you really want."

"I suppose I never thought about it that way." Despite her words, Cara still found it difficult to understand. After all, she'd been raised in an orphanage with two thousand other children. They'd had no money or privilege, and yet they'd had just as many rules governing their actions. "I suppose your brother—that is to say, his lordship—does very important things. In the government, I mean. The House of Lords, and all that."

"Do not refer to my brother as *his lordship* or other such nonsense. Not in my presence, at any rate. *Henry* is good enough. I prefer *Harry*, but for some reason he bristles when I call him that." Langham shrugged. "Harry's a straightforward, principled man who always does the right thing." He gave a snort. "Therefore, he's a terrible bore."

The cab was moving through Hyde Park. They passed many open carriages, as the day was fine. Most of the superbly dressed ladies and gentlemen appeared to be enjoying themselves, but a few wore expressions of mild ennui, as though such rides were so commonplace as to be dull. That was a shame. Cara would have been happy to trade places with any of them. She leaned back and sighed, giving herself over to the pleasure of daydreaming that one day she might join them.

Meanwhile, Langham had sunk into his thoughts, a frown drawing his brows together as he toyed with his cane.

"I suppose you have a large estate somewhere?" Cara asked. She imagined a vast tract of land and an ancient, imposing mansion. Something like what the Needenhams had, only even grander.

At the mention of the estate, Langham gave a little smile. "It's in Essex. A lovely place. It can be restful, and perfect for painting. Except for . . ." His voice trailed off.

"Except?" she prompted.

He inhaled deeply and straightened, waving away her question. "Look, we are entering Holland Park. It's a charming neighborhood. A lot of artists live here. I'll point out a few of their homes."

The names he rattled off as they passed stately homes surprised and impressed her. She had no idea so many painters lived in the same area of London.

When the cab finally stopped, they were in front of a town home that looked more modest than the others they'd passed, and yet to Cara's eyes it was still very nice.

"That'll be one and six, sir," the driver said once Langham and Cara had gotten down from the cab.

"Right, my good man," Langham replied. "Wait here. My money's inside."

The cabbie's manner switched from polite to brusque. "Make it snappy, if you please. I ain't got all day."

Langham led Cara up the steps to the house. Opening the door, he ushered her inside. "Georgiana! I've brought company!" he called out.

A woman came from an adjoining room. She wore a paint-splattered smock, but she was carrying a teapot. "Adrian and I were just wondering when you would show up." She offered a friendly, curious smile to Cara. "Welcome, Miss, er—?"

"Lend me two shillings for the cab, will you, dear?" said Langham.

The woman grimaced in irritation. "Hang on." She left them briefly. When she returned, she held coins instead of the teapot. "Here's one and eight," she said, dropping the money into Langham's hand. "You always tip too much."

"Georgiana, you are going to ruin my reputation for generosity among the fine cabmen of our city."

She pushed him toward the door. "Just pay the man so he can get to his next fare."

Langham went out the door and bounded down the steps.

"How do you do?" the woman said, extending a hand toward Cara. "I'm Georgiana Marshall."

"Cara Bernay."

"Come in to the studio." As she led Cara down the hall, she called out, "Adrian! Langham has brought someone for tea."

When they entered the next room, Cara's mouth fell open with delight. This was a room wholly dedicated to art. Everything suggested light and openness. The late-afternoon sun poured through a massive window along the wall to her left. At the far end of the room were two more large windows, set up high to allow more light throughout the day. There was even an overhead gaslight.

Canvases on a half dozen easels were positioned to catch the light from the windows. Tables were cluttered with every kind of art supply, including pencils, sketch pads, paint tubes, brushes, and palettes. She knew the large bottles on one table held solvent, for she smelled their astringent odor right away. Many people didn't like that smell, but to Cara it spoke of creation and endless possibilities.

Seated at an easel near the main window was a heavyset man with a bushy beard. He stopped painting as they came in, looking up to see the newcomer. Cara expected some word of welcome, but his eyebrows rose and he stared at her. Perhaps he was displeased at being interrupted. Remembering how often she'd had to set aside her painting just as she was getting to the heart of it because she'd been called to some mundane task, Cara sympathized. But as the man continued to look at her, she realized he didn't look angry but supremely interested. She began to feel her cheeks tinge under his scrutiny.

"Well, well," he murmured finally. He rose from his chair and walked toward them. He was very tall. "What did you say your name was?"

"She didn't," Georgiana said dryly. "I think you frightened her, looking at her like a bear anticipating his next meal."

Adrian laughed. It was a deep, sonorous sound. Just the sort one expected from a man his size. "I don't bite," he promised Cara. "Not really."

"I'm Cara Bernay. I'm so pleased to meet you. Is this your house? This is the most wonderful studio I've ever seen."

She spoke rapidly from nervousness, but he returned her rambling compliments with a pleased smile.

Langham rejoined them. "Adrian, this is Cara. She's a—"

"—model. I can see that," Adrian interrupted.

"I was going to say *painter*. But there's no reason she can't be both."

"I've been commissioned to do a mural for the interior of a new theatre," Adrian said, his gaze still on Cara. "I had in mind a painting of the Three Graces. I have models for Beauty and Grace. I only need Charm."

"He is *always* lacking charm, isn't he, Georgiana?" Langham put in.

Georgiana rolled her eyes but nodded at Langham's playful dig.

"How do you know I am charming?" Cara asked, genuinely perplexed. "You've only just met me."

"Ha! The artless way you asked that question tells me exactly what I need to know."

"Aren't the Three Graces usually painted in the nude?" Georgiana asked.

"Nude!" Cara squeaked in alarm. For the first time, she felt uneasy. Had she made a mistake coming here after all?

Her discomfort made Adrian chuckle. "Don't worry, my dear. This particular theatre aims to bring in respectable, middle-class patrons, and we can't risk offending them. I was thinking more along the lines of Greek robes. Enough to preserve modesty while accentuating each woman's face and figure." He took a step back, looking Cara over and considering. "Blue, I think, would be your color. Light blue with golden threads."

"You're right, she'd be perfect," Langham agreed. "You're using Augusta and Jane for the other two, aren't you? Cara will be a perfect complement to them. The round face, the pert chin, the golden hair. Not to mention those big blue eyes. She's a stunner of a different sort altogether. Not so languid and pale, or giving the impression of being two steps away from death."

"Oh, I should hope not!" Cara exclaimed. She felt decidedly uncomfortable again as the two men studied her. They might be looking at her with professional painter's eyes, but it was disconcerting nonetheless.

Georgiana took the paintbrush from Adrian's hand. "The tea is getting cold. Why don't we take a break?"

"I'll pay you for the modeling, of course," Adrian told Cara.

"Up front?" Langham asked.

"Are you her booking agent, then?" Georgiana teased.

"Don't give him any commission, Cara," Adrian warned. "He'll only drink it." As if to prove this, he picked up the bottle of gin and tipped a bit more into his and Langham's glasses.

At some point after the tea and sandwiches had been consumed, Langham had said something about the "sun being over the yardarm," and a bottle of gin had been brought out. This had made Cara nervous at first. She did not dare do more than wet her lips with the stuff, for throughout her life she'd heard admonitions about what terrible things happened to women who succumbed to drink.

Soon, however, she began to feel more at ease. Everyone was kind, and Georgiana's presence made her feel safe. Georgiana was down-to-earth with a wry sense of humor. She and Adrian had met a few years ago when one of his cousins had married one of hers. They had immediately bonded over their mutual passion for art and had been sharing this home for two years. Although not physically related, their status as cousins by marriage made their living arrangement marginally respectable. When Langham had come to London, looking for a place to live, they had invited him to join them.

When asked about her background, Cara shared some details about growing up in the orphanage in Bristol. She told them how she'd later worked as a scullery maid and then a parlor maid. She didn't mention the Needenhams or her work there. It wasn't *lying*, exactly, if one simply skipped over information, right?

As the day wore on, Cara knew she ought to go. But she had no desire to leave. This was the most fun she'd had in ages. She enjoyed the banter among these three. Such informal interaction between men and women was something she had never experienced.

"I asked about the payment for modeling because Cara is new to London and hasn't much money," Langham explained. "I want to help her out."

"And what big plans do you have for yourself in London?" Adrian asked her.

"I plan to become a painter." It was exciting to say it aloud. This was her new life. There would be no more living on her sisters' terms. "I know I might have to find other work as well, just to get on my feet."

"What makes you think you can find success as a painter?" Georgiana asked. She did not pose the question in a negative way but seemed sincerely interested.

"I read an article in *Victoria Magazine* describing how much more opportunity there is today for artists than in years past. Many people are commissioning paintings for their homes and for public buildings, and paying well for them. Some artists are becoming quite wealthy!" Even though Cara had been impressed with the article, she hadn't thought it could ever apply to her. Not until today.

"Some artists are living well off their earnings," Langham agreed. "Leighton, Watts, Burne-Jones. The rest of us are still working on it."

"But you are going to show your work at the Grosvenor!" Cara said. "Your paintings will be alongside those of famous artists."

Langham tipped his head. "I hope they don't put me to complete shame."

"Don't let Langham fool you with his false modesty," Adrian said. "He plans to be more famous than any of them."

Langham simply shrugged and grinned. "Georgiana, I believe she has a real talent for portraiture. Perhaps you can connect her with potential clients."

"It's possible," Georgiana replied. "But let's not get ahead of ourselves. She hasn't had training and is new to London. She will need a studio and supplies."

"Oh," said Cara, crestfallen. "I hadn't thought about that." Of course she hadn't. She'd had this mad idea in her mind for all of six hours.

"I don't wish to discourage you," Georgiana said. "Only to help you plan. Adrian will pay you for modeling. That's a start. Where are you staying?"

"I don't know," Cara said, feeling foolish. "That is, I will probably stay with my brother-in-law's family."

Langham said, "I vote that she stays here with us."

"Oh, I couldn't," Cara protested.

And yet the moment Langham said it aloud, Cara realized this was what she'd secretly been wishing for. It would be thrilling to live here, to have a chance to explore being a model and an artist. From what Cara had gleaned so far, Georgiana and Adrian made a reasonable living selling their art. Adrian had sold his more "lofty-themed" artwork, as Georgiana put it, to wealthy clients who needed to fill the walls of their grand homes.

Adrian's bushy eyebrows pulled together, and he and Georgiana traded glances. Neither one spoke, and Cara was suddenly embarrassed that Langham had put them on the spot like this. Why should they take in a virtual stranger? It was too much to ask. She set down her napkin, preparing to rise from the table. It was time to go.

Then, to her surprise, she saw Adrian and Georgiana give a tiny nod to each other, almost in unison.

"I suppose Cara might stay for a few days," Georgiana said. "Just to see how things work out."

"It would certainly make things easier for the modeling," Adrian agreed. "I can begin preliminary sketches tomorrow. The painting must be done before the theatre opens next month."

Relieved and happy, Cara grinned. Langham finished off the gin in his glass and sat back, crossing his arms and beaming.

"Is this what you meant about having an idea up your sleeve?" Cara asked him. "You thought I might stay here?"

"I saw it as a possibility. Now that I've heard your story, I'm sure I was right."

"It will be nice to have another woman around," Georgiana said. "However, sometimes you might need to remind these two that you are neither the cook nor the maid."

"It's a good thing, too," Cara said. "I'm terrible at both those things."

Georgiana smiled. "I think you are going to get along here just fine."

"Excellent," Langham said, slapping the table to indicate a done deal. He got up and began to rummage through a box of supplies at the far end of the studio.

"What are you looking for?" Adrian asked.

"I'm sure I packed somewhere in here what we need . . . yes, here it is." He pulled a bottle from one of the crates. "A bit of brandy to toast the new tenant."

CHAPTER

8

H ENRY LOOKED OUT at the rain, which was coming down in buckets.

Very large buckets.

"The rain will end in a day or so, my lord," said Mr. Thompson cheerfully. "I'm sure of it."

Henry and Mr. Thompson, the man hired to oversee the rebuilding project, were standing at the open door of the smaller house on the Morestowe estate. Although it was known as the dower cottage, his widowed mother would never consider inhabiting it. The place had been neglected for years and was nowhere near the grandeur of the family mansion. It would take a good deal of work to bring the kitchen and living areas up to modern standards. That was a project for another day, however. The mansion had to be finished first. Looking out at the pouring rain, Henry began to doubt whether that would ever happen.

Although Mr. Thompson had a near-legendary ability to foretell weather changes, Henry had a difficult time believing his prediction. "What makes you so sure?"

"Barometric pressure is rising, temperature is dropping. There's been a shift in the wind direction, too. Coming from the south now. Not to mention that I had a bit of forecast help from the Meteorological Office."

"So you use a smattering of science as well as tea leaves?" Henry said.

Mr. Thompson acknowledged Henry's attempt at humor with a smile. "I would say my strength is in bringing together many pieces of information."

From their vantage point, they could see the main house, which lay on the other side of the wide lawn. The roof of the entire east wing was still covered with large sheets of oilcloth to keep out the rain. Parts of the lawn were lost under pools of water, as was a good portion of the drive. It was going to be a challenge to get his carriage to the railway station. But Henry had to leave for London.

"In the meantime, we've been able to carry on with the refurbishment of the west wing," Mr. Thompson reminded him. "The plasterers are done, and the work on the baseboards is underway. Once that's complete, we'll start painting. You should be able to move in soon."

It was all good news, as far as it went. The family could live in the west wing, in the rooms normally used for guests, until the east wing was rebuilt.

After they'd reviewed a few more details, Mr. Thompson donned his mackintosh and strode off toward the main house.

Henry stood there awhile longer, looking at the soggy landscape. Even in this deluge, he could find some beauty in the scene. The wet summer had made everything green and lush. He'd always felt bound to this land, which had been in his family for generations. The hard circumstances he'd dealt with this year only made him love the place more. It was part of him, an extension of his soul. He wanted nothing more than to bring the estate back to its prime. There were more challenges to come, but somehow he would do it.

He closed the door against the rain and went to the room that originally functioned as a parlor. Now it resembled a business office. A large work table had been brought in, and the various plans and paperwork relating to the reconstruction were spread over it.

A smaller desk in the corner held Henry's correspondence and other documents that had been brought from his study at the main house. He pulled a key ring from his pocket and opened one of the locked drawers. This was where his housekeeper, the only other person with a key, deposited any correspondence that arrived for him. Today there was a small stack of items. Settling in a dusty armchair by the empty fireplace, he began to sort through them.

One item in particular stood out. It was from one of the best tailors in London. The one his brother used. Henry opened it and found a hefty bill for a new suit, completed just last week.

He could have kicked himself for missing the obvious answer. Langham had not gone tearing off to some seaside resort; he had gone to London. Langham wouldn't care that the city was melting in the heat or that the Season was over. Many homes in Holland Park, the artists' enclave Langham favored, had spacious lawns with shade trees, open to cooling breezes. Plenty of residents stayed there year-round.

Why had the bill come here, when Langham knew Henry was still in London? The answer was obvious. Langham had counted on Henry not seeing this for several weeks. He didn't want to disclose his whereabouts, even if he could not resist a new set of clothes—which, Henry noted with irritation, was expensive. Try as he might, curbing Langham's spendthrift ways had been a losing battle.

Henry placed the bill in a satchel, along with other correspondence that he would address once he returned to London. Now he had a way to find Langham. When he returned to the city, that would be his first order of business.

"Did I ever mention that I can do magic tricks?" Langham returned to their table and set down a glass of whiskey, covering it with his hat. "I can drink this, in one go, without touching the hat."

Georgiana groaned. "Even assuming you could, don't you think you've had enough?"

Langham waved away her remark like a pesky fly. "Then you should have asked to see this trick earlier."

Cara shared Georgiana's concern. The few days she'd spent at the artists' home had gone so well. The small bedroom they'd offered her was comfortable enough, and her days were full, as she'd begun to immerse herself in their world. The only thing that troubled her was Langham's tendency to drink too much.

They had been in this pub for hours. The evening had begun pleasantly, for the pub was frequented by many artists. Cara had enjoyed listening to their spirited debates about painting styles and techniques, and the gossip about whose work was at which gallery, and who had made recent sales. She and Georgiana were the only female artists there, although a few other women had accompanied some of the men.

Cara had spent the evening taking small sips from a single pint of beer, but many of the others, including Langham, had been steadily finishing off glass after glass. Gradually, as more and more pints of beer were brought out and consumed, the place got noisier and the talk became more raucous.

Langham's slurred speech and unsteady gait had already begun to worry her, and now he was going to top off the beer with whiskey.

Adrian rose from the table, reaching for Langham's arm. "Don't be idiotic. Let's go home."

Langham shook off his friend's grasp. "'There are more things in heaven and earth, Horatio, than are dreamt of in your philosophy.'"

"Horatio?" Cara repeated, confused.

"Langham always quotes Shakespeare when he's drunk," Georgiana told her.

"This is the last drink," Langham insisted, pointing their attention back to the hat covering his glass.

"You said that three pints ago," Adrian pointed out.

"Four," Georgiana corrected.

"Cara wants to see the trick, don't you?" Langham leaned toward her with a crooked grin.

Cara looked between the three of them, not wanting to be the deciding factor in this situation.

"See there, she does." Langham dropped suddenly to his knees and slid under the table.

"What are you doing?" Cara cried out in alarm.

The only response was three loud bangs as Langham struck the table from below. This was followed by a long, rude slurping noise.

"Come out from under there, Langham," Adrian ordered. "Don't be a buffoon."

Langham's hands appeared first, taking hold of the table. He then hoisted himself to a standing position. Once he had gained his feet, albeit unsteadily, he wiped a hand across his mouth.

"You can't really have drunk it," Cara said, giving the hat a doubtful look.

He waggled his eyebrows. "There's only one way to know for sure."

Cara couldn't resist. She picked up the hat to look under it. The glass was just as full as it had been moments before. Before she could even turn to Langham, he snatched up the glass. Tossing his head back, he downed the liquor in one swallow.

"Victory!" he proclaimed, slamming the glass on the table and dropping back into his seat. "You see, I drank the entire thing without touching the hat!" He began to laugh so forcefully that he held his stomach. "I . . . didn't . . . touch . . . the hat!" he gasped between bouts of laughter. He picked up the glass and sent it flying over his shoulder. It struck the wall and shattered, causing nearby patrons to jump in alarm. Their reaction only caused Langham to laugh harder.

"We're going home *now*," Adrian ordered. He grabbed Langham and pulled him to his feet. Georgiana got up, too, and Cara willingly followed.

They hadn't gone three steps before they were intercepted by the pub's owner, a big, beefy man with a grizzled chin. "Yer not goin' anywhere till you've settled the bill."

"Just put it on my account," Langham said breezily. "And the glass, too," he added, looking at the barmaid scooping up the shards from the floor. "You know I'm good for it."

"I know nothing of the sort," the pub owner returned. "You'll give me one pound, three shillings and sixpence, or I'll send a man to fetch the constable from the corner."

Cara gasped. Had they really spent that much? That was nearly two weeks' wages at her previous position. Adrian was correct that they'd lost count of how many rounds they'd ordered. Not to mention the cost of the glass that Langham had destroyed. Cara looked at her own glass, which was still half-full. After they had spent that kind of money, she felt almost guilty for not finishing her drink. As though finishing it might help justify the size of the bill.

Langham reached into his pocket and produced a gilt-edged card. "No need for the constable. Send your man 'round to this address tomorrow, and we'll get it settled."

The pub owner pocketed the card but didn't budge. "Do you think this is some fancy place that caters to swells? You think the likes of me can afford to run a place with no cash, hoping to get paid months from now?" He jerked his head around to call out to a worker clearing another table. "Bob! Fetch the constable. Now!"

Bob set down the dishes and made for the door.

"Wait!" Georgiana said. "I've got the money."

Bob paused, and the pub owner looked at her expectantly. "Well? Where is it?"

"It's in a pocket inside my skirt." Georgiana lowered her voice. "I will have to go to the ladies' privy to get it out."

The owner's eyes narrowed. "What new trick is this?"

Georgiana said coolly, "Send a barmaid with me if you don't trust me."

"All right." He pointed at Adrian and Langham. "But these two stay here."

He didn't seem to care one way or the other about Cara. She stood still, pressing her back against a nearby post, trying not to garner any attention.

Langham swayed, his face paling. Perhaps he was finally feeling the effects of so much alcohol. "I shall wait here, if you don't mind." He sent a defiant glance toward the pub owner as he sank onto a chair. "All this fuss is entirely unnecessary. In fact—"

He interrupted himself as his attention turned toward the door of the pub, where a man was just entering.

The new arrival was clearly not the sort of person who normally came to pubs like this. He wore a fine black coat and waistcoat. An

82

impeccably tied cravat stood out against the white linen shirt beneath. He and Langham caught sight of one another at the same moment. Two things were immediately obvious: these men knew each other, and neither was happy to see the other.

"Naturally," Langham said with disgust. "Just when we're starting to have some fun, in comes his lordship and ruins everything."

The man made a beeline for their table. "How long were you planning on slumming, Langham?"

Langham leaned back in his chair, arms crossed, and sent him an insolent smile. "Don't look so glum, Harry. Have a drink."

"I suppose I should be happy to have a brother who wastes my time by sending me on a wild goose chase across southwest England."

Cara drew in a breath. This was Langham's brother—the earl! She ought to have known immediately, if only from his aristocratic bearing and fine clothes. He was tall and handsome, although there was a hardness to his expression that she didn't care for. Perhaps he was the type of man who never smiled. Or never found a reason to.

"If you're not glad to see me, why bother seeking me out?" Langham sounded as disapproving as his brother. "Why can't you leave me be?"

The earl glanced around the pub, evidently aware he and Langham had become the center of attention. He spoke in a low growl. "We're not going to discuss this any further here."

He went round to the back of Langham's chair, clearly intending to hoist him to his feet.

"If I might have a word with you, sir," the pub owner interjected, dropping his belligerent tone for one more respectful. It hadn't taken him long to figure out this was a man of superior rank—one who likely had plenty of money. "I'm afraid I cannot allow this gentleman to leave the premises until he has settled his bill of two pounds. Perhaps you wouldn't mind helping him out, seeing as how you are a particular friend of his?"

Cara sucked in a breath, unable to believe he had bumped up the total so steeply.

"He's not my *friend*. He's my *brother*." His look of distaste made it clear there was no way Langham could possibly fill both roles. "And don't try to inflate the bill. Not even my brother could have drunk that much in one night."

"They were with him," the pub owner replied, indicating Cara and the others. "They've had supper as well as drinks, *and* bought rounds for their friends."

Langham raised his arm with a dramatic flourish and proclaimed, "'I like this place, and willingly could waste my time in it.'"

The earl sized up Adrian and Cara. His gaze lingered on Cara for an uncomfortably long moment. "You've hit up the wrong man. He has no money. You'd do better to aim your attentions elsewhere."

Cara stepped forward. "That's a terrible thing to say! Langham is our friend!"

In the context of this cramped and noisy pub, they might all look like ne'er-do-wells. But Cara wasn't going to allow anyone to belittle her. She boldly met the earl's gaze and was surprised to find herself thinking he had very nice eyes—dark and alert, showing confidence and intelligence but no friendliness. How much handsomer he'd be if he were not so formidable.

His brow furrowed. "You allow your friends to get so drunk they can't see straight?"

Cara was stung by this reproach. She'd wanted to curb Langham's drinking. But honestly, what could she have done?

"We have our own money, sir," Adrian said, speaking in a tone that was polite but not apologetic. "We were just getting ready to settle the bill and take him home when you arrived."

"You won't be taking him home," the earl answered. "I will." He turned to the pub owner. "I'll give you the two pounds—and an extra half crown if you help me get him to the carriage outside."

"Gladly, sir." The owner motioned to Bob, who immediately stepped forward, ready to lend his aid.

"But you can't just leave with him!" Cara protested.

Those aristocratic eyes once more turned to her. "Why not?"

"Well . . . because he's staying with us!" she sputtered.

His eyebrows lifted, and his mouth turned up just a little. She amused him, and this riled her more. She looked at Adrian, expecting him to offer some protest.

He merely said, "I think it's best if Langham goes with his lordship for now."

His response surprised her. Why was he so willing to send Langham home with his overbearing brother? This man could not possibly have Langham's best interests at heart.

The earl and Bob hoisted Langham from the chair. They half carried him as he stumbled forward, although the movement seemed to rouse him.

"'A horse, a horse! My kingdom for a horse!'" he shouted.

This drew plenty of guffaws from the other patrons.

The pub owner went ahead to open the door, and Cara and the others followed in their wake. Cara was worried. Langham had been helping her so much. What would she do if he didn't return?

The men got Langham into the carriage. Once the earl was seated next to him, he stretched out a hand and promptly dropped money into the pub owner's waiting palm.

"'Cry—God for Harry, England, and Saint George!'" Langham shouted, lurching forward as though trying to escape from the carriage. The earl stopped him, but his hand was still on the doorframe when the footman slammed it shut. He howled in pain. The footman offered profuse apologies.

"Just drive!" the earl barked.

The footman jumped into his place on the back of the carriage as the driver set the horses in motion.

Cara could only watch, flabbergasted, as the carriage rolled away.

CHAPTER

9

MUST YOU MAKE so much noise?" Langham groaned. In fact, the china had made only a tiny *clink* as the footman carefully set the coffee tray next to the bed.

Henry glared at his brother. "Must you drink so much that it leaves your head as tender as chopped steak?"

He ensured the door made a good solid *thunk* as he closed it after the footman left the room. He did not normally wish ill on people, but he did take satisfaction in seeing his brother wince again.

Langham dragged himself to a seated position and placed a palm against his forehead. "I admit I feel rather crapulous this morning."

Henry blew out a breath. After years of study at Oxford and Lincoln's Inn, Langham retained little more than an archaic word for feeling ill after too much drinking. He poured coffee into a cup and thrust it unceremoniously into his brother's hands. "What are you doing in London? You weren't to leave the sanitarium without the doctor's permission."

"You know what that *sanitarium* is," Langham returned sourly. "It's no health spa. It's for mad people." He took a swig of his coffee.

"There's nothing wrong with me. I'm perfectly sane. What's more, I have important business to attend to."

"I suppose your main office is located inside a dingy public house?"

"Mock me if you want; I don't care. Last week I met with Sir Coutts Lindsay, who owns the Grosvenor Gallery. I showed him my work, and he was highly impressed. He wants to display two of my paintings in the October show."

"And just what is he planning? A vanity show for wealthy dilettantes?"

Langham raised an eyebrow. "I'm glad we are still managing to convince people we're rich."

Henry was sorely tempted to snatch the cup from Langham's hands and hit him over the head with it. He might have done so, except his hand hurt like the devil from being slammed in the carriage door. "We'd be in a lot better position if you didn't keep wasting money. Or if you actually *earned* some. You need to find a real occupation, Langham. Maybe you don't mind playing a starving artist, but I'm the one who must ultimately pay those bills you're piling up."

"You needn't act so desperate. We all know you'll have the family fortunes repaired in no time. That LLC in Cumbria is set to make piles of money."

"Unfortunately, I was pushed out of the deal after the Duke of Crandall came on board."

Langham looked at him in surprise, then gave a nod of understanding. "Still harboring that grudge over your speeches against annexing the South African Republic? You'd think he'd reconsider, seeing all the trouble it has caused since."

"He also worries about my unstable brother."

"That's ridiculous." Langham looked truly affronted, which would have made Henry laugh were the situation not so serious.

"People talk. They know why you were in that sanitarium."

"Baseless rumors. I told you those fireplaces were bad."

"Be that as it may, that is where we stand. I need you to do your part to help this family. I've received tentative approval from the Council at Lincoln's Inn for you to return there in October—if you can behave yourself."

Heaving a sigh, Langham set his coffee cup aside. "Let me explain this again." He spoke with exasperating condescension. "I am never going back to Lincoln's Inn. Painting is my occupation. I intend to make money from my art."

"I can see how getting falling-down drunk in a pub is a good way to accomplish that."

"I'm not going to argue with you about it." Langham pushed back the covers. "If you don't mind, I'm going to bathe and get dressed, return to my lodgings, and get back to work."

"No, Langham. Your lodgings are right here. I can't have you off living somewhere like a bohemian." Henry wanted his brother where he could watch over him.

Langham frowned. "My clothes and supplies are at Holland Park Road."

"The address on the tailor's bill."

"So that's how you found me. I hoped it would be several more weeks before you saw it."

"When I went to the house, the maid told me the name of the pub where you'd all gone."

Langham must have caught the censure in Henry's voice. "Staying with Adrian is an excellent opportunity. I can learn a lot. He's a respected painter and making a fair living at it. You would know that if you'd bothered to look into it."

"I have looked into it, as it happens," Henry replied. "I know that most of Adrian D'Adamo's work involves scene painting and other commercial projects. I also know that he is living with a woman he calls his cousin, while his wife lives in India. Is that really what you call respectable?"

"I said he is a *respected* painter. *Respectable* is some adjective the blue-blood set and the middle class wring their hands over. Adrian's work is in demand. So is Georgiana's. They are seasoned artists, in addition to being decent people. That business about them being paramours is gossip, nothing more. Besides, do you really want me to set up a studio here? The only good light in this house is in the best parlor. I feel sure Mother would object to the room smelling of turpentine while she receives visitors during her at-home days."

Henry clenched his fists in frustration. He could not deny that adding Langham to this house would only increase tensions all around. But he could see no way around it, and it helped that the others were away for now. "It's only temporary. We're returning to Morestowe in a few weeks, and in the meantime, Mother has gone to Brighton with Amelia."

"Has she?" Langham lifted an eyebrow. "I thought she could not abide the girl. She seems to have it in for the governess, too, as I recall."

"Nevertheless, they have all gone together."

"Well, that sounds cozy." With this dismissal, Langham dropped his feet over the side of the bed. "I must get in some work while the light is good. I will sleep here, if you insist. But I have committed myself to producing two paintings for the Grosvenor, and I must paint in a proper studio if I'm to create work fit for it. Even *you* must be aware that the Grosvenor Gallery has an excellent reputation. The Prince of Wales himself attended the opening gala! It's difficult to get more haute than that. You might not think much of artists, but you have to admit that my being invited to show there cannot actually harm the family reputation in any way."

"I'm not prepared to admit anything of the sort. I haven't even seen your work, as you won't show it to your family. Suppose the critics agree that it is no good?"

His brother gave him a dark look. "Then you will be happy to see your brother fail at the wrong thing instead of the right one."

Langham's style of debating would have been effective in Parliament; he was a master at using his adversary's words to drive him into a corner.

Langham leaned over and pressed the call bell. "One benefit of being forced to live here is that there are servants to draw the bath." He pressed his hand to his head. "It will need to be a hot one to clear my brain. The sooner I get to the studio, the better. I need to see how Cara is getting along. She seems like a stray kitten at times, and she's bound to be unsettled by the scene you made at the pub last night."

A stray kitten? Casting his mind back, Henry could think of no one in that pub who fit such a description. Every woman there looked hardened from frequent visits to the gin trough. Except for the one with the fresh face and large blue eyes. "Do you mean the blonde standing near D'Adamo? She lit up like some kind of firebrand when I started to take you from the pub."

"That's the one. Miss Cara Bernay." Langham smiled. "She has more spirit in her than I thought."

"That wasn't Georgiana Marshall?"

"Oh, goodness, no. Georgiana is older and not nearly as pretty."

Miss Bernay's actions made more sense now. If she was somehow dependent on Langham, she'd be distressed to see him go. However, this information only aroused a new fear in Henry. Langham had been led astray by a woman before. Henry couldn't allow him to get entangled with another. "Exactly who is this Cara Bernay?"

"She's new to London. She wants to be a painter, and she's doing some modeling, too. She's a stunner, is she not?"

Henry wasn't fond of that slang word, but he couldn't deny she was beautiful. Based on what Langham had just said, she planned to capitalize on that trait to make her living. It brought to mind another expression making the rounds these days: *professional beauty*. These were often models or actresses and not generally known to have the highest morals. Henry found this a depressing thought. Despite the energetic way she'd tried to stand up to him last night, Miss Bernay had looked young and innocent. Perhaps she was, if she was new to London. Unfortunately, a career as a professional beauty would leave her jaded before long. Henry didn't know why it bothered him so deeply, but it did.

All the more reason he needed to keep a close eye on his brother. "We're moving back to the estate in a few weeks' time. There have been delays completing the east wing, but the rest of the house will be habitable soon. We can set up a studio for you there. In the meantime, you may continue to paint at D'Adamo's place. But I want to see what you are working on."

Langham replied to this pronouncement with a deferential droop of his head. "I thank you humbly for your kind permission, my lord."

Henry wasn't fooled. Langham was the one who called the tunes.

Henry just played along as best he could and tried to find a way to pay the band.

"You look stunning!" Georgiana enthused. "Simply beautiful."

Cara stood still as Georgiana fussed with the folds of the garment. To call what she was wearing a "gown" would not have been accurate, for this was loose and flowing, just like the picture of a woman from ancient Greece that she'd once seen in a book.

With the garment in place to her satisfaction, Georgiana began to weave flowers and a blue ribbon into Cara's hair. Cara watched her transformation in the mirror with fascination. Soon she would not only resemble a book drawing, but she herself would be forever captured in a real painting.

Her exhilaration was lessened only by her worries about Langham. They'd heard nothing of him since he'd been taken from the pub by the earl. She had no doubt he was all right, aside from the possible ill effects of too much drinking. Even though Lord Morestowe had sent murderous glares at his brother, Cara didn't think he would actually hurt him. After all, he was a member of the aristocracy! They didn't do such things—did they?

Cara shook her head and ended up pulling against Georgiana's hands.

"Is something wrong?" Georgiana asked.

Cara met her eyes in the mirror. "Do you think Langham will come back?"

"I'm certain of it. He's had run-ins with Lord Morestowe before. His lordship doesn't understand Langham's desire to be an artist. They are like oil and water, those two."

"How can you be sure he'll return?"

"He's got to paint, hasn't he? All his materials and works in progress are here. He's not going to abandon those."

Cara took some comfort in that. Still, she wasn't entirely at ease. "Suppose his lordship makes him go away?"

Georgiana paused to look at Cara more closely. "You're not falling in love with him, are you?"

"Of course not! It's just that, well, he's been so helpful to me. And he brought me here and asked you and Adrian if I could stay."

Georgiana went back to working on Cara's hair. "We have no objection to your staying here for now. We might leave, though, in a week or two. My family has been urging us to join them on holiday in Blackpool."

It was a reminder to Cara that, as much as she enjoyed being here, this was a temporary situation. Was she only putting off the inevitable—seeking help from her own family? Maybe she'd been foolish to think she could strike out on her own so soon.

"We can discuss all that later," Georgiana said, tucking the last bit of ribbon behind one of Cara's curls. "Let's go show you to Adrian."

As they went downstairs to the studio, Cara told herself to take things one day at a time. She'd seen many times at the orphanage that answers to prayers could come out of nowhere, and hardly ever in the expected way. Hadn't she experienced that already, given the events that had transpired since she'd arrived in London? This bolstered her soul and gave her greater confidence for the future.

Adrian was pleased with Cara's costume and set to work finding the best light to put her in. He had her stand on a raised platform and try several poses.

"But aren't there supposed to be three of us?" Cara asked. "Where are the other two?"

"That's what I'd like to know, too," Adrian replied with a frown. "They are late."

He'd hardly finished speaking when the doorbell rang.

"That'll be the ladies, no doubt," Georgiana said.

Cara caught a glimpse of their maid, Susan, hurrying down the hallway to open the front door.

A minute later, it wasn't the sound of ladies Cara heard approaching. It was men's voices. Langham strolled into the studio. Cara was overjoyed to see him, but her greeting snagged in her throat when she saw who was with him.

The Earl of Morestowe paused the moment he laid eyes on her. His raised eyebrows and slightly open mouth conveyed surprise—shock, even. It was no wonder. Her Grecian robes offered far less coverage than a proper frock. A shiver skittered across her bare neck and shoulders. She became acutely aware that the full length of her arms was exposed, along with her feet and ankles. Why hadn't she felt uncomfortable like this with Adrian? The whole atmosphere of the room changed with the earl's entrance. Embarrassment flooded through her.

In her confusion, she dropped her eyes from his bold look that seemed to take in every part of her. As she did so, she noticed the bandage around his left hand. She remembered how the coachman had accidentally shut the door on it the night before. Cara's heart, already aflutter from mortification, began to beat wildly. An idea played at the far edges of her mind, but she wasn't sure she dared to believe it.

CHAPTER

10

WHEN HE'D ENTERED the artists' studio, Henry had been prepared for any number of things. But not for this. He froze, hat in hand. He barely registered the room around him, because standing in the center of it, lit by sunlight, was a Greek goddess.

It was a testament to how startlingly beautiful she was that the sight of her instantly sent Henry's normally staid thoughts into such wild imaginings. He knew, of course, that this was the girl from the tavern. Cara Bernay, the "stunner." The would-be professional beauty. Her blue eyes grew round, her lips parting in surprise when Henry and Langham entered the room.

Henry swallowed, his mouth suddenly dry. This woman, who had been pretty even in a drab coat, had transformed from an ordinary human into a vision from some myth or heraldic tale. Her cheeks had the rosy bloom he'd noticed last night, but her neck and shoulders were pale as marble. Her gown was drawn in with a gold cord at her waist, displaying a figure perfect in every way. She was a statue come to life, with flowers in her hair and delicate blond tendrils framing her face.

Henry couldn't find the strength to look away. He was overcome by the urge to take in every detail of her. Try as he might, he could not dislodge the swarm of ridiculous thoughts taking over his brain.

Cara dropped her gaze. She held a bouquet of flowers, which she reflexively brought closer to her chest. Was she embarrassed to be seen like this? If so, why was she allowing herself to be captured by the painter's brush for posterity?

A curl bounced a little as she straightened and resumed her pose, her moment of uncertainty replaced with a jaunty lift of her chin. The grit she'd displayed last night blossomed in her eyes and posture, and her full red lips gave the barest hint of a smile. Henry was captivated, but there was a stab of disappointment, too. Cara Bernay was learning to throw off embarrassment as one more step on her road to becoming a professional beauty.

"What is this vision of loveliness?" Langham broke the awkward silence, opening his arms wide with warmth and approval. "Cara, you are perfect. Simply perfect. Not even Adrian will be able to do you justice."

D'Adamo gave a grunt of displeasure at this remark. He had paused his work when Henry entered. So had the other woman in the room, Georgiana Marshall. She stood at an easel by the window, also with paintbrush in hand. Neither looked pleased at Henry's arrival.

Cara turned her attention and a warm smile toward Langham. "I'm so glad to see you. I was worried you might be prevented from coming."

Her gaze slid briefly to Henry, but the warmth she'd been directing at Langham did not come with it.

Dropping his hat and gloves carelessly on a table strewn with painting implements, Langham went over to her. "You needn't have worried. My brother is an ogre, but he has not reached the point of locking me in my room."

"Not *yet*, at any rate," Henry warned, irritated at being talked about as though he weren't here and growing uncomfortable at the cool reception. "Langham, show me your work," he directed. This brought more disapproving looks from the others, but Henry didn't care. If he was to be considered an ogre, then so be it.

"I do not show unfinished work, so I won't show you the work in progress," Langham returned. "However, here is one that is complete." He went to a stack of canvases leaning against the wall. He pulled one out, unwrapped the burlap covering, and turned it to Henry's view.

The painting was perhaps four feet high. Judging from the clothing of the people in it, it was a depiction of some medieval tale. The scene was set in a garden. Everything was painted in minute detail, from the vines encircling the columns to the intricate patterns on the lady's gown.

There were two people in the piece, a man and a woman. They looked hurried, furtive, as though in a clandestine meeting. They seemed familiar, but Henry couldn't place them. Perhaps this was because their faces were partially obscured—the woman's face was turned away from the viewer, toward the man's shoulder, and the man was leaning into her, his lips pressed against one of her arms. The whole painting spoke of love and longing. It shocked Henry, because it grabbed at his heart in a surprising and painful way.

He said, astonished, "You painted this?"

Langham's eyes blazed with pride. "Perhaps now you understand what I've been trying to tell you."

A stillness overtook the room. Henry looked around to see that all eyes were on him as he studied the painting. The superior, almost haughty expressions of D'Adamo and Miss Marshall indicated the pride that they, too, had in their profession.

"Isn't it wonderful?" Cara said. "Langham is such a talented artist."

Her praise had a near-worshipful tone, and her eyes were shining. Henry wondered if she was in love with Langham. That thought worried him. What if Langham returned her feelings? Given Langham's history, how could he not find such a woman irresistible? And what dangers would it lead to? In this living situation, it would be too easy to cross the lines of propriety and—

Clearing his throat, Henry looked away from her and focused instead on his brother. "I won't deny it is good. I can see why Sir Coutts is willing to hang it in the Grosvenor."

His praise was given grudgingly, because he knew Langham would start preening. Langham did indeed indulge in a triumphant smile.

"Are you also a painter, my lord?"

This question came from Miss Bernay. It surprised him, for he was sure Langham would have already told her the answer to that question. But she seemed perfectly sincere, looking at him with friendly eyes. How could this woman appear so artless and yet also so alluring? A slant of sunlight perfectly highlighted one smooth shoulder, and for some reason this simple fact made it hard for Henry to breathe. "No, I am not," he managed.

"Henry does have a modicum of ability," Langham said, "but—"

"I haven't time for such things," Henry cut him off.

Langham's eyes narrowed, and his mouth flattened. He looked between Henry and Cara, his expression unreadable.

"I am a painter," Cara said, speaking with a lightness that indicated she had not noticed the tension in the air.

"So I have heard." He spoke more harshly than he intended, sounding as though he were belittling her. Cara looked startled at his rudeness. He said more gently, "I, er, wish you well in your efforts."

She beamed at him in response, and Henry felt decidedly unsteady.

Langham replaced the burlap over his painting. "Now, dear brother, if you will allow me to return to my work? My next *oeuvre* will be a masterpiece, too, but it is far from complete."

The others looked ready to see the back of him, too, except Cara. She was still smiling. Was she trying to win him over? If so, to what end?

Henry wasn't going to allow his younger brother to dismiss him so casually. "You will accompany me to the door, if you please."

Langham gave a little smirk at this order. "Yes, m'lord."

After giving terse good-byes to the others—and refusing to allow his gaze to linger too long on Cara Bernay—Henry walked out of the room with Langham. He paused when they reached the front entryway, satisfied they were out of earshot. "Langham, what do you know of that girl?"

"Cara?" Langham shrugged. "She's very sweet—as you have no doubt noticed. She has artistic talent, too. I think she has a good chance of succeeding as a painter. Would you like to see her work before you go?"

"No!" Henry didn't want to risk spending any more time in that studio. Cara had unsettled him too much already. "Where is she from? What's her background?"

"She grew up in Bristol and spent several years in service before coming to London. She's pretty, isn't she?" Langham lifted an eyebrow. "Is that why you are so interested in her?"

"No, that is *not* why I'm asking," Henry replied heatedly, although he was still trying to quell the odd sensations that had overtaken him. "I want to know if *you* are forming some kind of attachment to her."

"I think she is marvelous, but no, I am not 'forming an attachment.'"

"Why not?" he blurted, and immediately regretted it. He knew it would give the wrong impression.

Langham answered nonetheless. "My interests regarding that sort of *attachment*—which I assure you are honorable—lie in a different direction."

"Which are?"

"I'm not going to tell you. If I do, you'll interfere and ruin everything."

It wasn't the first time Langham had sent back a similar retort, but today it seemed to have extra venom. As though he harbored a long-standing grudge. Sometimes, Henry wondered whether his brother suspected that the sweetheart of his youth had been forcibly separated from him all those years ago. But Henry had no way of finding out, short of telling Langham the truth about the situation, and that was not something he was prepared to do. He returned to the topic at hand. "I'm worried that you've taken this woman under your wing when you know almost nothing about her."

"She needed a place to stay. She has relatives in the city, but for some reason she prefers not to stay with them. That is a sentiment I can well understand."

They stared at one another with mutual animosity. Henry seethed with frustration, taken by a powerful urge to shake some sense into his brother. Not that it would work.

Langham relaxed his posture and aimed a disarming smile at him. "Have you any money? I owe Adrian for a new canvas and paint."

It took extra audacity to ask this after the way he'd just insulted

Henry. But then, Langham never had any qualms about asking for money, no matter the circumstances.

Reluctantly, Henry reached into his pocket. But he wasn't going to let the money go without strings attached. He paused before dropping the coins into Langham's hand. "You are coming back to the house tonight, remember? You are to remain here only during the day—and to spend that time *painting*."

Langham gave him a supercilious grin as he pocketed the cash. "Yes, m'lord."

"Don't be late."

Henry strode swiftly out the door, fairly bursting from the house. He wanted nothing more than to walk off his agitation, but his carriage was still waiting at the curb. Taking a deep breath, he got in.

Two young ladies, walking arm-in-arm up the sidewalk, drew even with his carriage. One was a statuesque redhead, the other a shorter but equally slender brunette. Both wore the strange gowns preferred by the devotees of the Aesthetic Movement. Henry had come across a few of these types among the daughters of the upper classes.

He had brought his open landau, so although he was seated, the women could see him plainly. They must have noted the coat of arms on the carriage, for one of them said, "Good afternoon, m'lord." They both smiled and bobbed a curtsy, but Henry could see their actions stemmed from barely suppressed amusement rather than respect.

He tipped his hat, grateful that the movement of the carriage, which was already pulling away from the curb, kept him from having to do more. Why was he so uncomfortable around women today?

Before the carriage turned the corner, he sent a glance back and was not surprised to see the women walking up the steps to D'Adamo's house. More models. Or artists? At this point, Henry wouldn't hazard a guess. Not after seeing Cara Bernay looking so beautifully ethereal and yet insisting she was going to be a painter.

Henry's interactions with his brother usually left him irritated, but today he was more unsettled than ever. He knew it was because of Miss Bernay. So waiflike, and yet with flashes of inner strength. Clearly she was benefiting from forging this friendship with his brother. Had she really crossed Langham's path purely by chance? Even if she had, Henry was of the opinion there was no such thing as a "happy" accident. Something was bound to go wrong, and it would fall to Henry to make it right.

"That went well," Langham announced as he returned to the studio.

He looked amused, but Adrian gave a little *harrumph*. "I don't appreciate such high-handedness in my own home. I don't care who he is."

"Trust me, I will do everything in my power to keep him from returning. I'm sorry my brother is such a boor. However, I think he was positively smitten by Cara." He winked at her.

"Do you really think so?" Cara was still agog from the encounter. She'd been nervous at first, but that abated as soon as she'd come to the firm belief that she had been *meant* to meet this man. His injured hand proved it.

This thought made her smile, even though it was a secret she couldn't share with anyone just yet.

"You like him, too, it seems," Langham remarked.

"Yes, well . . ." She hesitated, not wanting to answer directly. There was no doubt the Earl of Morestowe was handsome. He was too stern and serious, but perhaps a man in his position had to be. Was there a friendlier side to him hiding somewhere, or was he truly so different from his brother?

A picture of Julia's frowning face came to mind. Cara rarely did anything right in her sister's eyes. She gave Langham a sympathetic smile. "He doesn't seem to approve of what you are doing."

"That's nothing new." Langham removed his coat, draped it over a chair, and began rolling up his sleeves. "He'll change his tune after my triumph at the Grosvenor."

"He did concede that your work is good," Georgiana pointed out.

"Small steps." Langham's reply held more than a hint of sarcasm. He grabbed his painter's smock from a nearby coat stand and prepared to work.

Cara was grieved at this discord between the brothers. Thinking

100

of her own situation only intensified this feeling. She was still angry at her sisters, for both had betrayed her. She intended to keep stoking that anger, because it was entirely justified. And yet, it did not keep an ache of longing entirely at bay. Despite their frequent disagreements, she'd never been completely cut off from her sisters, as she was keeping herself now. What were they doing? Were they thinking of her? Were they worried about her?

She sighed. "It can feel lonely, can't it?"

Langham paused in the act of laying out his paints. His gaze fastened on her. "You understand."

Cara saw a glimpse of unguarded sorrow in his eyes. A rare moment of vulnerability appearing from behind his mask of frivolity.

"Let's not get morose," Adrian admonished. "We've got work to do." As if to punctuate his remark, the doorbell rang. "Finally! There are Augusta and Jane."

The maid went to answer the door, and moments later, two women breezed into the room. They gave effusive hugs to everyone, including Cara, once Georgiana had introduced them.

"I'm terribly sorry, Adrian dear," Augusta said after the painter had chided them for being late. "It took us *ages* to get here. There was so much traffic, the omnibuses could barely move."

"We also stopped to curtsy to a real gentleman, whose carriage was just outside your door!" Jane added. "Is he a friend of yours? It's so *beneficial* to have well-to-do friends."

There was a pause. No one seemed inclined to discuss Langham's brother.

"Today the money's coming from me—*if* you will do your jobs," Adrian said finally. "Georgiana, will you take them upstairs and help them get into costume? Let's not waste the light."

The rest of the day was filled with hard work as they focused their efforts on the painting. There was plenty of laughter, too, for Augusta and Jane approached everything with a sense of fun. Cara quickly felt at ease with them. This was a good thing, because they spent much of the time in close contact. Adrian had them pose together with their arms intertwined, and they tried innumerable combinations and expressions before he was satisfied that he had found the right look.

Langham set up his easel at the opposite end of the room and spent the afternoon diligently at work. Perhaps his brother's critical attitude had only increased his determination to make a success of himself. Desire to rise up in defiance of a sibling's low expectations? That was a feeling Cara could well understand.

CHAPTER

11

I N THE DAYS THAT FOLLOWED Henry's visit to the studio, Langham was, amazingly, as good as his word. He came home very late, it was true, but he did come home. He would then sleep late the following day. At some point after midmorning, he would call for a bath and breakfast, and then he'd be out the door before luncheon.

Their paths generally did not cross, for Henry preferred to rise early and walk in Hyde Park before the heat set in. It was a poor substitute for being in the countryside, but it was the best he could do for now.

After about a week, Langham made a surprise appearance for dinner. Actually, it was not too great a surprise; Langham had sent a note to the cook that afternoon with a desired menu. Henry wasn't as irritated by his brother's unsolicited instructions to the staff as he might normally have been. He needed to speak with Langham, and dinner was as good a time as any.

While they ate their meal, Langham talked at length about painting. It would seem his rule of not *showing* a work in progress did not keep him from *talking* about it. He described various technical issues he had to surmount to get the image exactly right. He used a lot of unfamiliar jargon. Yet for all his talk about the studio, Langham made no mention of Cara Bernay.

"It's hotter than the devil these days, isn't it?" Langham said at one point. "We had to move our easels outside and paint under the trees just to find enough energy to work. How are the repairs progressing at Morestowe?"

This gave Henry the opening he'd been looking for. "I received a note yesterday from Mr. Thompson. Things are moving rapidly now that the rains have finally abated. The east wing will remain uninhabitable for another month, but the main portion of the house is nearly complete. We can move in next week."

Henry watched Langham carefully as he shared this news, wondering how his brother would react. The far end of the east wing was where Langham's rooms had been. It was the most damaged, since the fire had started in Langham's bedchamber. Langham claimed that heat or flames escaping from cracks in the "crumbling old fireplaces" had been the cause.

Henry had allowed this explanation to stand because it was the least embarrassing for the family. Privately, he was convinced his brother had set fire to the bed or chair while under the influence of alcohol or some other substance. He based this belief on his study of the ruins, plus the fact that it had taken Langham so long in those small hours of the morning to rouse himself, get away from the danger, and spread the alarm to the rest of the house. Henry could never get Langham to admit this—not even after a private confrontation—but he had been able to prevail upon his brother to go to a sanitarium, ostensibly to allow his smoke-damaged lungs to recover in the clean air of the pristine countryside.

Langham gave a grimace of distaste. "Oh, those cramped old rooms. There's barely space for a proper wardrobe in them."

"It's only for a month," Henry pointed out, ready to counter any argument his brother might make about staying in town.

"It will be deuced uncomfortable. But we have to go."

This took Henry by surprise. "You're ready to leave London?"

"Oh yes. The heat is sapping all my creativity. I need to get away.

I'm thinking of turning the dower cottage into a painter's studio. We don't use it for anything else, and the front room gets good light most of the day."

"I have no objection." It was a small accommodation. Henry was just glad his brother was willing to return to Essex and leave his artist friends behind. Even Cara, apparently. "How is D'Adamo's painting coming along?"

For some reason, this made Langham smile. Henry wouldn't have minded, except it seemed his brother's amusement was aimed at him. He raised his eyebrows and gestured for Langham to answer the question.

"Adrian works incredibly fast. I move at glacial speed compared to him. The painting is superb. But then, you've seen how beautiful the models are."

"Is Miss Bernay still modeling?" Henry's question came out a bit choked, as Langham's words had brought back the sight of her in that Grecian-style gown. He forced himself to breathe.

Langham's smile hadn't abated. It made Henry uncomfortable, but he didn't see why he shouldn't ask after her.

"Georgiana is giving her painting lessons. Cara would like to do portraits, and that's Georgiana's forte. Cara is not yet ready to advertise her services as a professional, but she'll get there."

"How does she plan to support herself in the meantime? Will she remain at the D'Adamo residence?"

Langham gave him a thoughtful look. "You seem to be taking a great interest in her."

"You were the one who picked her up like a 'stray kitten.' Don't you think that makes you somewhat responsible for her?"

"Do you want me to be?"

"I just don't want your actions to cause her any harm," Henry insisted. Why did his brother always put him on the defensive?

"I don't know what her plans are, exactly. Perhaps we can ask her about it."

We?

Henry didn't have a chance to ask what his brother meant. Dropping his napkin on the table, Langham rose from his chair. "I believe I'll pass on the brandy and turn in early."

Once again, Langham had surprised him. For him not to partake of a glass or two of brandy after dinner was unusual. Not that he hadn't consumed plenty of wine at dinner. Still, perhaps, in a small way, he was turning over some kind of new leaf.

"By the by," Langham added as they walked out of the dining room, "I need ten pounds."

Henry stopped short. "And just what is this for?"

"I have to purchase art supplies before we go to the country. Also, I need to give some remuneration to Adrian for the use of his studio. I think you can agree that's fair."

This need for money was, no doubt, the real reason Langham had made it home for dinner tonight. Such requests were inevitably bound up in their interactions. However, this sum was less outrageous than what Langham usually asked for. They went to Henry's study, where he withdrew cash from a locked drawer. If his brother really was working to meet his commitment to the gallery, that was an encouraging sign. Even if this foray into the art world went no further than that, Langham would have finally finished something he'd begun.

When Henry came home the following afternoon after completing a few errands, he knew something was amiss right away. The footman was waiting for him, opening the door before Henry could pull out his key. Normally, per Henry's instructions, they did not need to do this.

"Is something wrong, Samuel?" he asked.

"Not *wrong*, my lord. That is, not exactly."

His words were belied by the beads of sweat on his forehead. Or perhaps that was just due to the heat.

"Well, what is it?"

"Miss Amelia and Miss Leahy have returned from Brighton, sir."

Henry frowned. "And Lady Morestowe?"

"Her ladyship is not with them, sir. Miss Leahy is in the upstairs parlor, if you should wish to speak to her."

"Thank you." Henry made for the parlor straightaway, wondering what could have brought them back so soon, and without his mother. As he took the stairs, it occurred to him that the house seemed unusually quiet, given that Amelia was home.

Miss Leahy rose from her chair at the writing desk, murmuring a greeting as Henry entered the parlor. Judging from the open geography book and the paper lying next to it, she'd intended to plan a lesson for Amelia. However, the paper was blank. Miss Leahy looked agitated—a contrast to her usual calm manner. Dark smudges under her eyes indicated she might not be sleeping well. This set off new concerns in Henry's mind.

He said anxiously, "How is Amelia?"

"She is well, your lordship. She's presently in the nursery, working on her arithmetic lesson. I've asked her to make a drawing that illustrates 'five times four equals twenty.'"

"That seems an odd way to learn arithmetic."

"She seems to enjoy drawing, sir. I discovered I can keep her engaged if she uses the pictures to work out the problems."

Henry knew he ought to be pleased at Miss Leahy's perception and ingenuity. Instead, he felt a pang of dread. The older Amelia got, the more obvious her similarities to her father would probably become. At least those traits did not point to *him*, Henry thought with grim satisfaction. The gossips always assumed Amelia was his natural daughter. But in temperament—and now it seemed in artistic leanings—they could not be further apart.

Despite his misgivings, Henry could appreciate the calm in the house. "It seems you've discovered the secret to keeping her well-behaved."

"I had to use every trick at my disposal today, sir. She was unhappy that we cut short our trip to the seaside—as you might imagine. I've tried to keep her occupied with something she likes, and, well, I may have implied that the return to Morestowe was more imminent than it is."

She twisted her hands together, looking highly embarrassed at the admission that she'd more or less lied to the child. Considering that

Miss Leahy was always honest in her dealings with Amelia, something was clearly amiss.

"Why did you leave Brighton? And where is Lady Morestowe? The footman tells me she did not return with you."

"She has accepted an invitation to spend a few weeks in Torquay." Miss Leahy picked up a sealed letter that had been lying on the desk and handed it to Henry. "I believe this contains all the particulars."

Henry opened the letter. His mother wrote that she planned to spend a fortnight sailing on a yacht along the southwest coast with the Fitz-Wallaces. These were wealthy and well-connected friends of his mother, so Henry could see why she preferred that option to remaining with Amelia and the governess. "I'm sorry you felt compelled to return to London on account of this. You might have finished out the month there."

"Her ladyship told me that as well. However, another issue has arisen. My mother's health has been declining, and yesterday my sister sent word that things have reached a critical stage. I must visit her right away if I'm to see her before she—" The governess cut herself off, tamping down her emotions. "I apologize for the lack of notice, but I should like to leave right away, with your permission, sir. There's a train departing in an hour."

Now Henry understood the reason for her unusual behavior. "Of course you have my permission. It's only natural that you'd want to be with your mother."

After profuse thanks, she began to apologize for the lack of a lesson plan. Henry assured her not to worry, that they'd work something out. "You do plan to return at some point, don't you?" he asked.

"If I may, sir."

"Well, then. Do what you need to do, and keep me apprised of the situation."

"Yes, sir. Thank you, sir!"

Perhaps she had thought she'd be dismissed for leaving like this. Henry was sure his mother would have been only too glad to do so. But he wasn't about to get rid of this woman if he could help it.

And yet, even as Miss Leahy hurried from the room, he couldn't help worrying. What would he do with Amelia in the meantime?

Cara and Georgiana were sitting under a tree in the small garden, trying to find some relief from the heat, when Adrian came out the back door to join them.

"There you are," Georgiana said.

"I've some news," he announced. "A few days ago, I sent a note to Arthur Hughes, asking if I might bring you along to a garden party he's having the day after tomorrow. I got his reply today. He said that, as you are a friend of ours, you will be welcome."

Cara grinned in joyous disbelief. "Why would Mr. Hughes concern himself with me?"

"He does a lot of pastoral scenes. Country folk in fields and villages. Shepherd girls and the like. I think you'd be perfect for one of his paintings. He said he'd be glad to meet you."

Modeling for the famous Arthur Hughes! Perhaps this was the opening Cara had been looking for.

"Langham's also invited," Adrian added. "Where is he, anyway?"

"He went to the chemist's shop," Cara answered. "He said he wasn't feeling well."

Adrian frowned, sending a glance toward Georgiana. She gave a resigned shrug.

Cara sensed their worry. "Is there a problem with Langham's health? I heard a friend of his speak of recurring illnesses."

"He gets terrible headaches sometimes," Georgiana answered. "Sometimes he has to stay in a dark room for days. Other times, the tonic he gets from the chemist seems to solve the problem."

"I hope he's not becoming dependent on that stuff," Adrian said, shaking his head. "It's not good for his art. Makes him too nervous to work properly. He has real talent, if he will only get serious about making use of it." His gaze turned toward the house. "I see he's acquired his 'tonic,'" he added acerbically.

Cara turned to see Langham approaching, raising a bottle he was holding. "Anyone care for Vin Mariani?"

Georgiana rose from her chair. "I think Susan is making us more lemonade."

She brushed past Langham and went into the house.

"Cara, how about you?" Langham said.

Cara saw Adrian shake his head. She didn't know what Vin Mariani was, but apparently he and Georgiana disapproved of it. "No, thank you."

"Suit yourself." Picking up an unused glass from the small table, Langham dropped into the chair Georgiana had just vacated and began to pour himself a drink.

"What's the status of your painting?" Adrian asked him pointedly.

"It's been a wretched day. I've had a splitting headache since this morning." Langham lifted his glass. "This will help." He didn't seem to notice the disapproving look Adrian sent him. Or perhaps he was simply ignoring it.

"We've been invited to a garden party at the home of Mr. Arthur Hughes the day after tomorrow," Cara said, hoping to relieve some of the tension between the two men.

"Splendid. I've no doubt his place at Kew will be more pleasant than it is here in town."

"If you're not planning to do any work today, perhaps you should go home and rest," Adrian said. It was more of a directive than a suggestion.

Langham gave him a sour look. "I *am* on my way home, as it happens. I only dropped by to fetch Cara."

"Me? What for?" Cara said, startled.

"So that you may join me and Henry for dinner tonight."

"Oh! That sounds wonderful! But I thought you weren't feeling well. Besides, won't his lordship—Henry, I mean—be put out if you bring an uninvited guest?"

Langham gave a little snort. "Of course he'll mind—at first. He's far too fussy about such things. But he'll get over it." He leaned forward and looked her in the eye. "Your presence will be good for all of us. Remember, I live there, too. So you will be *my* guest."

In Cara's opinion, this made perfect sense. Not that she was inclined to contradict him. She wanted very much to go to Lord Morestowe's home. She sprang up from her chair. "I need to change my clothes first."

Langham poured himself more wine. "I'll wait for you here."

Just inside the house, Cara met Georgiana returning with a fresh pitcher of lemonade.

"Where are you going?" Georgiana asked.

"Upstairs to change clothes. Langham is taking me to his house for dinner."

"Just don't drink any of that stuff," Georgiana warned, motioning toward the bottle in Langham's hand.

"What is it?"

"It's cocaine mixed with wine. You would do well to stay away from it."

"Thank you, I'll remember."

"You're a good girl," Georgiana said. "I would hate to see Langham spoil you."

"I'm sure he wouldn't want to do anything to harm me."

"It doesn't have to be intentional."

Georgiana's words struck a chord deep in Cara's heart. There was great truth in them. After all, Cara had never intended to harm anyone, and look what she'd almost done to Robbie. It was a good warning to heed. Was Langham bringing harm to himself, and perhaps to others as well, with his actions?

Cara was so grateful for all he'd done for her. She hadn't thought of him as needing any kind of help in return. But perhaps he needed help of a different kind. He had said her presence tonight would be good for all of them. What did he mean? She didn't know, but she was more than willing to find out.

CHAPTER

12

Cara stood staring up at Lord Morestowe's four-story town home while Langham paid the cab driver.

This is where an earl lives, she thought, feeling a touch of wonder. The stately edifice was similar to those rented by the Needenhams whenever they came to town. Tonight, however, Cara wasn't going to take the narrow stairs down to the servants' entrance. Tonight, she was going through the main door as a guest.

She had nothing to wear that was truly suitable for visiting a member of the aristocracy, but she'd done her best to make herself as presentable as possible. Her best gown was secondhand, but she was wearing a new bonnet that she'd bought a week before the incident with Robbie. It might not be as fashionable as one from Paris, but Cara thought it was lovely. She wanted so much to make the right impression.

"You look very pretty," Langham told her, as though he had read her thoughts. "Henry will be charmed. You've nothing to worry about."

His words, along with the thrill she felt as he escorted her to the front door, erased her anxiety. She could already imagine a glittering table set with crystal glasses, bone china plates surrounded by polished silverware, and a bouquet of fresh flowers in the center. The Needenhams' table had looked like that whenever they had dinner parties. An earl must dine like that every day. This time, Cara would not be sneaking a peek into the dining room before the guests arrived; she would be sitting at the table herself.

A footman opened the door for them. As they walked into the brightly lit foyer, Cara took in the sight with delight. From the massive gilt-edged mirror to the painted china vase filled with flowers, everything spoke of gracious elegance.

She had only a moment to enjoy it, however. Such a home ought to exude quiet dignity. Instead, the place was in an uproar. Somewhere, a child was shrieking with anger.

"Oh, bother," Langham murmured. "Amelia is in one of her moods again."

"Who's Amelia?"

"Henry's, er, ward."

"*Ward?*" Cara repeated. This was something she'd never anticipated. The girl sounded very young. Why was she Henry's ward?

"A little monster, more like. She's been at the seaside. Unfortunately, she returned yesterday."

Lord Morestowe appeared at the top of the stairs and glowered down at them. "What are you two doing here?"

"I live here," Langham reminded him, returning his hard look. "I've invited Cara for dinner. You might take a moment to be civil to her."

This reprimand seemed to cause Henry to recollect himself. His rigid stance softened. "I apologize, Miss Bernay, but this isn't the best time for a visit."

Cara detected a glint of approval in his eyes as he took in her appearance. She was enjoying looking at him, too. At the moment he looked distracted and a little disheveled, but he was no less handsome. She smiled up at him. Now that she was here, Cara did not want to leave. Her mind whirled. Henry had a young ward. What else might she discover about him?

From a room above them came the sound of something crashing against a wall.

"What's gotten into her this time?" Langham asked, sounding more put out than concerned by the child's distress.

"The governess had to leave town unexpectedly to visit her sick mother. Amelia isn't happy about it, and as you can glean, her irritation at being stuck in London without her is increasing." Henry's hands tightened on the railing, his frustration evident. "I suggest you take Miss Bernay home immediately. It won't be a pleasant evening."

"Perhaps I can help," Cara offered. "I've had lots of experience with children. May I go to her?"

She didn't wait for an answer. This child was clearly upset, and whoever was in the room with her had no idea how to respond. Cara began taking the stairs. Lord Morestowe stayed where he was, frozen in surprise.

When Cara reached him, she said, "Please allow me a few minutes with her."

"But you don't know anything about her."

Cara continued past him. She knew her actions must appear impertinent, but surprisingly, the earl didn't attempt to stop her.

It wasn't difficult to figure out where the girl was. Cara simply followed the noise. At the back of her mind, she knew she ought not to get involved, but how could she ignore a child in need? She opened the door to find a girl who looked to be seven or eight years old fighting against two maids, each of whom had a hold of one arm.

"Please calm down, miss!" one of the maids was pleading.

"You've no right to order me about!" Amelia declared imperiously as she struggled to break free. "Where is Miss Leahy? Where is my guardian?"

Cara interrupted the proceedings. "His lordship has given me leave to handle this." She eyed the two maids. "Please leave us."

The women stared at her, dumbfounded. When they realized Cara fully intended to take on this situation, the look of relief on their faces was unmistakable. They let go of the girl. Cara stood poised by the door, ready in case Amelia should decide to bolt. But she looked so surprised at her sudden freedom that she merely stood there, staring at Cara with her mouth agape.

The maids slipped from the room. Keeping her eyes on Amelia, Cara closed the door behind them with an authoritative click.

"Who are you?" the little girl demanded.

"Miss Amelia, that is not the proper way to greet a newcomer," Cara chided.

"Why should I say 'how do you do?' if I don't even know your name?" Amelia countered without a trace of apology.

Cara had to admire her spirit. "Good point. My name is Miss Bernay. Didn't your guardian tell you I was coming?"

"No." The girl's eyes narrowed in suspicion. Her fist was still closed around a piece of broken vase, and she looked as though she were considering hurling it at Cara.

Cara made a little *tsk*ing sound. "His lordship can be absent-minded at times, don't you agree?"

"What are you doing here? Where is Miss Leahy?"

Clearly, this child was not going to be won over easily. It also seemed that Henry hadn't told Amelia why the governess had gone. He might have had his reasons, but whether they were justified was another question. For her part, Cara thought it best to be honest. "Miss Leahy's mother is not well, so Miss Leahy must go take care of her. Don't you think that is a kind thing to do—to help someone who is ill?"

Cara had found that asking a child questions was a good way to keep them engaged and less defensive. In Robbie's case, it generally worked better than direct commands. Even if he didn't respond verbally, in most instances Cara could tell from his expression that the questions had captured his attention enough to ponder them.

Amelia didn't answer. The look of consternation had not left her face, but her mouth moved, ever so subtly, her lips pressing together and then open again. She was unconsciously repeating the word *mother*.

That told Cara the route to take. If Amelia was Henry's ward, most likely she had no parents. She might be alone in the world, even though she had caretakers. This would surely inform her view of everything that happened to her. Cara understood the aching longing left in a child's heart after the loss of parents. But she knew Amelia needed more than sympathy. She needed to be led out of the idea that self-pity was a good excuse for bad behavior.

"I certainly would do the same as Miss Leahy if I had a mother," Cara said.

"Don't you have a mother?"

"No. She died when I was very young." With a sigh, she added, "My father, too." It always squeezed Cara's heart to say or even imply that her father was dead. Even if the rest of the world told her it was so, she refused to accept the possibility. But she said it now for Amelia's sake. "So it seems you and I are both orphans."

Unfortunately, this last remark turned out to be ill-advised. Upon hearing the word *orphans*, Amelia turned and flung the last piece of the vase against the fireplace with such force that some of the shards bounced off the bricks and landed at her feet.

Cara recoiled at the sound of the porcelain shattering. She prayed it would not send Henry into the room, because now she was getting somewhere.

Amelia turned back to glare defiantly at Cara, as though fully expecting to be reprimanded and ready to show that she didn't care.

Instead, Cara said calmly, "Yes, I have often felt that way myself. The world can be a cruel place. Even when those around us are trying to be kind."

Flustered by Cara's mild response, Amelia stared at her, her eyes wide and her mouth open in astonishment. She quickly rallied, though. "Miss Leahy should not have left. She is *my* governess. She ought to think of *me* first. We were having a perfectly lovely time at the seaside, and *she* ruined it."

"And just what is so wonderful about the seaside?" Cara said it in an offhand way, implying that going to the seaside was the most uninteresting thing in the world.

Amelia looked at her as though she were daft. "It's the *seaside*! There are waves and sea gulls and shells and cherry ices and sea bathing—"

"Can you not get cherry ices in London?"

Amelia blinked, taken off guard.

"You can see sea gulls down by the Thames, too, so I've heard, although I've not actually seen the Thames, so I don't know for sure. Have you been there? Walked along the Thames, I mean?"

Amelia's forehead scrunched as she attempted to keep up. "Of course!"

"What else can you eat in London? When the cook here makes your favorite dish, what is it? Because I have always loved Yorkshire pudding. I can't get enough of it."

As Cara spoke, she took a seat in a nearby chair. She was just close enough to chat comfortably without raising Amelia's defenses. She didn't think the girl was going anywhere now. Her attention was entirely focused on Cara. Her eyebrows were drawn together, as though she couldn't figure out who this strange woman was and why she was talking about outlandish things like never having seen the Thames.

"Cherry tart is wonderful, too," Cara went on. "Although cherry ices are better on really hot days. Shall we ask the cook to send out for some so we can enjoy them with our dinner tonight?"

"Have another drink, Harry," Langham said as he poured them each a fresh glass of port.

Henry was so preoccupied that he didn't even protest Langham's use of the hated nickname. "What in the world do you suppose is going on up there?"

It had been over two hours since Cara and Amelia had gone upstairs to the nursery. There they had rung the maid and requested a dinner of chicken pie and cherry ices. Henry couldn't see how rewarding the child's tantrum with her favorite foods could possibly improve her discipline. He had given his assent anyway, too astonished to resist. The cook had duly set about making the pie while a footman had been dispatched to Gunter's confectionery in Berkeley Square to purchase the ices.

Meanwhile, Henry and Langham had sat down to the dinner already prepared by the cook, although Henry had not eaten much. He'd been consumed with worry about his unruly ward and the woman he didn't know enough to trust and yet was somehow doing so anyway. And what must she think of them? According to Langham, Cara had only learned of Amelia's existence tonight. Yet Cara had taken up with the girl as easily as if they'd known each other for years. Henry couldn't believe any of it.

After dinner, they'd settled in the study to wait for Cara. The wait seemed interminable. Henry could only assume the peace and quiet in the house meant things were going well upstairs.

The clock was striking half-past nine when the door to the study opened and Cara finally joined them. As Henry and Langham rose from their chairs, she said cheerily, "Did you have a nice dinner? I know Miss Amelia and I did."

She was smiling so brightly that Henry had the impression she'd brought in extra light with her. Was she some kind of angel? He squelched the ridiculous notion. She had simply shown a knack for dealing with misbehaving children. Things were fine now, but another tantrum could come at any time. Without Miss Leahy, he felt powerless to control the situation.

"What is Amelia doing now?" he asked.

"She's asleep. Dinner made her sleepy, so I helped her into her nightgown and got her tucked into bed. She drifted off almost instantly."

"You are a miracle worker!" Langham exclaimed. He led her over to a chair. "Do sit down and allow me to bring you a glass of port."

She accepted the chair and received the wine with a surprised smile. She held the delicate glass carefully, as though worried she might break it.

Henry took the seat next to hers. "What were you doing up there, besides eating?" He was still astounded by the events of the past few hours.

Cara took a tiny sip of her port before carefully setting the glass on the table next to her chair. Her mouth moved a little, her lips turning in slightly. Henry thought she was taking a moment to savor the port. The movement seemed unconscious but was unaccountably beguiling.

She gave a little smile of enjoyment before setting her attention back on Henry. "We were talking, mostly, although she also showed

118

me her dolls and her toy boat. I told her she's a lucky girl to have such fine playthings."

"I must thank you. I'm grateful you were able to calm her down, although I must say that in general, I do not approve of trying to mollify unruly children." Henry wasn't sure why he'd added that last part. Perhaps it was his mother's warnings still ringing in his ears about how, by being too lenient on a child, one could raise a hellion.

"Don't be such a spoilsport, Henry," Langham chided.

"I know she acted badly," Cara said. "I made it plain to her that such behavior is unbecoming in a young lady. But I could only do that after I'd gotten her to give me a willing ear. She would not have received the reproof otherwise."

"And how did you do that—get her willing ear, I mean?"

"By listening to her first. A child throwing a tantrum usually does so because he or she believes they have a legitimate grievance, even if that is not the case. So I asked Amelia what was bothering her."

"And?" To Henry, this all sounded too simple.

"She's distressed about Miss Leahy's departure. She has grown fond of her governess. She is not, it seems, so fond of the maids."

"She doesn't like our mother, either," Langham put in. "It's a good thing she's not here just now."

"Don't be disrespectful," Henry said, sending him a sharp look.

Langham only shrugged.

"I know how much Miss Leahy has come to mean to the girl," Henry continued. "I knew there would be trouble after she left. But I couldn't refuse her request to visit her dying mother."

"Miss Amelia didn't know where her governess went or how long she'll be away. I think that was a mistake, because she began to imagine all sorts of reasons—primarily that it was her own fault, or that she'd driven Miss Leahy away," Cara explained.

"Why on earth would she think that? I told her Miss Leahy would return."

"Perhaps it sounded too vague for her to believe. It's easy for a child who has lost a parent or loved one to put the blame on themselves."

"Amelia was only four years old when she lost her mother." Henry chose his words carefully. He did not enjoy lying. Yet *lost* was accurate enough, even if the child's mother was still alive. "I thought if I told her Miss Leahy's mother was dying, it might raise Amelia's sorrows all over again."

Cara's eyes were warm with understanding, but she shook her head. "I'm afraid it doesn't work that way. At least, not in this situation."

Henry understood even less about children than he'd thought. "Thank you for calming her after my blunder."

Cara smiled, perhaps amused at Henry's self-deprecation. "I didn't know the whole story, so I promised I'd find out the details and tell Amelia all about it tomorrow."

"Tomorrow?" Henry was surprised that Cara would take the liberty of deciding to see the child again.

She looked at him with an abashed expression. "I might also have promised her—that is, it wasn't a promise exactly . . . I did say I would have to ask you first."

Her wide blue eyes were so innocent and yet so appealing that Henry felt an odd knot in his throat. "Just what were you going to ask me?"

"I said I might go out with her tomorrow. With your approval, of course," she repeated.

Henry was glad he was seated. This woman kept him strangely off-balance. "Where did you have in mind?"

"Amelia would like to take a walk along the Embankment. She mentioned an obelisk near the park and how much she enjoys watching the boat traffic on the river. And there's an organ grinder with a monkey who dances around to the music. It's one of her favorite places to visit. But I expect you know that already."

Henry didn't know that. At least, he would not have been able to answer the question if asked directly. He was aware of many of Amelia's likes and dislikes—primarily because she was so vocal about them. But he hadn't made an effort to catalog those details in his mind. His role as guardian was to ensure the girl was properly looked after by competent people. That was enough.

"It's not possible. I've too much work to do."

"Oh, you needn't go," Langham said dismissively. "Cara and I can take her."

Henry stared at his brother. This was the first time Langham had shown any inclination to spend time with Amelia. Should he encourage that, knowing Langham was her father? More likely he ought to take the safer route. Langham's bad habits and other problems would set a terrible example. Amelia needed to be inspired to do better, not worse. Henry had to admit the outing would stave off any problems that might arise if the child was forced to remain in the house all day with the servants, but he wasn't willing to let her go off with his irresponsible brother and a woman he barely knew.

On the other hand, perhaps he should find out more about this Cara Bernay. She had proven she could curb Amelia's tantrums, and she seemed to have taken a genuine interest in the child.

"No," he said. "I'm coming with you."

He was doing this for Amelia's sake, nothing more. There was no other reason he should set aside important tasks to traipse around London with his ward, or even with his brother, who he supposed ought to be spending that time painting.

Nor would he otherwise spend an afternoon in the company of this woman, even if he were intrigued by her eclectic traits. The alluring Greek goddess had shown she also possessed down-to-earth, almost motherly qualities. Henry needed to focus on that latter point—even if her warm blue eyes and her lovely full mouth, now smiling with satisfaction, tempted him to do otherwise.

CHAPTER

13

"How did Amelia come to be Henry's ward?" Cara asked as Langham accompanied her home that night.

"She is an orphan from another branch of the family, so she refers to us as Cousin Henry and Cousin Langham. Her family once had a large estate in Ireland, but that was lost. After her parents died, we took her in, as we were her closest living relatives." He shrugged. "That's the official story, anyway."

"You look as though you don't believe it."

"I hadn't heard anything about that branch of the family even existing before Amelia showed up. That doesn't mean they didn't. My father was dead by then, so I couldn't ask him about it. But I have another, more scandalous theory. One that involves Henry."

She gave him an incredulous look. "Henry, in a scandal?"

"It does seem hard to believe at first. But no man is entirely impervious to temptation. A year or so before Amelia was born, Henry fell in love."

"Oh!" Cara said in surprise. "What sort of lady was she?"

"She was the daughter of a man who owned a prosperous company in Shropshire that makes cast-iron products. Stoves, radiators, that sort of thing. She was the sister of Henry's best friend at university. One summer Henry visited him, and that's where he met her. According to his friend, it was love at first sight for both of them."

"She was the daughter of a cast-iron merchant?" Cara found it hard to believe that Henry, as proper as he was, had set his heart on the humble daughter of a manufacturer.

"Yes, and not only that, she was helping her father run the company!"

"So what happened? Were they not allowed to marry?"

"I see you understand how the match might be frowned upon. I don't believe they ever became engaged in any official sense. I was sixteen at the time, and my brother never confided in me about personal matters. I certainly couldn't get my parents to give me details about what happened. All I know is, a few months after they met, she went to the Continent with a wealthy aunt to tour France and Germany. She never came home."

"What?" Cara exclaimed.

"She died of a fever while they were in Paris."

"How terrible. Was he heartbroken?"

"To this day, I don't believe he has gotten over it. But what if she didn't die? What if she went to France to have a baby?"

"*Henry's* baby? Surely not."

"I told you it was a scandalous theory. The date of her birth fits easily into the timeline, so that's one thing that may or may not be a coincidence."

"If that's true, then what do you suppose happened to the woman?"

"Perhaps she remained sequestered away in France or in England somewhere. Maybe she only died three years ago, and that's why Amelia came to live with us."

"It's hard to believe Henry would do something so improper as to—" She stopped, embarrassed.

"Trust me," said Langham, "it happens all the time."

"But it still doesn't make sense. If he loved her, and if he got her . . . in trouble, why didn't he marry her?"

"That goes back to the problem of class differences, I suppose. Henry has to think of the dignity of his position. My father was intractable in that regard. So is my mother. She can't see that times are changing and that many wealthy people in England today have achieved their wealth through industry rather than inheritance. But my parents wouldn't consider anyone to be of equal rank with us who does not have family lineage going back to William the Conqueror."

"Surely you are exaggerating."

"Not by much."

"I see." Cara was crestfallen at this information. Would Henry truly walk away from someone he loved simply because she didn't have the right lineage? Cara was aware that members of the aristocracy preferred to marry among themselves, but she had hoped Henry was a different sort of man. He certainly didn't seem like the sort who would take advantage of a woman and then set her aside. The picture Langham painted of his brother was not a noble one.

"I've tried to get Henry to tell me what happened," Langham continued, "but he refuses to talk about it. I'm sure he's hiding something."

Was Henry really concealing such an important secret? The question was still occupying Cara's thoughts the following morning.

She'd risen early and was seated at a window with a sketch pad by daybreak. The rest of the house was quiet. After a week here, Cara had learned that no one else was likely to get out of bed until late morning.

Langham often talked about how the light was better in the afternoons, but Cara enjoyed the early-morning light, too. The world felt calmer, and everything had a sharp definition that seemed to fade when the sun was higher. This was especially true on summer mornings in the country. How odd that she'd wanted all her life to come to London, and now she found herself missing the countryside! She wistfully recalled days at the Needenhams' estate when she'd watched the predawn mist retreat from the fields with the rising of the sun.

Almost without thinking, she began sketching. In a few moments she realized she was drawing a portrait of Amelia. Cara had felt real empathy for the girl right from the start, but even more so once she'd heard the girl's story. If Langham's suspicions were true, that meant Amelia's father was with her every day, *and she didn't even know it.* This seemed to Cara an unutterable cruelty. She missed her own father so much. How would she feel if she were to discover he was there all along, seeing her, knowing her, without revealing himself? Who could do this and not feel terrible guilt about practicing such deception? Did this weigh on Henry's conscience? Was this why he had decided to come with them today?

There was another concern on Cara's mind. Last night she'd taken charge of a child for several hours. Everything had turned out well, and Henry had thanked her many times. Langham had been complimentary, too. But neither of them knew that Cara had broken the vow she'd made to God that she would never again work with children.

She hadn't meant to break that vow. She'd seen a child hurting and simply wanted to help. It wasn't until later, when she'd had time to reflect, that she realized just how large of an error she had made.

As she drew the full eyebrows over Amelia's hazel eyes, Cara thought back to her prayer on the morning when she was so desperately worried for Robbie. She tried to recall the exact wording of the vow. She knew beyond a doubt that she'd promised never to seek work as a nanny or a governess. That much was straightforward. But had she also been wrong to spend those hours with Amelia? If, during that time, it could be said she'd been responsible for the child's well-being, then it was contrary to her promise to God. It didn't matter that the girl's guardian and a dozen servants were mere steps away. And yet, wouldn't the Lord wish her to render kindness to a child if it was in her power to do so?

Cara sighed, looking at the portrait taking shape beneath her hands, even as unanswerable questions tousled her thoughts. With a light touch of her finger, she traced the little crease between Amelia's eyebrows. It was a worry line that should never be on a child's face. The poor thing must not be happy despite her luxurious living conditions. Her every physical need was cared for, but Cara perceived that she lacked the things that fed the heart. Langham's forehead had creased in the same way at times, generally when he was speaking of his brother. Something in the family was not well.

Even if Cara ought not to have meddled last night, did it follow that she should not keep her promise to see Amelia today? It would be another promise broken, and wouldn't that be a sin as well?

Her hand slipped, and Cara worked to erase the stray line. That done, she began to draw the child's neck and shoulders, the lace collar of her frock. She was such a pretty child when her face was not distorted with anger or obstinacy.

Cara decided she would go. It was a promise she had made, and besides, it was just for this one day. Henry and Langham would be there, too. Henry was the child's guardian. He would be in charge. Cara would simply be tagging along. She felt better when she thought of it that way.

With her pencil, she reshaped the corners of Amelia's mouth into a smile.

Henry was having breakfast the next morning when Amelia came in. He was surprised because he hadn't heard her usual *thump-thump* on the stairs. She stood in the doorway to the dining room, looking at him. She was dressed in a pretty dark blue frock with a matching ribbon in her hair. Apparently she hadn't given the maid any trouble this morning, or Henry was sure he'd have heard that, too.

He'd been pondering the events of the night before and thinking he ought to find ways to improve his relationship with Amelia. Here was a good time to start. He sent her a friendly smile. "Good morning, Amelia. Have you had breakfast?"

"Yes, sir." She was looking at him fixedly, in a slightly unnerving way. Something must be on her mind, or she wouldn't have bothered to come down.

He motioned toward the empty chair opposite him. "Would you care to join me?"

He'd never made this offer before, and he could see she was taken aback by it. Her gaze slid sideways toward the footman who stood by the sideboard, waiting in case Henry needed more food or coffee. Apparently deciding the man's presence was not objectionable, she came forward and slid into the chair.

Henry said, "I apologize for not telling you exactly why Miss Leahy had to leave us for a while. I am happy to tell you all about it now, if you like."

"Yes, please." Her words sounded more like an order than a mere response.

There was a *tap-tap* coming from underneath the table, and Henry realized it was the sound of Amelia's boot heels gently striking the chair as she swung her legs.

He motioned toward the footman, who moved smoothly to Henry's side. "Yes, sir?"

"A bit of orange juice for Miss Amelia, if you please." He looked at the girl. "Unless you would prefer milk?"

She straightened in her chair. "Juice would be nice."

The footman went to the sideboard and filled a glass from a pitcher. When he set it in front of Amelia, she nodded approvingly.

"That will be all for now," Henry said.

The footman nodded and left the room.

Amelia took a sip of the juice, looking at Henry expectantly.

"Miss Leahy's mother lives far from here, in Durham, which is in the northern part of England. It appears her mother is not doing well. In fact, she will likely die soon."

He paused, allowing time for the words to sink in. Amelia set down her glass, her attention fixed on him. Although she said nothing, her expression was somber, perhaps in sympathy for her governess.

"You can see why it was important for her to leave straightaway, and also why we don't know exactly when she will return. However, I have every confidence she will return to us."

He half expected some negative reaction. But to his surprise, Amelia merely nodded.

"In the meantime, we'll need to find a substitute to fill in for her," he added, emboldened by her calm acceptance of this information.

"Miss Bernay is good."

Perhaps the girl thought last night's interaction was a tryout of some sort. "Miss Bernay is not a governess."

The click of Amelia's boots stopped. "Who is she, then?"

"She's a . . . er, friend of your cousin Langham."

"Oh." There was a pause. "Miss Bernay said we were going to the Embankment today. And the Crystal Palace."

Surprised by this last bit of information, Henry set down his cup. "She did not mention the Crystal Palace to me."

Amelia idly pushed the empty glass from side to side between her hands. "I told her there are big statues of dinosaurs there, and she said they would be very interesting to see."

Henry leaned back and crossed his arms as he studied the girl, trying to decide if she had made the leap in logic by mistake, or if she had done it on purpose to see how far she could push her desires for this outing.

"She is coming today, isn't she?" Amelia asked, suspicion creeping into her voice.

For the three years that Amelia had been in his care, Henry had done his best to provide a stable home life, but she always acted as though she expected the rug to be pulled out from under her at any time. Perhaps that was partly a result of the frequent turnover in governesses. And yet Amelia herself had been the reason for that, making it more like a self-fulfilling prophecy. He didn't know what had started her on that downward spiral, unless the pain of her first few years on earth was embedded within her too deeply to overcome.

He said with a cheerfulness that was meant to be reassuring, "We shall all go together."

"You're coming, too?" She seemed surprised at this and, judging from her frown, displeased. Her legs began tapping against the chair once more.

"I have other things to attend to this morning, but we will leave after luncheon."

"But that's ages from now!" Amelia protested.

"If you can pass the morning quietly, then after we go to the river, we will see about going to the Crystal Palace as well."

There was a pause while she weighed her options. "Yes, sir. May I please be excused?"

"You may."

She slipped off the chair, but as she left the room, there was a spring in her step.

Henry couldn't help but think she had just proved herself an excellent negotiator.

CHAPTER

14

CARA COULD HEAR Amelia's approach long before the girl reached the parlor. "Why does Amelia deliberately make so much noise on the stairs?" she asked Langham.

"My mother reprimanded her once and told her a lady's step should be gentle and light. Ever since then, Amelia has been determined to do the opposite."

Despite the angry sound of her footsteps, Amelia did not look out of sorts when she entered the parlor. She wasn't exactly smiling, but Cara detected a tiny lift to her lips. "You came," Amelia said.

There was quiet emotion behind those simple words. Cara's heart went out to the girl. "You don't think I'd miss a chance to see the Thames, do you?"

Now Amelia's mouth widened in a true smile. "We're also going to the Crystal Palace to see the dinosaurs."

"Don't you think your guardian should approve that idea first?" Cara suggested. "I did not speak to him about the Crystal Palace."

"He has already approved it. We had a chat this morning at breakfast."

She said this with such a grown-up voice that Cara was tempted to laugh.

"Let's take the Underground," Amelia suggested.

Langham scrunched his nose. "Why on earth would you want to do that?"

"Because Cousin Henry never lets us ride the train."

"You are a contrary creature, aren't you?" Cara teased.

"I hate to disappoint you, Amelia, but Henry is coming today also," Langham pointed out.

"I know. Unless he's late. He's often late when he has to go to meetings." She sounded hopeful at this idea. "But if he does come, you can talk him into it!" She looked at Langham with pleading eyes. "Please?"

"You are not frightened at the idea of riding a speeding train through a dark tunnel?" He spoke in a macabre tone to scare her, but it had no effect.

"I think it would be exciting!" She turned to Cara. "Don't you?"

In truth, Cara was afraid of the Underground. Earlier this year, her sister Julia had been riding on the Underground when a terrible accident took place.

"The Underground is too hot and smoky," Langham said. "On a hot August day like today, it may well be unbearable."

"Maybe," Amelia conceded. But the expression on her face showed that Langham had done nothing to diminish her eagerness.

He gave an exaggerated sigh. "I suppose we can make a case for taking the Underground if you are so keen on the idea."

"Excellent!" Amelia said, once more giving a fair imitation of an adult.

Cara was about to remind them that the decision ultimately rested with Henry, when he himself entered the room. "My apologies. The meeting took longer than I anticipated."

His appearance had not altered, but today Cara looked at him with new eyes. Had he really done the things Langham had suggested? Could he stand here, as Amelia's father, and not give the poor girl the slightest indication of it? Cara hated that Langham had colored her impressions of Henry with these doubts about his character. She would

131

like nothing more than to discover Langham was wrong. But what if he wasn't? Surely there must be some way to discover the truth and do what was best for the child.

"We are taking the Underground to the Embankment," Langham informed Henry, presenting this as a fact rather than asking permission.

Henry frowned. "Why? Our carriage is just outside. Besides, the day is already warm. And inside those tunnels—"

"Yes, yes, we know it will be hot," Amelia interrupted impatiently. "But can't we go, just this once?"

Henry looked taken aback as he realized this idea must have been Amelia's, not Langham's.

Amelia's countenance had already darkened. She was steeling herself for his refusal. Cara fully expected it as well, for surely an earl would not ride on the Underground! Especially when he had his own carriage at hand.

Henry sighed, wiping his forehead as though he were overheated already. "All right. The Underground it is."

Cara looked at him with surprise and a touch of admiration.

Henry added with wry supplication, "May we take the carriage to the station?"

Amelia grinned and nodded.

As predicted, the Underground was oppressively hot and smoky. It was also crowded. The train platforms were jammed with people, which provided Cara with plenty of interesting faces to study while they waited for their train to arrive.

Despite the other drawbacks of this mode of travel, when they settled into the first-class carriage, they found the seating comfortable enough. Cara clutched the seat as the train hurtled through the pitch-black tunnel. But they arrived at the next stop without incident, and then the next one, too. Gradually she got used to the motion of the train and the way her body was thrown forward or backward whenever the train gathered speed or came to a halt. She did her best not to show her fear, but she had a feeling Henry knew anyway. More than once she saw him looking at her with slightly raised brows, but she couldn't tell whether he was concerned or amused.

In contrast, he seemed remarkably at ease. Perhaps he rode the Underground sometimes after all. At the station, he had paid for first-class tickets for all of them and then moved through the crowds with an assurance bred from a lifetime of privilege. Now he leaned back in his seat, looking unruffled despite the heat.

Langham, on the other hand, kept fanning himself with a newspaper he'd bought near the station entrance.

Before long another gentleman got on the carriage, leading a brown-and-white springer spaniel with him. It was the kind of dog Robbie had often asked to have. Amelia was thrilled when the man allowed her to pet it. As Cara watched the girl's joyful interaction with the gentle creature, she thought what a shame it was that Robbie's father refused him this simple pleasure. She also wondered, not for the first time, how the boy was getting along. Did he have a new nanny yet? Did he like her? Did she know how to handle such an energetic child? Just like Amelia, Robbie could be difficult at times, but he was a good boy at heart. And she hadn't even been allowed to say good-bye to him.

"Is everything all right?" Henry asked, perhaps noticing that her eyes had grown misty.

"Oh yes," Cara assured him. She took a deep breath and cleared her throat. "I think some smoke got in my eyes, that's all."

At last they reached Charing Cross station, where they got off.

Cara felt positively wilted, but Amelia looked only slightly worse for wear. Her frock had dog hair on it, and a strand of hair was loose where she had wiped the sweat from her forehead. But she beamed as Cara straightened her straw hat. "You see, I told you it would be fun!"

When they reached the Embankment, they turned left, keeping the Thames on their right. Boats of all sizes filled the river with noise and movement. The water glinted in the bright sunlight.

"That's a ferry," Amelia informed Cara, pointing, and then proceeded to name several others. "That's a fishing boat. And that's a yacht."

Despite the heat, many people were out enjoying the day. As they passed a family of five standing near the wall and looking out at the view, Cara could hear their comments and was certain they came from Devonshire. She was familiar with the accent because of the time she'd spent living near Exeter. Amelia's glance lingered on them, too, but Cara didn't think she was listening to their accents. She was looking at a little girl whose hand was being held by her father. Did Amelia wish for someone with whom she could do the same? She slowed down a little so that she was walking next to Henry. But she did not reach out to him.

Henry glanced down at her. "I suppose you'll want to stop at Cleopatra's Needle?"

"Yes," Amelia replied, beaming.

Looking at them together, Cara could almost believe Henry was Amelia's father. The girl was truly warming to him, especially after he'd allowed the ride on the Underground and did not object to her petting the dog. Perhaps she'd never seen a softer side of Henry before. Was he warming to her as well? If he was her father, would he one day have the decency and courage to admit it?

Cara was going to do her best today to show Henry the benefits and the enjoyment of spending time with one's child. And if he truly was only Amelia's cousin, it would still do Amelia good to have a man take on some of the role of a father.

After a while they reached Cleopatra's Needle, an obelisk covered with odd-looking symbols.

"Those are hieroglyphs," Amelia told her, looking pleased with herself for knowing such a large word. "It came from Egypt."

"It's impressive," Cara said, admiring the obelisk that stood higher than the nearby trees.

"I saw the workmen setting this up a few years ago," Henry said. "They built an enormous structure around it and lifted it with heavy chains and pulleys. It was fascinating to watch."

"I wish I could have seen that," Amelia said.

Langham gave Cara a look as if to say, *You see how alike they are.*

When they reached Waterloo Bridge, Henry said, "That's as far as we'll walk today. I gave my driver instructions to meet us on the next street. We'll take the carriage to the railway station by the Tower Bridge. The Crystal Palace is some distance from London, and the train is the fastest way to get there."

This news was immediately cheered by Amelia, who was as enamored of trains as she was of boats.

The trip went smoothly, and Cara was especially happy that this train ride was above ground.

"So much of what is inside the Crystal Palace is dreadful," Langham said as they neared their destination. "But the High Level railway station is a fine bit of architecture."

It soon became apparent what he meant. They got off the train and followed the stairs up to a corridor that led to the Crystal Palace. It was really more of a tunnel, curved in an S shape and brightly lit with gaslights. Rows of columns ran the length of it. They were covered in red brick, fluted at the top in a red-and-white mosaic, as lovely as any ancient tile.

They came out of the tunnel at the main entrance to the Crystal Palace. It was a magnificent structure, made of plate glass and cast iron. It was several stories high, with the roof rounded like a barrel in the center. Cara thought it resembled an overgrown greenhouse.

"The inside is like a museum of sorts, isn't it? Filled with the wonders of the world?"

Langham rolled his eyes. "Rather more like the bric-a-brac of civilization."

Amelia tugged Cara away from the door. "I bet the dinosaur park is way more interesting."

Cara caught Henry's eye. He was smiling, and her heart did a surprising dance. He was a good man. He had to be. If he had stumbled somewhere along the line—surely that could be rectified?

She turned back to the little girl whose eyes were alight with excitement. "Lead on," she said.

CHAPTER

15

A
S THEY CROSSED the wide green lawn on their way down to the park, they paused to admire two large fountains. Henry pointed out the tall towers on either side of the Crystal Palace, explaining that they were water towers that fed the fountains. Amelia enjoyed these, but it was clear when she was ready to move on.

They strolled farther down the hill until they reached the area of water and woods where the dinosaur statues were located. They were not hard to find. Some were very large, others perhaps five or six feet in length. Cara thought many of the smaller ones resembled oversized lizards, but the larger ones looked like nothing she'd ever seen.

"Well, what do you think?" Henry asked as Cara took in the scene. "Are these creatures that actually existed?"

"That's what they say," he responded with a shrug. "Many bones have been unearthed right here in England."

Amelia ran in and out among the statues, laughing. A few times she skirted the water's edge to view the ones that were partially submerged, as if they were just coming out from a good swim. There were small bridges over the marshy parts, and Amelia's happy step thudded on these as she went from spot to spot, seeking the creatures located between shrubs and tall reeds.

Amelia paused, pointing to the largest dinosaur. "That's called a stalactosaurus!" she called back to them.

"Surely that is not a real word," Cara said.

"It is!" Amelia insisted with a grin. She pointed toward another one—a giant lumbering thing on four legs with a neck as long as a giraffe's. "And that's a hipposaurus!"

"Well, she has the right idea, anyway," Henry remarked with amusement. "That's got to count for something."

"Why bother to put words on them at all?" Langham said. He sat on a nearby bench and pulled a sketch pad from the satchel he had brought with him. "A picture is worth a thousand words."

He began to sketch, his head bobbing up and down as his gaze moved between the paper and the view in front of him. Cara admired the ease with which he worked, and how quickly he could capture the essence of the scene with only minimal strokes.

"I would like to be able to draw like that someday," Cara said.

"It just takes practice." He pulled another pad from his satchel and a second charcoal pencil and extended them to Cara. "Why don't you give it a try?"

Accepting the proffered materials, she took a seat next to him on the bench. She looked at what Langham was doing and began to imitate his line strokes as he quickly drew an outline of a leafy tree. She liked the effect. She could probably learn a lot from watching Langham work.

After a minute, she glanced up, suddenly worried that she ought to be watching Amelia. Then she remembered she was not here as a nanny but as a friend. In any case, Henry's gaze was on the child. He had removed his hat, perhaps to cool down, for the late-afternoon sun was still very warm. He absently toyed with the brim as he looked thoughtfully at the girl playing among the unusual statues. Langham was viewing the scene with a painter's eye, but Cara wondered if for Henry it was more personal.

"She does like being outside," Henry murmured.

"I believe it is a good way to control tantrums," Cara told him.

"Children have so much energy. It's good to give them free rein once in a while."

He nodded. "I see."

"Clear communication can be helpful, too," Cara added. "From what I've seen, Amelia becomes frustrated if things aren't made plain to her, and she doesn't know how to handle those feelings."

"You seem to have a lot of experience working with children," Henry said, turning to look at her. "You have not, by chance, ever been employed as a nanny or a governess?"

Cara's breath caught. She didn't want to lie, but neither could she bring herself to directly answer his question. She dropped her eyes to her sketch and made a great show of carefully cleaning a smudged line with her finger. "Much of my experience comes from the orphanage. As we got older, we were called upon to help out with the younger ones."

"You're an *orphan?*"

Cara looked up again to see his eyes wide with surprise. Langham must not have shared this information. Even though it had helped her avoid Henry's direct question, Cara was almost sorry she'd brought it up. It was bound to make him think of her differently. Think less of her, maybe. "Yes, that's right."

"But Langham told me you have family in London."

"I have two sisters, but they are not in London at present. One is on her honeymoon overseas, and when she returns, she plans to attend the London School of Medicine for Women and become a licensed physician. My other sister is touring in the chorus of an opera production."

Cara listed these accomplishments to underscore that, although she and her sisters had been orphans, they had never been street beggars. She spoke in a straightforward manner, but her heart ached as she spoke of her sisters. She had been trying not to dwell on them, because that only made her miss them more.

"Your sisters have chosen interesting occupations." There was a slight lift to his brow that made Cara unsure what meaning lay behind his use of the word *interesting*.

"My sister Rosalyn is very respectable, even if she is on the stage," Cara assured him. "She's married, too. Her husband is the stage manager. I think people get the wrong opinion about singers. Some people don't think ladies can be competent doctors, either, but my sister Julia is going to be a leader in her field one day."

"You all seem to have come a long way, despite such a terrible start. In the orphanage, I mean."

Cara shrugged. "It wasn't as bad as many of those places are. We were treated kindly, even if everything was regimented and plain. But it could never be as nice as living with one's own family. It was good of you to take in Amelia. I suppose if you hadn't, she'd be in an orphanage today, wouldn't she?"

Henry flinched, signaling that Cara had struck a nerve. "Amelia is our relative. We would never abandon her."

"Goodness, no," Langham put in. "We couldn't have a Burke, however distant, being subjected to unspeakable horrors like an Oliver Twist. Although I suppose in this case she'd be an *Olivia* Twist."

He smiled at his joke, but Henry's hands tightened on his hat, and he gave Langham an angry look. "*Don't* say that," he growled.

Langham's rapid sketching paused. "My apologies," he said quietly.

Henry gave a sharp nod of acceptance. "I'd better make sure Amelia doesn't fall into the water."

He strode off toward the girl, who was in fact very close to the water's edge. But it was evident the comment had only been an excuse to leave them.

"Why did that make him so angry?" Cara asked. "It seemed a harmless joke."

Langham watched as Henry led Amelia back to the statues located on dry land. "It was my error. The woman he was in love with—her name was Olivia."

"Oh, I see."

Henry's reaction to her name seemed to indicate that his pain over losing her was great. And if she was Amelia's mother, wouldn't that add even more to his sense of loss?

Langham added the figure of Henry to his drawing, placing Henry's hand on the little girl's shoulder. Cara found it both poignant and sad. She sighed and returned to her own efforts.

Henry and Amelia trudged back up the hill.

"I'm tired," Amelia announced. "I'm thirsty, too." She came around the back of the bench to look over Cara and Langham's shoulders. "What are you doing?"

"We're drawing, of course," Langham answered. He held up his sketch. "What do you think?"

She scrutinized it. "You made the hipposaurus's head too small."

"You're a regular John Ruskin," Langham replied with a grimace. It was a reference to England's most famous art critic, but it naturally went right over Amelia's head.

She pointed toward Langham's pencil. "I want to try." She scooted around the bench and plopped down next to Langham.

He placed the charcoal in her hand and flipped the sketchbook to a clean sheet. "Let's see how much better you can do it," he challenged.

Amelia's hand paused just above the paper. "How do I start?"

Langham looked at her askance. "Haven't you been taught to draw?"

"No," she said simply.

"Why, that's scandalous! Henry, what kind of governess is not even teaching a young lady how to draw?"

"Actually, Mother is worried Amelia will make a mess."

"*Of course* she'll make a mess. That's how you learn. Is Mother truly concerned about the furniture? Or does she fear Amelia will catch the dreaded disease I have?"

Cara was surprised and saddened to learn that Amelia had been kept from drawing. It reminded her of her own childhood, although in her case, it was because writing implements and paper were strictly rationed. Sometimes Cara's fingers had fairly itched to draw something, and she had to scrounge for paper scraps to fill the need. She could not imagine why this joy should be kept from a child living in such affluence.

Henry didn't answer Langham's barb—not that Langham was waiting for it. Instead, he turned his attention back to Amelia. "First, look over the scene carefully and get a clear picture in your mind of what you want to draw. You'll need to decide what you want in the picture and what you don't want in the picture."

He paused, waiting as Amelia studied the closest group of dinosaur statues. She then gave a crisp nod, which Cara thought was not un-like the gesture Henry had given earlier. "Right. I want to draw the stalactosaurus."

For the next several minutes, they worked together as Langham gave her more instructions. He guided her hand a few times, but mostly he just allowed the child to attempt to draw what she had seen. The result was fairly good for a child's first try.

Amelia, however, was not impressed. "No, no, no," she blurted, suddenly scratching an angry dark X over the drawing. "It's all wrong."

"Amelia!" Cara cried in admonishment.

"I'm tired. And hot. And thirsty." Amelia thrust the sketchbook and pencil back into Langham's lap.

"Ah, the sign of a true artist," he said. "Our work is never as good as it appears in our mind's eye. That is why we keep trying."

"It's getting late," Henry pointed out. "Time to go."

"I don't want to go!" Amelia declared.

"You just said you were tired and thirsty. I'm sure we can find you something to drink, or maybe an ice, in the Crystal Palace."

"Can't you bring it here?" Amelia's voice had taken on a distinct whine that Cara recognized as the prelude to a tantrum. The girl's frustration with not being able to draw as well as she wanted had piled onto the end of a long and energetic day.

"We can't stay," Cara told her. She stood up and extended a hand to Amelia. "Let's walk there together, shall we?"

"No! I'm too tired!"

Langham winced at the piercing sound of Amelia's voice. He put away the pencils and the sketch pads. "I'll meet you there," he said and walked off, clearly eager to put some distance between himself and the whining child.

"We have to leave sometime," Henry told Amelia, no doubt thinking he was speaking reasonably.

"I'm too tired!" Amelia moaned. Then she began to cry. Great loud weeping sobs.

The panic in Henry's eyes showed he was at a complete loss. Cara supposed she ought to have known they would wear the girl out with all the walking in the heat, but she hadn't been thinking like a nanny today. She had merely been enjoying this outing as much as the child had.

She gave Henry what she hoped was a reassuring smile and then sat on the bench. She placed one arm on the bench behind Amelia, who was now crying with her hands to her face. Cara thought there was more going on than a typical child tantrum. She sat quietly, not speaking, looking over the child's head at Henry. Whereas Langham had only wanted to leave when Amelia became unruly, the stricken look on Henry's face told Cara he really wanted to find an answer. Cara admired him for that.

"Everything will be all right, my dear," Cara assured the girl. She gently lifted the straw hat from the girl's head, and Amelia turned and buried her head in Cara's shoulder. Cara held her in a loose embrace, allowing the child to cry herself out.

She thought back to the times at the orphanage when she'd been tired or sad or out of sorts. The staff there had always been kind, but they'd never shown individual affection. How could they? With two thousand children, it would have been impossible. At those times, Cara had been so grateful for her sisters—especially Rosalyn, who had often filled the role of a mother for Cara, giving her comforting arms to cry in.

Henry did not move or speak. He stood watching them both, waiting. Whatever his relationship to Amelia was, this situation could not be easy for him. When Cara was a child, she never thought about the lives of the adults around her, whether they had problems or worries. Now, of course, she knew very well that they did.

In time, Amelia's sobs died down. When the child was done, Cara waited another full minute before speaking. "Perhaps your cousin Henry will carry you back to the Crystal Palace."

Henry's look of panic returned.

To counteract this, Cara said brightly, "I'm sure you don't mind, do you?" Amelia was perhaps too old to be carried, but she was not tall for her age, and Cara thought Henry would have no trouble.

Watching the changes in his expression, Cara admired Henry's determination to bring himself around to the idea. It took several moments, but he finally found his voice. "Yes—that is, I'd be glad to, if Amelia is too tired to walk."

Amelia straightened, wiping her eyes. Pushing the hair from her face, she looked hesitantly at Henry.

"We're bound to find lemonade, or perhaps even cherry ices, in the Crystal Palace," Cara continued as a way of prompting the girl to make the right decision.

Heaving a great, hiccupy sigh, Amelia pulled herself to her feet. She and Henry looked at each other, both equally unsure what to do next. Cara suspected there had never been any real displays of affection in their family. It made her doubly glad she'd suggested this. She gave Henry a nod and an encouraging smile, and he hesitantly approached the girl. Then Amelia lifted her arms, and Henry scooped her up in a move that seemed natural, even if he'd never done it before. She laid her head on his shoulder, and he adjusted his hold to get her in a comfortable position. It was so touching that it left Cara misty-eyed, even as the three of them proceeded back up the hill to the Crystal Palace.

CHAPTER

16

I T WOULD HAVE BEEN IMPOSSIBLE for Henry to explain what was going on in his heart and mind just now. The sensation of this little girl clinging to him, trusting him to carry her, moved him more than he would have thought possible. He supposed he did love this child, even if he had often resented the responsibility of her care.

And what to think of the woman walking beside him? She had no reason to extend herself for Amelia as she had done today. He had watched her interactions with Langham as well, looking for signs that their relationship might be moving into improper territory. Yet he saw nothing between them other than an easy interaction that seemed, implausibly, like friendship. Perhaps they really were simply two people drawn together through their love of painting.

He ought to be glad that Langham's regard for Cara seemed to be progressing no further. He was already dealing with one woman who had used Langham's misplaced affection for personal gain. Amelia's mother kept pressing for more and more money, even though she had given the girl over to Henry's care. With his family's financial situation already in a precarious position, he did not need any more such problems.

At the same time, he found himself mystified that Langham's interest in Cara seemed so platonic. With her golden hair, round blue eyes, and smooth, pale skin, she was exactly the type of woman celebrated in poetry as an English Rose. She was also kind and seemed truly guileless. How could a man spend so much time with a person like that and not be tempted to fall in love?

Not that Henry was in danger of doing that, he hastened to assure himself. His heart was forever bound to Olivia. But for Langham, it would surely have been easy. Langham was too friendly with people he'd barely met, jumping over normal social boundaries. A few times this had blossomed into romances that had thus far been short-lived. Perhaps it was good that Cara did not seem to be entangled with his brother; perhaps she was not as naïve about these matters as she appeared.

Amelia's head moved against his shoulder, her soft hair brushing against his cheek. It spurred an urge to protect her, to do his best to make her happy—not merely as a provider, but as something more.

He wished Langham could be the one holding Amelia, and also that Langham knew this child was his. Henry thought that if what he felt right now was accompanied by the knowledge that he was the child's father, it would multiply into something inexpressibly profound. If he had seen some indication that Langham cared for Amelia, he might have been tempted to tell him the truth. But Langham had shown no real interest in her other than the few minutes when she had wanted to draw. He had physically distanced himself the moment interacting with her became difficult. This was not a man to try to shape into a father. He was too mercurial, too selfish.

Thinking over today, Henry recalled Amelia's fascination with the boats on the Thames and how she'd gravitated toward the water's edge in the dinosaur park. It reminded him of the first time he'd taken her to the seaside. She had been in his care only a few months, and it was her first contact with the ocean. She'd been enthralled by the waves sweeping in and out on the beach. She had looked for shells and squealed with delight as she'd chased the sea gulls. At her request, he'd taken her out in a small rowboat. He'd worried that she might get queasy as the boat rocked in the swells, but Amelia had taken naturally to it. Despite her little tirade just now, he was glad he'd been talked into coming here today. Perhaps it made up in some small part for having her holiday at Brighton cut short.

"How shall we find Langham?" Cara said as they approached the entrance to the Crystal Palace. "There are so many people here."

Henry did not hesitate, for he knew his brother well. "I suggest we try the restaurant."

Sure enough, they found Langham in the restaurant near the terrace. He was stretched comfortably in his chair, watching the passersby. There was a glass on the table in front of him.

Henry bent his knees, lowering himself until Amelia's feet touched the floor. Slowly, and it seemed to Henry somewhat reluctantly, she loosened her grasp. Once she was on the ground, she stood up straight and smoothed out her frock. She must have still been tired, though, for she lost no time taking a seat in one of the chairs at Langham's table.

"What are you drinking?" she asked, looking at his glass.

"Cherry brandy with a splash of aerated water. Very refreshing."

"Cherry! That sounds good." Amelia licked her lips at the mention of her favorite flavor.

"I'm glad to see you have regained your good temper," Langham said with a smile. "I know I have." He lifted his glass and drank the last of the brandy.

"Lemonade would be better for you, Miss Amelia," said Henry.

He pulled out a chair and seated Cara, embarrassed that his brother had not even bothered to stand. He was sure the drink Langham had just finished was not his first. Cara accepted the gesture, moving with simple grace. Even the pat she gave to her hair to check that all was in order seemed unconscious, without putting on airs. He noticed her delicate fingers had a few traces of blue and green paint at the fingernails. He wondered what her paintings looked like. What kind of subjects did she paint? Maybe he'd ask to look at them sometime.

"Something for you and the ladies, sir?" said the waiter, bringing

Henry back to the task at hand. He ordered three glasses of lemonade. "Make that four," he amended with a significant look at Langham. "We still have to get ourselves back to London."

"I have menus here, should you care for something to eat before the journey," the waiter offered.

"Yes, sandwiches, please," said Amelia. "And cream cakes."

"I'll do the ordering," Henry said. But he softened his reproof with a smile. Perhaps it was a good idea to eat something before they left. This way, Amelia could be rested and fed before they started back, just to ensure there was no repeat of her tantrum in the dinosaur park. He gave the waiter an order for sandwiches and cakes and added a plate of fruit as well.

Cara give a little sigh of delight. "It all sounds lovely." She was fingering the fine linen on the table and looking out at the manicured lawn and sparkling fountains. With her background, she probably had never been able to indulge in these kinds of simple luxuries. She would have had to watch every penny.

"I'm glad you're enjoying yourself," he said.

"Oh yes!" This enthusiastic response might also have been a reaction to the tall glasses of lemonade being set on the table by the waiter. As she studied her glass, she added joyfully, "Is that *ice?*"

Amelia's face scrunched a little, her expression clearly communicating her surprise that Cara would find such delight in something so mundane as ice in her lemonade.

When the food arrived, they made a jolly meal of it. Cara exclaimed over everything. Langham, perhaps buoyed by the brandy or else simply by his joy in the subject, talked to Amelia about drawing. Henry was surprised that she seemed willing to entertain the idea again after she had considered her previous effort to be such a failure. He supposed being strong-willed made her more resilient, too.

After the meal, they walked back to High Level station, Henry once more carrying Amelia. She was silent in his arms, and he could tell she was beginning to nod off. When they got on the train, he placed Amelia next to Cara, and it wasn't long before the child was fast asleep, snuggled into Cara's side.

"Thank you," Cara murmured to Henry as the train began its journey back to London. "It was such a treat to be able to accompany all of you today."

"Thank you for your help with Amelia," Henry returned.

Although he did not say it aloud, this day's adventure had been a rare treat for him, too. Spending the day in the company of this woman had been a big reason for it.

Everything went smoothly—until they got Amelia home.

While Amelia was asleep on the train, they'd all agreed that, to be sure the nursery maid was able to get her to bed without further incident, it would be best for all of them to go to the town home together. That way Cara could help out if necessary. Cara was pleased that Henry had this confidence in her. She could tell as the day progressed that he'd been growing warmer toward her. Their initial rough beginning had been smoothed over by their mutual interest in Amelia. Cara was sure Henry's love for the child was stronger after today. What good things might lie ahead for them all in the future? She decided she'd done the right thing by coming today, and God had blessed her for it.

When they reached the house, the front hall was brightly lit, and several maids and a footman were on hand to greet them. The light and activity roused Amelia. She stood in the hallway, rubbing her eyes, while Henry gave instructions to the staff.

"Here is Jeanne—she'll take you upstairs," Henry told Amelia, referring to the housemaid who also had duties in the nursery.

Jeanne offered the girl a smile, but Cara detected apprehension in her eyes. On the train Henry had shared that while Jeanne was more than competent in keeping the nursery and caring for Amelia's wardrobe, she was out of her depth when it came to dealing with the girl's behavioral issues.

Amelia turned toward Cara. "Aren't you coming?"

Cara shook her head. "Jeanne will help you to bed."

"But I want you to take me!"

"Don't argue, Amelia," Henry ordered. "You've had a nice day, and now it is time to go to sleep."

Amelia didn't budge, her eyes still on Cara. "Are you coming back tomorrow? We can go to Hyde Park! Or the zoo. Or the roller rink—that's so fun!" There was a hint of desperation in her voice.

Cara didn't answer. She and Langham were going to Arthur Hughes's garden party tomorrow. But even if she had been free, that didn't mean going out with Amelia was the best thing, nor even that Henry would approve it. That was his decision to make, after all.

"We'll talk about it tomorrow," Henry said.

"No, we won't. When you say that, it means no!" Amelia's voice got higher with each word.

Langham, who was waiting for this to be over so he could escort Cara back to the studio, put his hand to his forehead and murmured, "Not again."

Jeanne reached out to take Amelia's arm. "Come on, now, miss. Don't give his lordship a hard time." It was a halfhearted effort, though. It was clear Jeanne was a little afraid of the girl.

Amelia easily wrenched free of the maid's grasp. She stood in the center of the front hall, her face red and her hands on her hips, staring at the adults around her as though daring any of them to come after her.

Cara moved with an intuition honed by experience. She would take the girl upstairs, but she would do her best to ensure it did not count as a win or encourage such behavior in the future. She swept past the girl and began to walk up the staircase, speaking in a cool, authoritative tone. "Now, Amelia, I've told you before about keeping your voice calm. I know you are tired, but there is no excuse for not behaving well. Let's remember all the fun we had today and not spoil it, shall we?"

By now Cara had reached the first landing. She sent a quick glance back. As she had expected, Amelia had begun to follow her up the stairs, like being pulled by a magnet. Jeanne followed the girl, keeping a safe distance. Everyone else remained where they were, their faces turned upward as they watched this procession with surprise.

Crossing the landing and starting up the next set of stairs, Cara continued to speak reproving words she hoped the child would receive. She did this all the way up to the next floor and as they walked down the hall to the nursery. She opened the nursery door and ushered Amelia and the maid into the room.

Cara knew Amelia's physical exhaustion would eventually overtake even the strongest urge for resistance. The walk up two flights of stairs seemed to have mellowed her somewhat. Even so, the moment they were in the nursery, she turned, seeking Cara as though worried she would walk out.

Cara closed the door and stood with her back to it, holding the child's gaze. "If you hurry and get ready for bed, and allow Jeanne to help you, then I will tell you a special story."

There was a pause as Amelia stood there, her brow furrowed. It was a posture Cara had seen a number of times already. The wait wasn't long. Amelia walked over to Jeanne and then turned around so the maid could unbutton her frock. Jeanne gave Cara a look of surprised gratitude and then got to work.

Cara settled herself in a chair next to the bed and waited. She did not want Amelia to think of her as a servant. If she was truly going to reach this child, she had to remain in a position of authority.

"Thank you, Jeanne," Cara said as Amelia climbed into her bed. "That will be all for tonight."

"Yes, miss." Jeanne gave her a little curtsy and left the room.

Cara sat there, savoring a moment of stunned joy. Someone had curtsied to *her*. It was a nice sensation to be treated as a superior. One that Cara could get used to with no trouble at all.

Amelia tugged at her sleeve. "What's the story?"

Cara turned her attention back to the child. Amelia was settled into her pillows, looking at Cara expectantly.

"This is a story about a little girl who grew up in a *very* large house." Cara spoke as though she were reading from a storybook, and she used hand gestures to emphasize how big this house was. Remembering Amelia's reaction to the word *orphan* on the first night they met, Cara deliberately avoided saying the word. "The little girl lived in this big place with *hundreds* of other children."

Amelia's eyes grew wide. Her face brightened as she said, "*Hundreds?*"

"Do you think that would be fun, to have lots and lots of other children around? Perhaps so you could have someone to play with?"

Amelia nodded vigorously.

"It's true they had some nice playtimes together. But life at that big house wasn't as much fun as it might sound. You see, the children always had to obey the grown-ups—no arguing was ever allowed. They had no say about what *they* wanted to do. Most of the time they had to do things that weren't any fun at all, such as making their own beds and carrying big piles of laundry to the washing house. When they *were* allowed to play, they had to share among themselves what few toys they had. The food was adequate but oh, so boring. Sometimes it was butter beans three times a week. And I don't think they were ever once given cherry ices."

Amelia's face fell. "Oh."

"What's more, all of the little girls' frocks looked just alike. Their bonnets were made of plain straw and had few ribbons or bows. The boys fared no better. They were all dressed in brown or blue trousers and simple shirts. The children walked a lot, but they didn't go very far. Mostly to the schoolhouse or to church. They never went on holiday or got to go sea bathing."

"I'll bet the little girl didn't like living there," Amelia observed.

"She found it very hard," Cara agreed with a solemn nod. "However, there was *one* special day that this little girl looked forward to with great anticipation. It was a day in the summertime when the children went on a grand picnic. They walked for ages until at last they reached a big sunny field dotted with trees. They carried their own food with them in baskets. They ran and played tag and pushed each other high into the air on the swings tied to the biggest trees. That was always the best day of the year for this little girl. And do you know why it was so special?"

"Because of the swings?" Amelia ventured.

"No. It was because this day was a treat that only came 'round once a year."

"Oh." Amelia scrunched her face in displeasure.

Clever girl, Cara thought. She saw that this story would have a moral before Cara even got to it. But Cara pressed on anyway. "The little girl wished she could go on a picnic every day. She wished she could live in a house of her own and not have to share it with so many people. She wished she could have her own dolls and eat sweets every day. There were other things she wished for, too. She was sure that if she could just have all those things, she would be truly happy at last. But when she got older and met children who *did* have those things, she discovered they weren't always happy, either."

Amelia was frowning, not at all pleased with this ending. "Is this true, or just a fairy story?"

"It's all true. That little girl was me."

There was a pause. Amelia scrutinized her. Maybe she was trying to envision Cara as a little girl. Or maybe she was simply trying to digest the information Cara had just shared.

"I'll bet you can guess why I am telling you this story," Cara said gently.

Amelia answered reluctantly, "Miss Leahy and the countess tell me all the time that I ought to be thankful for what I have."

"Do you see now why that is? Life can feel hard and unfair sometimes—no matter who you are. But whenever we decide to be thankful for the things we *do* have, somehow the rest doesn't seem nearly so bad."

Amelia fidgeted with the counterpane. "Miss Bernay, did your mother and father live with you in that big house?"

Cara drew in a breath. In her desire not to bring too much sorrow to the story, she hadn't specifically mentioned that to have a mother and father was the thing she had wished for most of all. But Amelia had gleaned this anyway. With a sad smile, Cara answered, "No, they did not."

She didn't have to elaborate. Amelia understood.

"Are you happy, now that you are grown up?" Her eyes watched Cara's face, perhaps looking for hope that one day things might be better.

It was a difficult question to answer, and Cara was determined to be as honest as possible. She softly pushed a bit of hair from Amelia's face. "I won't deny that many things in my life have made me sad. Bad things happen to all of us. At those times, I reach deep down inside and find my happiness by being thankful for every blessing I have and every opportunity God has given me."

Amelia closed her eyes and gave a deep sigh. Perhaps it was only in response to Cara's gentle touch. But Cara hoped the lesson she'd been trying to convey was something the girl would take to heart.

CHAPTER

17

Henry stood outside the nursery door, riveted as he listened to Cara tell her story to Amelia. He'd been standing there when Jeanne had come out, and had quietly motioned for her to leave the door slightly ajar. He didn't feel guilty for eavesdropping. He was too impressed by Cara's tale, grateful he'd had an opportunity to hear it. She was telling it simply and honestly, unaware that anyone besides Amelia was listening. It gave him a vivid picture of what her life must have been like growing up, but it also illustrated her true character, confirming the positive things Henry had seen in her already.

Perhaps they were words he needed to hear, too. *"Bad things happen to all of us . . . I reach down inside . . . thankful for every blessing . . ."*

Cara came out from the nursery, stopping short with an exclamation of surprise when she saw him.

"I didn't mean to startle you," he said, speaking softly lest they disturb Amelia. "I came up to ensure everything was all right."

She looked so young, and yet to Henry, with her deep understanding of children, she seemed more mature and wiser than her years. Closing the door gently, she answered, "All is well. Amelia is asleep."

The gaslight sconces in the hallway were set low, but he thought there was a tinge of embarrassment on her cheeks when she added, "Have you been here long?"

"Not too long." He wasn't sure if he should reveal how much, if anything, he had overheard.

They walked together down the hallway. They both knew it was time for her to leave, although Henry found he was in no hurry to see this day end. "I must thank you yet again for your help with Amelia."

"I was glad to do it. But I'm concerned about the possibility of Amelia becoming too attached to me. Perhaps it's just as well that I'm unable to come back tomorrow." She pulled up short. "Not that you've invited me. I would never assume . . ."

"I hope you will come back." Henry's answer was honest and immediate. "Although I understand what you're saying about Amelia. I must figure out the best way for the two of us to get along. The servants, too, will need to learn how to handle her while Miss Leahy is away." It was a daunting challenge. "I hope you gave Jeanne some advice."

"If you approve, she might take Amelia for a walk every day. It will give her an outlet for her energy. She is tired out now from today's activities, but tomorrow she'll be ready to go again, as children always are."

"That's certainly true," Henry agreed, grimacing a little.

"I'm praying that Amelia will be a little less headstrong after today."

Henry's first inclination was disbelief, but he tried to change his mind to a more positive outlook. Perhaps he shouldn't discount the possible good effects of the time Cara had spent with the child.

"When will Miss Leahy return?" she asked.

"I don't know. It could be weeks. But we'll be back in our country house in Essex long before then. I think things will improve once we go there. Amelia will have more room to play, for one thing."

"And when will that be?"

"If all goes well, we leave next week."

"Oh! That soon?"

Her dismay was evident. Was she going to miss the child? Or Langham, perhaps?

"Langham will go, too," Henry pointed out, to test his theory. "I believe he'll be better off there." He wanted to keep his brother away from the distractions of the city that could lead him back to dangerous habits.

Cara nodded, although she looked a bit wistful. "Langham says it's lovely there. He told me he plans to set up a proper art studio. I hope he'll find time to give a few lessons to Amelia."

Henry was not excited about that idea, but he did not state this aloud, since he couldn't reveal his reasons. Besides, maybe he shouldn't hinder the child if she had natural aptitude and desire. His mother wouldn't like the idea, either, but Henry would deal with that when the time came.

They reached the bottom of the stairs, where the footman was waiting for any further instructions.

"Is the coach still outside?" Henry asked him.

"Yes, your lordship."

"Where is Mr. Burke? Still in the study?"

"No, sir. I believe Mr. Burke has gone to bed. He said he was suffering from 'a terrible pounding headache.'"

Henry didn't believe Langham was suffering from anything other than his own selfishness. However, his irritation at his brother's behavior was suddenly replaced by a different, contradictory feeling. He was content that this duty should fall to him.

He turned to Cara. "It appears I'll be escorting you home."

"Please don't trouble yourself," she protested. "Surely I'll be fine, if your coachman drives me there?"

Henry didn't doubt the sincerity of her words. But a picture flashed into his mind of a little girl, lost among a crowd of children, who had once longed for fancy things and a chance to stand out. After all the good she had done for him and Amelia today, Henry wasn't about to send her off like a servant.

He offered his arm. "I wouldn't hear of it."

It was a natural gesture, one he'd performed countless times in many social situations. He couldn't say why the feel of Cara's arm wrapped around his felt distinctly different. Maybe it was the expression on her face when she looked up at him with dreamy, pleased gratitude.

It wasn't late by London standards, and the warm night made it agreeable to be out. Once they were in the carriage, Cara leaned back and gave a contented sigh, her fingers lightly caressing the smooth leather seat. He thought again about the story she'd related to Amelia. If she dreamed of fine things, how was she happy to be living the bohemian lifestyle of a painter? Perhaps it was still a step up from the plain and structured life she'd led before. It might be true what Langham had told him, that many artists were gaining wealth and even a measure of respectability, but Henry knew they regularly disregarded customs that society counted as simple good manners. He found himself concerned about what would happen to Cara. He didn't want her to fall into bad ways. He sensed that she had a strong moral compass, and he hoped that would keep her on the right path.

"You mentioned you were not free to see Amelia tomorrow," he said.

He shouldn't even be asking for details of her plans. It was not his business, nor was it polite.

Cara didn't seem to mind. In fact, she responded happily. "Tomorrow we are going to a party, and I am going to meet Mr. Arthur Hughes. I might get another modeling job. Mr. Hughes paints a lot of pastoral scenes, and Adrian says I would be perfect for those. It would be wonderful if Mr. Hughes does hire me, because the money will help me buy art supplies of my own, in addition to paying for food. There will be other painters there, too. Langham and Adrian know so many people."

She spoke with breathless enthusiasm. Her thoughts were already returning to her prospects in the art world. Why shouldn't they? That was why she had come to London, after all. Not to be a caretaker for a child.

When they reached their destination, Henry helped her from the carriage and walked with her to the door. Not having a key, she rang the bell.

As they waited for someone to answer, he began to feel awkward, having no idea what to say. Cara seemed as much at a loss as he was. Her lips turned up in a little smile, acknowledging their mutual embarrassment. Even in the dim light, she was luminous. She'd make a perfect model, no matter what subject the artist was painting. Who wouldn't want to gaze on such a fresh and lovely face?

Henry's mouth went dry. He'd been admiring her all day, grateful for her beneficial interactions with Amelia. And, because he had eyes in his head, he was intensely aware of how lovely she was. All these things now piled up in his mind and left him powerfully drawn to her. He took a step back, needing to place more physical distance between them.

To his relief, the maid finally opened the door. "I thought it might be you, miss," she said to Cara. Seeing Henry, she gave him a curtsy.

Henry pulled himself together. He turned to Cara and tipped his hat. "Well, then. I'll just be saying good night." His words were crisp and perfunctory. He didn't think he had breath for anything else.

She reached out to take his hand. "Thank you for this lovely day."

It was simple, beautiful, and heartfelt. Her hand was warm in his. Everything he'd been feeling moments before threatened to overwhelm him.

Henry made some polite response and walked away before he could betray himself.

He thought about a lot of things during the carriage ride home. His powerful attraction to Cara troubled him. He hadn't felt anything like it since the last time he'd been with Olivia. But no one could take her place. How could he even think so?

He rubbed his face with his hands, trying to make sense of it all. Thanks to his brother's irresponsible actions, from leaving the sanitarium to everything that had followed, Henry was now driving alone through a hot summer's evening with his mind in turmoil. This astounding woman had been brought into his life. But it could not be for long, for she could not comfortably fit into any place in it. The milieu she inhabited was so different from his own. Langham might want to live in that world, but Henry never could. The two brothers might as well be living in separate countries.

Today's interlude had been just that—an interlude. A bit of pleasure that could not last.

It was good that they would leave for Essex soon. Until then, Henry had more than enough tasks to fill his days and problems to occupy his mind. As for Amelia, they would find some way to muddle through until Miss Leahy was back and life returned to normal. The child might be unhappy in the meantime, but it wouldn't last forever. And in any case, life didn't always present the most appealing options. That was a lesson Henry knew all too well.

CHAPTER

18

THE NEXT MORNING, Cara stood at her canvas, but she was
doing more thinking than painting. Georgiana and Adrian were
already absorbed in their projects. They'd gotten an early start
so they could accomplish a day's work before they all left for the garden party.

A brief rain shower had come with the dawn, leaving a breath of
coolness behind. Now a light breeze brought in the scents of the grass
and flowers to blend with the happy smell of oil paints. These were
ideal circumstances for painting, yet Cara couldn't concentrate. She
kept turning over in her mind all that had happened yesterday.

On the whole, everything had gone well. Amelia's episodes didn't
mar the day in Cara's opinion. Not when the rest of the outing had
been so lovely. Amelia had plainly begged for more such days in the
future, but Cara could not allow Amelia to think of her as a replace-
ment nanny.

She worried that Henry would think of her that way, too. He had
said she was welcome to return to their house, but there had been no
context to that invitation outside of visiting with Amelia again. And
he had asked whether she'd ever worked as a nanny. And yet, there

were times when his gaze had lingered on her, curious and warm, in a way that made Cara think he was interested in *her*, not simply her knowledge of childcare. Was she only imagining it? Perhaps his kindness to her yesterday, including the carriage ride home, stemmed only from gratitude that she had kept his ward happy and reasonably well-behaved for a day. The way he'd said good night confirmed that view. He had returned her warm thanks with a few stiff words before leaving as quickly as possible.

Langham, on the other hand, had spent the day speaking to her as a friend and fellow artist, but then he had disappeared, leaving Henry to take her home. She didn't think it was right to compare the two brothers, though. She already knew Langham had an inconstant nature that swung between extreme friendliness and casual disregard for others. Besides, maybe he really had taken ill. That seemed to happen to him a lot. Despite his unpredictable actions, he was a lot easier to understand than his brother.

"Your paint will dry on your palette if all you do is stare at your work," Georgiana said, noticing Cara's lack of movement. "Are you having a technical problem?"

"I am," Cara admitted, bringing her attention back to an issue that had baffled her before her thoughts began to wander. "It's difficult to properly capture light, isn't it?"

Georgiana walked over to look at Cara's painting. "An excellent technique for this is called Neo-Impressionism. It involves using tiny adjacent dabs of primary color to create the effect of light. I can demonstrate, if you like."

She began to show Cara the process, and for a time Cara forgot her other concerns. It was so satisfying to see the way the colors worked together to spark the effect of light.

They had been working together for several minutes when the doorbell rang. Since the maid was out on errands, Georgiana went off to answer it.

Cara began to clean her paintbrush. They would leave soon for Mr. Hughes's garden party, and she needed time to prepare.

"Cara!" Georgiana called from the hallway. "Come and see."

Cara hurried to the front hall just in time to see two men bringing in a large trunk on which were stacked two smaller boxes. Several days ago she had asked Adrian if she might have her things sent here from the Needenhams' estate, and he had no objections. "They arrived just in time!" she exclaimed. She had a parasol in there, and a nice summer frock. They would be perfect for today.

The deliverymen were young, perhaps sixteen or seventeen years old. They looked expectantly at Cara.

"Thank you so much," she said effusively.

They acknowledged her thanks with smiles and nods but didn't move. "We brought everything straight 'ere," said one of them proudly. "It arrived at the railway station not one hour ago."

"Didn't lose nothing, neither," the other chimed in. "Lots of things can get lost in this big, bustling city, you know."

"That is very good of you." Cara began to feel uneasy, wondering why they didn't leave.

"Wait here," Georgiana told them. "I'll be right back." She went off to the other room, leaving Cara with the men, who grinned. When Georgiana returned, she placed a coin in each man's hand. "There you go."

They tipped their hats and raced back to the street. Jumping onto their wagon, which was loaded with other deliveries, they set off.

"Thank you," Cara said to Georgiana, feeling foolish that she hadn't realized they were waiting for a tip. "I'll pay you back as soon as I can."

"Don't worry yourself," Georgiana said. She was about to shut the door when her attention was caught by something else in the street. "Well, look at that."

Cara looked outside. A carriage was pulling into place where the delivery wagon had been. It was Henry's brougham; Cara recognized the driver. The brougham's top had been folded down so that the plush seats were open to the fine day. Langham was the only occupant.

Seeing Cara and Georgiana, he gave them a wave and descended from the carriage. "Greetings!" he said as he came up the steps. "I've brought our transportation to Kew Green."

"That's Henry's carriage!" Cara said in surprise. "He let you borrow it?"

"It belongs to the family. I've as much a right to it as he does."

Adrian joined them in the hallway, grinning as he looked at the waiting carriage. "Bravo! We shall have a fun time of it, eh? This is a vast improvement over an omnibus."

"Are we ready to go?" Langham asked.

"We have to change our clothes," Georgiana said. "*Some of us* have been working this morning."

"I wish I had come earlier," Langham replied with feeling. "There is simply no peace to be had at Henry's house. I did well to get out of there before things got too loud."

"What do you mean?" Cara asked in alarm.

"Henry had to go out of town unexpectedly today, and a certain little girl isn't happy about it."

"Oh dear." Cara could easily imagine what must be happening at Henry's house.

"Don't worry about Amelia. The servants will keep her in hand. We've got a party to get to, remember?"

Reluctantly, Cara had to agree there was nothing she could do for Amelia at present.

The others helped Cara get her things to her room and then left to prepare for the party. Cara opened the trunk to retrieve her summer frock, which she remembered she'd placed at the top. As she pulled it out, a letter fell from the folds and drifted to the carpet. Cara snatched it up. It was from Julia. It must have arrived at the Needenhams' after she'd gone and been placed in the trunk by the housekeeper.

She placed the frock on the bed. They were leaving shortly for the party, but Cara wasn't going to wait even a minute to see what this note contained. She tore open the letter.

The first part of the message confirmed what Cara had learned from the Queen's College house matron: Julia and Michael had gotten married and left for South America just before Cara had arrived in London. As she read, Cara's anger resurfaced. Julia had behaved callously toward her sisters, both of whom would have wished to attend the wedding, and neither of whom wanted to see her leave England.

I cannot tell you why I am going, but I will say that I have the highest hopes for success, and that when I return to you, all will be forgiven.

Cara could hear Julia's voice as clearly as if her sister were here. But she could make no sense of the words. Julia had probably made them cryptic on purpose. If Julia thought this letter would somehow mollify Cara, she'd been dead wrong. It only confused and upset her more.

Rosalyn had no doubt also received such a letter. What had been her reaction? Cara could easily guess. In fact, their mutual indignation at Julia's actions might well have drawn them closer together than ever before.

If it had not been for their mother's watch.

Cara hastily refolded the letter and thrust it back in the trunk. She might have thrown the missive right into the fire, had there been one. Fighting to quell her irritation, she ordered herself not to waste a minute regretting her distance from her sisters. She had begun a new life here, and she was on her way to the home of a renowned artist. That must be her focus. She had goals of her own now. Heartaches must be placed in the past and not allowed to quench her dreams.

The ride to Kew Green in an earl's carriage to attend an exclusive party for artists ought to have provided Cara with more than enough to occupy her thoughts. There was a great deal of talking and laughing among the others as the carriage rolled westward out of London. Yet Cara couldn't help but wonder how Amelia was getting along. She felt sorry for the little girl who had so much and yet was so unhappy.

"Here we are!" Langham announced as the coachman brought the carriage to a stop in front of a red-brick town home that looked out over a large green with a cricket pitch.

A maid opened the door, and Mr. and Mrs. Hughes were waiting just inside to welcome them. Adrian shook the artist's hand heartily and greeted Mrs. Hughes with a kiss on the cheek. Cara hung back as Langham and Georgiana did the same. Adrian finally motioned

Cara forward. "Hughes, this is Cara Bernay, the woman I wrote to you about."

Arthur Hughes was a pleasant man in his early fifties with a kind face. "Welcome, Miss Bernay."

"Everyone is out back," said Mrs. Hughes, beckoning for the others to follow her.

It seemed they were the last to arrive. A lively conversation was already taking place among a dozen people seated at a long table under a tree. Cara was quickly introduced. Everyone else seemed to know each other. She joined the others at the table, supremely proud to have been invited here.

The party was all Cara could have hoped for—a happy perfection of delicious food and fascinating company. Mrs. Hughes and her two daughters brought out platters of cold chicken and fruit and pastries and a fresh apple tart. "The first of the season," Mrs. Hughes said.

The conversation among the artists enthralled and inspired her. It was a fine collection of news and gossip centered on the art world. Congratulations were traded for various critical and artistic successes, and in this regard, Langham held the spotlight for several minutes as they discussed his upcoming debut at the Grosvenor. As usual, the center of attention was the exact spot where Langham liked to be.

Nobody addressed too many comments to Cara, but she didn't mind. She simply soaked it all in. Georgiana tried several times to bring up Cara's desire to paint, but it never got any traction in the flow of talk as the guests moved from one subject to another. Cara knew she would have to prove herself first. That would take time.

"So what do you think, Hughes?" Adrian said at one point. "Do you think you can use Cara as a model for one of your upcoming works?"

"It's a possibility," Mr. Hughes acknowledged. "However, it would not be for several months. My family and I are going to Scotland, and I'll be working on another book illustration project. I'm coming home in early November; perhaps we can discuss something then?"

"Yes, that would be wonderful," Cara said.

The offer was both promising and discouraging. She had the prospect of work in the future, but how would she earn money in the present?

Mr. Hughes had already explained that the garden party was a send-off for his friends before most left for the countryside or a seaside resort. Cara, of course, had no such options.

"Don't worry, something will turn up," Langham told her as they rode back to London.

"I don't suppose you have another idea up your sleeve?" Cara joked, although she still felt disheartened.

"Possibly," Langham said with a wink, but he didn't elaborate.

When they reached Adrian and Georgiana's house, Cara prepared to disembark with them. Langham said, "I have a better idea. Why don't you come back to Mayfair with me?"

Cara hesitated as she considered this. "It seems rather late for me to go there unannounced."

"It's barely eight o'clock. There's even a ray or two of sunlight left. I'll bet Amelia is still awake. Wouldn't you like to see her?"

"I have been wondering how she is getting along," Cara admitted. "Do you think Henry will mind?"

Langham grinned. "Not a bit."

CHAPTER

19

H ENRY WAITED in the study until Langham—and Henry's carriage—came home. There was little else he could do, considering he had no idea where they had gone. Last night Cara had mentioned an artist, but he couldn't remember the man's name. He could only sit and fume and hope this wasn't going to be one of those days when Langham stayed out until all hours.

They had finally managed to calm Amelia. Perhaps it was just as well that Langham hadn't come home earlier. That way Henry could concentrate on one unruly child at a time. How had he thought he could handle both of them? He could not foresee days like today, when he had to go to Chelmsford to handle pressing financial issues related to the estate. Nor should he have assumed that Langham could be counted on to act like an adult.

At least he could cull one good thing from today. He'd happened to meet Nigel Hayward at the bank in Chelmsford and secured an invitation to visit him at Roxwell Abbey upon his return to Morestowe. It was a small step, but it might grow into a significant one.

The footman tapped on the door and entered. "They are arriving now, your lordship."

"They? Mr. Burke is not alone?"

"Miss Bernay is with him, sir."

Henry was doubly glad now that Amelia was quiet, although he wasn't proud of how he'd done it. He was also annoyed that he'd have to read his brother the riot act in Cara's presence. Did Langham purposely bring her, in hopes it would keep Henry from yelling at him? If so, he was seriously mistaken. Henry stalked out of the study so fast that the footman had to jump aside.

He reached the front hall as Cara and Langham entered the house. He closed the gap until he was nose to nose with his brother. "Where have you been? And why did you make off with my carriage for the entire day? Did it not occur to you that I might need it for other business? Did you make any kind of provision for the driver and the horses?"

Cara reacted to this tirade by shrinking back, placing herself halfway behind Langham like a frightened animal.

Langham's response was more languid. He rubbed his forehead as though Henry were the one giving *him* a headache. "Let's not make a scene, Harry. It's so tiresome."

Henry shoved a finger in Langham's chest. "You wait here."

He threw a glance at Cara, too, but he did not let it linger. He couldn't allow her remorseful expression to cool his righteous anger.

As Henry expected, the carriage was still at the curb. Whether Langham had dismissed him or not, Bryce, his driver, would know to wait for Henry's instructions. Bryce had been in the family's service for years, and he knew Henry would be furious about today's events. What made Bryce so valuable was that, in addition to being a good driver and conscientious with the horses, he was fiercely loyal and not the sort to run away from confrontation.

Bryce stood next to the carriage, hat in hand. He bowed his head as Henry approached. "Good evening, your lordship."

"Why did you do it, Bryce? And where has Mr. Burke taken you, that you should be gone so long?"

"I do beg your pardon for the inconvenience, your lordship. Mr. Burke saw me as I was returning from delivering you to the station. He asked me to take him to Holland Park. And, well . . . he is your brother, sir."

Henry took in a long breath, trying to calm his anger. It was true that Langham had a right to the family property, even if he didn't know how to use it properly. Since Langham was technically Bryce's superior—a mistake of the fates, if ever there was one—the driver would be in no position to refuse. "Did Mr. Burke have you cool your heels in Holland Park all day?"

"No, sir. We collected Miss Bernay and two others and drove to Kew Green."

Henry didn't ask Bryce why his brother should want to go so far outside London. Bryce wouldn't know anyway. He was simply following orders. Unfortunately, a trip to Kew Green and back would have added ten miles or more to the horses' workday. Henry spent a few moments looking them over and was glad to see they looked none the worse for wear. This was one of the best-matched pairs he'd ever owned, and he could not afford to replace them if they got injured. "Were you able to get some food during the day and keep the horses watered?"

"Yes, sir!" Bryce answered proudly. He placed a hand on the bay mare nearest him. "I take good care of my ladies. While Mr. Burke and the others were at their garden party, I found some refreshment for me and the horses. Kew Green is a right congenial place."

"Thank you, Bryce. I can always trust you to do your job well." Henry pulled some money from his pocket. "This should cover what you had to spend today, plus a bit more in appreciation for your extra trouble."

Bryce accepted the money with a smile. "Thank you, sir. All in a day's work, sir."

"It's not over yet," Henry said, remembering that Cara was still in the house. He gave Bryce instructions to wait and went back inside.

The hall was empty, save for the footman. "They are in the parlor, I suppose?" Henry asked.

"The study, sir."

When Henry walked into the study, he was not the least surprised to see Langham pouring brandy. Cara was perched on the edge of a chair, looking worried—an expression that heightened when Henry entered the room.

Langham walked to Henry, extending a glass. "An olive branch?"

"What were you doing in Kew Green?"

Since Henry had ignored the proffered glass, Langham took a drink from it himself. "Watching the cricket matches, of course."

"Langham . . ." Henry growled.

Langham held up his hands. "We were at a party hosted by Arthur Hughes. He's a famous painter and book illustrator. Perhaps you've heard of him. Or maybe not, since you don't follow news about the fine arts."

It was clear this conversation would be pointless. Langham was not the least bit contrite, and there was nothing Henry could do to make him so.

Cara stood and walked over to Henry. "I'm terribly sorry if we put you out."

"Don't say *we*. I'm sure it was not your fault."

"Even so." She offered a conciliatory smile. "How is Amelia?"

"She reacted badly to my leaving unexpectedly this morning. But she is fine now."

"I'm glad you managed to calm her down," Langham said. "How did you do it?"

"I reminded her that, as she is the child and I am the adult, she is not the one who decides what happens in this house."

"Oh, that seems calculated to appease," Langham returned dryly.

"I also told her—and this is unrelated to her actions—that we are leaving for Essex the day after tomorrow. She will be a lot happier once we are out of the city."

Henry had not liked the uncomfortable conversation that had ensued. Amelia had asked whether Miss Bernay could come with them. He had told her no but had not been able to give her a reason she could understand.

"But isn't she our friend?" Amelia had asked.

Henry had found it awkward to answer. Cara's exact status was not something he could precisely describe. He had settled for the easy answer that yes, she was their friend.

Whereupon Amelia had pointed out that, "The countess invites friends to our house all the time, and they stay for weeks and weeks."

Henry couldn't remember when guests had stayed *for weeks and weeks*, but apparently it had seemed that way to Amelia. Likely because she always had to be on her best behavior when there were guests in the house.

"Why are you pressing so hard to have an overseer?" Henry had asked the child. "I thought you'd be happy to be free from a governess for a while, to not have someone telling you what to do."

Amelia had shrugged. "Someone will. If not her, then you or the countess."

That matter-of-fact statement had bowled over Henry with guilt. But why should it? Of *course* people told Amelia what to do. She was a child, even if she didn't like to think of herself that way.

"May I go up and see her?" Cara asked, bringing Henry's thoughts sharply back to the present.

Henry shook his head. "She's probably asleep. She was tired out, so I had the nursemaid put her to bed early."

He left out the long, drawn-out discussion that had taken place before that. The one that had culminated in his promising Amelia he'd look into getting her a pony after they returned to Essex, providing she behaved herself in the meantime. He hoped that by bribing her to cooperate, he had not dealt a major setback to her proper upbringing.

"One reason we went to Arthur's house today was to see if we could find a modeling job for Cara," Langham said, launching into a new subject without showing any signs of following the current one. "We had no luck, though. Hughes and his family are going to Scotland for a few months."

"His lordship doesn't need to concern himself with whether or not I find work," Cara admonished, looking embarrassed.

"I think he'll be very interested, especially when I explain how everything is coming together for his benefit. For all our benefit, really. It's the perfect solution to our conundrum."

"Langham, what are you babbling on about?" Henry said.

"Miss Leahy will probably not return for several more weeks. That leaves you stuck with the problem of Amelia. Cara has no work at present. Everyone is leaving London for the long holiday. Therefore, I propose that she come to Essex to help look after Amelia."

"What?" Henry exclaimed. It was not at all the perfect solution. Henry knew this, because it was the exact idea offered up by Amelia. Once again, Henry marveled at how Langham and Amelia thought so much alike.

Cara's whole body stiffened. "No. I will not be a governess."

The vehement way she spoke surprised Henry. Her reaction seemed odd, given the warm interest she had shown for Amelia. She had been in service before, though. Had she been mistreated by her former employers? Perhaps that was why she was so adamant.

"We wouldn't think of lowering you to that role," Langham insisted. "You will be our guest. I suppose it is likely, however, that in the natural course of things, you would spend time with Amelia. For some reason that I cannot fathom, you seem to enjoy being with her."

That was certainly an odd way to frame an invitation. The way Cara's forehead wrinkled indicated she was thinking the same thing.

"Langham, she doesn't want to go," Henry said. "Don't press her."

But his brother was not to be deterred. "It will be just like yesterday, when we all went to the Crystal Palace and had such a lovely time. Wasn't it a wonderful time?" He looked back and forth between Henry and Cara.

"Life isn't only about having fun, Langham. I have work to do. *You* have work to do—if you are serious about getting your painting in front of the public."

In no way did Henry consider painting true "work," but he thought the mention of Langham's commitment to the art gallery would prod him to recognize the unsuitability of this plan.

"That's correct!" Langham said, seizing on Henry's words. "There is work to do. Cara is looking for work, too. She came to London to pursue a career in painting. But London is in a lull, and in any case, she needs training to hone her skills. Don't you want to help her out—especially after she has so generously assisted us with Amelia?"

There was no acceptable way to answer that question. Henry could only seethe in frustration that Langham had put him on the spot. It didn't seem any easier on Cara. She looked uncomfortable, and yet the rigid stance she'd assumed moments ago was softening. There was perhaps even a hint of hopefulness in her eyes. After all, Langham was promising her Utopia. But it wasn't as simple as he made it out to be.

"You haven't thought this through, Langham. How will she get training if she is living in the country?"

Langham waved a hand. "That part is easily accomplished. Mr. Perrine, the drawing master who used to give us lessons, lives in the village. He's retired now, but I'm sure he can be tempted to come out a few days a week. Especially if we include a nice luncheon. Cara, what do you say to that?"

"It does sound appealing." She threw a glance at Henry. "But I will not intrude anyplace where I am not welcome."

Now Henry felt like a complete heel. To say no at this stage would look like a rejection of her. There was also the question of finances. Mr. Perrine would expect more for payment than luncheon.

Surprisingly, Cara herself provided the objection. "What about Amelia? She is the reason we are even discussing this. As I said, I cannot be responsible for her."

"I had in mind that Amelia should attend the lessons, too, of course," Langham broke in. "Every cultured young lady should learn to draw and paint. Don't you agree, Henry?"

"Well, I—"

"We'll bring Jeanne to be the nursery maid, to keep her dressed and fed and all of those mundane details. Then, during the day, Amelia can come to the dower house with us, which we will turn into an art studio."

"Do you really think you will get your work done if there is a seven-year-old in the room?" Henry asked.

This point actually gave Langham pause. "Well, I doubt she'll be there all day. She's bound to spend a great deal of time running and playing outside and that sort of thing."

"And riding my pony." This was spoken by a voice near the door.

Henry turned to see Amelia in her white nightdress, her hair braided in two pigtails and her feet bare. She was holding a piece of paper.

"Amelia, you should not be downstairs," he admonished.

Cara was already crossing the room. "Good evening, Amelia. How are you?"

Amelia extended the paper she was holding. Cara crouched down to take it in her hands. "This is very good. Did you draw this from memory?"

Amelia nodded.

Langham walked over to look at the picture. "It's not bad," he said with the air of one giving grudging praise. "But there is room for improvement."

"The same is true for all of us," Cara pointed out with a smile. She stood up and returned the picture to Amelia.

"Did I hear something about a pony?" Langham asked.

Henry groaned inwardly. Nothing got past him.

"Cousin Henry says I may have a pony when we return to Essex. If I am a good girl," Amelia explained.

"Not that bribery ever works on a child," Langham said to Henry, his mouth turning up in a sly grin.

"A pony!" Cara exclaimed. "How exciting."

Amelia approached Henry. "May I have an art teacher?" She handed him the picture. "It's not bad, but there is room for improvement."

She repeated Langham's words without a trace of irony. Henry looked at the paper. It was a picture of the creature she had called a hipposaurus. Its legs were more spindly than the statue's, and the head looked a little misshapen. But what caught his attention was the figure of a man in the background. It was no mere stick figure, either. It was Henry, accurately portrayed, even to the forward peak of his hairline over his forehead. In the picture, he had a slight frown. It was clear he was far away because Amelia had captured the perspective of size relative to distance with fair accuracy. It struck some unnamable chord deep in his heart.

"Can Miss Bernay come with us?" Amelia's eyes were turned up to him beseechingly. "Please?"

Had someone shared with this child that a person could catch more flies with honey? Or had she simply figured it out for herself? Henry saw Cara place a hand to her heart and blink as though holding back

174

tears. Maybe the picture had touched her as well. He wondered whether it was for the same reason. Was it so obvious that he kept Amelia at a distance?

Cara gave him a wavering smile. It struck him how beautiful she was. Not merely pretty in outward appearance. An inner beauty manifested at unexpected times like a sudden spark of light. Whatever might have happened to her in the past, it had not diminished the kindness that defined her nature.

He realized now what Cara had been waiting for. There was something she wanted to hear before she would consent to Langham's suggestion that she go to Essex. And so, with a desire that finally outweighed his trepidation, Henry gave it to her. He extended the invitation himself with true sincerity.

"Miss Bernay, would you like to visit us in our home in Essex for a few weeks?"

She inhaled deeply, as though breathing in his words. Whatever her reservations, his invitation must have overcome them. Her smile broadened. Her blue eyes seemed to sparkle. Or maybe that was just a trick of the lamplight.

"Thank you. I should like that very much."

CHAPTER

20

T O BE TRAVELING to one of the finest country houses in
England—and as a guest, not a servant—was a pleasure Cara
had dreamed of for ages. As they rode in Henry's carriage toward
Morestowe, Cara imagined with delight all that was to come.

She sensed a similar excitement in the little girl sitting beside her,
even though in Amelia's case the reasons were quite different. She
must have taken this trip many times before. She'd dozed on the train
from London to Chelmsford, the town nearest the Morestowe estate,
but now she was wide-eyed and alert, gazing out the window as they
traveled the last few miles along the country road. The coachman had
brought a closed carriage due to the threat of rain. So far the rain had
held off, and patches of blue kept reappearing between the clusters of
gray clouds, sending down bright rays of sunlight.

Across from them, Langham leaned back in his seat, his head turned
to the window. He'd been unusually quiet since they had boarded the
carriage. He was either deep in thought or half sleeping; it was hard
to tell.

Henry had a newspaper open in his lap, but his gaze kept returning
to Cara and Amelia. "Are you glad to be going home?" he asked the girl.

"Yes." Amelia did not elaborate, but the smile on her young face spoke volumes.

Cara had brought a sketch pad with her, but for now she was content to take in the view and store it in her mind's eye for later. She took a deep breath, enjoying air that was fragrant with greenery and an occasional scent of blooms. What kinds of flowers flourished in this part of England in late summer? She was eager to find out. "Everything seems so clean here, after London, doesn't it?"

Henry smiled as he glanced toward the open countryside. "Yes, it does."

He had grown more at ease as they got farther from the city, although there was still a brooding in his eyes that indicated he still had a few serious issues on his mind. Was it family matters concerning Amelia and Langham, or was there more? Cara wanted to know, but not from mere curiosity or nosiness. She truly cared for each person in this carriage. It had always been easy for her to become attached to people she liked, but this felt altogether different. She prayed that these weeks together would bring about better understanding among all of them, and perhaps lessen the discord among these family members.

Like Henry, Cara had a touch of sadness that had not left her, even today. She wanted so much to share with her sisters the good things that had been happening in recent weeks. How astonished they would be! Since coming to London, she had embarked on a new and very different kind of life.

Being cut off from her sisters pained her, even if they had wronged her terribly. The thought of Julia on a boat in the vast ocean terrified her. Why had she done something so outlandish as to go all the way to South America? Until Cara found out, she was not prepared to forgive Julia, even if she did miss her.

The same was true of Rosalyn. How could she have treated their precious heirloom from their mother so carelessly? Cara could think of no good reason for it. Before leaving the Needenhams' residence, Cara had received letters from Rosalyn every week. Rosalyn would have learned by now that Cara was no longer employed there. Since she hadn't received any in her trunk, Rosalyn's letters must have been returned. Someone at the Needenhams' house, such as the housekeeper, might even have enclosed a note explaining the reason for it. If so, Rosalyn would doubtless be worried. Her sisters thought Cara was unable to fend for herself, despite the fact that she had managed just fine over the past four years since leaving the orphanage. Even after the disaster at the Needenhams', she had landed on her feet in a most interesting and wonderful way.

Cara had once or twice considered sending a short note to Rosalyn but had yet to do it. Thinking it over now, she decided to wait until she was settled in at Morestowe and had a clearer vision of her future. Then her sisters would be in awe at everything she'd accomplished.

Catching Henry watching her again, she gave him a big smile.

Henry was glad he'd purchased a newspaper at the railway station, because in the close quarters of his carriage, it gave him an acceptable place to focus his attention. It was hard not to stare at the two females seated opposite him. Their faces were turned toward the window as they chatted over what they were seeing, and Henry still marveled over the change in Amelia.

Cara seemed to have a calming influence on the girl. Miss Leahy's approach had been largely successful, but Henry suspected the governess hadn't addressed the child's emotional needs the way Cara had.

Amelia had spent much of today's train ride nestled against Cara, while Cara had placed a protective arm around her. One might even call it a motherly gesture. This was not something he'd ever seen Miss Leahy do. Henry worried over whether this growing bond would make things worse later, when Miss Leahy returned and once again took charge of the girl. This concern, like so many others, would have to be set aside for now—and probably added to a long list of things that might one day require payment with steep interest.

In the meantime, the trip was going smoothly, even though Amelia was a barely contained bundle of energy. She kept standing up to get a better view out the carriage window, only to fall back onto the seat with a giggle when a bump in the road caused her to lose her balance. Every now and then she'd touch Cara's arm to draw her attention to something outside. "That's an old coaching inn," she had explained to Cara when they'd driven past an abandoned set of buildings. "People don't use coaching inns so much anymore. Everyone takes the train now instead."

"I see," Cara said, taking in this information as though she'd never heard it before. She kept encouraging these tidbits from the child, sounding interested as Amelia pointed out other landmarks she was familiar with, from stone bridges to old thatched cottages.

Henry was surprised at how much knowledge Amelia had picked up about the area. She was a clever and observant little girl, and she was clearly happy to return to the place she considered her home.

Langham grunted as Amelia fell back in her seat again, her foot accidentally striking his leg. Until now, he'd been largely silent. He seemed *too* quiet. This was usually a sign his brother was depressed or out of sorts. Would this return to Morestowe bring back painful memories of what had happened before the fire?

Henry said quietly to Langham, "Are you feeling well?"

His brother shifted in his seat. "Well enough, I suppose. You did say Mother is still in Cornwall, didn't you?"

"Yes."

"Good," he said under his breath, closing his eyes again.

Langham had touched upon the same thing Henry was concerned about: their mother. When Henry had agreed to bring Cara to Essex, he had not had time to consider all the ramifications. At the time, it had not been too difficult a decision. It solved the problem of how to look after Amelia. Henry was counting on Cara to act as the de facto governess. He was sure she would naturally fill that role through her personal interest in the child, despite her insistence that she was coming as a guest and nothing more. However they chose to describe her presence was to Henry a mere formality. There would be plenty of benefits for Cara in return, including the expert painting lessons, so he considered it a win for all concerned.

How their mother would react when presented with this plan was another matter. If he'd merely hired a temporary governess, that would have been well and good. But the countess was not going to like the idea of a single young lady staying at the house, dining with them at meals, and participating in other activities generally reserved for family and "proper" guests. There was no denying that the situation was, as he was sure his mother would point out, "irregular."

He supposed he ought to send her a note so she would not be taken by surprise when she arrived. He could emphasize Cara's role in helping with Amelia, and surely that would appease her. However, he'd also have to make it clear that Cara was not to be treated as a servant. Coming up with the exact wording would require some thought.

Still, as Cara beamed at him and laughed with Amelia, he was glad she was here, despite whatever problems lie ahead.

When Morestowe Manor came into view, the first sight of it took Cara's breath away. Three stories high, it had an *H* shape, with the main house flanked by two long wings. Large windows looked upon the drive, and a wide flight of steps rose to the massive front door. There were a dozen chimneys, maybe more. The drive approached the house from the west, and Cara glimpsed a wide lawn that sloped gently away behind the house, unfurling like a boundless green carpet.

The only thing out of place in this perfect scene was the east wing of the house, which looked more like a new building site than an extension of a centuries-old mansion. Scaffolding lined one portion of it, and a crew of workmen were scrambling over the roof. Cara could hear hammering, even from this distance. Langham had told her that a fire had nearly destroyed this part of the house.

As they drew closer, Langham and Henry talked over what had been damaged and what repairs had been done. The fire had primarily destroyed the upper floor of the east wing, although smoke damage had spread to the main house. Some flames had also reached the rafters beyond the east wing. Henry had decided to replace the roof of the entire house. With a grimace, he pointed out that this was needed anyway, since no one could even remember when it had last been done.

As they talked, it was the most alert Langham had looked all day. Cara could see how much both brothers loved this place.

The house was nearly two hundred years old and had been in the Burke family for five generations. What must it be like to have roots so deep in one place? Cara could not name any of her ancestors. Any relatives beyond her immediate family were presumably dead. If her father were alive, Cara could ask him . . .

No, Cara corrected herself. *If Father were* here, *I could ask him.* She was never going to give up on that point.

Refocusing her attention outside the carriage, she noticed a second house a short distance away. It was not nearly so large as the manor house, but it looked pleasant. Tall windows and trellises of roses gave it a welcoming aspect.

"That's the dower house, where we'll set up the studio," Langham told her.

A wagon had been following their carriage, transporting the nursery maid and a few other servants. It pulled to a stop at a side door. Another wagon, which was filled with their baggage, did the same.

The carriage continued to the front entrance. Twenty maids and footmen, all in crisp uniforms, were lined up outside by the steps to greet the newcomers. To arrive in fine style at such a grand place made Cara feel like a princess.

As they alighted from the carriage, Cara was aware that many of the servants were looking at her curiously. "This is Miss Bernay," Henry informed them. "She will be our guest for the next several weeks."

Being familiar with how country houses were run, Cara easily identified the butler and the housekeeper. They stepped forward, and Henry introduced them as Mr. Jensen and Mrs. Walker.

"His lordship sent us word you were coming," said Mrs. Walker. To Henry, she added, "I have arranged the blue room in the west wing, as you directed, sir."

"But that's the guest wing!" Amelia protested. "Isn't Miss Bernay going to be near me?" She turned her eyes toward the damaged east wing and must have realized she wasn't returning to her regular room, even as Henry's next words confirmed it.

"We are all staying in the guest wing, Amelia. Miss Bernay's room will be next to yours. You are staying in the other blue room, the one with a sitting room attached. We have placed toys and books there, so it will make a nice little nursery for now."

"Oh." Amelia looked distinctly unimpressed. And disappointed.

"It will only be for another month or so," Henry continued. "You and Miss Bernay will have that top floor to yourselves. The rest of us will stay on the floor below."

"Let's go inside," Langham suggested. "It's too hot out here, and I'm famished. Is there luncheon?"

"Yes, sir," Mrs. Walker replied. "There is a cold spread set out in the small dining room for you to partake of whenever you are ready."

The *small* dining room. This house was grand enough to have two dining rooms. Cara was still marveling over this as they entered the house.

The front hall was everything she had imagined and more. A broad staircase with a carved banister swept up to a wide landing and then turned right, rising again out of sight to the next floor. The only thing out of place was an unmistakable smell of fresh paint and plaster.

"The layout of these looks different," Langham observed, indicating the many paintings that lined the foyer and the wide staircase.

"It might not be exactly the same as before," Henry answered. "Everything was taken down and cleaned while the new wallpaper was put up."

As they ascended the staircase, Cara allowed her fingers to trail along the banister. The varnish on the wood smelled fresh, yet the solid dark wood beneath her fingertips spoke of centuries of history. So did the paintings. The clothing styles in the portraits stretched back to the days of Charles II. Cara wished she could pause and study each one. She told herself there would be time for that later, and joy bubbled up within her.

Henry and Langham left them at the second floor. "Mrs. Walker will show you and Amelia to your rooms," Henry said.

"I know the way," Amelia answered. When they reached the third floor, she made a beeline for the far end of the hall. She hurried through the doorway and then disappeared to the right, presumably into the sitting room. Cara supposed she wanted to check on her toys and other things.

"Here's your room, miss," said Mrs. Walker, ushering her into the adjacent room. "I hope you'll find it comfortable."

Cara paused just inside the door, taking it in with delight. "Yes, I'm sure I will." From the four-poster bed to the massive oak wardrobe to the pretty dressing table near the wide window, the room spoke of elegance and ease.

The household staff was not only large, but efficient. Cara's trunk was already in the room, and a maid was unpacking it for her, lifting out the dresses. She gave Cara a smile and a curtsy.

"I understand you have brought no lady's maid, miss," said Mrs. Walker. "I've instructed Josie to help you as much as you need."

Cara gave them both warm thanks, and Mrs. Walker left.

"Shall I press this one for dinner tonight, miss?" Josie held up Cara's best blue gown.

"Thank you, Josie. That's very good of you."

Josie gave a little smile at Cara's words. Perhaps other guests had been more demanding or curt. It was easy for Cara to be kind; she'd been in Josie's position as a servant most of her adult life.

Somehow, in the midst of her elation, Cara remembered to send up a quiet prayer of thankfulness to God for bringing her here. She walked over to the window and looked out at the wide lawn below. It was peaceful, green, and open. A landscape that spoke to her of a boundless future.

CHAPTER

21

HENRY WAS THE FIRST to arrive in the parlor before dinner. He was not surprised at this. Langham never arrived anywhere on time. Tonight, Henry had sent Jensen to deliver a reminder that there was a guest in the house and Langham should not be late. Whether that did any good remained to be seen.

He supposed Cara was still busy with Amelia, or perhaps getting dressed for dinner. His mother was always punctual, but he'd been to enough house parties to know this was not the norm. Those ladies took their time getting every detail of their evening attire just right. Cara no doubt fell prey to the same vanities.

As he waited, he thought over the two very different letters in his stack of correspondence this afternoon. The first, from his mother, had related the news that she would be delayed another week because she'd been invited to a house party on the Isle of Wight. The Prince of Wales would be the premier guest, so naturally his mother had accepted the invitation. She did not approve of His Royal Highness's dissolute manner of living, but royalty was royalty, and someday he would be their king. With the Countess of Morestowe, protocol and pragmatism always won out over personal preference.

One benefit of her change of plans would be a greater likelihood of calm here at the estate. Amelia and Langham would be happy about the countess's absence. Henry sighed. He did not like that there was so much friction in the family, but it was a problem he did not know how to solve.

The second letter was from Jacob. It had been far more welcome, to be honest. Jacob was coming to Morestowe and would accompany Henry on his visit to Lord Nigel Hayward's estate.

The footman standing at the parlor door inclined his head as someone approached from the hallway. Henry stood, and a moment later, Cara entered the room.

Her gown was simple, but it was a flattering shade of blue that not only matched her eyes but took them to a deeper hue. Her hair was pinned up in a manner more elaborate than usual. The effect was that she looked elegant in an unpretentious way.

"I hope I haven't kept you waiting." She glanced around the room. "Langham isn't here yet?"

Henry resisted the urge to snort. "No."

Jensen entered the room. "I have a message from Mr. Burke, your lordship. He is not well and will not be coming down to dinner."

Henry's irritation flared at this news. "He was perfectly fine this afternoon."

Cara, on the other hand, looked concerned. "I suppose it is another of his headaches?"

The butler gave a nod in response.

"He did tell me those things could come on suddenly," she said. "Perhaps it was caused by the journey. All that jostling and smoke."

Henry had another theory. "Excuse me," he said to Cara and left the parlor, motioning for Jensen to follow.

Once the two of them were in the hallway, Henry said quietly, "What has Mr. Burke brought in his bags?" He knew the butler would understand what he was asking and why.

"We don't know for sure, your lordship. There was nothing unusual among his clothing and personal items. However, he did not allow the footman to unpack several smaller bags, which he said contained art supplies that he would take to the dower house himself."

Henry could imagine what might be in those bags besides art supplies. There would be a range of "medicines" to treat his headaches. Some could be dangerous if taken too liberally—which Langham could be counted upon to do. "Keep an eye on him, will you? Take up some tea or broth every hour or so, or use whatever reason you can find to enter his room on a regular basis."

Surveillance on Langham was not a pleasant task. He could be difficult to deal with when he didn't feel well. Fortunately, Jensen had plenty of experience. He gave Henry an understanding nod. "Certainly, sir."

Jensen was about to walk toward the kitchens to collect the first round of tea when Cara called out, "Excuse me. I don't mean to interrupt, but I've had an idea."

Henry turned to see her standing in the doorway to the parlor. He hoped she hadn't overheard his instructions to Jensen. "Yes?"

"I've been thinking about a remedy that my sister Julia recommends. She's a nurse and will soon be a doctor." This explanation was provided for the butler, who raised his eyebrows fractionally in surprise. "She recommends massaging the temples and back of the neck with a mixture of lavender and peppermint oil. Perhaps that could help Langham."

Although Henry doubted this could be a useful remedy, he sent a glance toward the butler. "Jensen, do we stock such things?"

"I can ask the housekeeper, your lordship."

"Thank you." The butler thus dispatched, Henry considered what to do next. There was no point returning to the parlor, so he offered his arm to Cara. "As we are all here, we may as well go in to dinner."

As they walked toward the dining room, Henry was vividly aware of the precariousness of his situation. He would be dining alone with a young female who had come as a guest to this house without a chaperone or escort of any kind. The detailed rules of society had never been his primary concern in life, and yet as the Earl of Morestowe, he did have a certain reputation to uphold. From the point of view of propriety, this was the very reason they ought not to have brought Cara here. They had justified it in a number of ways: she was here as the guest of the Burke family as a whole, not one person in particular; she was studying to be a painter and therefore a colleague of Langham's; she was here to offer temporary help and guidance with Amelia.

None of those reasons had taken into account Langham's unreliability and his tendency to disappear for days on end. Henry hoped the "headaches" would not turn into multiday affairs, as they often did. For now, he would simply make sure there was a footman or other servant in the room with him and Cara at all times. This was for her protection as well. She might be of lower-class background, but that didn't matter. He would not do anything that could damage a lady's reputation. Some might say that, as Cara had recently been paid to model in questionable clothing for a public painting, she had already crossed a line of honor. To Henry's mind, that was all the more reason to prevent any whiff of scandal arising from her visit here.

When they reached the dining room, Henry seated Cara. It was easily done, without a trace of the awkwardness he had experienced when seating some ladies at dinner parties. Where had she learned this subtle art? Some women simply had a natural grace. Olivia had been an example of that. Even now, after all these years, Henry felt the familiar grip around his heart at the thought of her.

He waited until the first course had been served before opening any conversation besides that related to the meal service. He thought it best to keep to the usual banal topics. "Are you finding your accommodation comfortable?"

"Oh yes, it's lovely. A maid helped me unpack, so that took no time at all. Then I visited Amelia's room. She is sad not to be in her familiar nursery, but was mollified at seeing so many new playthings."

"I'm glad to hear it. We had to replace all her books and toys, which were destroyed in the fire. I wasn't able to get exact copies of everything, but I did the best I could." He had been concerned that Amelia would find an excuse to throw another tantrum. Cara must have found a way to keep the child's mind occupied. "I suppose you asked her to show you everything?"

"Actually, she was feeling energetic despite our long journey from London, so we took a walk around the grounds. Then we went to the stables. She showed me exactly which stall she expects to keep her new pony in. The groom, Mr. Hart, was pleased to hear there would be a new addition soon." She paused to take a sip from her water glass, but Henry could see a smile playing around her lips.

"I did tell Amelia it might not happen right away. I hope she has retained that bit of information."

"Children are notorious for their selective memory," Cara said. "You might need to clarify that point again."

"I presume she remembers that in the meantime there will be art lessons?"

"Oh yes!" Cara looked as excited as a child herself. "First thing tomorrow, we'll go to the dower house to set up our studio."

"I wouldn't plan to get too early of a start. Not if Langham is involved. Especially as he is experiencing one of his, er, headaches."

"Perhaps it won't linger. We must ask the butler how he is getting on—oh, look, there he is."

Jensen was indeed just entering the dining room. "Mrs. Walker informs me that we have both of the requested items on hand, sir. Shall I take them to Mr. Burke?"

"That would be wonderful!" Cara said, even though Jensen had addressed himself to Henry. "Please tell him what I said about applying it to his temples and the back of his neck. It can be applied directly, or you can put it on a cotton cloth first. Perhaps a valet or footman can help administer it?"

Henry was just glad she hadn't offered to do it herself. She seemed willing to dive into everything and did not seem aware of any impropriety.

Jensen looked to Henry for approval. Henry nodded. "Very good, sir," Jensen said and left the room.

Cara smiled. "If Langham will follow those instructions, I feel certain he'll be good as new by tomorrow."

"If not, I'm afraid you'll be on your own. I'll be busy in the morning with other things." He and Mr. Thompson were reviewing the ongoing renovation work, plus he wanted to tweak the prospectus he planned to give to Hayward. Although Cara was technically a guest, Henry had no time to organize a schedule of activities for her. She needed to know that, for the most part, she and Amelia would have to entertain themselves.

"We'll muddle through just fine," Cara assured him. "We popped into the dower house today, and I can see why Langham says it has excellent potential for a studio. The front room is so open and bright."

"Tomorrow afternoon we'll be receiving another visitor here. Jacob Reese is a friend of mine. He owns a cast-iron business. His company is responsible for the new radiators we're installing throughout the house."

"Like the one in my bedroom? I've never seen a radiator with such lovely designs on it before."

Henry nodded, pleased she had noticed. He supposed that as an artist, she would have an eye for details like that.

"It seems luxurious to have reliable heat," she went on. "So much better than a fireplace."

"Less dangerous, too." If this observation came out too wryly, Henry couldn't be blamed. That night when half the house was in flames and he was frantic to ensure his family and servants were all safe was something he hoped never to live through again.

Understanding flickered in Cara's eyes. She'd seen a portion of the damage that had been done and could no doubt imagine the rest.

Henry wasn't going to allow the conversation to move into morbid territory. Changing to a more conversational tone, he said, "Mr. Reese's company makes other items as well. Tomorrow he's bringing new benches for the garden. We'll also discuss the possibility of installing a fountain."

"A fountain! Amelia will be overjoyed."

"She does like water," Henry agreed. "It won't rival the ones at the Crystal Palace, but it will have a pool large enough for her to float her toy boat."

"You're a very conscientious guardian to provide things to make Amelia happy."

She gave him a look of admiration that he wasn't sure he deserved. He hoped he wasn't spoiling the child. His mother had accused him of this. Yet Cara thought he was doing good things for Amelia, and Henry found he was inclined to give her opinion more weight.

He just wished she wasn't looking at him with such radiance. It made him supremely uncomfortable.

There was a pause in the conversation as the servants brought out the next course. Henry was glad Jacob was coming tomorrow. With three people at the dinner table, it would feel more like a party and less intimate. He was sure Jacob would not be critical of Cara's presence, especially after Henry explained why she had come. His friend knew all about Henry's troubles with his ward and his brother.

Henry noticed, as he had at the previous course, that there was a tiny lag between when he picked up his silverware and when Cara did. She seemed to be watching him for clues. Perhaps she'd never eaten at such an elaborately set table. The staff had been trained by the countess to always put on their best whenever a guest was in the house, but in this case, Henry worried whether Cara would feel out of her depth. If she was daunted, though, she didn't show it. He even thought she gave a little sigh of satisfaction when, after she had placed her soup spoon in her empty bowl at exactly the same angle as Henry had done, the footman had understood the sign and deftly whisked it away. No doubt she thought it a luxury to be waited on in such a fashion.

He was brought out of his musings by Cara's next statement. "Langham mentioned your friend. He said you met Mr. Reese when you were both students at Oxford."

If Langham had told her about Jacob, he'd surely told her about Olivia. The delicate fish he was eating stuck in his throat. He took a sip of wine to force it down.

Sure enough, Cara said, "Langham told me Mr. Reese had a sister, whom you also knew."

Henry's grip tightened around his glass. "Yes. She died some years back."

That was all he was going to say about it. Even if he were inclined to say more—which he wasn't—he wouldn't do it at dinner with the servants nearby. If there was one thing Henry guarded fiercely, it was keeping his private life private.

Cara's expression softened with sadness, but Henry did not like sympathy of any kind directed at him. Especially as it confirmed that

Langham had told her too much about Olivia and about Henry's feelings for her.

Leaning back in his chair, he forced his hands to relax. "I'm glad you're setting up a work space in the dower house. Mr. Perrine will be here the day after tomorrow to give you and Amelia your first lesson."

Cara easily took up this new thread of conversation. Even so, as they discussed what would be needed at the studio, she directed a thoughtful look at him from time to time. She had not completely forgotten the previous subject.

When dinner was over, Henry suggested they go to the parlor. It was the polite thing to do, even though he'd have to figure out how to keep a servant there to ensure no gossip could arise.

Cara said, "Thank you, but I believe I will turn in for the evening."

"A good idea," Henry responded. "We've had a long day." Even so, his relief was mixed with an uncomfortable realization that he would have liked to spend more time with her.

"Besides, I thought you'd want to check on Langham," Cara added.

This had not been on Henry's mind at all. He supposed he'd grown callous over Langham's episodes of supposed ill health. Cara's naïve expectation that he should care enough about his brother to offer help—well, this chastised him.

As they walked up the staircase, Cara paused before a portrait on the first landing. "Today as I was coming downstairs with Amelia, I was quite taken with this one. I asked Amelia about it, but she said she hadn't seen it before. From the clothing, I guess it is fairly recent—perhaps two decades ago?"

Of all the paintings in the house, Henry was pleasantly surprised that this should be the one to catch her eye. It was a portrait of Henry and Langham as children, playing under a large oak tree. Their mother was seated in a chair, watching them, and their younger sister, Charlotte, who was three years old at the time, was standing in her lap. "I like it, too. I had it moved here when we were rehanging the paintings. I suppose you've guessed who those boys are."

"I have. How charming you are, teasing that dog."

"That was Ranger. Our constant companion."

"And the little girl?"

"That was my sister, Charlotte. She died about a year after this was painted."

"Oh," she said softly, with empathy. "Does it pain you to think of her?"

"I moved the painting here on purpose. It is a bittersweet memory, as you can imagine. And yet I prefer to place my sister where she can be remembered, not relegated to a dark corner."

"That is a lovely sentiment."

"My mother may have different ideas when she sees it. She still mourns deeply, even after all these years."

Cara directed a look of sympathy toward the likeness of his mother in the painting. "Who can blame her? A mother's love must be fathomless."

Henry could hear a note of longing in her voice. She would naturally grieve for her own parents, being orphaned so young.

"Her ladyship looks like a strong woman, though," Cara added. "I can tell by the way she holds herself and the set of her chin."

"*Strong* is a good word to describe her. As you will see when you meet her."

"Should I be afraid?" she asked, a twinkle in her eye.

"Perhaps." He spoke lightly to match her tone, but also to mask the truth. There was bound to be trouble in some form when his mother arrived. The only question was how bad it would be.

"Are there any portraits of Amelia?"

"No."

"Why not?"

"We . . . that is . . . I suppose we are waiting until she is older. She's a little hard to pin down at the moment."

Cara smiled at his joke, but after a moment it faded, and she said with some hesitation, "Henry . . ."

"Yes?"

"When Langham told me about Amelia's history, he hinted that perhaps the official story isn't entirely true." She looked at him with wide eyes, beseeching him to answer.

Henry forced himself to squelch the anger that always arose whenever his brother indulged in the same gossip as people who knew nothing of the situation. It was reprehensible. Langham now had Cara thinking Henry was Amelia's father. Unfortunately, Henry could not defend his honor—ironically because he was honor-bound to uphold the story his parents had fabricated years ago.

It troubled him to have to lie to her. It troubled him even more that he had an urge to tell her everything. He'd never been tempted to unburden himself to anyone. Why now, with this woman he'd known only a few weeks? He selfishly wanted to retain her good opinion of him. It suddenly mattered very much. But it was impossible to tell her the whole truth.

He decided to share what he could. Knowing she cared for Amelia told him how to craft his answer. He gave a quick glance around to ensure no one was within earshot before speaking low and earnestly.

"If we've chosen not to divulge every detail about how Amelia came to live with us, it is for *her* sake. It's wrong to allow any stigma to attach to an innocent child. She deserves to be raised as a proper young lady. That way, when the time comes, she'll be welcome in polite society. I don't want anything to prevent her from being able to make a good marriage, to live happily and well."

Cara took a moment to consider his words. He saw objections rising to her lips. "But—"

"I want only the best for her. Please believe that." He met her gaze, trying to make her understand he couldn't tell her more.

"I understand," she said at last. Her eyes were sad, but she smiled.

Henry's heart lurched in his chest. For all he knew, she still thought he was Amelia's father, but at least she was willing to accept things as they stood and not prod further. "Thank you."

They continued on, not stopping again until they'd reached the second landing, where Cara was to continue upstairs.

She turned to face him. "I would like to say again how immensely glad I am to be here."

"You are most welcome. I hope you will enjoy your stay." The rote words came out automatically, which was a good thing, because the sight of her pleasing face turned up to his was suddenly doing strange things to his insides.

"I know I shall. I feel at home already."

Before he could figure out what to make of that, she turned and went on her way. He averted his gaze, determined not to watch her as she ascended the stairs. What was wrong with him?

He shook his head and walked down the corridor toward Langham's room. He was met by the butler along the way. "What's the news?" Henry asked. "What did Mr. Burke say to the idea of the lavender and peppermint oil?"

"He agreed to give it a try."

"Really?"

"He said that since the suggestion came from Miss Bernay, it would be rude not to."

That was something, at any rate. How strange if it actually worked.

Henry decided not to visit Langham after all. The butler's report was good, so he would leave it at that.

He went to his room but sat brooding for a long while.

It was it likely his mother would object to having that painting where it might be seen every day. He had placed it there in an effort, perhaps, to remind them all of the times when they had been more close-knit as a family. Perhaps recalling those times might make his mother a little kinder in her dealings. It might be a vain hope, but he thought it worth a try.

Henry had a feeling Jacob would like Cara. He would see her goodness and appreciate her sincere faith in God. He would see how she was helping Amelia and agree that bringing her here was a good thing. The two of them would get on well.

Though he had no idea why, Henry was pleased at the thought.

CHAPTER

22

Jacob arrived in the afternoon with a wagonload of cast-iron benches. Henry met him on the front drive.

"Where is Amelia?" Jacob asked as he and Henry exchanged greetings. "She always runs out to greet me."

Jacob had long taken an interest in the girl. Being a father himself, he went out of his way to be kind to her whenever he visited. As a result, he was one of the few guests Amelia liked. It was just one more reason Henry counted this man a good friend. Jacob didn't know Amelia's true parentage, but Henry was sure that even if he did, he would treat her no differently.

"I know she wants to see you," Henry assured him. "She's engaged in an interesting project. I'd be happy to show you."

"I'm intrigued," Jacob answered.

First they got the wagon unloaded, the horses taken to the stable for rest and watering, and the two men Jacob had brought with him handed over to the housekeeper, who led them to the servants' hall for their own rest and refreshment.

Finally, Henry and Jacob walked to the dower cottage. Along the way, Henry updated his friend on the issues with the governess and why they had brought another woman to the estate.

"It sounds as though you were fortunate to find this Miss Bernay," Jacob observed. "Especially if she is helping Langham as well as Amelia."

"Yes, she even recommended that he administer lavender and peppermint oils for his headache, and it actually seems to have worked. Langham rejoined the world today at noon, instead of being out for a day or more."

"So she is a miracle worker, too," Jacob said with a smile.

"I just hope we can convince my mother of that when she comes."

His friend nodded. "Her ladyship can be rather set in her ways."

He spoke without rancor, even though he'd often tried to break through her icy reserve. She had grudgingly accepted Henry's friendship with Jacob, and she certainly appreciated the monetary benefits that resulted from their business dealings. However, Jacob's middle-class background meant she would never see him as an equal.

For his part, Henry was determined to treat honest, hardworking men like Jacob with the respect they deserved. He hoped the attitudes of others in the aristocracy might one day move in that direction as well.

They heard the talking and activity through the open doorway before they even entered.

Henry would not have believed Langham or Amelia capable of such industry if he hadn't seen it with his own eyes. Langham had commandeered two footmen, and under his direction they were carrying a tall cabinet out of the room to the parlor at the back of the house.

The front room was filled with easels, canvases, and boxes of supplies. The plain wooden worktable that had functioned as the adjunct office of Mr. Thompson was now placed along a wall. Amelia was helping Cara pull items out of a crate and place them on the table. So far, they had laid out pots and tubes of paints, a stack of paintbrushes, and a variety of tools whose uses Henry could only guess at.

Amelia was the first to see them enter. She ran over to stand in front of Jacob, beaming up at him. "Mr. Reese! I'm so glad to see you."

Pulling something from his pocket, Jacob said, "I've brought you a little present." As he extended it toward Amelia, Henry saw it was a small bag from a confectioner's shop. "I hope your guardian won't mind my giving you sweets."

"Cherry candy!" Amelia squealed. She tore open the bag, inhaled the cherry scent, and immediately popped one into her mouth.

"Don't eat them all at once," Henry admonished.

"I won't," Amelia answered, her voice slurred from the candy.

Cara watched this scene with a serene smile. As Jacob's attention turned to her, Henry thought he read surprise on his friend's face. Perhaps this was not the type of woman he'd expected. Henry had made it clear Cara was not a governess in the vein of Miss Leahy, but he hadn't mentioned the age difference between the two ladies.

Cara offered her hand as Henry introduced them. "I'm so glad to meet you. I understand you are Henry's dearest friend."

"I'm flattered to think so. I have already heard many good things about you as well."

They both sent a glance at Henry, and he felt a flush of embarrassment. Jacob would have noticed her use of Henry's Christian name, and Henry had just spent the past several minutes extolling her virtues. Henry was mortified, lest his friend get the wrong idea.

He turned away to survey the room. "It looks like you are well underway."

"We are turning this house into an art studio," Amelia informed Jacob.

"Is that so? How exciting."

"Did you come to help us?" Cara asked.

Her question was directed primarily at Henry. Even though the lilt in her voice told him she was teasing, he was surprised to find her suggestion sounded appealing. He decided it must be a reaction to the happy buzz of excitement here. After all, he had never been interested in painting. That had been Langham's domain.

Henry shook his head. "Actually, we've come to see if you're ready to return to the house for tea."

"Splendid idea!" Langham said, entering the room. "I think we're at a good stopping point." He turned to the two men who had been helping him. "That will be all for today."

"Mr. Jensen likely needs your services," Henry told the footmen.

"Yes, your lordship," they said and left the cottage.

"We are *nearly* to a stopping point," Cara corrected Langham. She went over to a stack of easels folded up on the floor in a corner. "Amelia, where shall we set up your easel? Do you like this spot by the south window?"

"*My* easel?" Amelia responded.

"Yes, we brought it from London. It will be your very own."

Amelia looked so excited that one would think she had never received a gift in her life.

Jacob must have thought so, too. Speaking with a smile, he murmured to Henry, "I don't think my gift of sweets can compare to that."

They began to set up the easel, Cara showing the child how to adjust the horizontal bar for height, and the way to set the back legs so the canvas would be at the desired angle for painting. "This will be yours," Cara reiterated. "You can even paint your name on it, if you like. Or add any other decorations you choose."

If Henry had known this was all it took to make Amelia so happy, he would have done it long ago. But was it the act of painting itself, or the fact that she was part of some important activity with these two people? Maybe she was lonely for companionship. There had always been people around her, but they were adults in supervisory roles. The grown-ups did not exist to keep Amelia entertained, but allowing her to join in their activities might be beneficial.

It was one reason he found himself readily agreeing when Amelia said, "May we all take tea together?"

Cara couldn't deny a certain fascination with Jacob Reese. He was Henry's best friend, and even more interestingly, the brother of the woman Henry had been in love with. If Amelia really was Henry's daughter by Olivia, that made Jacob her uncle. If so, was Jacob aware of this? Was that why he was so kind to Amelia? He truly went out of his way to include her in the conversation during tea.

For her part, Amelia had been fairly well-behaved while having tea with the grown-ups. Perhaps Jacob's presence helped, because he appeared happy to listen to her chatter about a variety of subjects, including their recent visit to the Crystal Palace.

Langham excused himself before the rest of them had finished eating, saying he wanted to return to the studio and do some painting while there was still good light. "I'll see you at dinner," he had said, making it clear he wished to spend the time at the cottage alone.

Cara couldn't blame him. They'd been so busy preparing the studio that they hadn't actually done any work. Langham would be anxious to get to it. He also looked as though he was wearying of Amelia's company. Her manner had become progressively sillier, egged on perhaps by Mr. Reese, who encouraged her to talk about the dinosaurs and other things that interested her.

But Cara recognized this last burst of energy that signaled a child was fighting off tiredness. Not long after Langham was gone, Amelia's vitality began to flag, and she kept interrupting herself with yawns. They had worked hard at the dower cottage, and there had been no opportunity for her to rest. "I think it's time we went upstairs," Cara said.

"But I haven't finished telling Mr. Reese about the stalactosauruses!" she protested, even as she tried to suppress another yawn.

"I believe you've told him quite enough," Henry returned. "And in any case, Mr. Reese and I have work to do before dinner."

It didn't take much more cajoling to get Amelia to acquiesce. Especially as Cara was going upstairs with her.

"You are coming down for dinner, aren't you?" Jacob asked before she and Amelia left. "I feel I've barely gotten to know you—what with all the conversation being on other things." He sent a smile and a wink to Amelia as he said this.

"Yes, of course." Cara was pleased to see Mr. Reese so amenable to chatting with her. There was so much she wanted to know. Aside from her natural curiosity about the man himself, she felt he was the key to understanding Henry.

Tonight's dinner was going well, Henry thought. Perhaps he felt less pressure, as there were four people at the table tonight. Even Langham had shown up, claiming he was "positively famished" after so much hard work at the studio that afternoon.

Henry had barely managed to conceal an eye roll at his brother's comment. He didn't see how it could compare to the work he and Jacob had been doing. Henry was expending every effort to repair the estate and keep the family finances afloat. It wasn't easy. Getting cut out of a deal by the Duke of Crandall would make it hard to attract other members of the aristocracy to back his plans. They often bowed to the duke's point of view in such matters. It didn't exactly make Henry a pariah, but it certainly didn't help.

Fortunately, Jacob's business insight, his contacts with wealthy men not of the aristocracy, and above all his solid faith that God would help them, all left Henry feeling better about his prospects than he had this morning.

At one point this afternoon, they had also spent a few minutes discussing Cara. Henry had told Jacob what he knew of her background. Knowing Cara was likely to ask Jacob a lot of questions about him and his family, Henry had requested that his friend be circumspect if the subject of Olivia should arise.

"She was my sister, so of course I will answer questions about her if asked," Jacob had pointed out. "However, I will keep confidential the more personal bent of your feelings for her."

Happily, so far this evening it had not been an issue. Jacob had chatted with Cara in that friendly and diffident way he had that put people at ease and got them freely talking about themselves. At one point, he professed himself intrigued by her background and the unusual career choices her sisters had made.

"Cara has had a few interesting adventures herself," Langham said. "Cara, tell him about the time you hid from the police in a big washing kettle."

The footman was at that moment setting a dish on the sideboard, and it landed with a bit of a clatter. The servants were trained not to listen—or at least, to *act* as though they were not listening—but they were not always successful.

Cara looked embarrassed. "Perhaps I shouldn't have told you that story. I wouldn't want anyone to get the wrong impression of me."

"Nonsense, they're dying to hear it," Langham insisted.

"I certainly am," Jacob said with an easy smile.

He wasn't the only one. A glance at his footman showed Henry that the man was "not listening" very carefully.

Cara looked around the table, and Henry held his breath in anticipation. He couldn't imagine what this story was about, but there was no doubt his curiosity was piqued.

When at last she overcame her qualms and spoke, her words spilled out in a rush. "I visited London last spring. It was my first visit to the city, and I spent the day walking around with my sister Julia. But then we had to go to Bethnal Green, because she needed to help a woman deliver a baby. We ended up staying late, and it was very dark, and we walked past a gin shop just when some trouble was happening. One of the ladies who was with us ran in to help her friend, and then the police arrived." She paused. Her forehead crinkled a little. "The bobbies were after the bad people, not us," she added.

"Thank you for the clarification," Jacob said, still smiling.

The narrative was so unexpected and told so breathlessly that Henry had trouble taking it all in. "And then what happened?"

"There was a terrible brawl, and people were running everywhere, but I was able to slip away. I saw the kettle—a great big one for washing sheets and things—and I hid in there until everyone was gone. It was a good thing I did, because they took my sister Julia to jail. If I hadn't escaped and gone to find the barrister Michael Stephenson, she might never have gotten out! That is one thing she will always have to thank me for, because now she and Mr. Stephenson are married."

Henry stared at her. He was pretty sure there were some big gaps in that story. "They took your sister to jail?"

"That was just a misunderstanding. She did nothing wrong. As I mentioned before, she is going to be a doctor."

"Yes, that explains everything," Langham quipped. He clearly enjoyed this tale immensely. No wonder he'd prompted Cara to share it.

Jacob looked both charmed and impressed. "It must have been difficult to keep up your courage in such a situation. How did you manage it?"

"I was scared at first," Cara admitted. "Especially when I got out of the kettle and was all alone, not knowing what to do next. But then I reminded myself that God would help me, so I prayed. We were taught in the orphanage that God would supply our every need if we pray to Him and keep believing until the answer comes."

"That's true," Jacob replied. "Did you say you were taught this in the orphanage?"

Henry could understand Jacob's surprise. Last year, when he'd been collecting information for a Parliamentary report on the conditions of the working class, Henry had visited several London workhouses. He'd seen the treatment of the destitute people there, including young orphans. They were repeatedly admonished by their overseers to be thankful for the meager rations and grim housing that barely sustained them. But thinking back to the night he'd overheard Cara describing her childhood to Amelia, Henry knew she'd been raised in a very different kind of place.

"The orphanage was founded by Mr. George Müller," Cara explained. "He never seeks out donors or gifts; he only prays his needs to God. It has worked all this time, and of course he teaches us to do this as well."

She told them a few stories about times when food or other supplies had been sent to the orphanage, arriving just as they were needed. Henry reflected that if a person truly believed God was doing those things, it would enable them to live with a great degree of fearlessness. This was a quality he had definitely seen in Cara.

It was clear Jacob was impressed as well. That would be no surprise, given her stated faith in God and her pluckiness. Things his friend would admire in anyone.

"I can tell you'll go far, Miss Bernay," Jacob said. "You mentioned earlier having been in service in Devonshire. What made you decide to leave that position and move to London? One would think, given your first introduction to it, that you might not be so keen on returning."

Cara had been too open, perhaps, about her past. It had been so easy to talk with Mr. Reese. To suddenly withdraw from answering his question would make her look guilty about something—which, of course, she was.

"It seemed like the right time." Her cheeks warmed at edging so close to a lie.

"Cara wants to be an artist," Langham chimed in. "What better place than London? I hope you'll come 'round to the studio tomorrow and see some of her work."

"That may not be possible," Henry said. "We're driving to Roxwell Abbey tomorrow, and we'll need to start right after breakfast."

Langham looked perplexed. "Roxwell Abbey?"

"We're going to see Lord Nigel Hayward," Jacob clarified.

Cara was just taking a sip from her glass. Upon hearing Lord Nigel's name, she gasped so sharply that she inhaled some of the water. She hastily set down the glass and covered her mouth with her napkin to stifle a cough and clear her throat. Having startled the others, she gestured to assure them she was fine.

"I'd heard the marquess gave Hayward that property after his decrepit uncle died," Langham said. "Are you making a social call to welcome him to the area? Or is this something to do with the mining scheme?"

"Both, I hope," Henry replied.

"It certainly will make our country dances more lively to have Hayward at Roxwell Abbey. And Hayward's bride, too, of course, once they are married. I saw their announcement in *The Times* last week, but her name has slipped my mind. She's the daughter of a baronet, I believe."

Cara was fortunate that Langham had everyone's attention, because she needed time to compose herself. They were speaking of Lord Nigel Hayward! The man who was courting—

"Miss Sarah Needenham is her name," Henry supplied.

The Needenhams had successfully gotten their daughter engaged to the man after all. Cara didn't know whether to be happy for her, or mortified that they might be so close. She said tentatively, "How far away is Roxwell Abbey?"

"About ten miles."

"Why don't we all go?" Langham suggested. "Make a party out of it. Amelia would love the drive, and Cara might like to see some of the surrounding countryside."

No! Cara wanted to scream, but she could say nothing. She sat mute, desperately hoping that her terror at this idea didn't show on her face. She didn't think Lord Nigel would remember her. He'd never even had occasion to speak to her, for she was only the nursery maid for Miss Sarah's young brother. But what if Sarah and her parents were there?

"That's not possible," Henry answered. "As I said, Jacob and I may get into business matters with him. Besides, Mr. Perrine comes tomorrow. You'll need to be here."

Cara felt a rush of relief.

"Make sure you invite him to visit us," Langham said.

Henry nodded. "I'll do that."

Somehow Cara made it through the rest of the evening, but she had to use all her wits just to remain coherent. She kept turning this startling new information over in her mind and thinking through the possible ramifications. Was this God's way of telling her to be honest about her past and why she'd come to London? Perhaps she should tell Henry everything. But would he then worry that she might accidentally put Amelia in danger? Worst of all, his opinion of her would surely plummet. She could tell he thought well of her, and she didn't want to lose that.

On the other hand, she was only going to be here a few weeks. Lord Nigel might not pay a call during that time. Perhaps it was better just to leave things as they were. The chance that her name would come up tomorrow, or that Lord Nigel would connect it with the Needenhams' nursery maid even if it did, was surely negligible.

Wasn't it?

Tomorrow might be a very long day.

23

H ENRY AND JACOB sat in the library of Roxwell Abbey, waiting for Hayward to finish reading the prospectus. This was apparently the room where Hayward's great-uncle had spent most of his time during his declining years. It had a comfortable and well-worn aspect, and the books looked as though they had actually been read. A refreshing breeze came through the open French doors.

Hayward had received them cordially. They'd spent an hour or so catching up, for their paths had not often crossed in the years since they were at Oxford. He was as genial and easygoing as Henry remembered.

After luncheon, Henry had finally been able to turn the talk to business. Hayward was receptive to the topic and agreed to read the prospectus. He was taking his time with it, which Henry regarded as a positive sign.

At last, Hayward set the documents on a nearby table and stood up. "This is very interesting. How about we go for a walk while we discuss it?"

They went out the French doors to a small terrace and down to the gardens. "Please excuse the state of the place," Hayward told them.

"It's in desperate need of sprucing up. My great-uncle didn't concern himself with landscaping toward the last."

As they strolled through the gardens, Hayward described some of the projects he planned to initiate, both on the grounds and in the house. He seemed in no hurry to speak his thoughts on the proposal. Henry perceived that Hayward was in the polite and roundabout process of declining. Henry looked at Jacob. His friend met his gaze with a conciliatory half-smile that showed he was thinking the same thing.

Leaving the gardens, they walked along a field bordering the stables. Four horses and a pony grazed in the afternoon sun. "I plan to enlarge the stables so I can do some breeding," Hayward said. "It's a passion of mine. I've just bought a horse I want to run in the Derby next year. At present he's at my father's stable, which has a proper exercise track."

As he spoke, the horses wandered over to them, either looking for treats or just out of curiosity. The pony, a chestnut with splashes of white on its muzzle and forelegs, gave Jacob a nudge with her nose.

"I don't suppose this one is for racing," Jacob said with a smile.

Hayward grinned. "That's Maisie. I believe my cousin's daughter rode her whenever they came to visit my great-uncle. He rather doted on that girl. She's outgrown the pony now, though."

Henry reached out to pat one of the horses but was too on edge to fully participate in the casual conversation. He kept waiting for the ax to fall. He decided it was better just to get it over with. "So, about that prospectus . . ."

"Yes, forgive my rambling." Hayward answered as though he were at fault, even though Henry had rudely changed the subject. "It's clear your mining venture has solid potential. I've no doubt it will be a great success when you find the right investors."

"I understand," Henry said. He was disappointed but not really surprised.

"Much of my funds, such as they are, will be needed to fix up the house and grounds. As you can see, I have some work to do to make this a pleasant place to bring my bride next spring. What money that is left over is tied up in an export company in Liverpool."

"I don't suppose his lordship might be interested?" Jacob ventured, referring to Hayward's father, the Marquess of Dartford.

Hayward looked away for a moment, studying the landscape. "I don't wish to be untactful, but my father is a close friend of the Duke of Crandall, and . . ."

"You don't need to say anything more," Henry interjected. There was probably some truth to the reasons Hayward was giving for declining, but even if there weren't, Henry couldn't fault him for not wanting to place himself in a position that might antagonize his father.

"I hope this won't cast a pall on our relationship," Hayward added. "Being neighbors, I'd like us to be on friendly terms."

He proffered a handshake, which Henry accepted. "Certainly. I hope you will pay us a visit soon."

"I should like that. My fiancée and her family are coming here in a few weeks. In the meantime, I'll be working hard to get the place presentable." He added with a smile, "I don't want Sir John to backtrack on his permission to marry her!"

The subject of business being effectively closed, they walked back toward the house.

After a few steps, Hayward paused. "I've just thought of something. You were telling me about your little ward, Amelia. Would she be interested in Maisie?"

Mr. Perrine arrived promptly at ten o'clock. Although he was nearing seventy years old, he still had a spry step. He came in a small one-horse carriage, which he even drove himself.

Henry and Jacob left soon after breakfast, but Cara had started worrying long before that. She'd spent the night and early morning vacillating between revealing everything to Henry and keeping things just as they were.

She had hoped to speak with Langham, curious what Henry and Jacob were trying to accomplish during their visit to Lord Nigel's home, but Langham had sent word that he'd been up late and would join them at luncheon. This left Cara alone with her questions and concerns. They never completely left her mind, even during the lesson. It was fortunate that the drawing master's attention was primarily centered on Amelia.

Once the lesson got underway, it was apparent that Mr. Perrine had a wellspring of patience and experience when it came to working with strong-minded children. Amelia naturally wanted to rush headlong into painting with a full palette, as the studio was filled with tempting supplies. Mr. Perrine had to carefully explain why she must first master drawing with a pencil in order to understand the basics of proportion and perspective. After an hour and a half of rigorous instruction, he ended the lesson by encouraging her to draw whatever she wanted. Her choice had been no surprise, and Cara thought there was already marked improvement in the way Amelia drew the figures.

Mr. Perrine clearly enjoyed working with children. "That's what keeps me young," he quipped as they enjoyed a cold luncheon under the trees after the lesson. "I take great satisfaction in helping them develop their raw talent. And, of course, you never know what they'll come up with." He chuckled. "Dinosaurs, for example."

When Langham arrived, he greeted Mr. Perrine jovially, like an old friend. He also complimented Amelia's drawing, which she had brought to luncheon.

"I am drawing in pencil for now, until I master proportion and perspective," Amelia told him, echoing Mr. Perrine word for word. She turned to the drawing master. "When do we begin painting with colors?"

"As soon as you are ready—and the more you apply yourself, the faster you will reach that point," Mr. Perrine promised. "Perhaps one day you will rival your cousin Langham. But you will have to work very hard." He turned to Cara. "Langham was one of my best students. I always knew he had the potential to be a great artist. I tried to persuade his parents to send him to the Royal Academy."

"Unfortunately, my father was having none of that," Langham put in sourly. "All of the Burkes have gone to Eton and Oxford, and I was to be no different."

"You've made superior progress, even so," Mr. Perrine said. "I saw a few of your paintings in the studio, and they exceeded my high expectations. I wonder if you and I might review them together for a few minutes before I leave."

"Shall I run and call for your carriage, sir?" Amelia said, always glad for a reason to go to the stables.

"Are you that excited to see me leave?" he replied with a chuckle. But it was clear he took no offense.

"We'll go together," Cara told her.

Mr. Perrine and Langham crossed the lawn to the dower house, deeply immersed in conversation. The drawing master might enjoy working with beginners, but he clearly loved discussing advanced techniques with skilled painters. Spending time with someone who was knowledgeable and passionate about art would surely be a balm to Langham's soul, as he seemed to be facing so many objections from his family. Cara could not understand why they had been so adamantly against art studies for him.

Amelia tugged at her hand. "Let's go!"

Before setting off, Cara spoke to the two maids and the footman who were clearing away the luncheon dishes. "Thank you so much. The meal was delicious, and this setting under the trees was perfect."

They paused, surprised to be addressed like this. Cara didn't know if she was breaking protocol to do so. She only knew that she'd been in their position once, invisible to the people they worked for and expected to do their jobs seamlessly. They had succeeded, for neither Langham, Amelia, nor Mr. Perrine seemed to give a second thought to the fact that they were being waited on so fastidiously. Cara wanted the servants to know that she, at least, had noticed.

They looked at one another, perhaps unsure how to react.

"You're very welcome, miss," one of the maids said.

"That's kind of you, miss," the footman added.

Cara read pride in their faces at having their good work acknowledged. She made up her mind that she would do her best never to take such service for granted now that she was on the receiving end of it.

She and Amelia went to the stable, where the groom, Mr. Hart, hitched Mr. Perrine's horse to his carriage. They all rode it together the short distance to the dower house, which Amelia found to be great fun.

As Mr. Perrine and Langham emerged from the studio, Cara could see that their time together had been good for Langham, as she'd anticipated.

It wasn't until Mr. Perrine had driven away and Amelia had gone to inspect some butterfly bushes in the little garden beside the dower house that Cara was able to speak with Langham alone. "Why was your father so set against your going to the academy?"

"He said I needed proper discipline and I wouldn't get it at an art school."

"Were you that much in need of discipline?"

Langham's lips quirked. "I am *always* in need of discipline. Haven't you caught on to that by now?"

It was hard to be amused at this because she heard the pain beneath his words.

"I was sixteen and would have been among the youngest pupils at the academy. But my father said no, off to Eton you go." He heaved a sigh. "He told me I had to pull my weight, find a 'real' profession. Just as Henry tells me now."

These were not problems Cara had ever associated with the aristocracy. She'd thought they had nothing to do but enjoy their leisure pursuits. But in the short time she'd known him, she had yet to get the impression that Henry had any leisure time at all. "What is the business venture mentioned at dinner last night? Something about a mine?"

Langham scrunched his nose. "The family is in need of money, so Henry has decided to sully his hands with business and trade."

"How can he be in need of money? He's an earl!"

Langham laughed at her naïveté. "Blue blood is often in need of gold coin."

"But all this—!" Cara indicated the beautiful landscape all around them.

"It costs money to run and maintain. Farm rents no longer cover it all. Henry was locked out of a lucrative investment opportunity by a powerful duke who doesn't like him. We have a copper mine in Cornwall that could bring in a lot of money. However, it takes a great deal of capital to get the operation going. Henry needs investors. He's hoping he can get Hayward to be one."

"It's critically important, I suppose?"

"I expect the future of our family depends upon it." The words were heavy, but Langham spoke nonchalantly, as though he had a sense of fatalism about the family falling to ruin.

"What if Lord Nigel turns down the offer?" Or worse, she added to herself, what if that should happen, and it should somehow be her fault? She supposed it was an unreasonable fear, but then, fears were rarely reasonable.

"He'll get it straightened out somehow." Langham fanned himself with his straw hat. "Let's get back inside. There's money in painting, even if Henry refuses to believe it."

Langham was soon lost in his work. Cara was starting to recognize when his focus was exactly where it needed to be. He seemed unaware of anyone around him.

With Amelia happily engaged outside, Cara decided to spend time on the portrait she'd begun of the child. It was a first pass in watercolors, based on some of the drawings she'd made over the past weeks. Perhaps one day she'd attempt a proper portrait in oils. Whether she could match the skill on display in the other paintings at Morestowe Manor remained to be seen.

In the end, she found it impossible to concentrate. Her mind kept returning to Henry, trying to envision what might be happening. They would be traveling home by now, for it was nearing teatime. Would he return in jubilation at having secured the financial deal he needed so badly? Or was he coming in anger, having learned a criminally negligent woman was spending time with his ward? She would not rest easy until she knew that nothing terrible had come from today.

Setting aside her work, she went looking for Amelia. She found her lying on her back on one of the garden's marble benches. At first, Cara thought she was dozing, but then she saw the girl had a rose in her hand that she must have picked from one of the nearby bushes. She was staring up at the clouds, twirling the flower in her fingers and singing. It sounded like a lullaby, but it wasn't one Cara had heard before.

Happy rosebud, happy May; baby sleeps till break of day.
When the dew falls on the nest, robin sleeps on Mama's
    breast.
Never worry, never frown; Papa soon returns to town.

"That's very pretty," Cara said, approaching the girl. "Where did you learn it?"

Amelia sat up, looking startled. "It's just something I remember from before. From when I was little." She rose from the bench. "Is it teatime? I'm hungry. Can we eat under the trees again?"

As they returned to the house, Cara thought over Amelia's words. It was tempting to smile at the idea of a seven-year-old saying *when I was little*, but perhaps there was something to it. Henry had said Amelia came to live with him at age four. Did she retain some memories of her life before that time? If so, how clear were they? Cara had been six years old when her mother died. Her memories were imperfect and yet powerful, especially the sensation of being wrapped in her mother's arms.

Had Amelia's mother sung that song to her? The child had obviously heard it enough times to retain it over the years.

Cara hesitated to ask any further questions. Remembering Amelia's violent reaction when Cara had said the word *orphans*, she thought it best not to ask about her mother, but only to accept whatever the child might offer.

Cara was able to arrange tea under the trees. Langham did not emerge from the dower house, so they began to eat without him. Cara knew he would come in his own time.

Amelia seemed content to linger at the table after tea, and Cara, too, felt no desire to leave. There was still no sign of Langham. Nor of Henry and Jacob, for that matter. It occurred to Cara that perhaps she and Amelia were waiting here in anticipation of Henry's arrival. This spot afforded a good vantage point for seeing carriages as they came up the long drive from the main road.

Before long, they saw the carriage in the distance. Amelia sprang up and began running toward them before Cara had even risen from her chair. The reason for the child's excitement was plain to see: trotting behind the carriage on a lead rope was a brown-and-white pony.

Cara hurried in Amelia's wake, desperate to get a good look at Henry's face and glean what state he was in.

He pulled the carriage to a stop, grinning at the sight of Amelia running toward him and shrieking with glee. As his gaze moved from the girl to Cara, his smile seemed to change, but not to fade. She had the impression he was happy to see her. The burden she'd been carrying all day slipped from her shoulders.

CHAPTER
24

"I T'S A PONY!" Amelia, still breathless from running, had stopped
a few feet away from the creature, every fiber of her being vibrating
with joy. "Such a pretty pony!"

Henry had been hesitant at first to accept the offer, even though
Hayward named a reasonable price for the pony and all its tack, including the custom-made sidesaddle. Plus, Henry could keep the pony
for a month before making a final decision. Even though acquired so
inexpensively, the pony would still cost money to maintain. But seeing the way Amelia had raced toward them, and her expression now
as she understood the horse was for her, made him glad a thousand
times over that he'd done it. He'd just have to add Maisie's expenses
to his growing list.

The ten-mile ride from Roxwell Abbey had given Henry plenty of
time to brood over the setback and discuss the matter with Jacob. His
friend had encouraged him to press forward, insisting there were others who would be able and willing to back this project. On some level,
Henry knew this was true; however, it was harder for him to match
Jacob's confidence that the answer would come at exactly the right time.

If watching the child sprint over the wide green lawn had been pleasing, so was the sight of Cara as she followed. She was not wearing a hat, and the summer breeze played with loose wisps of her hair. Although moving rapidly, she still looked graceful. She paused about twenty yards off. Meeting his gaze, she beamed in answer to his own smile and then waved before closing the gap between them. That simple gesture vibrated a tiny chord deep in his soul.

Had he stared too long at her? He turned to see Jacob looking at him with amusement. "Yes?" Henry prompted, more an accusation than a question.

"You're smiling."

"Of course I'm smiling. I've just made a little girl very happy."

"That must be it." But Jacob's lopsided grin implied he'd had something else in mind.

Henry covered his discomfort by busily securing the reins and jumping down to join Cara and Amelia. "This is Maisie," he told them.

Amelia turned to look at him. "Is she . . . ours?"

Her eyes shone with joy, giving Henry a pleasant sensation of satisfaction and happiness all rolled up together. "We have Maisie on trial from Lord Nigel, but yes, if she works out, we can keep her."

It was clear from Amelia's broad smile that she interpreted this as a yes. She didn't foresee any issues with Maisie "working out." She tentatively reached out to pat the pony's neck. It nudged her in return, and Amelia giggled as Maisie's movement pushed her slightly off balance.

"She is very pretty," Cara said. "Look at the charming white streak on her nose."

"Shall I drive the carriage to the stable while the rest of you continue with Maisie?" Jacob offered. He was still sitting in the box seat, smiling down at them.

"Thank you, that's an excellent idea," Henry answered, more than willing to stretch his legs after the long drive.

He loosed the pony's lead rope from the carriage, and they waited until Jacob was far enough ahead for the dust to settle behind him before they began walking toward the stable.

Cara looked over the child's head at Henry. "It seems your trip to Roxwell Abbey was successful."

"Yes, it was good to see Lord Nigel again. And it was fortuitous that he had this pony that his cousin's daughter had outgrown."

Henry left it at that. The most important thing he'd hoped to accomplish today had *not* happened, and that was perhaps what Cara was subtly asking about. But Henry didn't want to discuss the family's financial matters. Certainly not in front of the child. "Amelia, Lord Nigel tells me Maisie can be much too clever at times. But he insists she's not naughty, just cheeky. What do you think of that?"

Amelia's eyebrows drew together as she thought over this description of the pony's character. Apparently deciding she would be the winner in whatever tussles lay ahead, she said confidently, "Maisie will be nice for me."

"That's the spirit," Cara said, laughing.

By the time they reached the stable yard, the assistant groom was unhitching the horse from Henry's carriage. The saddle, bridle, and other items for Maisie that Hayward had included in the deal had been unloaded onto a bench, and Mr. Hart was inspecting them.

"This is a right fine saddle, your lordship," Mr. Hart told him. "Excellent workmanship." He walked over to Maisie. "This is the little lady it's intended for, eh?"

Hart gave the pony a thorough inspection, looking in its mouth and running practiced hands over its back and legs. "She looks healthy, sir." He had to work to get the horse to lift its hooves, but eventually he got a good look at all of them and pronounced the horseshoes to be in fine shape, too. As he set down the last hoof, Maisie gave a snort and sidestepped impatiently.

"She's a plucky one," Hart said with a grin. He winked at Amelia, who had watched the entire process with fascination. "But then, so are you, Miss Amelia!"

Amelia grinned, considering this a compliment. She was generally more manageable in the country than in London, but lately Henry thought he saw a different aspect of her demeanor. He thought Cara was the catalyst. Then again, it could be nothing more than evidence that Amelia was enjoying a summer with the freedom to do the things she loved without too many restraints.

Although he could never say this aloud, he was sure a big part of Amelia's satisfaction was the continued absence of his mother. When she returned, things could revert to the way they'd been before. It might even be worse, because although she'd resisted starting Amelia on riding lessons, once they began, she would want to be involved. The countess was a highly skilled horsewoman and deplored ladies who did not learn to ride properly. Her standards were high, and she would impose them on Amelia from the start.

"When can I ride her?" Amelia asked, startling Henry by asking the very question he was considering.

"Tomorrow."

"Hooray!" Amelia bounced so much from excitement that her feet nearly left the ground.

"Doesn't she need a teacher? And riding clothes?" Cara interjected.

"Mr. Hart will make a fine teacher. He has a lot of experience." In fact, when Henry had hired him two years ago, a big factor had been Hart's fifteen years of experience working for a large family in Colchester. Hart had overseen the riding lessons for their four daughters. His training method was one of the best Henry had heard of. It was bound to get Amelia confidently riding before the countess returned to Morestowe. That prospect made Henry eager to get started.

"I recommend the young ladies wear their gymnastic costumes for the first several lessons," Mr. Hart said. "That will help us ensure the positioning of the legs is right and that she is seated properly in the saddle."

"Do you have such clothes?" Cara asked Amelia.

The girl nodded. "Miss Gunther used to make me do *cal-is-then-ics* on the lawn." She spoke the long word carefully, although her face scrunched in distaste at the memory.

"This will be more fun, won't it?" Henry said, not wanting her to dwell on memories of her rigid former governess.

Amelia reached up to pat Maisie's neck again. This time the pony didn't seem to notice. It swung its head toward the stable and whinnied.

Mr. Hart chuckled. "They always know when the others are getting fed. She wants her share of the rations, too."

"Excellent idea," Henry said. "In fact, I'm heartily looking forward to my own dinner. We missed tea."

"May I come to dinner with you?" Amelia asked, even though she knew full well she was supposed to eat in the nursery.

"You are not quite ready for that," Henry said firmly. "Besides, you should get to bed early so you will be rested for riding lessons in the morning."

"But I haven't had a chance to talk to Mr. Reese yet!" Amelia countered. Apparently, the fact that she'd talked his ear off at tea yesterday didn't count.

"I'll be around tomorrow," Jacob said. "In the meantime, you shall have my undivided attention right now as we walk back to the house. Why don't you tell me about your art lesson?"

Taking hold of her hand, he began to walk briskly, leaving Henry and Cara to follow. Amelia skipped to keep up with him and launched into a description of Mr. Perrine and what he had taught her.

"I'd forgotten all about the art lesson," Henry admitted. "How did it go?"

Cara gave him a brief account of the day. He was glad to hear things had gone well.

"Roxwell Abbey is nice, I suppose?" She changed to this new subject without preamble.

"It's a pleasant enough place. Its upkeep was neglected by the former owner, but Lord Nigel has many plans for it."

"Did he happen to say anything about his fiancée?"

"Only that Miss Needenham is the most charming, beautiful, and gracious lady ever to walk the earth."

Cara laughed. "Theirs will be a happy marriage, I think."

"No doubt."

"She wasn't there, I suppose? I mean, visiting with her family?"

Henry wondered why Cara should take a particular interest in the woman. He supposed that, like most ladies, she enjoyed reading the society columns and following the lives of the well-to-do. "I believe Lord Nigel said she's been staying with her aunt this season, and they are presently at another house party."

"And you told him all about Amelia, I suppose?"

This was beginning to feel like an inquisition, even though Cara maintained a tone of friendly interest. He glanced at her before answering. "He already knew I had a young ward. I did little except add that she is a strong-minded young lady. We both agreed she and Maisie were likely to understand one another very well."

Cara smiled at this. She did not ask any more questions, though he still had the feeling something was on her mind. Perhaps she was trying to ascertain whether they had talked about her. The truth was, Henry had been careful not to mention her. He didn't want to say so outright because the explanation would have embarrassed them both. Hayward was aware of the rumors surrounding Amelia's parentage. He had not been rude or snide about it, but Henry could tell Hayward believed he was her father. Because of this, Henry felt mentioning the single, unchaperoned young lady staying in his home wouldn't do his reputation any favors.

Much later, after Amelia had been put to bed and the rest of them had reconvened for dinner, Henry wished he'd been able to tell Hayward about her after all. Cara had a certain charm in her own right. Tonight she wore a very becoming pale pink gown, and her hair had once again been prettily styled by the maid. She had quickly learned how to navigate the intricacies of the dinner service; although this was only her third night at the house, Henry thought her manners were as good as anyone's. Despite her humble beginnings, she seemed to fit in naturally to these surroundings. There was much laughter as she and the others discussed the events of the day and anticipated tomorrow.

He began to feel almost guilty, as though he had done her a disservice by concealing her existence from Hayward. Certainly Jacob had not been in favor of it. That had been clear from his expression as they had discussed the issue on their way to Roxwell Abbey. But, perhaps because he understood the constraints of Henry's social position, he had raised no objections.

"There is one thing I forgot to mention about today," Cara said. "This afternoon when I went to join Amelia in the garden, I found her singing a lullaby. Are you familiar with it?"

Henry shook his head. "I have heard her humming from time to time and sometimes singing under her breath, but I've never been able to catch the words."

"She told me it was something that she remembered 'from before.' Might that mean from before she came to live with you?"

"That seems unlikely. She was so young." Henry spoke with conviction, but he knew this statement was wishful thinking. He hoped Amelia didn't remember too much about her former life. Was that wrong of him, to want to deny a child her memories? Over and over, Henry kept trying to do the right thing and found himself in a moral morass anyway.

"Perhaps you can wheedle the information out of her," Langham said to Cara. "She seems much happier to talk to you than to any of us."

"Just let it be," Henry replied fiercely. "Do *not* question the child further."

He saw the others start in surprise at the force of his words. Or perhaps they were reacting to the clatter of his fork hitting the plate too sharply.

There was a long, uncomfortable pause. Cara dropped her eyes, looking embarrassed. She set her own fork down with extra care, perhaps unconsciously trying to counteract Henry's actions. Jacob sent Henry a frown that was questioning and disapproving at the same time. Langham raised his wineglass to signal a refill from the footman.

Henry regretted that he'd spoken so roughly. He did not regret his demand, however. Although Amelia could be difficult at times, she had an independence and reserve that functioned like an emotional shield. As far as Henry knew, she had not shared her innermost thoughts with anyone. He had seen that as a good thing. The last thing he needed was for Amelia to say something that might point to Langham being her father. Whenever such information was revealed, Henry wanted to be in charge of the time and place.

It was Jacob who finally broke the silence. "I'm looking forward to watching the riding lesson tomorrow. My son will be learning to ride soon. Perhaps I can glean some techniques for teaching him—even though, of course, he will not be riding sidesaddle." He said this with a smile, trying to lighten the mood. "Do you ride, Miss Bernay?"

"Oh no, I would be afraid to."

"Perhaps you will feel differently after tomorrow," Henry said. He spoke kindly, hoping to make up for any hurt feelings he might have caused.

Her response was a tremulous smile, and that only made Henry more uncomfortable. Had he just tacitly offered her riding lessons? He hadn't intended to. There were too many impracticalities to the idea. Despite that, as well as her statement about being fearful of riding, Henry had no trouble envisioning her in a smart riding habit, perched confidently on a fine horse. He shook his head, trying to clear the image. He reminded himself she was leaving in a few weeks, and things were not likely to progress so far as her acquiring appropriate riding attire, let alone mastering the art of riding.

Even so, the vision kept returning to him long after they had all said good night and gone their separate ways to bed. Alone once again with his thoughts, Henry sat at his bedroom window for a long time, looking out at the moonlit landscape and wondering if his heart would ever feel truly settled.

"You see how easy it is, miss! Mind you keep your torso facing forward and your hands low. . . . That's right!"

Mr. Hart called out these commands and encouragements as Amelia rode the pony around a circular fenced-in area near the stable. It was perhaps more accurate to say the child was being carried, because she did not hold the reins. Those were knotted loosely at the pony's neck. Amelia's hands gripped only a short whip lying across her lap.

In the center of the ring, Mr. Hart held a long rope attached to Maisie's bridle. He used a whip to gently guide the pony's movements. He walked in a small circle to follow the horse as it traced the perimeter over and over.

Cara stood at the fence along with Henry and Jacob. Henry was dressed in riding clothes so he could help as needed. He had set aside his jacket due to the heat, but Cara thought he looked exceedingly handsome in his white shirt, brown riding trousers, and high leather boots.

Out in the ring, Amelia appeared pleased and comfortable, her body adjusting to the pony's movements as needed. Her gymnastic costume consisted of a navy blue knee-length tunic with red trim over short matching pantaloons and dark stockings. On her feet were ankle boots of flexible leather that she often wore when playing outside. Cara could see why Mr. Hart had recommended this clothing.

Cara also now understood the use of the two curved horns near the front left edge of the saddle that arched out from one another in a *V* shape. Amelia's right leg was draped over the top horn. Her left leg was snugly fitted under the curve of the bottom horn, which Mr. Hart explained was called the leaping horn because it helped a lady keep her seat when jumping the horse. Her left foot was securely fitted into a stirrup.

Mr. Hart had kept the pony at a walk until Amelia showed she could keep her body positioned correctly and maintain her balance. A few minutes ago, he'd set the horse to a trot, and Amelia was still riding with ease. Although breathless from the work and concentrating intently on what she was doing, she also managed bursts of laughter at the thrill of successfully riding.

"How does she keep from falling off?" Cara asked. "She's not holding on to anything!"

"That's the point of the whole exercise," Henry answered. "This is how she'll learn to keep her seat without riding the bridle."

"It's ingenious," Jacob agreed.

After the pony and rider had made a dozen or more loops around the ring, Mr. Hart signaled for Henry to enter. Henry slipped through the gate and joined the groom at the center, deftly taking over the rope and whip.

"This is wonderful!" Cara enthused to Mr. Hart as he came out of the ring.

"Don't go away—we're just getting to the good part," he answered with a wink, and went inside the stable.

Henry began to alternate the pony's pace, setting it to a walk, then a trot, then down to a walk again. In this way, Amelia learned to react to the changes in Maisie's speed and gait. It was clear she relished the challenge. At one point, she called out to Cara, "See how well I am riding!"

Cara loved watching the two of them work together like this. Oh, if Henry was really her father, how could he not say so? Especially now, as he watched her with obvious approval and, Cara thought, affection.

Cara realized this could be a good time to ask Jacob some questions, since they stood alone at the fence. "Henry really is good to her. At times he seems exactly like a doting father."

She watched to see if the word *father* might produce any reaction, but Jacob simply nodded in agreement, accepting Cara's comment at face value. "Henry's a good-hearted man. I keep telling him that he needs to—" He paused, finishing his sentence only with a shrug.

"Langham told me he was in love with your sister, but she died in France." It was beyond impertinent to bring this up, and she immediately felt bad when a shadow crossed his features. "I apologize, I should not have mentioned it."

"I don't mind. It's been nearly eight years, and if you want to understand why Henry is the way he is, you need to know about Olivia. He still mourns her in a way that I do not believe is healthy."

"Why do you think he has such a hard time accepting her death? Do you think it's because she was so far away when she died?"

He shook his head. "I believe he accepts that she is dead, but for some reason he's unable to get past it. I don't know why, because even though we are close, he won't share his reasons with me." He gave a sad shrug. "Who can explain the intricacies of the heart?"

Turning back to watch Henry and Amelia once more, Cara pondered Jacob's words. She felt sure that if Henry was Amelia's father, Jacob didn't know it. And to think that Henry harbored such deep feelings for his lost love! "I suppose Olivia was an extraordinary person." She felt herself getting choked up as she asked, and perhaps a little jealous, too, although it was terrible to feel such a thing.

"Yes, she was special." Jacob gave her a kind smile, as though he were focused more on her distress than his own sorrow.

Mr. Hart reemerged from the stable, followed by the assistant groom, both carrying bales of hay. The men went inside the ring and laid the two bales side by side.

At this point the pony was at a walk. When it reached the bales, it put its head down to sniff them, which unbalanced Amelia. She wobbled and grabbed the upper horn, readjusting herself after Henry prodded the pony to raise its head and keep going. Maisie stepped over the bales and continued moving around the ring.

"Mind your balance, Miss Amelia," Mr. Hart called out. "You want to stay low and back in your seat. Are you ready to jump?"

"*Jump?*" Amelia and Cara repeated at the same time, although in Cara's case it was from alarm.

Henry set the pony once more into a canter, calling out further instructions to Amelia. "Just remember what you learned about holding your position. Sit back in the saddle and keep your hands low. If you feel unsteady, squeeze your upper legs together hard against the horns."

Cara held her breath as the pony completed another loop around the ring and once more approached the hay bales. Mr. Hart and the stable hand stood on either side of the bales, ready to step in should there be a mishap.

The bales, not even two feet high, presented no trouble for the energetic pony. It took them in a smooth, swift jump and resumed its canter. Amelia's torso tipped back and lifted slightly from the saddle. Her hands rose as well, but she worked to bring them down. When the horse landed, she was still firmly in her seat.

"Excellent!" Henry exclaimed. Cara and Jacob applauded enthusiastically.

Amelia let out a whoop of triumph. "Can we do that again?"

Mr. Hart grinned at Henry. "I believe she is a natural, sir." He called out to Amelia, "Watch your hands this time. Sit back, and don't allow the motion to toss you back too far."

They came around again. Once more, Maisie took a short leap over the hay bales. This time, Amelia moved virtually in unison with the pony.

Henry slowed the horse to a walk. Amelia was so happy at her success that she'd begun laughing more than concentrating. "Perhaps that is enough for the day. Don't you think so, Mr. Hart?"

"Yes, sir. I believe that was a good first lesson."

Henry began looping the rope, shortening the distance between him and the pony until he was standing next to it. He handed the rope to Mr. Hart, who held the pony's head while Henry helped Amelia down. Cara thought the girl might protest, but Amelia was still overtaken with the giggles, laughing even after her feet had touched the ground.

"Do you like riding, then?" Henry asked. But he needn't have, because the answer was clearly written on Amelia's face. "Let's take her in," he said. "I believe she's ready for a brush down."

He allowed Amelia to help him walk the pony back to the stable. Mr. Hart and the assistant groom went with them, once more leaving Cara and Jacob alone.

"I can tell you are fond of the girl," Jacob said. "Henry told me you've taken on her care—in an unofficial capacity. That's admirable. Especially when they had a hard time finding someone who would do it for money!"

Cara smiled. "I suppose I empathize with her, given that we both seem to be without parents."

If Jacob noticed the odd phrasing, he didn't show it. "Do you really wish to devote your life to art?"

"Yes, of course! That is, I think so."

His eyebrow rose. "You *think* so?"

"My sisters both have a calling for their lives. They've always known it. At least, I think Julia has always known. Maybe Rosalyn didn't know right away, but when the opportunity to sing professionally was presented to her, she leapt in with both feet. And she is so happy and successful now! So I've wondered a lot about what my calling might be. I think it must be painting. I've always enjoyed drawing, and I love to study fine works of art whenever I can."

Jacob was looking at her with a bemused expression probably caused by her rambling.

She gave him an apologetic smile. "I suppose what it comes down to is that, to be honest, I never thought about painting as a *career* until I met Langham."

"I see."

"That doesn't mean it isn't the right thing for my life," Cara insisted. "As I just said, Rosalyn—"

"Perhaps you have other abilities. Perhaps talents just as good, or even greater, that are yet untapped."

Cara stared at him, taken aback. "It would be nice to think so, I suppose."

"Why not ponder it a bit? It may not come to you right away, but give it some time. Do you wish to get married someday?"

"Oh yes!"

"And to be a mother?"

That question was harder to answer. "There is something . . . that is, I haven't figured out how God feels about that."

He smiled. "I should think it would be obvious."

"Yes, but in my case there are, well, circumstances that might make it questionable."

"I will pray that you find the answer you are looking for."

"Thank you," Cara said, truly grateful. "I can see why you wanted to go into the church. You would have made a splendid minister."

Jacob tilted his head in a modest acknowledgment of her compliment.

She turned back as Henry and Amelia reemerged from the stable, the little girl's hand in his, both of them laughing. If he was not her father, he was as good a substitute as any child could wish for—and not just because he could provide these nice things. Their walking hand in hand signaled that some emotional bonds might be forming as well, something Cara knew from experience that a child craved. Perhaps that was enough for now.

CHAPTER

25

I WISH YOU COULD STAY LONGER, Mr. Reese," Amelia said.
Amelia and Cara had come out to the front drive after luncheon
to say their good-byes as a footman loaded Jacob's luggage into the
carriage. Jacob's wagon and men had been dispatched yesterday for
the long drive back to the foundry. Jacob would take the train back,
a faster and more comfortable ride. Jacob had asked if he and Henry
might drive to the station together, and Henry was happy to oblige.

Jacob looked fondly at the girl. "I would like to stay, too, but I must
return to my family. My little boy will be missing me." He looked at
the packet of cherry sweets in Amelia's hand. It was nearly empty now.
"He'll be looking for his present, too, you know."

Amelia grinned and popped another sweet into her mouth.

Cara's good-bye was more effusive. She took Jacob's hand, shaking it
energetically. "It has been so lovely meeting you. Thank you—especially
for the nice things you said to me yesterday."

He smiled warmly back at her. "I'm glad it was of help to you."

Henry didn't know what they were referring to, but he wasn't surprised they had got on so well, or that his friend had shared something
that helped her. That was Jacob's way.

After Amelia and Cara had showered Jacob with another round of fond wishes, Henry and Jacob got in the carriage. Cara and Amelia waved as they drove away.

"Cara is a lovely woman," Jacob observed once Henry had turned the carriage onto the open road. "It's evident you and Langham enjoy having her here."

"And Amelia, too," Henry pointed out.

Jacob nodded. "Over these past two days, I've seen what a difference she's made in that girl's life. You are lucky she agreed to come."

Henry gave him a look. "I thought you didn't believe in luck."

Jacob grinned in return. "You're right. I don't. But you have to admit that an interesting set of circumstances brought her into your life."

"I know you are a religious man, Jacob, but you cannot attribute everything to divine intervention."

"Perhaps not."

Henry recognized his friend's habit of seeming to agree when he actually felt quite differently. Henry didn't want to press him, though. It could open a conversation he did not want to have.

They rode in silence for a while. They were within a mile of the station when Jacob said, "Henry, there is something I would like to say to you before I leave today."

There was no mistaking the seriousness of his tone. Henry didn't answer. He kept his eyes on the horse, concentrating on his driving, knowing his friend would speak his mind with or without Henry's permission.

"I think it's time you faced one particular truth that you've been avoiding for eight years."

With that kind of introduction—especially the mention of eight years—Henry knew this was about Olivia. He grimaced but said nothing.

"I thought that in time your heart would heal of its own accord and I wouldn't be obliged to point this out to you. But I feel now is the time to do it."

Jacob looked at him with the kind of sympathy one generally reserved for the newly bereaved. Whatever was coming, it was likely to open up fresh torrents of pain. "Are you so determined to hurt your friend?" he countered.

"You will always remember Olivia for her youth and beauty. She will never grow old in your eyes, because you knew her only in the summer of her prime. She will always have an unsurpassed perfection—her grace and poise, her kindness, even being an excellent woman of business."

"You make this sound like an accusation. Would you have me forget all the good things about her?"

"I think you should honestly acknowledge the context in which those things existed."

Henry shook his head. "What am I not acknowledging?"

"I believe Olivia cared for you deeply. But she was also dedicated to the foundry. As our father grew more frail, she took on more and more responsibility. She did it not because she had to, but because she loved the work. She thrived on all of it: sleeves pushed back, hard negotiations with vendors, long evenings poring over the accounting and finding ways to make those numbers add up the way they should. She loved the grit and grime and excitement of it all. She found fulfillment in a job well done. And, although it required so much from her, it also gave her a sense of freedom."

"But those are exactly the reasons I fell in love with her," Henry insisted. "What's the problem?"

"You would have taken her away from all of it. If she married you, she would have had to leave her world for yours. To marry into the aristocracy brings with it an entirely new set of demands that are much different from the sweat and heat of the foundry."

Henry had known this, but he'd always been able to justify it in his mind. "She would have excelled as a countess, too."

"I've no doubt of it. Yet it would have meant losing an important part of who she was. This was the hard conversation she could never bring herself to have with you. She was fearless in so many things, yet this daunted her. The whole situation unsettled her. Falling in love with you shook the foundation she'd laid for her life. It left her with fearful questions. After all, you had not known each other long. What if the love you felt for her turned out to be a passing infatuation? What if she married you and left her other life behind, only for you both to realize it had been a terrible mistake?"

"How could she even consider those things?" Henry said in disbelief.

"Olivia never made any decision lightly. She looked at a question from every possible angle. I believe she accepted that invitation from our aunt because she felt the need for some distance between the two of you. Especially after you never actually declared your love for her outright before you returned home."

"I loved her! I will always regret that I did not declare myself. I told myself she must know how I felt. Ironically, I assumed her decision to go to the continent was proof of that. I thought she was going in order to round out her education, acquire some culture. I thought it meant she knew I was going to ask her to be my wife, and she wanted to be prepared for it."

Jacob said nothing for several moments, and Henry thought perhaps he had persuaded his friend of the error of his thinking.

"I cannot say whether you are right or wrong," Jacob said at last. "Olivia is gone, and the deepest thoughts of her heart are gone with her. But I feel led to remind you that all of that is in the past. It is unchangeable. You must put it behind you and look to the future."

Henry had been wrestling with this problem for years. He shook his head, his eyes stinging with tears. "I cannot figure out how to do that, Jacob."

"Maybe you can." Jacob's voice was calm, confident, consoling. "Maybe that road is before you, if you will only open your eyes. Maybe it's right in front of you."

"You are speaking in riddles."

They pulled into the station yard, and Henry brought the carriage to a halt. In his agitation, he reined in the horse too hard. He tied the reins and jumped down, giving the horse a pat in silent apology.

After pulling his luggage from the back of the carriage, Jacob came to stand face-to-face with Henry. He extended his right hand, grasping Henry's hand hard when he reached out to shake it.

"You must think about what you really want, Henry. And what you honestly need. Let us be clear: I'm not saying there was anything good about Olivia's death. I'm only saying that perhaps God had a different plan for you all along. You've just been too wrapped up in grief to see it."

Henry found it ironic that just a short while ago he'd been thinking about how Jacob always helped people. The words his friend spoke now burned worse than salt on any wound. It was impossible to think Olivia might not have married him. That she would have preferred the foundry to life with him. It was insulting that Jacob should even imply it.

Henry couldn't bring himself to say another word. He turned on his heel, climbed into the carriage, and drove away.

Henry fumed all the way home, although he tried not to take it out on the horse this time. He kept the mare at a measured pace, which also gave him time to think. Once he returned to the house, the other business of the day would force itself upon him. He had promised Mr. Thompson he would go to the east wing to inspect the work going on there. They'd run into some issues that required his attention. Nothing in his life ever ran on a smooth course.

What had led Jacob to say all those things? It was as though he were deliberately trying to ruin their friendship. But *had* Henry been nursing an idealized memory of Olivia all these years? He wasn't ready to concede it.

As he turned onto his property, Henry surveyed the landscape. Everything was picture perfect. Even the house, damaged as it was, was impressive. Survivor of time and of fires, Morestowe Manor was venerable and beautiful. Had Olivia truly thought she would not be happy here? Had she imagined she'd be restricted to deciding the menu and organizing house parties? There was so much more to running an estate—overseeing the rents and working with the tenants being just a few of them. He would have welcomed her help with all of it. His biggest mistake was that he hadn't made this clear enough. He had let the opportunity slip through his fingers.

Henry delivered the carriage to the stable hands with as few words as possible. Still wrapped up in his thoughts, he walked toward the main house. He planned to spend a few minutes alone in his study before going to see Mr. Thompson.

"Cousin Henry!" Amelia's gleeful voice stopped him in his tracks. She and Cara were coming across the lawn from the dower house, hurrying to catch up with him. They both carried paper and drawing implements.

He took a deep breath, working to compose himself. "Where are you going? It's too early for tea."

"We are on our way to the garden," Cara said.

Amelia was swinging her pad and pencils, a bundle of energy. "Cousin Langham said we should go outside and practice drawing the flowers or something."

He could tell she had quoted him verbatim. She seemed happy at Langham's suggestion and not the least bit aware that he'd really just told her to leave him alone. When Langham had first proposed that Amelia could be involved at the dower house studio, Henry knew it wouldn't be long before his brother found her presence tiresome. Especially if she was wound up, as she seemed to be right now.

"Would you like to come with us?" Cara offered. "It's such a lovely afternoon."

"I have other things to attend to. Enjoy yourselves."

She made a little movement to keep him from walking off. "Why not come and sit with us for a few minutes?" She spoke kindly, looking troubled at his gruff manner. "It's a good time to try out those new benches Jacob delivered."

The mention of Jacob only made his anger rise up again.

"Cousin Langham told me a joke," Amelia said. "Do you want to hear it?"

"I don't want you repeating any of Langham's jokes." Henry knew there was little in his brother's repertoire that was suitable for children.

"I've made sure he only tells her the harmless ones," Cara assured him.

He might as well get it over with so he could go. "All right."

Amelia opened her arms wide. "Life is short."

He stared at her, confused. He did not understand this joke at all. But then Amelia grinned, and he saw that she'd been pausing for effect.

232

"It only has four letters in it!" She started laughing, jumping up and down and acting silly. Much the same way that Langham laughed at his own jokes.

Henry was not prepared to be bombarded like this. "Don't do that!" he barked. He scrunched up his eyes, pinching the bridge of his nose, his soul still burdened with the dark thoughts he'd been nursing.

Amelia's laughter stopped. He opened his eyes to see both ladies staring at him—Amelia with a hurt expression, and Cara with earnest concern.

"I apologize for my brusqueness," he said and began to turn away. He ought to leave before he caused any further damage.

Cara laid a hand on his arm. "Please come with us." Her voice was gentle, entreating. Too kind for what Henry deserved.

"Are you sure you want that?"

"It's why I asked." She spoke firmly, but Amelia did not look so sure.

It was the child's expression that told Henry what he must do. He could not take out his anger on her. "Perhaps a turn in the garden will do me good."

They skirted the house and made their way to the garden behind it. Even though it was early September, there was still plenty of color. His gardener had designed the garden so that something was blooming nearly year-round.

Cara chose one of the benches and set her things on it. "This one will be good, I think. A nice view of those dahlias."

"I don't want to draw." Amelia had not recovered from Henry's sharp words. He recognized the petulance in her voice; he was beginning to realize it was born of a sense of rejection.

"Why don't you go and play?" Cara suggested, taking the pad and pencil from Amelia's hand.

Amelia ran to the far end of the garden. She was a resilient little thing, and soon she was looking for butterflies and following them as they flitted between the plants.

Henry sat brooding, watching Amelia at play, while Cara opened her sketch pad. After a moment he glanced down to see her hand moving across the paper as she drew the garden scene, including a girl beaming at a butterfly. The sight of it choked him up a little. He was growing to like Amelia more and more, especially since Cara had helped bring out many of her better qualities. He remembered her laughter yesterday during the riding lesson as she successfully landed the jumps. He truly wanted her to be happy despite her rough start in life.

Quiet minutes stretched by. Cara seemed too wrapped up in her work to say anything. Or perhaps she sensed he had no desire to talk.

Henry felt the intensity of his anger ease as he listened to the birds and the buzzing insects and the breeze that occasionally stirred the flowers. He loved it here. He was required to spend portions of the year in London due to social obligations and his work in the House of Lords, but this estate was always the place he returned to. It was why he worked so hard. This land was a part of him.

"This is a nice place, isn't it?" Henry said it more to himself, not really expecting a response.

"It's very nice," Cara answered.

"Anyone would be glad to live here, don't you think?"

"I think it would be wonderful to live in such a place."

Henry had only been musing aloud, not intending to draw such an effusive response. He turned to see that she had also turned toward him. Her expression was warm and bright, her face close to his, her lips parted in a smile. He thought of the day he'd seen her in D'Adamo's studio. She'd been breathtaking then, but somehow she looked even better here, perfectly framed by the garden's greenery and flowers. At ease in her surroundings. Undeniably appealing.

Henry understood what Jacob had been trying to do. His friend was a romantic, it seemed, in addition to having an unshakable conviction that simple faith could smooth the roughest path. But it wasn't as easy as that. Even supposing Henry was ready to look for a wife—which he wasn't—things were infinitely more complicated now than they'd been that summer when he'd fallen in love with Olivia.

He'd been a brash young university student then, ready to defy the wishes of his parents. A woman whose family owned a foundry— even a prosperous one—would not be considered suitable for a man who would one day inherit an earldom. He had not known it then, but that was the last time he might have had the freedom to make such a choice.

Since then, he'd come into the title and all the responsibilities that came with it. Burdens that often outweighed the privileges. Marriage to Olivia would not have changed any of that, of course. Nor could it have changed the past five years of bad crops. But they would have faced those challenges together. He was sure she would have come to love this place and find it worth fighting for. And four years ago, when his father died and his mother was forced to tell him about the existence of Amelia, they would have dealt with that problem together as well. Perhaps then Henry would not have been subject to the rumors he'd endured since bringing the girl to live with him. It had not been an easy choice. He'd only known he could not allow his own niece to live in poverty when he had the means to give her a better life.

What would Cara do if she knew Langham was Amelia's father? She cared so much for the girl. Yes, memories of Olivia had held Henry back. But so, too, had the embarrassments and disasters in the years since her death, especially those caused by his own family members.

"Langham told me your family is facing some financial issues. Is that what's troubling you?"

"Partly." He wished Langham were not so free with information that ought to be kept private. "How did you two get onto that subject?"

"There was mention of a copper mine at dinner the night before you went to Roxwell Abbey. I asked him about it. Does Lord Nigel want to get involved?"

"No."

"Was there a specific reason?"

He looked at her, wondering why she was so interested, and tried to sort out how much he was willing to share. "His funds are tied up elsewhere."

"Oh, I see. Well, that's too bad." Somehow, though, she looked relieved.

"If you happen to know any rich industrialists who might like to invest in my mine, I hope you'll put me in touch with them." He couldn't believe he was making a joke at a time like this, with so many troubles and painful memories crowding his heart. Yet it made him feel strangely better.

"I'll keep that in mind."

Her smile and the inner light reflected in her bright blue eyes really were extraordinary. Her kindness was a balm, yet everything else about her produced emotions too conflicting for one person to survive.

He stood up. "There are things needing my attention." He cleared his throat, not quite meeting her gaze. "Thank you."

As he walked away, he didn't hear her say anything in response. Somehow, though, he felt she knew what he'd been trying to convey.

CHAPTER

26

I've been thinking about something Henry said to me. It was a joke, but maybe there is something to it." Cara had wanted to talk to Langham about this for a day or two. Since he had taken a break from his painting, she thought this was a good time. "We were talking about the challenges he's having with finding investors for the copper mine."

Setting aside his palette, Langham rolled his eyes. "Our perennial worry."

"He said if I happen to know any rich industrialists to put him in touch with them."

Langham looked at her with interest. "Do you know any?"

"No, but you do. In a way. Isn't Louise's sister, Mariana, going to marry one?"

"Philip Everson. Yes, it looks that way."

"Since you've been writing to Louise, I thought perhaps you could mention it."

He shrugged. "It's a tenuous connection. Why should our mine matter to him?"

"You may be in-laws one day."

"Cara, you are an incorrigible romantic, aren't you?"

"It's the best kind to be," she quipped in return. "But really, the way Mariana was talking, she wants to help you and Louise get together. Why not give it a try? If you can help get your family on better financial ground, wouldn't that bolster your cause?"

Langham nodded, thinking it over. "I suppose you're right. It can't hurt to try. I'll mention it in my next letter to Louise."

Cara went back to her painting, but she couldn't resist humming to herself. She had a feeling that all sorts of things were going to turn out very well.

"Why can't we go down to the woods?"

It wasn't the first time Amelia had asked this question. Cara had been careful whenever the two of them were out alone never to stray from sight of the house. "I don't know the way, and I would not want us to get lost."

"But I know the way. I know all the paths in the forest, and in the deer park as well."

"I'm sure you do. However, I would prefer that we have your guardian or your cousin Langham along if we decide to go that far." That was Cara's standard answer, although the real reason was that she was doing her best to keep her promise to God. Even to be out here walking the pasture that edged the stables seemed to be pushing it. Over the past few days, Cara had found herself alone with Amelia more often than not. Henry always seemed to be busy, and Langham was more and more absorbed in his painting.

There had been another art lesson and another riding lesson as well. But in both cases, neither Henry nor Langham had been present. Cara had sensed Amelia's disappointment and had done her best to keep the child from feeling neglected. They had just spent an hour at the stables, but Amelia was still antsy and looking for outdoor amusements.

"Why don't we walk to the east garden?" Cara suggested. "We haven't really explored there yet."

Amelia agreed, although she did not look happy about it.

The path to the east garden skirted the drive. As they walked along it, a carriage approached from the main road. Amelia shielded her eyes from the sun to get a better look. "Oh no." She stamped her foot. "I *told* you we ought to have gone to the woods. That's the countess."

The carriage came to a halt as it drew alongside them. The driver jumped down and opened the door, assisting the Countess of Morestowe as she descended from the carriage.

She took a long look at them both, and her expression indicated that her assessment was not good. The dust from the road and the stable yard had settled on their shoes and clothes.

Amelia stared brazenly back at Lady Morestowe. Cara could almost feel the animosity between them. Henry had put the case mildly when he'd said the two did not get on well. There was an evident dislike between them that ran deep.

"Good afternoon, your ladyship." Cara curtsied but then immediately wished she hadn't. It was probably the correct thing to do, but it made her feel like a servant again.

Unfortunately, the countess received this signal clearly and addressed Cara accordingly. "Who are you? Where is Miss Leahy?"

It was Amelia who answered. "Miss Leahy's not here. Her mother is dying. This is Miss Bernay."

As she spoke, the girl placed her hand in Cara's. It wasn't clear whether Amelia was seeking protection or offering her support against Lady Morestowe's onslaught. Either way, it warmed Cara's heart.

"Is this true about Miss Leahy?" the countess demanded.

"Miss Leahy's mother is ill, ma'am, and Miss Leahy has gone to stay with her until—well, we're not sure when she'll return."

"I should like to know why I wasn't apprised of that situation. How did Lord Morestowe locate you? Through an agency? What's your background?"

"I am here as a guest, ma'am."

The countess looked affronted at the idea. "How can that be?"

"Hen—his lordship invited me here. I am an acquaintance of Mr. Burke."

Amelia crinkled her nose and looked at Cara in surprise. It was probably a reaction to hearing her use formal designations for Henry and Langham after they'd spent the week talking so casually to one another. But Cara wanted to make the best possible impression with the countess.

"An *acquaintance* of Mr. Burke? That sounds singular."

"I expect it does, ma'am." Cara began to understand why this woman was not so warmly thought of by her family. She gave all evidence of being harsh and unyielding.

"I shall go to Lord Morestowe and find out what this is about," the countess informed them. Returning to her carriage, she added, "Mind you don't get into any trouble."

Cara wasn't sure whether that admonition was aimed at her or Amelia.

As the carriage drove away, Cara was tempted to laugh. Lady Morestowe's overreaction was so absurd as to be almost funny. Amelia was not at all amused. She stuck her tongue out at the retreating carriage.

"You can't tell me you've had that woman staying here as your guest. Don't you understand that is courting scandal?"

Henry sighed. His mother had come straight to the study to find him the moment she'd arrived. It was too bad she had seen Amelia and Cara on her way up the drive. Henry had hoped to break the news to her first. "I can't imagine it's really so bad as that."

"What family is she from? It certainly couldn't be one with a good reputation if she is off gallivanting on her own."

"She isn't from a family—that is, not in the sense you're thinking of. She was raised in an orphanage in Bristol and recently moved to London. She's someone Langham befriended. You know how he does."

She frowned. "I do." Her tone conveyed her irritation at Langham's tendency to go around befriending people. "Where, exactly, did they meet?"

"At the Grosvenor Gallery." That was not exactly the truth, but Henry decided it was close enough. He'd already written to tell her Langham had left the sanitarium and had been with him in London, although he had not gone into detail as to the particulars. "Miss Bernay is interested in pursuing a career as a painter, so Langham invited her to come here."

Perhaps it sounded like he was trying to shift blame to his brother, but that wasn't the case. The ultimate decision to bring Cara here had rested with Henry.

His mother was of the same mind. "And you agreed to this plan? Really, Henry, you ought to know better. The only way a young unmarried woman can stay in this house is if she is one of the servants. To stay as a guest, she must either be a relative of ours or accompanied by a family member. How can you expect to keep a good reputation if you forget basic rules of propriety?"

"There is another reason I decided to bring Miss Bernay here." Henry was careful to refer to Cara in this formal way when speaking with his mother. Heaven knew what palpitations she would suffer if she found out they'd been using each other's Christian names. "She is helping us with Amelia until Miss Leahy returns. She has a knack for handling children. In fact, she's worked wonders with Amelia in a very short amount of time."

"You might have informed me about Miss Leahy going away and leaving us in the lurch. I would have come back to oversee things."

"I thought we could manage for a few weeks. I didn't think it right that you should have to cut short your holiday with Lord and Lady Stafford."

"Yes, well . . ." There was a pause as his mother considered something. "So we may say Miss Bernay is acting as a temporary governess. That makes things marginally more acceptable. You are paying her something for this, I suppose?" She sounded almost hopeful.

"No, we are not paying her. She prefers not to be labeled as a governess, no matter how temporary."

His mother's lips pursed. "Why not? If she's from an orphanage, the job could only be a step up."

"It would appear her aspirations are higher."

Henry was referring to Cara's interest in becoming an artist, but his mother's shocked expression indicated she took his words another way. "You don't think Langham is in love with her, do you? Or that she has designs on him? We cannot afford another of *those* problems. Aside from everything else, there will be the never-ending begging for money. Just like Amelia's mother."

"I truly believe there's no danger of that." Henry didn't point out that Langham might have had dalliances with any number of women over the years. He thought it best to concentrate on the current concern and not bring up new worries.

"Then what does she get out of this?" Her eyes narrowed as she began to entertain a new suspicion. "She might very well set her cap for you, you know. That would be quite the plum indeed."

Henry was not about to allow his mother to go down that path. "I already pointed out that she has been helping us with Amelia. She wants to be an artist. I have engaged Mr. Perrine to come out twice a week to give them both lessons. I know you object to her being here. However, things are working well, and I do not intend to change them."

His mother fanned herself in exasperation. "No, Henry. Something *must* change. We have guests coming, and this will put us in a terribly awkward position."

"Guests? Who?"

"Although I am still put out that you did not keep me informed about Miss Leahy, I will say it's a good thing I went to that house party in Cowes. I was able to do some work on your behalf. For all of us, really. I made the acquaintance of Mr. Stanley Myers."

Henry shook his head. "Are you speaking of the millionaire from Pittsburgh? The steel magnate?"

She gave a satisfied smile. "Yes, that's the one."

"What's he doing in England?"

"What do all Americans do? They come here for business, of course. And perhaps to lap up a bit of history and culture. He told me he is interested in speaking to you about the copper mine. He said he trades in—oh, how did he put it? 'Futures and commodities.' That's it." She looked pleased with herself.

This was unbelievably good news. Henry had just spent two days thinking morosely that his plans would be stalled into failure unless he could bring himself to apologize or make things up with Jacob. And yet here was a completely unforeseen and interesting possibility—and courtesy of his mother, no less.

As trying as their relationship could be, there were times when she proved herself surprisingly adept in unexpected ways. "Wouldn't it be better to meet in London? Half the house is still under reconstruction."

"That's a terrible idea. The city is too hot. We can receive them here with greater comfort, even with the limited space. Besides, I've already extended the invitation. They will be here in two days. Mrs. Myers is accompanying him. I explained about the fire and that we are just getting the house back to its previous grandeur. They are not the least bit concerned, and in any case, I've no doubt that our house far exceeds theirs, even in its present state."

Henry sighed. "Fine. We'll do what we have to, I suppose."

"Speaking of which . . ." She gave him a pointed look. "You can see why this Miss Bernay should stay out of the way while the Myerses are here. We simply cannot risk our reputation or the embarrassment."

"Do you think the Americans are really as concerned about such things as we are?"

"More so." His mother gave a little laugh. "I think they do it to compensate for their feelings of inferiority to Europeans."

Henry ought to have known his mother would find a way to gain her own purposes on her own terms. The last thing he wanted was to humiliate Cara by asking her to live as a governess. She would not be able to participate in any events involving the guests, and she would have to eat dinner with Amelia or in the servants' hall. "How long will they be staying?"

"Two or three days only. They are on their way to France."

That was something, anyway. He could ask Cara to do it as a favor and frame it as a minor inconvenience. She was already aware of the financial issues at stake. Henry felt she was just kindhearted enough to agree to his request. One thing he would not do was make it a command. She deserved better than that.

"Well?" his mother prodded.

"I'll discuss the matter with her tomorrow. However, tonight she dines with us. I insist upon it." It wasn't often that Henry invoked his status over her as lord of the manor. When he did, he fully expected his mother to acquiesce.

She gave him a hard look followed by a crisp nod and left the room.

Leaving Henry feeling that he had both won and lost at the same time.

"The placement of the paintings on the main stairs is completely wrong. They will need to be taken down and rehung."

By Cara's reckoning, this was the third pronouncement by the countess this evening. The first had been that she intended to visit the dower house tomorrow to "see what you've done to it." She had said this in a way that conveyed she didn't expect to like it.

The second had been her insistence that she would be at Amelia's next riding lesson. "If the child is going to ride, we must see that she learns correctly. Mr. Hart may be competent, but no man can ultimately be the best teacher, because he has no personal experience of riding sidesaddle."

Despite the discord between Lady Morestowe and Amelia, Cara thought the countess's presence at the lessons could turn out to be a good thing. During dinner she'd learned that Lady Morestowe was an excellent horsewoman. If she shared her expertise, she would be spending enjoyable time with Amelia. Perhaps they could finally find common ground.

As for the paintings in the front hall, Cara had known from her first night here that Henry expected his mother to object to his changes. Sure enough, he said, "They shall remain as they are. I set them that way for a reason."

Not having seen them before the change, Cara had no reference point. However, she thought Henry had done well. She'd found snippets of time to study the paintings every day. They were pleasing not only in their content but in the way they had been grouped. During her visit to the Grosvenor, Langham had explained that the gallery had acquired a good reputation for knowing how to hang paintings to their best advantage. There was apparently an "art" to that, too. Henry claimed to have no artistic talent or interest, but she thought he had a good eye, nonetheless.

"Sometimes change can be good," Henry added.

"Hear, hear," Langham interjected.

He was drinking heavily tonight and was in the "happy" stages of his cups right now. It bothered Cara. She had begun to think he was putting such behavior behind him.

"I will not argue with you about it now," Lady Morestowe told Henry. She threw a glance in Cara's direction as she spoke. "In any case, there isn't time to make changes before the Myerses come."

"Myerses? Who are they?" Langham asked.

"Mr. Myers is a steel magnate on his first visit from America," Henry explained. "He's interested in learning more about the investment opportunity of the copper mine."

"That's wonderful!" Cara said. "I was sure something would turn up." She had been praying about it ever since their conversation in the garden.

"We are fortunate that I made his acquaintance at the home of Lord and Lady Stafford."

"Mr. Myers was at the Staffords' house party? He's newly arrived from America and already hobnobbing with the Prince of Wales?" Langham took another sip of wine. "But then, I shouldn't be surprised. His Royal Highness loves Americans. They are so much less stuffy about things." He followed this observation with a hiccup.

Henry exchanged a glance with his mother. It seemed fraught with meaning. Maybe they were upset about Langham's intemperance. Cara had not seen him this drunk since the night Henry had taken him out of the pub. It might also be the reason Henry looked less happy than she might have expected, given this good news about the wealthy American.

Langham finished his wine and set the glass on the table. "Did you know they took 'God Save the Queen' and put their own words to it? Cheeky blackguards."

Sending her son a dark glare, Lady Morestowe rose from her chair.

"It's time for the ladies to retire to the drawing room." She said this with such gravity that Cara decided it was pronouncement number four.

Following her lead, Cara stood. So did the men, as Cara knew etiquette required. However, Langham began to sing, "'Long live our noble Queen! God save the Queen!'"

"All right, Langham, off we go." Henry took his brother's arm and began to pull him from the room.

Langham made only a playful show of resisting, shouting, "But wait! I haven't finished the song!"

Cara remained in place, frozen in embarrassment. The countess also had not moved, but in her case, it was because she was rigid with anger. Even from the dining room, they could hear the brothers making their way up the stairs and Langham's joyful taunt, "'Cry—God for Harry, England, and Saint George!'"

"I see he has not improved one bit since I saw him last," Lady Morestowe said in disgust.

"With all due respect, ma'am, he has done this very little during the past few weeks. I think—that is, I hope and pray—that this is only a minor setback. I've been encouraging him to think about his painting and to concentrate on doing things that will help him improve his art."

Cara spoke these words from the heart, intending to offer comfort. However, the countess only gave her a cold stare. "What is your purpose for being here, Miss Bernay?"

"I was invited to come, your ladyship."

"It's clear you finagled an invitation. My question is, why did you accept?"

At that moment, Cara was tempted to wonder herself. She understood why Amelia was so ill-behaved in this woman's presence. Two stubborn natures would be like fire meeting fire. Unsure how to answer, Cara stammered out a reply. "I am, er, most grateful for the opportunity to enjoy time in the countryside. And to receive art lessons. Also, I believe I am helping Amelia."

"That is all?" Lady Morestowe pressed.

What else did she want? Cara felt her cheeks tinging pink, aware there were servants in the room observing this condescending inquisition. If the countess wished to humiliate her, she was doing a very good job.

"I understand you are having some success at keeping control of Amelia. But I warn you right now that it is already too late for Langham."

"How can you say such a thing? He's your son!" Cara couldn't help but come to his defense, even if Lady Morestowe was so formidable.

The countess arched a brow. "You will do well to stick to your business, Miss Bernay, and not insert yourself into ours."

The fifth pronouncement of the evening came down as a rebuke, and Cara bristled at the unfairness of it.

"If you will be so good as to excuse me, I have had a long travel day and will be retiring early."

"Yes, of course," Cara murmured, although the Countess of Morestowe was not asking permission.

CHAPTER

27

Henry left for his morning walk earlier than usual. He had a lot to sort out, and he could think better when he was away from the house. Not that he was likely to run into Langham or his mother; both preferred to remain in their private rooms until late morning. In addition, Langham would be sleeping off the effects of last night.

He didn't like that his mother had been so cavalier, treating Cara like a servant. He certainly didn't like the idea that, for the next few days at least, he had to ask Cara to act like one. She had comported herself so well during dinner. He could see she'd been nervous, and yet, aside from picking up the wrong fork during the fish course, he had noticed no faux pas of the sort that would give his mother an excuse to look down on her.

By the time he'd come back downstairs after he and Jensen had wrangled Langham to his room, both ladies had dispersed. *"Her ladyship professed herself tired after a long day, and Miss Bernay said she quite understood."* That was the report from one of the footmen who'd been serving dinner. Henry could glean plenty from that statement, although the footman had been wise enough to say no more.

Henry admired the way Cara had remained relentlessly cheerful. Her obvious joy at hearing about Myers and his upcoming visit was a perfect example. But that only made Henry feel guilty, because he knew what he had to ask of her. He would see little of Cara and Amelia while the Myerses were visiting. He would make it up to them by planning an excursion of some sort after the Myerses had gone. Perhaps a picnic by the creek. Amelia would like that. So would he, come to think of it. It would be his way of showing his appreciation for their sacrifice.

As he came out of the woods, he decided to look into the art studio. He had not been there since Jacob's visit, and he was curious to see how things had progressed.

His last encounter with Jacob had been on his mind a lot over these past few days. After his anger had cooled, he had tentatively begun to consider his friend's words. He'd wanted to sound them out, to test them in his mind and heart. There had been hard truths to accept. Maybe he wasn't ready to believe Olivia might never have married him; perhaps he didn't need to. Perhaps he needed only to accept that it was time to move on.

Certainly, after last night he knew something had to change. This family could not continue on as they were. Henry had to find a solution. He'd realized that his old, lingering sorrows had been stealthily replaced by a very different sort of ache. He wanted to step away from the overtrodden pathways of thought that, painful as they were, had been too easy to follow again and again. It was, in short, a longing to begin anew.

Approaching the dower house, he was surprised to see someone already there. Through the window, he saw Cara seated at her easel, alone in the studio. Here was an opportunity to speak to her privately.

Catching sight of Henry, she waved. Something stirred within him—a heady sensation that heightened his senses. There had only ever been one other person who could make Henry feel this way.

He waited for his heart to protest, as it always had at the idea there could ever be anyone else. This time, though, his heart urged him forward.

Early morning sun bathed the studio in golden light. After last night's dinner, Cara was grateful for the peacefulness of the place. She had withstood Lady Morestowe's attacks, but she felt bruised from the experience.

Cara had already gotten in the habit of coming here in the mornings, when she could have time to herself to paint. Later, after Amelia had been dressed by the nursery maid and given her breakfast, Cara would bring her out here. It was better to let Langham have the studio to himself in the afternoons. That was when he seemed best able to work and least tolerant of having others around. Especially Amelia, who often proved too much of a distraction. It was a schedule that worked for everyone.

Today, however, she worried that Langham might not appear at all. Would the events of last night bring on more physical maladies? It was surely no coincidence that the day of Lady Morestowe's arrival was the first time Langham's drinking had been so obviously out of control since they'd left London. Her ladyship seemed to bring out the worst in everyone. Was there any way to change that? The thought was daunting. If Langham was so set in bad habits at the age of twenty-four, how much more would the countess be?

Maybe her ladyship had been correct in stating that Cara should stick to helping Amelia. Cara planned to be extra diligent, doing anything she could to shield the child from Lady Morestowe's hurtful ways, which were likely to bring back Amelia's tantrums. Cara had begun to dread the prospect of the countess being at the next riding lesson. What if, instead of drawing them closer, it spoiled Amelia's love of riding?

She sat back and surveyed the work she'd done on her portrait of Amelia. Cara was rather proud of it. She hoped to capture Amelia's vulnerability as well as her imperious nature. The child was both clever and sensitive, and Cara prayed the girl would find a way to flourish.

Looking out the window, Cara was pleased to see Henry crossing the lawn. She watched him appreciatively. She loved his long strides and the way he always moved with a confident air, even when his mind seemed focused on other things.

Catching his eye, she waved. He lifted a hand in return. She hastily tucked in a loose strand of hair and smoothed her skirt. Not that these things could improve her appearance very much, for she was plainly dressed. But he was used to seeing her this way by now.

A few moments later, he entered the cottage.

"Good morning," Cara said cheerfully.

He paused just inside the door. "You're here early." He was looking at her intently, but she could not gauge his mood.

"It's the only time I can find to myself. Not that I mind. I am thankful to have this opportunity at all."

"I apologize for my mother's behavior last night. Langham was out of order, too, yet I feel my mother's ungracious attitude toward you was the greater wrong."

Something about the way he was looking at her made her pulse quicken. "Thank you, that's very kind. I did not take offense . . . but perhaps I am a little afraid of her after all."

"You shouldn't be. You have the bigger heart."

Cara savored this compliment, and most especially the admiration in his eyes as he said it. It would make enduring any number of Lady Morestowe's barbs worthwhile.

"What are you painting?"

"It's a portrait of Amelia."

Henry walked over to her, standing beside her to look at the picture. Cara delighted in the solid warmth of his presence. It felt just like when they'd shared the bench together in the garden. She had loved those few minutes together. Even though she'd quietly kept drawing, inside she had been alight with pleasure. Since then, she'd often relived in her mind that moment when they'd turned to one another, seemingly so close, before Henry had pulled away.

"I like it," Henry said as he studied the painting. His mouth quirked. "She looks like she's about to demand a cherry ice."

"So she does," Cara agreed with a laugh.

His mouth broadened into a true smile. He looked so handsome at these brief, unguarded moments. He sobered a little, though, as they continued to look at each other. "It's clear to me how much you care for Amelia, and I'm grateful."

"Believe it or not, she is easy to love, despite the times when she's unruly. I suppose my heart went out to her right away, as she is an orphan."

Something flickered in Henry's eyes. "Yes, well . . . she does have family, though—Langham and my mother and me. Even if we are a poor substitute for actual parents."

"You are doing an excellent job. Langham is more intermittent in his attention, but I think he loves her, too, in his way."

"Yes, he does. That is, I hope so."

She did not say anything about the countess. Nor did Henry. His brow furrowed. "Cara, there is something I need to ask of you. It's a request only, and I hope you will be good enough to accept it in the spirit in which it is set forth."

"I hope the question isn't as complicated as what you just said, or I'll have no idea how to answer," she teased.

He tried to give her a smile. "You are correct. I don't know quite how to say this. I'd like to give you some background first. You remember how important it is that I secure investors for the copper mine."

"I remember."

"This opportunity with Mr. Myers is one I cannot afford to lose— that is, for any other reason than that he finds the investment itself not to his interest."

"For any other reason?" Cara repeated. "I don't understand."

"It's vital that I make the right impression. Despite Langham's remarks last night about Americans, they are in fact very conscious of propriety, and, well, there is no denying that your being here is somewhat unusual. . . ."

Cara's heart sank. She saw where this was going. "Are you asking me to leave?"

"No!" Henry answered quickly. "I'm asking only if you will consider spending all your time with Amelia while they are here."

"You want me to pretend to be the governess." As far as Cara was concerned, this was worse.

"I am *asking* only. You are well within your rights to refuse. The only reason I dare to ask is because you have been so understanding and sympathetic about the tough situation our family is in right now. Because you are so kind, I am hoping that you will be amenable to this plan." He gave her a look that was both pleading and apologetic. "It will only be for a few days, and I will be eternally grateful."

Cara was certain this was Lady Morestowe's idea. For that reason alone, she wanted to object. But if she did, she would run slipshod over Henry's feelings. He was asking this favor with true humility. It showed he held her in high regard. Surely that must be the guiding factor in her decision. Did she want to help Henry? Yes, she did. The way he was speaking to her now, and the way he was looking at her, gave her hope that the idea that had presented itself to her the day they'd met at Adrian's studio was more than an idle fantasy. It would come true. This was but one step along the way, and even though it was unpleasant, it would pass.

"I am not amenable. But I agree to it wholeheartedly. For your sake, and for Amelia."

His entire body seemed to exhale in relief. "Thank you." They were simple words, but infused with real emotion. "You are beautiful."

Her breath caught as she realized the deeper meaning of his compliment. It was not about physical things; it was about two souls understanding each other.

She smiled up at him, willing him with all her heart to take the next step. He searched her face, and she watched, fascinated, as something appeared in his expression that she had not seen before. It was as though he were slowly, cautiously allowing himself to feel the desire he'd kept buried deep within him. The moment was suspended deliciously in time, simmering with promise. At last, when the time was exactly right, he leaned forward and pressed his lips to hers.

For long delicious seconds, they both savored it. He reached up to caress her cheek, to place a gentle hand behind her head and pull her closer, to kiss her again, deeply and more fervently. She leaned into him, for like him, she could not get enough. It was as perfect as Cara had dreamed a first kiss would be.

But then she felt his lips widen in a smile. She opened her eyes to see that his gaze had slid to his left, where she had been holding her paintbrush with an extended arm so it would not smear paint on either of them. They both laughed, which effectively ended the kiss, although it did seem funny.

Henry cleared his throat. "I seem to have, er, interrupted your work."

"Oh, that's quite all right," Cara teased, albeit breathlessly. "But maybe I should clean this." She was painting in watercolor, so it took only moments to dip the brush in a nearby pot of water and wipe it clean.

Henry watched her throughout the procedure. She couldn't tell exactly what was going on in his mind. The corners of his mouth tilted upward, but his eyes were troubled. If he was having misgivings, it did not dampen Cara's feelings, for she was sure they would pass. Her own heart soared with elation.

She set the brush aside, not knowing what should come next. He stepped forward but did not entirely close the gap between them. "Cara, I—"

She leaned toward him. "Yes?"

But he stood, not speaking, as though at a loss for words. Suddenly his attention turned toward the window. "I believe Amelia is coming."

Cara followed his gaze. Amelia was skipping up the path to the cottage door. She was dressed in her gymnastic costume, anticipating another riding lesson.

Disappointed as she was, Cara wanted to laugh. "I suppose she didn't want to wait for me to fetch her." She placed a tentative hand on Henry's arm. "We will continue this conversation another time, yes?"

"Yes, we must." He covered her hand with his own, caressing it gently. Then he lifted it to his lips. The kiss he placed there sent a thrill to every part of her. Still caressing her hand, he added, "We'll have to postpone it until after this visit of the Myerses is over. Can you wait until then?"

There was no mistaking how passionate that kiss had been. Filled with love, it could only be a promise of a perfect future.

"Yes," Cara said, smiling. "I'll wait."

They were going to give Amelia the reins today. She didn't know this yet, however. Mr. Hart was still keeping the pony on the lunge line while they made a series of loops around the ring as a warm-up.

Henry was nervous, but not because he felt Amelia wasn't ready. This was the first lesson with his mother present. She and Amelia had not interacted with one another since meeting on the driveway, and both had been content to leave it that way. But today they would see if the two could work together when engaged in the sport they both loved.

So far, things were going well. The countess approved of the pony, and she'd even expressed a reasonably good opinion of Amelia's form in the saddle.

"Did you talk with her?" his mother asked as they watched Amelia take another turn around the ring.

Henry sent a quick glance in Cara's direction. She stood on the other side of the ring, beaming as she watched Amelia. So far during this lesson, she had kept clear of Henry and the countess, although several times she met Henry's gaze across the ring, her eyes shining with affection.

It was hard not to look at this kind, beautiful woman who was chipping away the sorrow that had encrusted his heart for years. He had so many things to say to her, and so many things to ask. He had not intended to kiss her. But he had, and new ideas had sprung up so quickly that they left him as breathless as the kiss. But the headiness taking hold of him could not negate the fact that there were obstacles ahead. Those could not be ignored or easily surmounted. For now, he focused his hopes on this meeting with the American businessman. It could be an important step toward reaching his goal and enable him to pursue his future on his own terms. "Miss Bernay has agreed to step into the role of governess while the Myerses are here."

"She seems strangely happy about it," his mother observed.

"She believes she is helping us, and that is a great satisfaction to her."

"Are you sure that's all it is?"

He did not miss the suspicion in her voice. She knew her son well.

He would have to stay on the offensive to deflect her concerns. "You should not always ascribe bad motives to everyone, Mother. It's neither charitable nor wise."

His mother sniffed but made no reply.

Mr. Hart brought the pony to a halt and began to gather up the lunge line.

"We can't be done already!" Amelia complained, recognizing this movement as signifying the end of a lesson.

"No, miss, we're just getting started," Mr. Hart assured her. "You've learned how to *sit* on a pony; now we're going to teach you how to *ride* one. Today, you get the reins."

"Hooray!" Amelia raised her arms and wiggled with excitement.

"Act with some decorum, child!" the countess called out. "Remember that it is possible to become a perfect horsewoman while remaining a perfect lady."

Henry went into the ring and held the bridle while Mr. Hart unhooked the rope and loosened the reins. During this process, Amelia settled back into the saddle, but her face also settled into a pout. Henry knew this was a reaction to his mother's words, not the prospect of guiding the pony on her own.

He said quietly, "Remember that you are a very good rider, Amelia. The countess will give you a lot of directions today. Just think about *what* she is saying, not *how* she is saying it. She is an excellent rider, and her instructions will help you. Can you do that for me?"

Amelia gave a little nod, but her glower didn't lift. "I still wish she wasn't here."

Henry responded with an understanding smile. "Fair enough."

Henry and Mr. Hart instructed Amelia on the proper way to hold the reins, how to use them to steer the pony, and the methods to get the animal moving and to a halt again. Cara paid close attention. It had been a scant two hours since that wonderful kiss, and she had already thought of a hundred things she would need to learn or improve upon in order to be a proper countess. Riding was one of them. She would have to get over her fear and become an excellent horsewoman. That was just one of the many ways she would fulfill her new role.

Cara would remember that kiss forever. It was the moment her world was turned upside down and finally placed exactly where it should be. It was true that Henry had not declared himself outright, but Cara wasn't worried. Not after the way he'd looked at her when he said that yes, they would talk again. And the way he'd kissed her hand—oh, who would have thought such a simple gesture could hold so much meaning? She gently touched the spot on her hand where Henry had placed his lips. How could this not be exactly what God had intended?

There were still plenty of issues to work out, of course. Cara was not so naïve as to think everything would be easy. One glance at the countess, who had thrown her only dark glares all morning, told her that. Cara would have to work extra hard to win over the Countess of Morestowe to the idea that someone with humble origins could marry her son.

Seeing the woman's frown aimed at her again, Cara responded with a friendly smile. Even though it was not reciprocated, Cara was determined to keep trying. Surely there was some way to reach that woman's heart.

Returning her attention to Amelia, Cara decided that as soon as she and Henry could discuss things, she was going to press until she got the true story about where the girl had come from and who her parents were. Surely he would tell her now.

"Remember," said Mr. Hart, summing up his directions to Amelia, "to start her moving, use your voice, then, if needed, the kick and the tap with the whip. Are you ready?"

Looking determined, Amelia nodded. Henry and Mr. Hart stepped back from the pony. Amelia made the clicking sound with her tongue that they had taught her. Maisie's ears flicked, but she didn't move.

"Try again," Mr. Hart directed.

Amelia tried again, louder this time. She accompanied it with a nudge from her left foot, which was in the stirrup, and a tap on the right side of the horse with her whip. That did the trick. Amelia smiled triumphantly as the pony began to walk.

"Hold your hands steady!" the countess ordered. "Changing the positioning of your hands can signal that you want a change of pace. You don't want to give the horse conflicting commands."

She had barely finished speaking when Maisie stopped suddenly and put her head down and to the left. Taken by surprise, Amelia slipped from the saddle and went right over the pony's head and into the dirt.

"Amelia!" Cara cried out in alarm.

Mr. Hart grabbed the reins while Henry hurried to the girl. He helped her to her feet and gave her a quick once-over to ensure there were no injuries.

Amelia looked stunned, but only her pride seemed hurt. "Why did Maisie do that?"

"Ponies can be right ornery creatures sometimes," Mr. Hart said. "I think it's because they're so smart. They want to know that you know what you're doing. So you must be firm with her. If she tries to put her head down, you must pull up and back and do the other things I taught you to force her to keep moving forward."

"Are you ready to try again?" Henry asked.

Amelia wiped some of the dust off her arms and clothes. "Yes," she answered firmly.

Henry helped her back on the horse. Once more, Amelia got the creature moving. This time they made it successfully around the ring. Amelia sent a proud grin at Cara as she passed by. But on the second loop, for no reason that Cara could see, Maisie came to a sudden stop and put her head down. Once more, the child tumbled to the ground.

This time, Amelia scrambled to her feet before Henry could reach her. She didn't look stunned, only angry.

"For heaven's sake, child," the countess said in exasperation. "Mr. Hart told you what to do. Pull up, pull back. Use your foot and whip to keep the pony going forward. And remember to grip the horns with your upper legs so you can't be forced off the saddle."

Amelia didn't even look in the countess's direction, just resolutely got back in the saddle. The next time Maisie tried the same trick, Amelia was ready. She pulled back so hard on the reins that the pony whinnied in protest and began to back up.

"Whoa!" Mr. Hart said, taking hold of Maisie's bridle. "Calm down, Maisie, that's a good girl. Easy, now."

Amelia looked shaken. "I pulled back! I pulled back!" she insisted loudly.

"You pulled too hard," the countess said. "You must get the horse to respect you, but not to fear you. This is the balance you must learn if you wish to be a good horsewoman."

Cara thought this sounded like good advice, even if it was rendered too harshly.

"She's right," Henry told Amelia, but his voice was kinder than his mother's, a tactic that echoed what Cara had been thinking. "This is something you will learn with practice, so you mustn't get discouraged."

"Maisie has what we call a good mouth," added Mr. Hart. "That means she'll be responsive to the pressure from the reins as you pull back. So be firm, but don't yank. That will only hurt her."

"I can do it." Amelia positively radiated determination, and that made Cara proud. She was going to conquer this.

In the end, it took several more tries, although Amelia did not fall off the horse again. She came close a few times, but she hung on and worked the reins to lift the pony's head while she coaxed it forward. With each tussle, Cara thought she saw the child growing more confident. At last, she and the pony seemed to understand one another.

During this process, Cara noticed the countess's tone change from scolding to grudging approval. Once or twice her eyebrow even lifted, expressing something that looked like admiration.

Then, without any prompting from anyone, Amelia urged the pony into a trot.

Amelia had traveled at this speed before, but only while on the long rope with Mr. Hart in control. Cara gasped, instantly worried, because the faster the horse was moving, surely the greater the likelihood of injury if Amelia should fall. There were similar looks of surprise from the others, but they decided not to stop her. Henry and Mr. Hart did their best to follow them, calling out instructions as pony and rider went around the ring. Cara was relieved that today there were no hay bales. She was sure Amelia would have attempted to jump over them.

"That's very good, Amelia," Henry said after a time. "Now you need to bring her to a halt. Collect the reins and remember everything you've learned, and you'll be fine." He spoke firmly, but Cara thought she detected a note of worry in his voice. What if something went wrong?

The countess, on the other hand, had only praise to offer. "Excellent, child!"

"Whoa." Amelia pulled back on the reins, bracing herself in case the pony tried to resist or made any unexpected movements. "Whoa."

The moment the pony slowed to a walk, Henry and Mr. Hart got near enough to grab the bridle if needed. They held off, though, to see if Amelia could bring Maisie to a full stop by herself.

She did.

"Excellent!" the countess cried again. She went through the gate and strode up to Amelia. "You still need to work on keeping your torso facing forward, but on the whole, that was well done."

Cara could not believe she was hearing these words from the countess. Judging from the looks on the others' faces, they couldn't, either. Amelia met the countess's gaze. If the two weren't exactly smiling at one another, they were close to it. With Amelia seated on the short pony, she and the countess were practically eye to eye. Henry stood by them, and Cara could see pleased expressions on the three people who were, for the moment, in harmony with one another. The scene impressed itself on her mind, and she was sure that someday she would paint it. This was a perfect moment in a perfect day that she would always remember.

CHAPTER

28

"THERE IS SOMETHING I need to speak to you about, Henry, before you go."

Henry looked up from his letter, perturbed to see his mother standing there. He was working hard to finish his stack of correspondence before he had to leave for the railway station to meet Mr. and Mrs. Myers. It was aggravating enough that his mother had insisted he go, rather than sending their perfectly capable driver and footmen to do it.

Setting down his pen, he stood up. "I thought we went over everything."

"Yes, everything is ready. I am sure they will all be pleased with their visit."

Henry eyed her. "What do you mean *all*?"

"That's what I wanted to talk to you about. Miss Florence Myers is a lovely young lady, and I'm sure you will enjoy meeting her. She's the daughter of Mr. and Mrs. Myers. She's coming with them."

A daughter. Henry could have kicked himself for not researching Myers enough to know he had a daughter. He could already feel his anger rising that his mother had kept this key piece of information from him. "You wouldn't happen to know the *age* of Miss Myers, would you?"

"I believe she is nineteen. A fresh-faced and lovely thing. Charming, too, in her way, although her accent is atrocious. She is enamored with the idea of marrying into English aristocracy, and thanks to her father's successful business, she brings a very nice dowry with her."

"You want me to marry a rich American girl for her money? That's preposterous!" He ought to have known his mother was hiding something. He ought to have known she would not rest until she had bullied and badgered him into what she thought best for his life.

Always sanguine when she had the upper hand, his mother never flinched. "You needn't sound so negative. This would be an excellent way to reestablish our fortune. Many of these American girls have no refinement or understanding of proper etiquette. But those things can be learned if the girl is willing and has an ounce of common sense."

She spoke as offhandedly as if she were discussing the weather. It wasn't the first time she had tried to steer him toward some lady based solely on the size of her dowry. In the past, though, she had kept the field to Englishwomen.

"Why didn't you tell me about Miss Myers before now?"

"Because I know how you are. I knew you would reject the idea out of hand. However, I also know we cannot wait any longer to fix the family fortunes—not to mention it is long past time for you to get yourself an heir."

Henry now understood why this plan of Myers's coming to discuss business had seemed too good to be true. It was. "This isn't about the mine at all, is it? It's about bartering a title for money."

"Why can't it be about both?" His mother threw up her hands. "Honestly, Henry, you're behaving as churlish as a schoolboy."

"I suppose this is also why you insisted that they come here. They will want to inspect the place where their daughter might spend the rest of her life. Aren't you concerned they will be taken aback when they see half the house is still not livable?"

"Quite the contrary. They will be impressed at the new construction and renovation. The Americans may be enamored of our titles and our ancient traditions, but they want their comforts, too. Lady Ashton told me her American daughter-in-law does nothing but complain about her huge drafty manor house with faulty plumbing. When the Myerses come here, they'll see our house is stately, historic, *and* has modern conveniences."

Henry thought this was about the least admirable reason that could be devised for marrying someone. "So everything—the house, the grounds, *me*—is to be presented for Mr. Myers's approval? I will not forgive you for putting me in this spot, Mother."

"You might very well change your tune. You haven't even met Miss Myers yet. You may even like her!"

"Well, that would be a blessing," he retorted.

"Henry, the Myerses are coming—all three of them. Mr. Myers is willing to discuss *everything* with you, from business partnerships to nuptials. This is an unparalleled opportunity. You might as well make the most of it."

Henry objected to this entire scheme, but what could he do? It was too late to stop them from coming; his mother had made sure of that. Nor was there time for him to talk to Cara.

During the ride to the railway station, he considered his options. If he could present the investment opportunity on attractive enough terms, maybe Myers would be willing to negotiate a deal without marriage to his daughter being a stipulation. Henry would do his best to make that happen, even though it might be a false hope.

But another issue troubled him far more. Now he knew the real reason his mother had insisted Cara step into the shadows while the Myerses were here. She had intended all along to bring a prospective bride into the house, and she could not have Cara's presence hindering her aims.

The idea that Henry should sell himself to the highest bidder was galling enough, but it was worse because of what had happened yesterday between him and Cara. When she discovered the presence of Miss Myers, would she think Henry had only been dallying with her? Of course she would. She would be hurt and angry and think him the worst sort of cad. He could only hope to set things right as soon as he could—and pray that it would be possible.

Mr. Stanley Myers was a big, burly man with a booming laugh and the kind of confidence bred by success. He was just the type of person Henry would have guessed a millionaire American to be. As they rode through the countryside to the house, Myers asked many questions about the area and how the estates were run, questions Henry might have found rudely direct from any Englishman. With Mr. Myers, he sensed only a genuine interest in how things worked, the natural curiosity of a businessman and a foreigner. So he answered the questions as honestly as he could without getting into details he considered confidential.

Mrs. Myers was more solemn, but nearly as vocal. She seemed obsessed with following the correct protocol for everything. Several times she offered a gentle rebuke to her husband, which he seemed not only to tolerate but to find amusing. The deferential treatment she gave Henry indicated she was awestruck by English nobility. Henry began to feel she viewed him as some wildly exotic being, which made him uncomfortable. He was used to receiving respect from others due to his rank, but this woman's manners bordered on excessive.

Miss Florence Myers, on the other hand, was more difficult to figure out. She was pretty enough, he supposed. In truth, it was difficult to tell, because she'd held a handkerchief to her nose from the moment they'd arrived at the station. From what he could see, though, her nose and eyes were red and swollen.

"I hope you did not find the journey too arduous," Henry said to her when there was a lull in the conversation. He could not think of a more polite way to ask after her health, for she was clearly indisposed.

"I am well, thank you." The answer came out bland and flat, as though she were merely repeating words as she'd been taught. Her voice was muffled from the handkerchief. Henry thought he heard a sniffle as she dabbed the delicately embroidered linen to her nose.

"My daughter is suffering from allergies," Mrs. Myers said. She sent her daughter a look that seemed more reproving than sympathetic. "I'm sure she will recover soon."

Henry wasn't sure how a person "recovered" from allergies, but it would be rude to point that out. Mr. Myers said nothing but sent a troubled glance in his daughter's direction.

"This must be the venerable Morestowe Manor!" Mrs. Myers said as the house came into view. "Why, it's magnificent! So stately and grand. Isn't it lovely, Florence?" She didn't wait for an answer. Instead, she turned to Henry and said, "How old did you say it was, Lord Morestowe?"

Her forced brightness was painfully obvious, but Henry was happy to turn the conversation to a new topic. He'd seen enough of Mrs. Myers to understand that her question stemmed from her admiration of England's long history. "It was built in 1726, ma'am. The land and the title were given to my ancestor by King George—the *First*," he emphasized. He understood, albeit from a different point of view, how the Americans felt about the third monarch of that name. "As you can see, we are in the process of rebuilding the east wing. We suffered a fire last winter."

"I've heard old houses can be dangerous," Miss Myers said. It was the first real observation she'd put forward. Although her nose and mouth were concealed by the handkerchief, Henry had the impression she was viewing the house with far less enthusiasm than her mother.

"I assure you, you will be perfectly safe," Henry said. "We have found a blessing in this catastrophe, in that we are now modernizing everything, including the fireplaces. We are also installing a system of radiators for more efficient heating."

He hated himself for saying these things, because they were exactly what his mother would wish him to say in order to impress upon the Myerses how wonderful the house was. And yet Henry was proud of the place. He wasn't going to deny that. "I have every expectation that you will enjoy your visit here."

"I'm sure we shall!" Mrs. Myers responded eagerly. "Lady Morestowe has described to us how delightful the grounds are and the many pleasant activities to be enjoyed here. I believe there will even be a croquet match. Florence loves to play croquet, don't you, dear?"

Miss Myers nodded, and the tiniest spark of happiness appeared in her eyes. Henry had no idea how a person with allergies could be so enamored of a lawn game. But then, he did not really believe that whatever was troubling her had to do with allergies.

He'd encountered many simpering mothers and their daughters who were angling for marriage to Henry and the title that came with it. He'd assumed the Americans would be worse, and his initial impressions of Mrs. Myers seemed to confirm that.

However, he felt unexpectedly sorry for Miss Myers. He doubted that her reticence stemmed from shyness. He did not think she wanted to be here. Perhaps he could talk with her alone and find out what was really going on. This was not likely to be difficult, because if her parents and his mother were determined to get Henry and Miss Myers engaged, they would arrange lots of time for them to speak privately, if chaperoned. If Miss Myers was an unwilling participant in this game, that was knowledge he could use.

He wasn't going to lose Cara. Whatever it took, he was going to find a way out of this situation before the damage was beyond repair.

CHAPTER

29

C ARA STOOD at her easel, painting the wildflowers growing near the brook and keeping an eye on Amelia as she played nearby. The child had removed her shoes and stockings and was splashing happily in the ankle-deep water. Cara felt a little envious. Given how warm the day was, she imagined that the cool water dancing over her bare feet would have been deliciously refreshing.

She understood now why Amelia had plagued her so often about coming here. With shade trees, open meadow, and this little gurgling brook, this spot in the woods was idyllic in every way. She was glad Langham had wanted to come today, enabling her to say yes to the excursion. Though if he hadn't come, she might have brought Amelia here anyway. After all, Henry was the child's guardian. Therefore, when Cara became Henry's wife, she would take on that role as well. It was God's way of telling her she was forgiven. Cara was sure of that. Why else would He have placed Amelia in her care?

Langham's current project was set outdoors, and he wanted to get the details of the landscape just right. He had been engrossed in his work all afternoon, pausing only when they had enjoyed a picnic of sandwiches and biscuits. At the moment he seemed unperturbed by the noises Amelia was making, absorbing them as part of the cacophony of sounds around them.

Cara decided playing the part of the governess wasn't so bad if it enabled her to spend lovely afternoons like this, removed from the countess's company. The riding lesson had led to a thaw in Amelia's relations with the countess, but that didn't mean the woman's attitude toward Cara had altered.

Someday that would change, though. Cara had spent the afternoon dreaming of all the good things that would come after the Myerses' visit. Perhaps Mr. Myers would give Henry the financial backing he needed for the mine. If not, there was still the possibility of getting Mr. Everson. As he'd promised, Langham had written to Louise. There hadn't been time to hear back, but Cara had a good feeling about it. One way or another, something would work out.

"Look, Cousin Langham! I caught a tadpole!" Amelia shouted, squealing with laughter as the creature squirmed in her cupped hands. It slipped free and plopped back into the water, but Amelia only grinned and pushed a bit of hair from her forehead with her damp hands. "I'm hungry. Are there any more biscuits?"

"I'm afraid not," Cara answered.

"Perhaps it's time to return home," Langham said, brought out of his concentration by Amelia's calling to him. "I'm famished. One benefit of having guests is that Mother will ensure dinner is spectacular."

"I have found all the dinners to be wonderful. It's hard to imagine them being any better." Cara couldn't keep the wistfulness out of her voice.

Langham shook his head. "I still don't think it's right, Henry and Mother asking you to play the part of a servant. Not after we invited you here as a guest."

"I don't mind. It's only for a few days." Cara hadn't told Langham how her relationship with Henry had changed. It was a secret she kept in her heart, waiting to be revealed when the time was right. "May I look at your painting?"

Langham did not generally like to show his work, though he'd at times made an exception for her. He nodded.

Cara came over to look at it. "It's lovely," she said, although the word did not really do it justice. "How well you've captured the place. Even the trees are influencing the mood of the painting. How did you get that effect with the shadows?"

"I'm glad you asked," Langham said proudly. He held out his palette. "See how I have the colors arranged? This is the first step."

They launched into a fascinating discussion that was cut off by Amelia proclaiming once again that she was hungry. They packed up and began the walk back to the house. Cara was dismayed to see that Amelia had splotches of mud on her clothes. Jeanne might not thank her for the extra work to clean it, but Cara thought it important that a child should be able to play and run freely.

They stopped at the dower house to put away their canvases and supplies. Amelia pointed toward the drive as they emerged from the studio.

"Look, a carriage is approaching!"

"That must be Mr. and Mrs. Myers," Cara said.

Langham squinted to get a better look. "That's odd. There are four people in the carriage. I can't imagine Mother went to the railway station."

As the open carriage reached the main house, it was easy to see it held two men seated opposite two women. Henry and the other man got out of the carriage, while one of the ladies leaned over and whispered something into the second—and much younger—lady's ear.

"It isn't the countess," Cara said, surprised at what she was seeing. The young woman stood, offering Henry a smile along with her hand for him to help her down. This was easily accomplished, as the lady's actions were smooth and graceful. She was pretty, too, dressed in a summer frock that was dazzling both in its rich pink color and the tasteful way it showed off her perfect figure. A cold feeling of dread began to creep into Cara's heart. "Do the Myerses have a daughter?"

"Mother didn't mention it." Langham's voice went hard as he added, "But then, she wouldn't." His fists clenched. "Henry must have known, though. He might have had the decency to say something to us."

"What—what do you mean?"

But Cara knew, even before Langham answered.

"Mother has found a match for Henry. Someone who undoubtedly has a nice fat dowry."

"No," Cara murmured, feeling as though the wind had been knocked out of her. "No."

"Miss Bernay, are you all right?" Amelia peered up at her with concern.

"I . . . just need water and a bit of rest," Cara stammered. "Why don't we use the back stairs? Then we won't risk disturbing the guests."

Unfortunately, avoiding them wasn't going to be possible. Lady Morestowe came out to the main steps to greet the Myerses, and spotting Cara and the others, she motioned for them to come over.

"Good," Langham murmured. "I plan to find out just what is going on."

He stalked across the lawn. Cara and Amelia hurried to keep up. As they reached the newcomers, Cara's embarrassment blossomed. She knew she looked dirty and disheveled, and so did Amelia. The contrast to Miss Myers was unmistakable. She was perfectly coiffed, and a lovely hat and delicate white lace gloves completed the ensemble. Her gown looked even more perfect up close than it had from a distance. Jealousy, that terrible sin, only fed Cara's mortification.

The countess made the introductions. She mentioned Cara only briefly and almost as an afterthought. She didn't even bother to say why Cara was there; the Myerses would make their own assumptions that she was the governess.

Mr. Myers was friendly in his greeting, shaking Langham's hand and giving a tip of his hat to Cara and Amelia. Langham's response was cool and perfunctory toward the guests, and he sent several glares in the direction of his brother and mother.

"So you are Lord Morestowe's little ward!" Mrs. Myers said cheerfully to Amelia. "Lady Morestowe has told me so much about you!"

"She did?" Amelia's eyebrows rose in surprise, then settled as she gave a suspicious frown. "What did she say?"

Mr. Myers laughed. "She said you're a precocious little girl! We can see she was correct."

"I apologize for our unkempt appearance," Cara said. "We've spent the afternoon down by the brook."

"Well, that sounds charming," Mrs. Myers burbled. "Lord Morestowe, perhaps you might give us a tour of your lovely property while we are here?"

"I'd be happy to," Henry replied, a stiff smile on his face.

He looked supremely uncomfortable, which Cara was glad to note. That was entirely as it should be, given the terrible situation he had put her in.

"You'll want to get Amelia inside and cleaned up," Lady Morestowe directed.

Thus dismissed, Cara nudged Amelia forward.

"Oh, Miss Bernay, there is one more thing before you go."

"Yes, your ladyship?" The humbleness with which she had to speak left a bitter taste in Cara's mouth. She sent an accusatory glare at Henry. She thought the look he gave in return was beseeching, but surely she was wrong about that. After all, she'd been wrong about everything else. So utterly wrong.

"Given that we are still renovating the east wing," the countess said, "our sleeping space is limited. Miss Myers will be staying in the yellow room on the third floor, just down the hall from you and Amelia. I trust that you will give her every consideration, especially remaining quiet in the mornings."

"Yes, ma'am."

She could tell Miss Myers wasn't any happier with this arrangement than Cara was. Not that the lady seemed happy about anything. She looked as though she'd been crying. But Cara wasn't going to spend any time feeling sorry for her.

She took hold of Amelia's hand and set off, anxious to get away from them all. Everyone else followed, although they remained in the front hall while Cara and Amelia took the stairs. She didn't know if Amelia comprehended the dark undercurrents of all that had just transpired, but she certainly must have felt them. She began to take the stairs with pounding thumps, just as she used to do in London.

"Amelia! Don't do that!" Cara scolded, more mortified than ever, knowing the guests would blame her for Amelia's bad behavior. In a lower voice, she begged, "Please stop, for my sake."

Hearing her desperation, Amelia relented and resumed a normal step.

Before they rounded the corner at the first landing, she could hear the countess telling the Myerses, "I'm afraid our ward has gotten a little out of hand these past few weeks. Miss Bernay is only a temporary governess. The real one will return to us at the end of September."

Never had Cara felt so thoroughly humiliated. She did not think she could ever forgive Henry for standing by and allowing it to happen. That seemed the worst betrayal of all.

"That was low, even for you, Mother." Langham paced the study in frustration. Henry's anger was just as intense. He stood stock-still, glaring at his mother while she sat calmly in a chair, presiding over this meeting like a queen.

Somehow, they'd been able to act as though everything was perfectly fine after Cara had taken Amelia upstairs. The countess had showed off the main area of the house to their guests and gotten them dispatched to their rooms to rest and prepare for dinner. It was a miracle that Langham had managed to control himself during this time. Even so, his stiff and acerbic manner, though aimed primarily at Henry and their mother, could not have gone unnoticed by their guests.

"I have already explained to Henry my reasons for what I did," their mother said archly and without a trace of apology. "All you need to know is that Miss Myers is a worthy marriage prospect—one we cannot dismiss lightly."

Langham turned on Henry. "Are you seriously thinking about marrying someone just for her money? I know you were devastated by losing Olivia, but I didn't think your heart had turned to stone."

"Langham, keep your voice down!" their mother admonished. "We don't want the entire household, from staff to guests, hearing this conversation."

"Yes, it would be terrible to reveal what grasping, coldhearted people we are."

"You don't know anything about it," Henry said. "The situation is complicated." He wanted to add that Langham had multiplied their troubles by his irresponsible behavior over the years, but what would be the point? That argument had never yet penetrated Langham's thick skin and hard head. "I do not agree with Mother's tactics, but now that we are in this situation, we must make the best of it." He didn't like the way his mother smiled in triumph at his words. "However, let me clarify that I do not intend to do anything merely for money. I will do my best to get acquainted with these people and discover what they want."

Langham's reply was a sneer. "I should think it's obvious what they want. A title for their American princess."

"And what's wrong with that?" the countess demanded. "Miss Myers would make a perfectly adequate wife and countess. She is lovely, well-educated, reasonably cultured—"

"And rich." Langham hit the point hard. They all knew it was the most important one.

"While they are here, I will extend them every hospitality," Henry told his mother between gritted teeth. "However, one thing I will *not* allow is your public treatment of Miss Bernay as a mere servant. She has agreed—very kindly, I might add—to remain out of the way during the Myerses' visit. But I will not have you shaming her, as you did today. It was unconscionable and mean."

"Well, hoorah for Henry's chivalry," Langham put in dryly. "Somewhat belated, don't you think?"

"I will do my best to make it up to her." Henry knew this sounded weak, but he couldn't say more in their mother's presence. If he could persuade Myers on the business deal, then something could be salvaged from this mess. If Henry was free financially, he would be able to marry Cara. He hadn't realized the depth of his feelings for her, not even after the kiss they had shared. It came to him, full-blown, as he'd seen Cara today, disheveled and with paint stains on her fingers. With her compassion and decency and tender heart, she would be so much more than "adequate" as a wife and countess. Refined social behavior and "cultured" speech were mere outward trappings that could be acquired later. The most important qualities were intangible, and Cara possessed them.

"If you don't want me to speak to Miss Bernay, then she had better keep out of the way," his mother snapped. "She can keep Amelia with her, too. There is no need to trot the child out before the Myerses again, now that they've met her. The last thing we need is her bad manners ruining everything." She stood. "Now, if you two are finished with your ranting, I am going to prepare for dinner. I expect both of you to be on your best behavior." She spoke as though Henry and Langham were children.

Langham looked ready to retort, but Henry took him by the arm and motioned for him to stay quiet. With one last reproving look at the both of them, the countess left the room.

"Henry, what has gotten into you?" Langham asked. "You can't tell me you are turning into our mother."

"Will you tell Cara that I didn't know about Miss Myers? Will you tell her I am sorry for what happened today?"

"You should tell her yourself."

"How in the world am I supposed to do that? I won't even see her. I certainly can't go knocking on her bedroom door. Even you must see the impropriety in that—not to mention that Miss Myers is staying on that floor. You'll see her, though, tomorrow at the dower house."

"Do you truly expect a secondhand message to have any effect?"

"Cara will understand. She . . . she knows me well enough by now." He looked away, embarrassed, not wanting to reveal more. Not yet. He could not risk jeopardizing this opportunity to secure their future. "Will you please be nice to these people at dinner? Will you do it not because Mother demands it but because I ask it? These next few days could make a big difference to us all."

Langham gave him a cold look before answering. "Fine. I won't like it, but I'll do it. I hope you know what you're doing."

"So do I," Henry answered with feeling.

Cara finished reading the note Jeanne had brought up to the nursery while she and Amelia were eating breakfast. She folded it and put it in her pocket. Amelia looked at her questioningly, even as she chewed her porridge.

Cara gave her a cheerful smile. "Her ladyship says we are not required to attend the adults at tea or any other events. She suggests that we spend most of the day at the dower house and its garden. Doesn't that sound nice?"

This was the kind of news Amelia would normally welcome, and yet now she frowned.

"Is something wrong?" Cara asked.

"It's my fault Countess is being mean to you. She was always mean to Miss Leahy, too."

It was hard to tell whether Amelia said this because she understood the true meaning of the note—that they were to stay far away from the others—or whether the mention of the countess had merely brought back the memory of their run-in with her yesterday. Cara might have bet on the former because Amelia was a perceptive child.

"It's not your fault. You've done nothing wrong. We shall enjoy these days on our own, yes? We can work on the practice tasks that Mr. Perrine set for us."

"And another riding lesson," Amelia said, brightening. She seemed to have lost all interest in her art lessons now that they had acquired Maisie.

"Perhaps. We'll ask Mr. Hart."

"Do you think Cousin Henry will come to the lesson?"

"I don't think so. He'll be busy with the guests."

Amelia nodded. "Countess said we were to be quiet, but it seems to me that Miss Myers is the one making all the noise."

"What do you mean?"

"I passed her door this morning, and I could hear her talking really loud to someone else. It must have been Mrs. Myers. They were arguing. *Very loudly,*" she added again, to prove her point.

"I hope you were not eavesdropping." Though in fact, Cara was very curious to know what they'd been arguing about.

Amelia shrugged. "I only heard a little. Something about her not behaving correctly. The usual things."

It was sad that Amelia always associated adults with harsh reprimands. As though there were no way to correct a child with love and kindness. It hurt Cara's heart, and it was one reason she had decided to stay and act as Amelia's governess despite the hard way she had been used yesterday. She might have expected such treatment from the countess, but it was unforgivable coming from Henry.

It was heartbreaking, too. Cara had spent the night in anguish, tossing over and again in her mind what she should do. She could not simply leave the house. Even if she had the ability to do so, she could not abandon Amelia to the countess. And so, although her heart ached, she was going to stay. Besides, as soon as she had an opportunity to confront Henry, that was exactly what she planned to do. It might be unrighteous pride, but she would not be treated like that, not even by an earl. Not even by a man she had thought she loved. Simply because she was no longer fooled did not mean she would walk away without speaking her mind.

But all these things would have to wait. There was nothing she could do today. She directed a smile at Amelia. "Have you finished eating? Let's gather our things and go over to the dower house."

"Can we go to the stables first and visit Maisie?"

Cara didn't bother to correct the child's grammar. Today was not a day for browbeating, but for finding peace and pleasure where they could. "Yes, that's an excellent idea."

CHAPTER

30

"THIS IS IMPRESSIVE," Myers said. He tapped the prospectus, which they had just finished reviewing together. "Did you really assemble this yourself?"

They had spent the two hours since breakfast in the study, discussing a variety of topics mostly centered around manufacturing. Myers had not been shy in detailing his rise from a poor messenger boy to a millionaire. He pointed out several times that it was accomplished not only through hard work, but by recognizing opportunities overlooked by less-diligent men, and then making the most of them. "I'm a good negotiator, too," Myers had said after sharing how he'd bought two rival companies and managed to merge them to everyone's satisfaction. "That is an indispensable quality for success."

Henry appreciated being able to spend time with such a successful man and gain valuable insight from him. He was gratified by the compliment about the prospectus, because he did not think Myers was the type of man to give false flattery, especially when it came to business. "I am the main author of it, although I received valuable input from Jacob Reese."

"Ah yes, the owner of the cast-iron business you told me about. They

277

are a big competitor to several American companies for the market in South America. Did you know that?"

"Yes, sir. Although I am a silent partner in the business, I am familiar with all aspects of the company and offer suggestions when I can."

"I wish I had someone like you working for me—or several, for that matter. I spoke with many gentlemen at that house party in Cowes, and none of them had a head for business like you do. Take for example the way your large landowners handle the farming rents. One viscount told me he relied on his estate agent and lawyers to keep up with those details. But I asked myself, who is keeping up with *them?* In America, you can't just allow the lawyers a free hand." He chuckled. "I'm guessing it's no different on this side of the Atlantic."

"You are correct on that point," Henry acknowledged with a smile. "I confess I'm surprised at how interested you are in the nuts and bolts of business over here."

"Well, I have a personal reason for it. There's a good likelihood my daughter will settle here one day." He paused, giving Henry a significant nod. It made Henry realize that while they had been talking, he had in fact been completing his first interview as prospective son-in-law. He supposed on some level he'd known that, but he hadn't wanted to dwell on it.

"If my daughter does settle here," Mr. Myers continued, "I think it likely I'll spend a bit of time here as well."

"But what about your business in Pennsylvania?"

"That's easily managed. I make good use of the transatlantic telegraph to keep up with pressing matters. Not to mention that one can get comfortably across the ocean now in just a few days." He rolled his cigar between his fingers. "What would our ancestors have thought of that, I wonder?"

"It does seem a miracle," Henry agreed. "I am glad to know your family is enjoying your stay in England."

"Oh yes. We find the welcome much more congenial here. In New York, Mrs. Astor would not give us the time of day. We are new money, you see. *Parvenus.*" He pronounced the word with a distinctly un-French accent: *parr-vee-nooz.* "Whereas over here, we just spent a week in the company of the Prince of Wales." He gave a self-satisfied chuckle. "As my wife remarked to me the other day, Mrs. Astor will be astounded when she reads that tidbit in the society columns."

"Since you plan on spending a lot of time in England, I hope you will seriously consider this investment opportunity." Henry pointed toward the prospectus.

Mr. Myers nodded thoughtfully. "I certainly will give it serious consideration. As I said, I admire your business acumen."

This seemed a major step in the right direction. "I'm happy to answer any further questions you might have—"

"I'm sure I'll have plenty," Mr. Myers said, cutting him off. "Let me think it over. For now, shouldn't we rejoin the ladies? It's nearly lunchtime, and I believe Lady Morestowe has some amusements planned for us in the afternoon. My wife and daughter are looking forward to getting to know you better. My daughter is lovely, don't you think? I've given her the finest education for ladies that money can buy. She charmed everyone in Cowes."

Henry's heart sank. A marriage match was still clearly the most important negotiation on the man's mind today. Henry wasn't yet willing to give up hope that he might be able to get somewhere with Myers without having to marry his daughter. However, he'd gone as far as he could for now. Sometimes negotiating involved biding one's time. Besides, he still wanted to find out how Miss Myers truly felt about things.

He stood up. "Yes, I'm looking forward to this afternoon as well."

If Henry had been told there were similarities between the Countess of Morestowe and Mrs. Myers, a woman raised in poverty in a coal town in West Virginia, he would never have believed it. Yet the two women were getting along famously. They spent luncheon gossiping about all that had happened at Lord and Lady Stafford's house party in Cowes. They covered plenty of other topics, too. Their primary point of agreement seemed to be that if a young lady was wealthy and beautiful, she was the perfect match for any aristocrat. As though these were the only variables that mattered in that equation.

Miss Myers seemed to have "recovered" from her "allergies." Her nose and eyes were no longer red, and she suffered no ill effects when they ate luncheon outside on the terrace. However, she still had a certain pallor to her cheeks and had indulged in a number of quiet sighs.

Mrs. Myers kept dragging her daughter into the conversation and prompting her to respond to questions and observations. Miss Myers complied, although Henry got the impression that her heart wasn't in it. Henry's mother likewise prodded Henry to join in, and he'd done his best to be a good host and keep the conversation light and genial.

Throughout it all, his thoughts kept returning to Cara. The terrace was located at the back of the house, with a view of the gardens and a stretch of lawn where a croquet game had been set up. The dower house wasn't visible from the terrace, since it was located on the opposite side of the main house, and Henry was glad of this. It would be difficult to keep any of his attention here if he could see what was going on over there. He hoped Langham had relayed his message to her. He prayed that she would understand.

Finally, when luncheon was over, the countess suggested that Henry and Miss Myers take a walk to inspect the setup of the croquet hoops. "Florence is an expert in croquet," Mr. Myers said proudly. "She is also very good at lawn tennis."

"I hope to learn to ride soon," Miss Myers added. "I understand that is quite the thing here in England."

This comment earned approving nods from both mothers. Henry wondered if Miss Myers had been coached to say this, but her enthusiasm seemed real.

"I understand you and Lady Morestowe are excellent riders," Mr. Myers said to Henry. "Perhaps we might visit your stables? I'd love to see them."

"Yes, certainly." Henry said this in an upbeat manner, although he dreaded the idea that Cara and Amelia might be there. He didn't want a repeat of yesterday's encounter between Cara and his mother.

He stood and moved to help Miss Myers from her chair. "Shall we go have a look at the croquet lawn?"

"Yes, you two go on. We'll join you shortly," said Henry's mother.

Henry noticed the significant looks she exchanged with Mr. and Mrs. Myers as he and Miss Myers left the terrace together.

"How are you enjoying your visit so far, Miss Myers?" Henry asked as they walked through the gardens on their way to the croquet lawn.

There was a slight pause before she answered. "It's lovely here."

It wasn't exactly an answer to his question. "I expect it is not as exciting as a large house party in Cowes. I suppose there were many yachts there, too?"

"Yes, there were!" she replied with the first true smile she'd displayed today. "We were invited to visit several of the larger ones for dinners or parties."

"It sounds exciting." In truth, Henry had gone to the annual regatta there last year and had not much enjoyed himself. But that might have been because he'd been bombarded by society matrons trying to bring their daughters to his notice. "I suppose you met a lot of interesting people at those parties?"

"I met so many people! All very kind, of course. One was a gentleman by the name of Mr. Wesley Carrington. Are you acquainted with him?"

Henry tried to dredge up the name from his memory. It seemed he had heard the name, but he couldn't place it. "I don't believe I've had the pleasure."

"Mr. Carrington is a banker in London. He is not nearly as rich as my father, but he has a home in one of the nicer parts of the city. Also, he has a wealthy uncle who never married, and he expects to be named heir to his uncle's fortune one day."

Henry began to think this line of conversation might lead someplace interesting. "It seems you became well acquainted with this gentleman."

"There was nothing untoward, I assure you!" She added guiltily, "I shouldn't even be speaking of him." She threw a glance backward, as though to ensure her parents had not snuck up on them.

Henry cleared his throat. "Miss Myers, perhaps we might speak plainly. It's clear your parents have come here because they thought that we—that is, that you and I—"

Miss Myers turned on him with eager eyes. "Have you ever been in love, Lord Morestowe?" Evidently she'd decided to throw all caution to the wind.

He swallowed. "Well . . . that is . . ."

"I know you want to marry me, and my parents have assured me this is best for me. You do seem like a nice gentleman. However, I feel I should be honest with you. My heart will always belong to someone else."

Henry stared at her in surprise. He was starting to like these Americans and their forthright way of communicating. "I see. You are speaking of this Mr. Carrington?"

"Yes!" Her eyes shone at the thought of her beloved.

Henry recognized the fervor of first love. It was something he remembered well. "I gather your parents object to him as a suitor?"

She nodded, sighing. "By the time he declared himself and I approached my parents about it, they had already arranged this visit. They insisted there was no going back. They said Mr. Carrington *might* get an inheritance one day, but you are already an earl." She placed a hand to her mouth in embarrassment. "Forgive me. That sounded grasping and rude. I do not mean to offend."

"Why are they so determined to marry you into the aristocracy? Your father is enormously successful. It seems your family has everything they could want."

"My maternal grandparents were Irish immigrants. They lived hand-to-mouth, barely eking out an existence. My grandmother was once in service to an Irish earl, and she fed my mother with stories of how grand it was. My mother decided one day she would be rich, just like them. But she didn't stop there. She wants me to marry an English lord. To her, that is the pinnacle of success."

"So that is *her* dream, not yours."

"That's not exactly true. I was so excited about this trip to England! It does seem so grand to be able to say one is a duchess or a countess! But that was before I met Wesley—I mean, Mr. Carrington."

"Believe me, I understand." Henry thought of the way his plans in life had been upended.

"I shouldn't have told you. My mother will punish me if she finds out." She looked at him with pleading eyes. "You won't tell her, will you?"

"The situation will require some tact on our part. Is that why you were crying yesterday?"

"Yes. My mother told me if I ruined things she would never forgive me." She began to wring her hands. "Oh dear, I *have* ruined everything. You will never marry me now. We will all go home in disgrace, and it will be entirely my fault!"

It would seem Miss Myers was a young lady whose emotions ran high. He would never have guessed that from her subdued appearance yesterday. Her parents must have been doing all they could to suppress this aspect of her nature. "Is your father as adamant about this scheme as your mother is?"

"He is now, I suppose," she answered despondently. "To be honest, I don't think he'd have ever thought of it were it not for my mother. Coming to England was her idea. But he supports it. And of course he wants me to marry well."

"Will you allow me to speak to your father?" Miss Myers's eyes widened, and Henry realized how that sounded. "I don't mean to ask for your hand." He found a strange irony in having to reassure a young lady of such a thing. "Perhaps I can find a way to feel him out and find a solution to our dilemma."

Everything had just gotten better *and* worse at the same time. He was risking a lot to turn away this opportunity. But he would be free to give his heart where he wanted.

Miss Myers took hold of his hands. "Oh, Lord Morestowe! You are so kind and understanding! How can I ever thank you?"

"Nothing is solved yet," he reminded her. "Let us say nothing of this to anyone. I will look for the right moment to speak to him."

CHAPTER

31

ACH TEAM STARTS at the stake at their end of the field," Amelia explained to Cara. "They hit their balls through those hoops, and the two teams pass each other as they work toward their opposite sides. Whenever you reach a hoop at the same time as someone from the other team, that's when things *really* get interesting."

"I see." Cara and Amelia were watching from Amelia's bedroom window as Henry and the Myers family played croquet.

It felt a bit like spying, and perhaps it was. But it hadn't been intentional. They had come back to the house so Amelia could change clothes for her riding lesson. After putting on her gymnastics costume, she had noticed the game.

"It's very fun to play," the child had informed Cara. Upon learning that Cara had never played croquet, Amelia insisted they spend a few minutes watching so she could explain the game.

"I wish we had been invited to play," Amelia said. "And Cousin Langham, too." She giggled. "He always cheats, but it's so funny when he does."

Cara was only half listening. She was focused on Henry and his interactions with Miss Florence Myers. It was clear they made up one team, while her parents comprised the other. The countess observed from a chair under a nearby awning.

Everyone seemed to be having a lovely time. Tears stung Cara's eyes as jealousy drowned out any sensible or honorable emotions. Were all her hopes about to be dashed because of this rich American girl?

Langham had told her about Henry's insistence that he did not know Miss Myers was coming. This had been the countess's doing. But if Lady Morestowe had gotten her way in this, might she not also prevail over Henry in the matter of marriage? Her opinion would hold enormous sway. Even Langham had gloomily admitted this could happen.

Miss Myers placed an expensively shod foot on her croquet ball, which was set against the ball her mother was using. With a swift *thwack* of her mallet, she sent the other ball flying to the edge of the playing field.

"Ooh, she dismissed her mother!" Amelia exclaimed. "That's what you call it when you hit someone's ball far off course. Maybe it would be fun to play with Miss Myers after all."

Everyone on the croquet lawn seemed to approve of this move. Even Mrs. Myers laughed with delight, despite being greatly set back. All offered a round of applause and smiles to Miss Myers. Including Henry. Cara's throat pinched, making it difficult to breathe. Miss Myers was beaming at Henry far too often and much too brightly. His answering smiles were warm and friendly. They did not necessarily indicate he was falling in love with her, but then, Henry was very good at hiding things.

Cara leaned against the window frame and closed her eyes, not wanting to see more.

"Are you all right, Miss Bernay?"

"Yes, fine." Cara offered Amelia a wobbly smile. "We'd better get going, if you want that riding lesson."

With this reminder, Amelia immediately forgot all about croquet. As she bounded down the steps, eager to get to the stables, Cara followed, wishing she could forget so easily what was happening on the back lawn.

Watching Amelia as she went through her paces on Maisie, Cara had mixed emotions. She kept recalling the elation she'd felt the last time they were here, when she'd been convinced she was going to marry Henry, be a mother to Amelia, and live at Morestowe forever. She had reveled in that kiss she had so wrongly mistaken for a promise.

Cara would have given almost anything not to have seen the looks and smiles passing between Henry and Miss Myers today. But she *had* seen them. And perhaps it was better to have her eyes opened than to remain a naïve fool. Miss Myers was rich, and she was pretty enough, especially with her exquisite wardrobe and a maid who styled her hair perfectly. She was clearly more suited to be a countess.

Cara, on the other hand, was going to be an excellent artist. She brought her mind back to the decision she'd made earlier today. She would take up her plans for her art more seriously, and as soon as possible. When Adrian and Georgiana returned from Blackpool, surely she could live with them again.

It would be hard to leave Amelia. And this wonderful place, which had already grown dear to her. And Henry—

She choked back a sob, raising a hand to cover it. But no one was watching. She willed herself to think only of the future and of her greatest strength: she was very good at starting over.

No sooner had she reminded herself of these things than she saw Henry, Miss Myers, and Mr. Myers approaching. Miss Myers had a delicate hand placed lightly on Henry's forearm. They stopped halfway around the ring from where Cara stood, and the Myerses' attention was immediately drawn to the horse and rider.

Henry, on the other hand, looked straight at Cara, almost as if he'd been searching for her. She fancied that her heart paused, held in check by the intensity of his gaze. What was he thinking?

The moment ended when Miss Myers tugged at Henry's arm and pointed toward Amelia. "Look how accomplished she is, and how well she is riding. And so young! Why, I am positively jealous!"

Gripping the fence to steady herself, Cara turned her attention back to the ring. Amelia had the pony in a brisk trot. As Miss Myers had noted, the girl was poised and confident.

Seeing Henry, Amelia called out a greeting. To her credit, she appeared to catch herself before she made the mistake of raising a hand, since she was supposed to keep them low and close to the saddle. She settled instead for a lift of her chin and quickly returned to the job of keeping the pony on course.

"Very good, Miss Amelia!" Mr. Hart called out, noting her self-correction. "Good afternoon, your lordship! We are having an excellent session today."

"Yes, I can see that," Henry answered. He looked pleased and proud of Amelia's progress.

"I'm sure one day you will ride as well as she does, my dear," Mr. Myers said to his daughter.

Her nose crinkled. "I hope I shan't have to dress like that. What odd clothes."

"She's wearing that while she is learning," Henry explained. "We'll have her fitted up with a proper riding habit soon."

"That's a fine-looking pony," Mr. Myers observed. "I don't ride myself, but I'm a good judge of horseflesh. I'm an excellent driver, too, if I may boast a little. I especially like those four-in-hand coaches. I suppose you have other horses at your stables as well?"

"Naturally. Would you care to look around?"

"I'd love to."

Henry sent another glance in Cara's direction, and this time, Mr. Myers noticed. "Good day to you, Miss Bernay!" he called out in his cheerful, robust manner. He waved for her to join them, and she had no choice but to comply. When she reached them, he said, "Do you enjoy watching these lessons?"

Miss Myers sent a disapproving frown toward her father. Did she think he shouldn't be talking to the governess?

Cara lifted her chin. "I am paying close attention in hopes of using the information in the future. I want to learn to ride someday."

She enjoyed seeing Miss Myers's look of incredulity. Cara had promised to play the part of a governess, but she saw no reason a governess couldn't harbor a desire to ride horses.

Mr. Myers didn't seem to find it outlandish at all. He merely said,

"A fine goal! Perhaps you two can watch the lesson together while Lord Morestowe and I inspect the stables."

Miss Myers looked taken aback by this suggestion. But then a look passed between her and Henry. When he gave her a tiny nod, Miss Myers seemed to understand.

She brightened and said, "Yes, that's an excellent suggestion!" Her admiring gaze lingered on Henry as he and her father walked toward the stable. "Lord Morestowe is very nice, isn't he? He seems just the epitome of an English lord. I believe he is a man of his word." She spoke dreamily. "But that's the way all English gentlemen are, I suppose."

Cara sensed a lot of meaning behind those sentiments. She told herself firmly that it didn't matter. They watched the lesson for several more minutes without speaking.

"I suppose her ladyship and Mrs. Myers did not wish to walk out to the stables on this hot afternoon?" Cara finally ventured.

"I beg your pardon?" Cara's words seemed to call Miss Myers out of her reverie. "Oh yes. My mother was worn out by the croquet match." This statement was accompanied by a sly smile. Cara remembered the way Miss Myers had sent her mother's croquet ball flying to the far end of the field. Perhaps she'd done it more than once. "Lady Morestowe offered to stay with her."

Mr. Hart had Amelia bring the pony down to a walk, and they came around to where Cara and Miss Myers stood.

"Where's Cousin Henry?" Amelia asked.

"He's gone with Mr. Myers to inspect the stables."

"They'll find 'em in good order," Mr. Hart said proudly. He tipped his hat to Miss Myers. "Do you ride, miss?"

"Not yet. I'm eager to learn, especially after seeing this young lady doing so well."

Mr. Hart gave a nod. "I've had a lot of experience teaching ladies to ride."

Cara caught the meaning behind his words. Mr. Hart would know the gossip no doubt being passed around by the rest of the staff: that Miss Myers was the prospective future mistress of this estate. Therefore, he would expect the duty of training her to ride to fall on him one day.

Maisie shifted and gave a little snort, as though impatient to be moving again. Amelia held the pony in check, speaking a few words in its ear.

"What is your pony's name?" asked Miss Myers.

"Her name is Maisie," Amelia answered readily, still warmed by the compliment Miss Myers had extended about her riding. "She's a handful, but she's cheeky, not naughty."

"Is she?" Miss Myers said with a laugh. "I think that sounds like the best kind of horse."

"It is, once they learn they must not throw you off."

Miss Myers's eyes widened in surprise. "How do you manage that?"

"They have to respect you, but not fear you. Here, I'll show you." With a click of her tongue, she set the pony in motion. Mr. Hart must have decided this was all right, because he raised no objection when she guided the horse around the ring. As she went, she described what she was doing, as if she were the one giving lessons. Both Mr. Hart and Miss Myers seemed to find this amusing.

Cara was proud of Amelia, but also envious at how well she and Miss Myers were getting along.

After a few minutes, Henry and Mr. Myers returned from the stables. Amelia immediately urged Maisie over to them. "I've been showing Miss Myers how to ride," she told Henry proudly.

"Shall we wrap up the lesson for today, your lordship?" Mr. Hart suggested.

Henry nodded, and even Amelia seemed ready to stop. She allowed Henry to help her off the horse. Cara loved seeing them together. She could see the bond between them getting stronger. It made her happy, even if the feeling was laced with sadness at the thought of leaving.

"Good-bye, Maisie! You behave for Mr. Hart!" Amelia said. Mr. Hart grinned as he led the pony away.

"Who's ready for tea?" Henry said.

"I am!" Amelia responded without hesitation.

"Shall we all go back to the house together?"

Cara could think of no reason to object. As they began walking, Amelia said to Miss Myers, "We saw you playing croquet today."

"Did you?"

Amelia nodded. "We could see you from my bedroom window."

Henry looked troubled at this, and Cara could imagine why.

"I saw your foot shot," Amelia continued, and the two of them walked on together, with Mr. Myers joining them.

Henry took Cara's arm to hold her back. "I want to tell you how sorry I am that I—that is, I had no idea that—"

"It's all right. Langham told me." Cara shrugged. "It's water under the bridge." Maybe she was as good an actress as her sister Rosalyn.

He seemed taken aback. Perhaps he was expecting anger or recrimination. "I'm going to London for a few days with the Myerses. When I return, I'll be bringing Miss Leahy with me. She has wrapped up her mother's affairs and will be resuming her post. Then—"

"Cousin Henry!" Amelia had turned and was beckoning for him to join her. It seemed her comfort with the newcomers only went so far.

Henry gave Cara an apologetic smile. "When I return, we'll have that talk. Remember?"

How could he even bring that up? That conversation was supposed to be about something else altogether. Not about how and why he was going to never see her again—which was what had to be coming. Cara nodded but averted her gaze. She was angry, yes, but so mortified at her own foolishness that she couldn't even look at him. Her steps remained slow as Henry hurried to catch up with the others. As they returned to the house, Cara continued to follow some distance behind. It seemed fitting.

CHAPTER

32

H ENRY SAT PATIENTLY while Myers considered the information Henry had just shared with him. He pretended to take an interest in the cigar he was holding, even though he was only smoking it as a gesture of goodwill after Myers offered it to him.

Myers did not look happy. Henry had expected this. By suggesting that Myers consider Carrington as a suitor for Florence, he was tacitly and politely declining to offer for her himself. This had clearly been a blow to the American's plans.

"I won't say I'm not disappointed," Myers said at last. "After meeting you and your family, I would have been pleased to see a connection forged between our two dynasties, as it were." He eyed Henry. "Are you sure there is nothing wrong with Florence—other than this pesky business about Carrington?"

"Sir, your daughter is lovely and charming. I find no fault in her at all."

"Except the fault of being too honest." Myers shook his head. "I suppose I have only myself to blame. She's my only child, and so clever and sharp-witted. I've always allowed her to speak her mind."

Henry was relieved Myers seemed to be taking this so well. "I was concerned you might think I was intentionally misleading you during your visit to my home. I would never do such a thing."

Myers took a moment to survey the room; they were in the lounge at Henry's club. "I understand why you asked to meet me here. When our women learn what we've discussed today, there will be all kinds of emotional outpourings—positive and negative."

"Yes, that was my thought as well."

"I think they all three had particular goals they were determined to pursue, no matter what." Myers leaned back in his chair. "I was happy to go along with my wife's desire that Florence marry an English lord, especially as it seemed to be Florence's dream as well. We took this trip to England with high expectations, but things did not turn out exactly as we planned. I'm not such a tyrant as to force my daughter into a marriage she does not want. However, the corollary is that I will do anything to get her into a marriage of which I approve."

Henry nodded. "I understand."

"You laid out very kind reasons why you're not going to pursue this match. You've been generous in your compliments toward Florence and our family. I can't help but think there is an element of self-sacrifice in it. Many men would not hesitate at the chance to marry a young lady with such an appealing dowry."

"I would like to think I have higher principles than that. However, I will admit I had hopes we might nonetheless strike another kind of deal—one that has nothing to do with marriage." He held his breath while Myers considered this.

After a moment, the American shook his head. "I'm sorry to disappoint you, Lord Morestowe. I think for now it's best if we go our separate ways. I wish you all the best, and I have no doubt you will be successful with your mining enterprise."

"I understand." It was disappointing but expected.

Myers rose to his feet. "I suppose I had better get back to the hotel and face the onslaught that will follow when I tell them about this conversation."

Henry wasn't looking forward to telling his mother, either. She would be livid. But it wouldn't be the first of her storms that Henry had weathered.

"It will be hard on my wife, as she had her heart set on this," Myers said as they walked toward the door. "But if this Wesley Carrington proves to be suitable, perhaps she'll be mollified in the end. I'll check into his background right away. If I find any evidence he's nothing but a fortune hunter, he'll get nowhere near Florence. I may be softhearted when it comes to my daughter, but I didn't get where I am today by giving away the store."

Henry could believe this. "I put out a few inquiries. From what I've learned, Mr. Carrington is telling the truth about his current circumstances and the prospect of an inheritance when his uncle dies. In addition, he seems to be solidly in the circle of His Royal Highness's good friends. If your daughter marries Mr. Carrington, she'll have greater entrée to the royal family than I could give her."

Myers looked pleased. "I'll keep that in mind when I try to win my wife over to the idea." As they paused to shake hands before parting, he said, "There's just one more thing I'd like to ask you. It's mere shameless curiosity on my part, and you don't have to answer."

"I'd be happy to, if I can."

"By the time you met Florence, she'd already given her heart to this Carrington fellow. Whether that was a foolish mistake remains to be seen. Throughout our conversation, you never gave any hint that you might have your eye on someone else. Even so, I can't help but wonder if that was a factor in your decision."

"You are very perceptive, Mr. Myers."

"It wouldn't happen to be your governess, would it?"

Henry stared at him in admiring surprise. "Was it that obvious?"

"I may be perceptive, but I'm no mind reader," Myers replied. "In my factories, I always pay attention to what the men on the floor are saying. The same principle can be applied to these big country houses. My valet overheard a comment in the servants' hall—that Miss Bernay had been dining at your table in the evenings, and in every other way being treated as a guest—until we arrived. I'm sorry she was demoted on our account. I hope you'll do something to make it up to her."

Henry could think of a thousand ways he would like to do that. "That's kind of you to say."

"What's her background? I assume she has no money or position."

"Miss Bernay is . . . a friend of the family, you might say. However, we were not lying that a reason for her being there was to help with Amelia. She has a lot of experience working with children. She was raised in an orphanage."

"An orphanage! Well, well." Myers looked impressed. "Yet you obviously feel she has the potential to rise to better things. I hate to be a braggart about my native country, but that does seem more of an American point of view than an English one." He accompanied this remark with a little grunt. "Except in New York. Those people seem overly interested in people's pedigrees. But I believe that will change in time."

"I feel the same way about English society."

"As you are aware, my wife and I both had hardscrabble childhoods. She didn't marry me for my money or social position. No, sir. We didn't have a dollar between us. My Maybelle and I married for love, and we're still happy today, despite one or two differing opinions." He chuckled. "Or maybe three."

Henry smiled.

Myers reached out again to shake his hand. "I wish you all the best, sir."

"And to you."

As Henry watched the American stroll off down the street, he felt troubled. He was sure he'd made the right decision, but that didn't make the road ahead any easier.

Henry returned to his club. He sat in the lounge, brooding over what steps he should take next. The path seemed to be clearing, yet many obstacles remained.

To marry a woman with no dowry was folly for a man in his position. Not only was someone of his social standing entitled to a wealthy and well-connected bride, but the financial burdens he carried made it seem imperative. And yet hadn't he been determined to succeed on his own? It was too soon to give up on the idea of making the mine work.

Also, there was no reason crops might not be better in the coming years. The future was, as it had always been, in God's hands. He would keep working, and he would keep praying for help and guidance.

Then there was the question of his mother. This was both a hard and an easy problem to tackle. She might attempt to make his life miserable if he married Cara, but she could not stop the marriage from happening.

Perhaps the thorniest issue was how little he knew about Cara's background. He had no doubt that she was a good person, and yet he could not afford to risk his reputation if it were discovered that her family had skeletons in their closet. As the Earl of Morestowe, he had responsibilities he could not shirk, no matter how much he might want to.

Henry mulled over what he knew of Cara based on their previous conversations. There was that mad story of her hiding from the police in a giant washing kettle. That alone ought to be a warning. It had the potential to make a laughingstock of him and the family name. But would it? Cara had made it clear that both she and her sister were absolved of any wrongdoing.

As he considered this, another detail of the story came to mind. Cara had said the barrister, Michael Stephenson, was now her brother-in-law. Henry knew who this man was. The widely publicized lawsuit that Stephenson had won for the Earl of Westbridge had made his name well-known among the peerage.

Henry rose from his chair and walked to the other end of the club's lounge, which had paper and pens available for its members' use. There were many things Henry didn't know about the future, but this was one thing he could do. He would see about arranging a meeting with Stephenson.

"She really does have a flair for this, doesn't she?" Langham said, joining Cara as she watched Amelia's latest riding lesson.

By now Amelia had graduated to a larger ring and was riding fully on her own. Mr. Hart was still there, giving instructions, but these were finer, more subtle corrections to her posture and movements. One side of the ring had a set of raised benches covered with an awning, providing a place where Cara could sit comfortably while watching. She had brought her sketch pad and was doing her best to capture horse and rider.

This was the first lesson since the Myerses had come to the stables three days ago. Cara had spent most of her waking hours since then at the dower house, launching wholeheartedly into her painting. That had been easy yesterday, when the Myerses were still here and Amelia had been invited to join them in a croquet match. She and Henry had won against Mr. Myers and his daughter. Amelia had related all the details to Cara later. In any other circumstances, Cara would have counted it an achievement that the girl had spent a congenial afternoon with the adults. Instead, she had found it painful, like a harbinger of the separation that was to come, even though she knew it was wrong to feel that way.

Shaking off those thoughts, Cara brought her attention back to Langham. "Are you feeling better?"

"Right as rain. Your prescription once more did the trick."

Yesterday Langham had stayed in his room, complaining once more of a headache. Cara thought his recovery might actually have something to do with his relief at the Americans being gone. She suspected he might ordinarily have enjoyed such gregarious people, but he still held a grudge toward his mother for the underhanded way she'd brought Miss Myers into their midst.

Cara had watched from an upper window yesterday as Henry and the Myerses had boarded the carriage for the railway station. She had seen with painful clarity the pleased smiles on everyone's faces— especially the ladies. It was easy to imagine what was happening in London. Henry would be concluding his deals with Mr. Myers. Would one of those be a marriage contract? Remembering what Henry had said about wanting to speak with her when he returned, her heart had filled with trepidation. The dreamlike wonder and excitement of those beautiful moments in the dower house had mostly vanished in the glare of the days that had followed.

"Well, that's impressive!" Langham said as Amelia confidently took the pony over a low hurdle. "I wouldn't expect anything less, though. Not if she is Henry's daughter. Both he and Mother are excellent riders."

"You are not?" Cara asked.

He shook his head. "I prefer driving—and much too fast, according to my mother and brother." He grinned. "But that's what makes it exciting and therefore worth doing."

"Are you taking a day off from painting?" she asked, since he wore a nice suit instead of the paint-splotched clothing and boots that were his usual working attire.

"That's right. As the old saying goes, 'All work and no play makes Jack a dull boy.' Besides, we have a guest coming today. Nigel is always great company."

"Do you mean Lord Nigel Hayward?"

"That's right. He sent a note proposing to visit, so I wrote back and said by all means come over. Even though Henry is gone, I saw no reason he shouldn't come, and Mother agrees. I might even do Henry a favor and pester Nigel some more about that mining deal. Nigel likes me. Besides, Mother and I are both anxious to meet his fiancée. She's coming with him."

Cara gasped. Her mind instantly went a thousand places as she tried to decide what to do.

Langham saw her dismay. "Don't worry, you shan't have to play the role of governess. I'm sure that's what my mother would like, but we're done with that. I fully intend to introduce you to Nigel and Sarah—although I suppose for today I ought to call her Miss Needenham, even though I detest being so stuffy and formal—as our family friend."

"No!" Cara blurted, panic rising. "I mean, that won't be necessary. Perhaps I'll just stay away anyway. To, ah, make things easier. I'm sure her ladyship would prefer it, and, really, I have no objection."

Her words came out so stilted that Langham tilted his head and looked at her in surprise. "Don't tell me you're afraid of my mother. I'll lose all respect for you if that is the case."

"Of course not. It's just that, well, I do think things will go better for everyone if I were absent."

No sooner had she spoken than they heard the sound of a carriage approaching.

"It's too late now," Langham observed. "Here they are."

The carriage did indeed hold Miss Sarah Needenham, her aunt, and Lord Nigel. The countess made the fourth person in the carriage, which showed they must have spent time at the house before coming to the stables.

Langham hurried over to them, calling out his greetings before the carriage wheels had even stopped. Cara, desperately wishing she was anywhere but here, brought a handkerchief to her nose, though it would only buy her a few seconds of anonymity. Caught between the urge to flee and the desire not to draw attention to herself, she decided to remain seated. She even hunched down a little in the vain hope they might forget she was there. Meanwhile, out in the ring, Amelia was so busy conquering the low jumps Mr. Hart had set up for her that she didn't notice what was going on beyond it.

Lord Nigel's attention went immediately to the pony and rider even as he and Langham helped the ladies out of the carriage. He grinned in appreciation. "I had no idea Maisie was capable of such things! My little cousin did not take her through such excellent paces."

He and the others spent another minute watching Amelia and exclaiming over how well she was doing. Cara could feel sweat trickling down her neck as she waited for the inevitable.

Sure enough, Langham finally said to them, "Allow me to introduce you to a family friend."

He turned and motioned for Cara to join them. Reluctantly, she got up from the bench. She could feel her legs shaking as she walked. She watched Sarah Needenham's face, waiting for the recognition to set in. She hoped that when it did, Sarah might have some compassion, since the two of them had gotten along well and had not seen each other since before the incident with Robbie.

Miss Needenham blinked several times in bewilderment and disbelief. Her expression became an angry stare when Langham said, "This is Miss Cara Bernay. She's visiting us for a few weeks."

"Our normal governess was called away by a death in the family," the countess added, clearly wanting to keep that pretense going with these new guests.

"You can't tell me *you* are acting as a governess!" Sarah's words shot out fast and hard, startling everyone so much that they practically jumped.

Cara took a deep breath. She kept her hands flat against her sides so that no one could see them shaking. "As Mr. Burke has noted, I am here as a friend."

"Do you two know each other?" Lord Nigel asked his fiancée.

Sarah pointed an accusing finger at Cara. "This is the woman who nearly killed my brother!"

CHAPTER

33

I KNEW SHE WAS TROUBLE the moment I laid eyes on her." The countess was so livid that her face was red.

Lord Nigel and the others had gone, their visit cut short by Sarah's accusations and the ugly scene that had followed. But that had been nothing compared to what Cara was facing now that she and Langham were alone with the countess.

They were in the parlor, but Lady Morestowe refused to sit down. She preferred to berate her son while standing and using furious gestures to punctuate her words. "This is why you can't just bring people you barely know into your house. Why, she might have killed us all!"

"What happened at the Needenhams' was an accident! That has been clearly explained." Knowing that Langham generally hated unpleasant altercations, Cara was grateful that in this instance he did not hesitate to answer his mother with the same fierce intensity she was leveling at him. "Cara is not a murderer. You should be ashamed even to imply it."

"*I* should be ashamed?" Lady Morestowe repeated. She pointed a finger at Cara. "You are the one who should be ashamed. Hiding your past, and worse—taking on the responsibility of looking after a child when you know you are a danger to children."

Cara stood speechless, engulfed in guilt. The countess's attacks, while vicious and exaggerated, were also true.

"Is there no way to be forgiven for past mistakes?" Langham challenged.

"No," the countess answered without hesitation. "Some mistakes leave an indelible mark. You heard what Miss Needenham said about her mother. She is still devastated even though the child didn't die. She might never recover from it."

This was one accusation from Sarah that had surprised Cara. On the day she'd left the Needenhams', Lady Needenham seemed worn out and subdued, but not devastated. Had Sarah been overstating the case?

Cara decided there was at least one defense she could give. "With all due respect, your ladyship, I made it clear to his lordship and to Mr. Burke that I was never to be considered a governess. Furthermore, I was never with Amelia anywhere that was not in the immediate vicinity of another adult. I was determined that an accident such as occurred with Master Needenham would never happen again."

"You see that, Mother?" Langham said. "She has atoned. She acted with great caution and care. You were the one who insisted she play the part of governess—*and* treated her as such. She never asked for it nor wanted it."

"I will not be lectured in my own house." The countess advanced on Cara. "You will pack your things and leave immediately."

Langham stepped between them. "You will not dismiss her as though she's a mere servant. She's my guest, and she will stay."

Lady Morestowe drew up, looking surprised at her son's impertinence. "You are not the master of this house, Langham."

"No," he replied forcibly, "*Henry* is." He paused to let that sink in while the countess glowered at him. "Therefore, things will stay as they are until he returns and says differently. You don't love Amelia anyway. You don't even like her. What do you care if that little girl lives or dies?"

Cara's mouth fell open in shock. She could only thank God that Amelia was not in the house so she could not overhear anything. Mr.

Hart had been perceptive enough to see the terrible altercation beginning and had taken Amelia to the stables to keep her occupied with looking after Maisie.

Langham's words, brutal and ugly, had stopped his mother cold. She was visibly shaken. Cara had a vision of that painting of the little girl who'd been lost so long ago. Was Lady Morestowe thinking of her, too? Cara saw her deep intake of breath as she struggled to keep her composure. "That was cruel, Langham. It was unworthy of you as a gentleman and my son."

Langham said, more gently, "Mother, please listen to reason. There was no harm done. You cannot deny how much better Amelia has been over the past few weeks. Cara has been a good influence on her. You've seen the results yourself. Why can you not focus on that, instead of one past mistake?"

Cara thought—hoped and prayed—the lady was softening.

She rallied though, her anger returning. "What about the harm done today? She embarrassed us in front of our most eminent neighbor. His father, the Marquess of Dartford, already holds a grudge against Henry, which has damaged his political and social life. Do you realize what greater fodder this will give him? You can be assured Lord Nigel will tell him everything. This entire mess will be a major blow to Henry's reputation and standing."

Cara bowed her head in shame. Despite her best intentions, her actions kept bringing harm to others. Even to a man she loved.

"I am willing to wait until Henry returns," the countess added. "He'll be only too glad to remove this woman from our home. Fortunately, his marriage contract with Miss Myers should be settled before word of today's events has time to spread."

"You can't tell me he's serious about Miss Myers!" Langham exclaimed.

A satisfied smile returned to his mother's face. "Why else do you think he accompanied them to London?"

"He said he planned to meet Miss Leahy and bring her back."

She smirked. "As though the governess were not capable of taking a train on her own."

It was difficult to argue with that.

Seeing that she'd regained the upper hand, the countess said, "Until Henry returns, I insist that Miss Bernay not have any oversight of Amelia."

"Fine," Langham answered tersely. "Amelia can spend her days with me."

He looked poised to fight, expecting his mother to resist. Instead, she nodded. "It wouldn't hurt for you to take on more responsibilities with the girl. In fact, I think it's an excellent idea."

"You do?" Langham looked as puzzled as Cara at this pronouncement.

"You may both go now," the countess informed them.

Cara left the room in a daze. One thing was clear: the Countess of Morestowe still held the real power in this family, and she wasn't about to let anyone get in her way.

"I'm sorry about all this," Langham told her as he accompanied her up the stairs. "I don't know what is going on with Henry, but let me exhort you not to take everything my mother says at face value."

Cara's shoulders drooped as she walked. "There was truth to what she said, though. I'm sorry to have brought such embarrassment to your family."

"Such balderdash. Mother worries too much about this idea of a spotless reputation. Henry is the one who extended the invitation for you to come here, even if I first suggested it. He knew the circumstances were unusual, but he did it anyway."

Cara shook her head. "But Henry didn't know about the Needen-hams. When he learns what happened today—"

"Just have patience. He'll return in a few days, and then we can sort out everything. I know he's a slave to duty and all that, but I still can't imagine him marrying Miss Myers."

"Why not?"

"He doesn't look at her the same way he looks at you."

That simple statement took Cara's breath away. She paused on the stairs, feeling her cheeks grow pink.

Langham gave her a knowing nod. "I've been convinced for a while now that you and Henry would make a fine match. No one has brought him out of his shell like you have."

"You are an incorrigible romantic, aren't you?" She echoed Langham's words to her on the day she'd spoken to him about Louise. She couldn't quite manage the cheerful tone, though. She sighed. "There was a time when I thought Henry cared for me. But if he hasn't already changed his mind, he soon will. And in any case, there's Miss Myers—"

"Don't give up the ship!" Langham interjected. "I've been watching the post closely these days. What with Louise and I sending our letters by way of Georgiana, and her being in Blackpool, our private postal network is spotty. But I expect to hear from her any day now. If we can get confirmation that Everson is interested in funding the mine, perhaps Henry won't feel compelled to marry Florence. Then our problems will be solved!"

It was something Cara would love to believe. But she knew Langham was oversimplifying the issue. Even if all those other things worked out, there was still the countess.

Furthermore, the social obstacles were real and could not be ignored. Cara had been wrong to think they could be so easily overcome. She thought back to that afternoon at the creek when she'd been dreaming of a life with Henry. At one point she'd even envisioned that she and Sarah Needenham would become friends. They'd be neighbors, after all, and married to men of high station. But today, Sarah's disdain for her had been plain. Cara sensed it was due not only to what had happened with Robbie, but to class differences between them that could never be bridged.

As she and Langham continued up the stairs, they passed portrait after portrait of the blue-blooded men and women who made up the Burke family tree. The faces staring at her from those frames seemed determined to remind her that she didn't belong here.

Perhaps they were right.

They made it through nearly the whole of the next day before Amelia caught on to what was happening.

Cara remained in her room all morning. She heard the child trip gaily down the hallway after breakfast, heading outside. No doubt she thought Cara would already be in the studio, as she often was. Jeanne had instructions to stay with her, either at the studio, the dower house garden, or the stables, until Langham arrived at the studio later that morning. Even though the countess had not expressly forbidden Cara to interact with Amelia, Cara thought it better to begin the weaning process now in the hope that it would make their separation easier when the time came.

After eating a light luncheon brought up to her room by a maid, Cara collected her sketchbook and pencils and went out to the garden behind the main house. She was restless, needing fresh air and sunshine. She also did not want to be in the house if Amelia was brought back to change clothes for a riding lesson.

Irresistibly she gravitated toward the bench where she and Henry had sat together. Memories flooded her mind: the child playing among the flowers; the warm, fragrant breeze; and most especially, how she'd been able to help Henry through his anger, and the door it had opened between their two hearts.

She would never understand why everything that had seemed a true gift from God would soon most certainly be gone. Wiping away a tear, Cara turned in her sketchbook to the drawing she had begun that day of Amelia chasing butterflies. She had never completed it. She decided to do so now, especially as the memory lived vibrant and clear in her mind's eye.

The afternoon advanced. Cara remained in the garden, but her thoughts were on Amelia and Henry. She prayed for the whole family—even the countess. It was the only way she could think of to atone. At last, a gnawing in her stomach told her it must be time for tea.

She pulled out her watch to check the hour. Looking down at it, she knew what else she must do when she returned to London. It was time to go to her sisters and sort out their differences. Her desire to be reunited with Julia and Rosalyn was so strong that everything else paled in comparison.

Cara heard the crunch of steps on gravel. She turned to see Langham approaching. He looked haggard, but he managed a smile as he reached the bench and sat beside her. "Have you spent the day out here?"

"Most of it. How is Amelia?"

"Things were going well enough until we returned to the house for tea. That was when she noticed you weren't in your room. We'd told her you were not feeling well today, so there was a bit of a row when she realized you had deliberately spent the day away from her. She was offended as well as confused. Especially when we couldn't tell her why you had done it."

"Oh dear. Perhaps I should go in—"

Langham put out a hand to stop her. "Between Jeanne and my mother, they have her in hand. There is something I'd like to discuss with you first, if you don't mind."

His tired expression showed there was more on his mind than Amelia's tantrum. "Of course. What is it?"

"Last night I couldn't sleep. Everything about this situation bothered me. I was angry at my mother, angry at Henry. It seemed to me they were worried about all the wrong things and ignoring the things that were truly important. Amelia's welfare, for instance."

Cara nodded. "I've spent hours mulling over that same thing."

"I thought it was high time we cleared the air about who Amelia is and where she came from. If Henry plans to marry someone, don't you think that person deserves to know the truth about his ward?"

"Yes," Cara answered with feeling. "But how can that happen? Henry refuses to discuss it."

"I know," Langham said with a grimace. "So I decided I would find out for myself. Last night while everyone was asleep, I went to the study to look through Henry's papers. I know where he keeps the key to the cabinet that holds his private correspondence. At the back of a drawer, I found the answer to my question. I've spent every hour since then wondering if I ought to regret it."

"Why?" Cara asked, startled. "What did you find?"

Langham glanced around, though Cara doubted anyone could approach without their knowing. "I found a stack of letters from a woman who is clearly Amelia's mother, and who is clearly still alive."

Cara drew in a breath. "Is it Olivia?"

"No. Her name is Delia. She is not someone Henry knew. She is someone *I* knew."

His words were heavy. He looked at the ground, shuffling a toe in the gravel and shaking his head.

"Are you saying Amelia is *your* daughter?" Cara was so shocked at the idea she could barely say the words. "How could you not know—or even suspect?"

She asked as kindly as she could, but Langham spit out his answer as though it was an accusation. "I don't know! It doesn't make any sense! I mean, it does, but it doesn't!"

"Perhaps if you told me what you know, that would help sort out your thoughts," Cara said gently.

He took a slow breath, as though trying to calm himself. "You're right. Well, one summer, when I was sixteen, which was about eight years ago—no surprise, considering Amelia's age—I had a habit of walking to the Boar's Head Inn. That's a tavern in the village. I'd go there once or twice a week, whenever I could sneak away. I found the company there more congenial than at my house."

Given what Cara had seen of the Burke family, she could easily believe this. She nodded, waiting for Langham to continue.

"Delia worked at the tavern. She was a few years older than me, the daughter of a farmer, although she lived in a room above the tavern. We became friendly. I would stay late, and sometimes when her work was done, she and I would sit on the grass by the narrow river that runs through town. We'd look up at the stars, talking." He shrugged. "And drinking." Another pause. "And—" He gave Cara a sideways glance. "Well, other things. Although we never went so far as—that is, I don't think we did."

Cara's eyes widened in surprise.

He held up his hands. "I know what you're thinking—how could I not know? Well, one night toward the end of summer, I purloined enough money from my father's purse to buy a very nice bottle of brandy. Delia and I drank the entire thing, and we had a jolly good time doing it. We passed out cold at some point. We were discovered under the bridge at daybreak by my father, who'd gone out searching for me. You can imagine how angry he was. He dragged me home and kept me under lock and key until I was sent off to school three days later."

"Did you have any contact with her after that?"

"No. And here's the thing—I could swear in a court of law that nothing happened, and yet there seems to be proof to the contrary." He pulled a piece of paper from his pocket. "Here's one of the many letters I found. It's the most recent, dated not even a month ago. It appears she owns a millinery shop, but it isn't doing well."

He handed the letter to Cara, staring at the ground while she read it. It was addressed to Henry and signed by Delia Stover. Its purpose was to request money. One paragraph in particular tugged at Cara's heart.

> *I have kept my word and not spoken of this to anyone. Nor have I asked to see my dear girl, though being apart from her these years has been a sore trial and has broken my heart a dozen times over. Won't you consider all that I have given up for her sake and find charity in your soul to give me a little more help? More than once I have been asked how I came to be in such straightened circumstances, and it is hard work to keep telling those lies. I fear that if things go on like this, one day I might accidentally let slip the truth—and that would be a terrible misfortune for everyone.*

Cara refolded the letter and handed it back to Langham. "You don't think it's possible that somehow Delia and Henry . . . ?"

He shook his head. "Henry was off hiking in Wales and later falling in love with Jacob's sister." He slapped the letter against his hand. "All this time, Henry has believed I fathered Amelia, and he never told me! I'd wager my mother knows, too."

"Why wouldn't they have told you?"

"I don't know. But I've got to get to the bottom of it. I've spent most of the day with Amelia, looking at her in a new light, as you might imagine, trying to see if there are any similarities." He shook his head. "Her dark hair and hazel eyes aren't like anyone in our family. Delia had dark hair but blue eyes." He shook his head again. "You can see why I find this so confusing."

"Well, Amelia likes bad jokes," Cara offered. "And don't forget her fascination with drawing and painting."

"But she's not very good at it, is she? I know she's only seven, but I worked with her today and I can't see any great talent there, waiting to be developed. Mr. Perrine mentioned the same thing to me privately, although he naturally gives her encouragement and praise. I do like Amelia, though. More than I'd realized." He looked earnestly at Cara. "If Amelia is my daughter, I want to set things right. I want to do what's best for her. It's incredibly sobering."

"Will you wait until Henry comes home and then confront him and her ladyship at the same time?"

"No." He stood, shoving the letter into his pocket. "I can't risk that they will tell me more lies."

"But how can they, when you've seen the letters?"

"They'd find a way. I've got to find Delia and talk to her myself. I'm going tomorrow."

"Tomorrow?" Cara repeated, rising from the bench. "Why so soon?"

"I've got to do it before Henry comes back." He grasped her arms. "Listen, Cara. This is so important. I've done plenty of things in my life that were not exactly laudable. Henry has accused me of being a master at shirking responsibility, and perhaps I have been. I'm certainly no saint. But I'll tell you this: I couldn't live with myself if I thought a child of mine was growing up thinking she had no parents."

This was exactly the sentiment Cara had tried to draw out of Henry. She understood now why she hadn't been able to do it. "That *is* laudable, Langham, no matter what else you may have done."

He gave her a tiny smile of thanks. "I'm taking the early train, and I'm taking Amelia with me. And you, too. I can't take care of her by myself."

"But, Langham!"

"You saw from the letter how much Delia pines after Amelia. Don't you think she'd want to see her again?"

"But then what?"

"I don't know. We'll figure it out. But I can't leave you both here at the mercy of my mother."

That certainly was not a pleasant prospect, but still Cara wavered.

"Please say you'll go. I'm desperate for answers. I've been running this over and over in my head since I found those letters. I can't wait another day."

Cara's head was still spinning. "I don't know. . . ."

"I asked Mother yesterday if there was never any forgiveness. I see now why she answered the way she did. She said that some things can't be recovered from. But I believe she's wrong. She and Henry have been holding this over my head, and I didn't even know it. Surely you understand my need to set things right?"

He stared at her beseechingly, not letting go until she finally gave a nod.

"God bless you," he said fervently, giving her an impulsive hug.

Cara felt shaky, almost light-headed. Was she doing the right thing? She didn't know, but neither could she refuse Langham's request. "I'll talk to Amelia tonight," she said as Langham released his hold. "What should I tell her?"

CHAPTER

34

CARA WAITED until Jeanne had gotten Amelia to bed. Once the maid had gone downstairs, Cara went to Amelia's room and eased the door open a few inches.

The room was quiet. In fact, everything about the evening had seemed unnaturally quiet. According to the maid who'd brought dinner to Cara's room, Amelia was no longer rebelling against orders. Instead, she was acting with stoic calmness. "It didn't seem natural for her," the maid had confessed. Cara was concerned about this change in Amelia's behavior. Perhaps she was beginning to accept abandonment as a matter of course.

As Cara stood there, she heard the child begin to sing to herself. It was the lullaby Cara had overheard in the garden. It hadn't occurred to her before, but perhaps Amelia sang this to herself every night. Cara remembered her own mother used to sing her to sleep. After her mother had gone and they moved to the orphanage, Rosalyn had performed that role. It hadn't been the same, but it had been comforting nonetheless.

Perhaps this trip to Galway Hill, where Delia's millinery shop was located, was a good idea after all. If this woman was Amelia's mother, surely there could be some way to make things better for the child.

Cara still worried, though. There had to be a reason Henry had kept this a secret. She hoped it only had to do with the family reputation, and not with the mother herself. Tomorrow she would find out. As Langham had pointed out, learning the truth could be painful, but surely it was better than being kept in ignorance. Cara had been learning this hard lesson ever since she'd left the Needenhams.

She entered the room and closed the door behind her.

Amelia's singing abruptly stopped. "Who's there?"

"It's Miss Bernay."

Amelia sat up. "Where were you today?" The question was filled with anger and accusation. Cara didn't blame her.

She lit the lamp on the bedside table, setting it to a dim, soft glow. "I'm sorry I couldn't be with you today," she said as she seated herself on the edge of Amelia's bed. "I had some things to take care of. It came up rather suddenly, and I didn't have time to tell you. But I've been planning an adventure for us."

"What kind of adventure?" Amelia still sounded suspicious, but there was a hint of excitement, too.

"We're going on a train ride tomorrow."

"The train? Where to?"

"It's a surprise."

"Is it to the seaside?" Amelia persisted, squirming with pleasure at the idea.

"Perhaps that will happen another time." Cara chose her words carefully, aware this would probably be her last outing with the girl. "We will have to get up very early. I'll come wake you and help you dress. We'll have to be very quiet, because her ladyship might still be sleeping, and we don't want to disturb her."

Amelia nodded. She understood this meant the countess wasn't coming, and a ghost of a smile showed her happiness about that. "Is Cousin Henry coming with us?"

She asked with such hopefulness that it hurt Cara's heart. The child had really become attached to him. If Langham was her father, it might take some work to move her affections in his direction. However, what Cara had seen of Langham today told her he was willing to do whatever was needed to make that happen.

"Tomorrow it will be just me and you and your cousin Langham, just like when we were together by the brook. Doesn't that sound fun?"

"I suppose so."

It wasn't surprising that Amelia wasn't overly enthusiastic. After all, Cara had given her only a few details. She was just glad the girl was willing to go.

"Would you like me to read to you before you go to sleep?"

"Yes!" Amelia answered happily, settling back in her bed while Cara found a good story.

Later, when Amelia was clearly about to doze off, Cara closed the book and set it aside.

"Miss Bernay?" Amelia said as Cara rose to leave.

"Yes?"

"Will you tell me next time you have to go and arrange something?"

Cara's heart went out to the girl, all the more because she knew she couldn't truly make that promise. "I'll do my best."

As they approached the house, Henry took in the view with increasing anticipation. He couldn't wait to see Cara again, to tell her what he'd discovered from Michael Stephenson, to share her happiness when she was reunited with her family—including the father she'd been mourning all these years.

Miss Leahy was in the open carriage with him. She wore black in remembrance of her mother but was ready to return to her duties. Henry had told her enough about what had transpired while she was away that she'd be able to disregard whatever comments his mother made on the subject.

He was confident Amelia would be happy to have her governess back again. He didn't even worry about the child's reaction to seeing Cara leave, because Henry had decided he would do his best to convince her to stay. He didn't know how he was going to work it all out, but there had to be a way.

He expected to see Amelia running to meet them. Surely the girl would want to greet the governess she'd always liked, even on days when she was cross. The grounds were quiet, however, as the carriage rolled to a stop. Henry got down and handed Miss Leahy out of the carriage.

Miss Leahy, also familiar with Amelia's habits, noticed the lack of greeting, too. "Where do you suppose Amelia is?"

"Perhaps they are at the studio. Or the stables."

But even as Henry spoke, he had a feeling something was amiss. He couldn't explain why. Something about the way the dust settled in the drive just felt wrong.

It wasn't until they went inside and Henry heard the commotion upstairs that he realized why no one had noticed the arrivals. "Wait here," he instructed Miss Leahy and headed for the staircase.

He heard his mother's shrill voice, which became clearer as he raced up the stairs. He followed the sounds to his mother's private parlor. She stood in the middle of the room, angrily waving a piece of paper as she interrogated the butler. "This is absurd! Are you sure you've searched everywhere?"

"What's wrong, Mother?" Henry asked as he entered the room.

"The maid found this note in the nursery this morning when she took up Amelia's breakfast. The child is gone—and so are Langham and that woman."

"Amelia wrote you a note?"

"Don't be daft. Langham wrote it, very prettily informing us they've decided to take a trip."

Henry snatched the paper from his mother's hand and scanned it. Sure enough, the note stated that the three of them were going away for a day or so and—in Langham's typically nonchalant words—they shouldn't worry.

Whatever this adventure was, he couldn't see it boding well. "It doesn't say where they're going. Do you have any idea?"

"Not in the least."

"What about Mr. Hart? Or any of the stable hands?"

"I've just come from the stables, my lord," Jensen said. "Mr. Hart has confirmed that none of the horses are gone."

"How far could they get if they are traveling on foot?" his mother said.

"They might have walked to the railway station," the butler suggested. "It's three miles by road, but if you walk through the southwest field, it's nearly a mile shorter."

"I'll ask at the station," Henry said. "If Langham was there, someone is bound to remember."

"We may now add kidnapping to that woman's charge!" his mother bellowed as Henry made for the door.

Henry had no idea what that meant, but he wasn't going to take the time to find out.

"Why yes, your lordship, Mr. Burke came through here this morning." The ticket agent answered Henry's question without hesitation. "Your ward was with him, sir. Miss Amelia is turning into a pretty little girl, if I may say so. There was a young lady with them, too."

"Where were they going? To London?" That would make it easier to find them—unless they didn't return to D'Adamo's place. Then they'd be lost anywhere in that giant city.

"Let me see . . ." The ticket agent lifted his cap and scratched his forehead as he thought back to this morning. "No, sir, it wasn't London," he said, replacing his cap. "It was somewhere north. Shropshire, that's it."

Shropshire.

That one word brought forward a niggling worry Henry had been trying to suppress. "You're sure about this?"

"Yes, sir. Took the nine forty-five on the Great Northern line."

Henry could only surmise that Langham had learned about Delia Stover. How he had done so, Henry didn't know. Taking Amelia to see her mother now would be incredibly foolish. Their carefully crafted story—a pack of lies, he readily admitted—was in danger of falling apart in a messy and unpredictable way. As angry as Henry

315

was, he was most worried about the harm to Amelia at being abruptly confronted with this sordid situation. She was too young for such things.

What was Cara's role in this? Had she tried to talk sense into his brother, or was she a willing participant? Either way, she was equally at fault.

Henry now had to chase them down and try to mitigate whatever damage might be done. He reached into his pocket for money. "When is the next train?"

When they reached the little town of Galway Hill, they obtained directions to the address on Delia's letters. The millinery shop was located on a narrow street several blocks from the town's main thoroughfare. It was flanked by other dingy shops that gave the area a slightly unsavory feel.

A sign on the door read, *Back in One Hour.*

"That's perplexing," Langham said. "One hour from when? And why would she close shop in the middle of the day?" He stepped back, inspecting the building. "It looks like someone lives above the shop, but I don't see any exterior stairs. It must be reached from the inside."

Cara peered in the window. She could see no one, but there was a light just beyond a curtained doorway at the far end of the shop. Pointing toward it, she said, "Maybe she lives at the back."

They still had not told Amelia why they had come here. Cara had persuaded Langham that it might be best to wait until they could discover the truth. Amelia held Cara's hand, but her nose scrunched in distaste as she looked at the down-at-heel street. Overcast skies only added to the gloom.

Despite the sign indicating the place was closed, Langham tried the door. Surprisingly, it was unlocked.

A bell over the door rattled as they entered. They stopped in the center of the shop and looked around. At a glance, it was easy to see why Delia had written to ask for more money. The whole place had a sad air. There were not many hats on display, although shelves behind the counter held spools of ribbons, feathers, and other materials. Perhaps Delia made her wares to request.

"Is anyone here?" Langham called.

A terrible, rasping cough came from the back room. "I'm coming." The response sounded tired and annoyed.

After a moment, a woman came through the curtained doorway, coughing into a handkerchief. She must still have been in her twenties, but the world-weariness emanating from her face and posture made her seem much older. She stopped in her tracks, swaying a little, staring at Langham in disbelief. "Langham! What are you—?" Her gaze landed on the child. "Amelia?"

Cara felt Amelia's hand tremble in hers. "No," said Amelia flatly, tightening her grip on Cara and leaning into her side. "No."

"So they figured it out," Delia murmured, still looking at Amelia. She didn't seem to notice the way the child clung to Cara. "I never thought they'd send you back, though. I thought you'd be safe and happy, living the good life, all fancy. It's more than I ever had."

There was a pause. Cara was stunned at the woman's suggestion that Henry would simply return a child, like tossing a fish back into a pond. Langham looked equally taken aback.

"How pretty you are," Delia said as she studied Amelia. "You was always a pretty little thing, right from the beginning. But your eyes! And those full brows. You take after your father now."

Cara and Langham exchanged a confused look.

"What are you talking about?" Langham said.

Delia turned her bleary eyes to Langham. "Do you mean his lordship still doesn't know?" She started to laugh, but this dissolved into a coughing spasm that shook her entire body. She doubled over and would have fallen, but Cara and Langham dashed forward and took her by the arms.

They half carried her back through the curtained doorway, behind which was a kitchen area with a small table, and set her on a chair. Moaning, Delia flopped over, landing facedown on crossed arms, and promptly passed out.

Langham picked up a small brown bottle next to the teapot and inspected it. "Laudanum. I think we need to find a doctor. Who knows how much she's taken?"

Cara brushed the hair from Delia's face. There was blood on her sleeve and around her mouth. Cara looked around for the handkerchief. Realizing Delia must have dropped it during her coughing spasm, Cara went back to the shop to retrieve it.

As she picked it up, she realized with a jolt of horror that the shop was empty. The door to the street was still open from when Amelia had run through it.

CHAPTER

35

The railway station was located perhaps half a mile from the center of town. Henry decided to cover the distance on foot, despite signs of an approaching storm. He was filled with pent-up energy after sitting on the train, worrying over what could be happening here.

He'd never been to this little village before. Everything had been done through correspondence. On the day Delia had delivered up Amelia, they'd met in his solicitor's office in Chelmsford. Even though her address was burned into his memory, Henry had no idea how to find it. After asking directions from several people, he finally found the place tucked away on a narrow side street.

Dusk was falling. In the gathering gloom, a faint light coming from the back of the shop was clearly visible. Henry walked back there and found Langham sitting by himself at a small table. He was slumped in a chair with a wet towel folded over his eyes. Henry was alarmed to see no sign of the others.

"Langham, it's Henry."

Wincing as though the mere sound of Henry's voice caused him pain, Langham removed the cloth from his eyes. "Well, if it isn't the good brother."

Henry took a seat opposite him at the narrow table. "Where are Cara and Amelia? Are they with Delia?"

"Delia is upstairs, sleeping off the effects of too much laudanum. The doctor says she'll recover from that, although she's not likely to survive the other things wrong with her." Langham spoke matter-of-factly, but the pain in his eyes was evident. "Fortunately, there was some left in the bottle, although not nearly enough. My head is splitting in two."

"Where are Cara and Amelia?"

"Amelia ran off. Cara went to find her while I went for a doctor for Delia. I haven't seen them since. I wanted to search for them, but I didn't want to leave Delia. And in any case, my head—" He scrubbed his hands over his face as though trying to push out the pain.

"Why did Amelia run off? What's happened?"

Langham met Henry's gaze. "I shouldn't bother explaining anything to you, seeing as how you never felt it important to tell me you've thought for years that Amelia was my daughter."

"Well, now you know." Henry paused as what Langham had said registered. "What do you mean, I *thought* she was your daughter?"

"The doctor and I roused Delia enough to get her to her bed. She told me a few things before she passed out completely. As she is probably dying, she thought she might as well confess. Or maybe her tongue was simply loosened by the effects of the laudanum." He attempted a smirk, even as he pressed his hands to his temples. "*In laudanum veritas.*"

"What did she tell you?" Henry pressed.

"I am not Amelia's father, although you and our parents found it too easy to think so."

"What? How can that be?"

"She was seduced by a man who was a guest at the inn. He was an estate agent researching a nearby property for a wealthy client. He promised Delia many things, but then he left when his client decided not to buy the land. When Delia discovered she was with child, she used that incident when Father found us together as an excuse to pass off the child as mine. Lucky for her, Father believed her and immediately set about keeping things quiet. So quiet, in fact, that no one even informed *me*."

He straightened enough to send Henry a malevolent glare. "Little did I know that I spent the past eight years working diligently to live down to your low opinion of me."

Henry slammed a fist on the table, filled with rage at his father for making the decisions that had placed them in this situation.

The sound caused Langham to moan. He placed the cloth back over his eyes. "Go ahead and be angry, but for pity's sake, do it elsewhere."

"I'm sorry, Langham." Those words were far from adequate. Henry's disgust was aimed not only at his parents, but at himself. He had helped to perpetuate the lie when he might have acted differently. They might have cleared things up and saved years of trouble and heartache. They had suffered precisely because those who could have spoken up did not.

And yet, what would have happened to Amelia if they hadn't taken her in? The thought pained him as he looked around at these miserable surroundings. He loved her. He wasn't going to abandon her.

The important thing now was to find Cara and Amelia. He'd seen and felt the gathering storm as he'd walked here from the station. What if Amelia had gotten lost in the outdoors, and Cara was searching the countryside for her? To be in a strange place at night, with weather like this, could not be safe.

He rose from his chair, wanting only to get out the door. To find the two people who had come to mean so much to him. To ensure they came to no harm.

Henry laid a gentle hand on his brother's shoulder. "I'll do whatever I can to make it right."

A muscle twitched, but otherwise Langham didn't move.

Henry turned and bolted from the shop.

Cara had searched through the town, down the alleyways, and even along the hedgerows on the roads skirting the town. Amelia was nowhere to be found. It was only as the moon began to rise and cast pale light on the countryside that Cara noticed a lake, edged by boats, on the far side of a field. She took off across the field, drawn toward the water as surely as Amelia would have been. The short masts rising from the sailboats would have been a magnet for the child.

Once at the lake, Cara walked out onto the dock. She carefully looked in every boat, in case Amelia was huddled inside one of them. But there were no signs of life, only a variety of supplies, from boat oars to oilcloth bags for rain gear and other essentials.

When Cara reached the end of the dock, she looked out over the broad lake. Heavy cloud cover blocked out most of the moonlight, but Cara's eyes slowly acclimatized to the night landscape. On the far side of the lake, trees lined the shore. In between, there was only the vast expanse of water.

Or was there something else? Cara strained, willing her eyes to see better. After a few moments, she was sure. There was a darker spot on the lake, a small rowboat. It was drifting, carried along by the strengthening breeze. Cara thought she could make out a child's head rising barely above the rim of the boat.

"Amelia!" she called out, her voice echoing across the water.

The head rose a little, but then sank lower. Cara called several more times, but the girl refused to answer.

It would be just like Amelia to find a boat and push out onto the lake. She'd always associated boats with freedom and escape. But as thunder rumbled in the distance, the situation was precarious, if not deadly dangerous.

"Amelia! I'm coming for you!" Cara yelled, certain the child could hear, even if she didn't respond.

Cara retraced her steps up the dock, intending to run back to town and summon help. She was sure to find men at the pub who knew the owners of these boats.

A flash of lightning stopped her in her tracks. Even if she ran as fast as she could and then found people willing to rush back here with her, she would still be gone for half an hour. Her conscience wouldn't allow her to leave the child alone that long. Not with the storm looming.

To her left, tied behind one of the sailboats, was a small rowboat similar to the one on the lake. Lifting her skirts, Cara clambered into the boat. Once she was firmly balanced inside, she fumbled with the ropes to free the rowboat from its moorings. The wind was stronger now, bringing occasional splatters of rain.

When the rope finally fell away, Cara pushed hard against the sailboat, thrusting her rowboat out into the deeper water. With shaky hands, she set the oars into position. She had never rowed a boat before, but she'd seen others rowing along the streams that skirted the Needenhams' property.

She was clumsy at first, but it didn't take long to catch on. With each stroke, she gained a better feel for how to move the boat in the direction she wanted to go. There was another streak of lightning, illuminating droplets of light rain falling on the lake. Cara kept rowing, gathering speed as she became accustomed to the oars.

Amelia stood up, waving her arms. "Go away! I don't want you here! I want to be left alone."

Cara's heart jumped as Amelia's boat wobbled. "Please sit down!" she cried, pushing the oars harder to close the gap. "I know you're upset. Let's get you to safety, where we can talk."

"All grown-ups ever do is talk. Go *away!*"

But even as she spoke, she sat down in the boat. Cara was about to take this for a good sign until she saw what the girl was doing. Amelia lifted an oar, but it slipped from her grasp and fell out of the boat. She lunged for it, trying to grab it before it hit the water. Her sudden movement caused the rowboat to pitch, flinging her overboard.

Cara shouted with terror as the child disappeared under the water.

Amelia's head popped up to the surface and she coughed, flailing her arms and gasping for air. Her boat had been pushed away by the force of her fall and was out of reach.

Cara rowed harder, desperate to reach the child. She couldn't swim, but she thought that if she got close enough, Amelia could grab onto the side of her boat.

To Cara's horror, the child began to swim *away* from her. Amelia wasn't even trying to reach her own boat. She was swimming toward the center of the lake. What she thought she might gain by this, Cara had no idea. Amelia probably didn't know, either. She was simply desperate to get away.

She couldn't outpace Cara, though. How she even stayed afloat was a mystery; it was evident that the weight of her dress hampered her. Surely it wouldn't be long before the layers of wet cotton acted as a lead weight to sink her.

Cara caught up to her, slipping alongside. She lifted one oar out of its socket and extended it toward the child. "Amelia! Grab onto this! *Now!*"

Amelia stopped and turned to face the proffered oar. She reached up and grabbed it, taking hold and yanking hard. Cara was leaning over the side of the boat, and the surprise force of the child's tug pulled her far enough that the boat tipped. Her balance shifted, and Cara fell into the lake.

She gasped as cold water encircled her. Her mouth filled with the taste of brine and fish. She tried to spit it out, but there was only water everywhere, pressing in on her. She reached upward, as though if she could find the water's edge she could somehow pull herself up. But her heavy clothes fought against her. She heard Amelia's muffled voice calling her name. She thought she saw the child's legs, still in stockings and boots, kicking at the water above her. She even had a sensation as though the child had grabbed her sleeve and was tugging at her. It was to no avail. Guilt was dragging her down. Her own wrongdoing had brought this. Another child was in danger and would probably die because of her.

No! She struggled, fighting the water, desperate to find the top. Lack of air was making her faint. Dizzy. The water was growing darker. The small hand she'd imagined holding on to her had let go. Cara was glad for this. She would not take the child down with her. Perhaps Amelia might survive.

Perhaps . . .

Cara's last conscious thought was a prayer: *Please, God, save her.*

CHAPTER

36

HENRY SCOURED THE VILLAGE, looking for Cara and
Amelia. He looked into shops and taverns, and asked everyone he saw if they had noticed a young blond woman and a
little girl, or perhaps either of them alone. The closest he got was one
man who remembered Cara searching for a little girl, but he did not
remember which direction she'd gone.

Finally, having no idea what to do next, Henry stood at the edge of
the village. From here, there were only open fields and a road leading
out into the country. A signpost noted the next town was three miles off.

There was no one about. Everyone had hurried home to avoid being
caught in the rain. Henry sat on a low fence, trying to devise a plan.
Where could he possibly look next? How could they have simply disappeared? The wind was picking up, and he could feel occasional drops
of rain on his face.

The wind carried something else, too. A woman's voice, crying out
Amelia's name.

The sound had come from behind him, distant but clear. Henry
jumped to his feet and turned around. He scanned the fields, which
gently crested before turning downhill again. And on the far side was

a lake. Cara called out louder this time, the fear and urgency in her voice prickling down Henry's spine. He climbed over the fence and broke into a run.

The stiff wind chased the clouds, allowing intermittent light from a crescent moon. As he reached the water's edge, Henry could make out two rowboats in the distance. Cara stood in one of them. She called out Amelia's name, extending an oar toward the water. Henry was barely aware of his feet pounding on the boards of the dock as he ran toward the sound. He had just reached the edge of the dock when he saw Cara topple from the boat into the lake.

Henry stripped off his coat and yanked off his boots. There was no time to come up with another plan. He took a shallow dive off the end of the dock and began swimming furiously the moment he hit the water. It was cold enough to render him breathless at first, but before long, the physical exertion of pushing through the water began to warm him.

He hadn't seen Amelia. He prayed she was in the second boat as he pumped his arms and legs as fast as he could. He had to reach Cara before she sank too far, while he could still find her and pull her to safety.

As he got closer, he saw Amelia's head pop out of the water. He cried her name. She was a reasonably good swimmer for her age, but the water was far too deep here. Add to that the weight of her clothes and shoes, and she could easily drown. She didn't seem to hear him. She didn't even look in his direction, but instead disappeared beneath the water again. Her backside and feet rose up in the air before they too submerged, and Henry realized she was not sinking but rather diving. She was probably looking for Cara. He couldn't help but admire the girl for that, and yet a child and a drowning woman were a recipe for disaster.

Keeping his eyes pinned to the spot where Amelia had disappeared, Henry redoubled his efforts. It made for awkward swimming, but he couldn't risk losing their position. As it happened, he knew immediately when he was in the right spot. The water churned, evidence of a struggle beneath the surface. He took a few precious seconds to catch his breath and then to inhale deeply, knowing he would need plenty of air. Then he dove.

The water was far from clear, yet he saw Amelia instantly. Her white petticoats stood out in the gloomy depths. She was struggling, one arm flailing and her two feet kicking. Her other hand grasped Cara's wrist. She was trying to pull her toward the surface. It was futile for the child to even attempt this, and Cara wasn't making it any easier. She thrashed, frenzied from fear.

Henry swam to Amelia and took her arm to get her attention. She pulled back in fright until she recognized him. He pointed toward himself and then to Cara, and then took hold of Amelia's waist and pushed her upward. He was trying to communicate for her to rise to the surface, that he would go after Cara, and she understood. She was also likely out of air, for she willingly swam upward. Henry, too, already felt the strain of holding his breath.

He turned back to Cara. She no longer struggled. She was sinking, arms floating. She was unconscious. That would make the rescue easier—provided she wasn't dead. He shoved that fear aside, lest panic overtake him. He swam to her, turning her floating form so that her back was to him. Wrapping one arm around her waist, he began to fight his way back to the surface.

Her soaked clothes made her doubly heavy. Henry kicked and stroked at the water, using all the force he could muster, fighting to raise them both to the life-giving air. He was beginning to see spots, but he pushed all the harder. He could make out Amelia now. Everything below her shoulders was still submerged, but she seemed stationary. Then he saw the darker shadow of an object next to her. She had grabbed the side of the rowboat.

He was so close. He kept pushing, willing himself to rise. Just when he thought his lungs would burst, he broke through to the surface. He gasped, sucking in air—and water, too, for it was raining hard, pelting the lake's surface and thudding on the wooden boat.

Amelia clung to the side of the boat. She stared at Henry and Cara with wide, frightened eyes.

Cara was still a dead weight in his arms. He couldn't even tell if she was breathing. He grabbed hold of the boat himself, which gave him some rest from the sheer work of supporting her. But he couldn't stay here long. He had to get Cara to land, and he could see no way to get any of them back into the boats.

He pulled Cara toward him. Holding her tightly. Willing her to be alive.

She made a gurgling, gasping sound, and water poured from her mouth. She was alive! She coughed and heaved in a spasm as more water poured forth. She was still unconscious, but it was a good start.

"Amelia, I have to take her to shore and get the water out of her lungs. It has to happen quickly. Can you stay here and hold on? I'll be back very soon."

"No! I want to come with you. I can swim."

He looked toward the shore with its dock and line of boats. The best he could gauge was that they were about a quarter of a mile away. "It's a long way," he told her. "I won't be able to help if you get tired. It will be all I can do to get Miss Bernay back."

"I can do it!" she insisted. "I'm too cold to stay here."

Henry could see her shivering, and her lips were turning blue. The rain and the stiff breeze were adding to the chill. A series of lightning bolts punctuated the danger of leaving her here. Henry had no choice. He could only pray to God that their one way out would work.

He pulled himself up higher, looking in the boat for anything that might help the child if she faltered. He saw an oilcloth rucksack shoved into the corner and strained to reach it. With his fingertips he just barely got hold of it, dragging it to him. He pulled it from the boat and dropped it into the water. It floated.

"Keep hold of this," Henry instructed.

Amelia pulled the rucksack to her side, cradling it under one arm.

"Are you ready?" he asked.

She nodded.

"Let's go."

Now that they were floating on top of the water, making progress was not as difficult. Having air to breathe also made the task easier. "Stay with us, Cara," he murmured as they went. "Stay with me."

He could not have fallen in love *twice*, only to have the woman taken from him both times. He knew all men must endure hardship, but surely the Lord was not so cruel as to let his heart be torn out like this a second time.

Nor, surely, could the Lord allow harm to come to the child. But they were swimming at night in a thunderstorm. Henry couldn't imagine a more dangerous scenario.

As they swam toward shore, Henry veered from the boat dock, aiming instead for the beach that lay south of it. He could hear Amelia splashing along behind him, occasionally moaning and grunting in effort. He looked back and saw that she now grasped the rucksack with both arms, placing much of her weight on it. She was clearly tired, and tears were streaming down her face, mingling with the raindrops. She used only her legs to provide forward momentum, but it was working.

"We're almost there," he said to bolster her, for she could see the approaching shoreline with her own eyes.

The moment when he dropped his feet down and felt the sand beneath them was pure elation. He walked the rest of the way to shore, pulling Cara behind him. The wind had whipped up small waves, which now pushed them those final steps ashore. The shoreline was rough, covered with pebbles. Henry stretched Cara out, then turned and waded back in, scooping Amelia into his arms to bring her the last few yards. She clung to him, sobbing now, letting go of her fortitude in an agony of relief.

Henry hugged her tightly, and the realization of just how much he loved her hit him with full force. "You are strong and brave, do you know that? I couldn't be more proud of you." As he spoke, he walked, returning them both to Cara. He set Amelia down on her feet, but she resisted leaving his arms. "Will you help me now? We must help Miss Bernay. She did not come out of this adventure as well as you."

She was still sobbing. "I didn't mean to pull her in. I didn't know she couldn't swim. Why can't she swim?"

It might have sounded like recrimination, but her voice was high-pitched with panic and she was twisting her hands together, looking at Cara with anxious fear.

"One day," said Henry, "you and I will teach her."

He dropped to his knees and gently rolled Cara onto her side. He gave vigorous slaps to her back in an effort to get her body to expel any water still in her lungs. After several tries, it worked. More water came out of her mouth, and this time as her body convulsed, Henry thought her eyes fluttered open briefly before closing again.

"She's going to be all right," he said, determined to believe it.

Amelia dropped down beside him, shivering, her fearful gaze transfixed on Cara. "What do we do now?"

"We get her home," Henry replied.

Later, they would sort out this mess, come to terms with all that had happened. For now, he drew Amelia close to him once more. He found he was taking as much comfort from the hug as she was. "We all go home."

Henry paced the second floor of Galway Hill's main inn, just as he'd done all night and now into the morning. He was exhausted yet too restless to sit in the chair the innkeeper had brought him. Henry couldn't rest until he knew for sure that Cara and Amelia were going to be all right.

Reaching the end of the hallway, he paused at Amelia's door and placed an ear against the wood. The room beyond was quiet and still. The doctor had assured him she was sleeping soundly, and there was nothing more Henry could do. Turning back, he walked the other direction until he reached Cara's room. There he stood, waiting and praying.

It was barely dawn, and few people were stirring. Henry was surprised, therefore, to see Langham coming up the stairs. His brother's clothes were crumpled and unkempt. He also wore a contrite expression that Henry had never seen before.

"How are you feeling?" Henry asked, although he could easily guess. His brother looked completely devastated.

Langham answered the question with a grimace, then pushed some straggling hair from his face. "I need to explain. And apologize."

"There will be time later to discuss all this."

Langham shook his head. "I need to do it now." He continued without waiting for a response. "I want you to know I came here with the best of intentions. When I discovered Delia's letters and thought I might be Amelia's father, I was determined to right the wrongs I had committed—albeit unknowingly. I had some idea that I'd turn over a new leaf, maybe try to cobble together a family with Delia and Amelia—" He paused, shaking his head. "All I did was make things worse, and the mistake was nearly fatal."

Henry didn't know how to answer. His thoughts could not be entirely pulled from the woman who lay just beyond the door next to him.

"It's a good thing you came, or who knows what might have happened. And it would have been my fault." Langham looked away for a moment, clearly choked up and doing his best to hold the emotion at bay. "That's a burden that I can only thank God I was not made to bear. Most especially, of course, for their sakes—an innocent child and one of the best ladies I've ever met. In some way, Cara reminds me of our lost sister. I hope that she may yet be that to us—and more."

Henry had an inkling what Langham meant. It was his hope, too.

"Last night I berated you because you accepted the accusations laid against me. Everyone—you and our parents—was so ready to believe I was that person. And yet, who could blame you? My life has provided the perfect context for such a lie."

No matter how battered his heart was from yesterday's events, Henry did not wish to see his brother so weighed down with condemnation. "You're a good man, Langham. We've disagreed on many things, but I never doubted your generosity of heart."

"Even so, I want to tell you that I plan to turn over a new leaf. I will be better and different from now on."

"I'm glad to hear it."

"No, wait." Langham held up shaking hands to stop Henry from speaking further. "I *want* to tell you those things. But I won't. I know about the Bible's admonition to 'boast not thyself of tomorrow.'" He let out a tiny laugh at Henry's lifted brow. "You didn't think I listened to the minister's sermons when we were children, did you?"

Henry allowed a brief, sardonic smile. "No, I did not."

"Well, as I said, I will not tell you these things. I will only *prove* them in the doing."

Langham's humility was real. Henry saw a resolve that was not likely to fade. For the first time in years, he was proud of his brother. "I've been at fault, too. I'll need to join you in that endeavor."

Henry extended a hand; he wasn't sure why. They had rarely indulged in these types of gestures over the years. He just felt the need to do something.

Langham took hold of Henry's hand, and then pulled him in for an embrace.

CHAPTER

37

SEARING PAIN in her lungs brought her to consciousness.
Cara awoke, startled to find she was in a soft bed, swaddled in blankets. A small lamp on the dresser at the foot of the bed sent a warm glow through the room. She coughed, unable to help it even though it brought only more pain, as though her lungs were on fire.

Immediately a woman was at her side, helping her lean forward, holding her until the coughing fit was done. "There you go, miss," she said. "I knew you'd come 'round."

"Who are you?" Fear took hold of her as she remembered the sensation of Amelia's grip loosening just before she lost consciousness. Someone from the town must have been close enough to rescue her after all. But had they found Amelia? "Where is Amelia?" The hoarseness in her voice caused by her burning lungs was magnified by horror at what she might hear.

The woman gave her hand a comforting pat. "She's right down the hall, tucked into bed. Poor thing was exhausted, but no other harm came to her."

Cara began to cry. The tears quickly turned to sobs, as the relief seemed too great to bear. Amelia was safe. Whatever terrible consequences would come to Cara—and she had no doubt that plenty would—the child was safe. God in His grace had once more answered her prayers. She covered her face with her hands but could not stop the tide of tears.

The woman gently pushed a handkerchief into her hands, waiting patiently until Cara's sobs began to subside before speaking again. "I'm Mrs. Lowell, the innkeeper's wife," she said, answering the question Cara had initially blurted out. "You gave us a scare, but I knew you'd pull through. You're young and strong, that's what I told his lordship. I said, 'She's young and strong, sir. You've no need to fret.'"

"Hen—Lord Morestowe is here?" Suddenly Cara was desperate to see him, desperate to face the brunt of his fury and get the worst of it over with. Coming here may have been Langham's idea, but she had agreed to it. Henry would hate her after this. Not that it mattered. After all, he was going to marry Miss Myers, who would certainly be a better mother to Amelia. She wasn't likely to go haring off to the countryside and put a child's life in danger. Cara tried to wipe away her tears, but knowledge of her own terrible inadequacies kept them coming.

"His lordship is just outside. Hardly budged all night, although after diving in the lake and swimming all that way to rescue you, he must have been as worn out as Miss Amelia."

Cara stared at her in shock. "Lord Morestowe rescued me?"

"Aye, that he did." Mrs. Lowell beamed. "I haven't had much dealings with aristocrats, but I know they aren't all as polite and gracious as he is. Not to mention so heroic."

Cara tried to picture Henry swimming with her in his arms, bringing her to shore. The scene was almost too fantastic to imagine. It stirred so many emotions, leaving her deeply embarrassed and yet overwhelmingly grateful. How had he known? How had he been there? She owed him her life.

There was no way to repay that. No way to counter the anger he'd be feeling.

Whatever happened, Cara would always love him with all her heart.

It would make life without him that much harder, but it was a love she would always cherish.

Henry was still pacing the hall, but now he was pondering what Langham had just told him. The revelation that Cara had hidden her previous employment as a nanny, and her reason for doing so, was troubling. It also explained why Cara had been so adamant about not wanting to be a governess. She was perhaps still wracked with guilt over what had happened to the little boy. Unlike his mother, Henry believed it had been a simple, if serious, mistake and not evidence of some deep flaw in Cara's nature. It was one more issue they would have to address—once he was assured Cara was out of danger. At the moment, that was all he cared about.

He paused again outside Cara's room. This time he heard voices—evidence that Cara was awake. He rapped on the door. "How is Miss Bernay?" he called. "May I enter?"

"Certainly, sir," Mrs. Lowell responded.

Henry opened the door, eagerly glancing toward the bed. Cara was propped up against the pillows, a blanket pulled up to her chest. Her long blond hair had been tied back but was now askew, falling out of its ribbon. Her nightgown, one of Mrs. Lowell's, was far too large, swathing her in excess cotton. Her eyes were puffy, and her nose was red. In short, she looked lovely.

He cleared his throat. "How are you feeling?"

Her gaze was fastened on him as he approached the bed. Her wide blue eyes shone with unsuppressed admiration. "You saved my life—and Amelia's, too. I—" She stopped as words failed her.

As much as he loved the way she was looking at him just now, he felt uneasy to hear it put in such terms. He didn't want to admit that things had gotten that close to disaster. She was here, she was safe, and she was alive. Those were the only facts his heart was willing to hold.

He wanted more than anything to take her in his arms. For the moment, he had to content himself with sitting on the narrow wooden chair next to her bed, drawing it as close to her as possible.

"You must be furious with me," Cara said, mistaking the reason for his silence.

He shook his head. "Langham told me what happened. I believe you both meant well."

"We never dreamed it would turn out as it did. I thought—"

Henry held up a hand to stop her. Turning to the innkeeper, he said, "Mrs. Lowell, I'd like to have a few minutes with Miss Bernay. If you could wait just outside."

"Certainly, sir," the lady agreed readily enough, although she looked surprised at his request. Henry was asking to be left alone in a room with a woman. He didn't care.

Neither, apparently, did Cara. She picked up her narrative the moment they were alone. "I thought it would be good for Amelia to see her mother. I lost mine so young. I understand what a terrible chasm it leaves in your heart. But Delia was not at all what I imagined her to be. She collapsed, and I had to run after Amelia while Langham tended to her—"

"It's all right," Henry said gently. "You don't have to explain."

His soft answer seemed to take her by surprise. And no wonder. She must have expected him to berate her soundly. Something he might well have done, except that he loved her too much.

Cara said tentatively, "How is Delia?"

"She is not well. We'll do all we can to help her. We may move her to a sanitarium, although I have spoken to the doctor, and he doubts it will make much of a difference."

"I was afraid of that." She plucked absently at the counterpane as she turned a remorseful gaze on him. "Now I think this will only open fresh wounds for Amelia, and I feel so guilty. Delia thought you were sending the child back to her! But of course, that can never happen. Langham is determined to be a good father to her."

"Yes, well, about that . . ." Henry told her what he'd learned from Langham.

By the time he'd finished, Cara's eyes—those large, sweet blue eyes— were wide with amazement. "Then Amelia is no relation to the Burke family at all? What will happen to her?"

"She isn't going anywhere. I fully intend to raise her as my daughter. She is headstrong, yes. But she's also clever and fearless and resilient. Just like you."

Cara shook her head. "I'm foolish and naïve and too full of daydreams. I lose children!"

"That's true," Henry agreed calmly.

"So you know about Robbie, too."

"Yes." He took hold of her hands. "I would like to hear all about it, but not now. It can wait."

She regarded him as though gratefully drinking in the kindness he was offering. She looked so frail and too sorrowful.

"This trip was Langham's idea," he reminded her. "Unfortunately, I can't very well send *him* away, much as I'd like to." He gave her a grin, although he only managed to draw a weak smile in return. "However, I do think you should not return to Morestowe. There is a certain protocol that must be followed, especially after all that has happened. I want to ensure there is no room for the gossipmongers—"

"I understand," Cara interrupted, seemingly so disheartened she didn't want to hear more.

"I don't think you should be living under my roof, since I intend to begin courting you officially and properly," Henry finished as though she had not spoken. "With your permission, of course. And that of your f—" He stopped short. He'd almost said *father*, giving away the most glorious secret. "Family," he finished.

Cara didn't even notice the way he'd faltered. She was looking at him in disbelief. "But you're engaged to Miss Myers! Or you will be soon."

"No. What gave you that idea?"

"Your mother told me. And when you spent those extra days in London, I knew you must be working out the details."

"Is that why you were willing to go on this ill-advised journey with Langham, even though you knew I'd be upset?"

Her head drooped. "I suppose I felt I had nothing left to lose."

He gently lifted her chin. "We didn't have time to discuss everything before I left, but even so, I thought you must know how I feel about you."

"I—I believe a woman needs those things explained clearly," she answered, managing to inject reproach into her words even though her countenance was beginning to lift with hope.

He needed that reproof. He'd been guilty of the same wrongdoing toward Cara that he had done to Olivia. He'd assumed his feelings were known instead of speaking them outright. He'd allowed circumstances to prevent him from boldly declaring himself. He vowed never to allow that to happen again.

"I love you, Cara."

It felt wonderful to say the words, to get them out into the open air so there could be no mistaking his intentions.

He expected her to say the same thing in return, but she looked too thunderstruck to answer. After several long moments, she said, "I suppose Miss Myers was terribly disappointed."

How like Cara to be worried about the feelings of her rival! Her compassionate nature was one reason among thousands that Henry loved her. "You needn't be concerned on that score. There is someone Miss Myers fancies more than me. She told me so at her first opportunity."

Cara's eyes fluttered wide. "How can that be?"

Henry laughed. "I'm going to interpret that remark as your acceptance that I may begin courting you."

Cara was never one to hide her feelings. They always bubbled up to the surface. At this moment, he was overjoyed to see only love in her eyes.

She answered, in glorious understatement, "All right."

Henry saw, rather than heard, her answer. He was focused on her beautiful mouth. Her lips were pale, which was no surprise, given the ordeal she'd been through, but still ripe for a kiss. So he leaned forward and gave her one.

He kept it sweet and gentle, assuming she was still fragile after her near-drowning. But it wasn't long before she responded with increasing fervor, pulling him closer, and he thanked God that this woman was willing to be his.

Sometime later, Henry came to his senses. He sat back, realizing it wouldn't do their reputations any good if someone walked in on them.

They stared at each other, smiling in joyous wonderment. But then

Cara's expression turned pensive. "I hate to throw cold water on my own lovely fairy story, and yet . . . your mother will be so angry. She's never liked me."

"I'll admit she warned me you were laying a trap to ensnare me. She told me you had 'set your cap for me,' or some such expression."

A twinkle appeared in Cara's eye. "I'm afraid that's true. In a way."

"What?" He looked at her incredulously.

Her mouth twitched. "You see, I was sure you were the man I was going to marry, although this belief was sorely tested." She smiled, but her amusement seemed aimed at herself. "I must sound as silly as ever."

"I'd be happy to hear you explain it better."

"It began the night you came to take Langham from the public house. You took him out to the carriage, and the two of you climbed inside, and Langham was shouting, 'Cry—God for Harry, England, and Saint George!'" She lifted one hand and spoke in a deep voice that was a credible imitation of his brother.

"I remember it well," Henry said, grimacing and yet laughing at the same time. Only Cara could get him to see the humor in the mess his brother always made of things. "Go on."

"Langham tried to get out of the carriage, and you stopped him. And the coachman accidentally slammed the door on your hand." She gave him a critical look. "You cried out something terrible, as I recall."

"Guilty as charged," Henry admitted. "And—?"

"Well, that's it, really. It was confirmed when I saw you the next day with a bandage on your hand."

He shook his head, mystified. "I don't follow."

"Ah, right, I forgot. You don't know about the others."

He lifted an eyebrow. "Who?"

"My two brothers-in-law. You see, they both had injured hands when they first met their future wives—my sisters. Well, Nate's was injured already. Michael's was injured the first day they met, just like yours. So naturally I took that as a sign."

"The fact that I injured my hand was a sign that I was destined to marry you?"

"I knew you'd think it nonsense. But there it is, just the same."

She tried to look abashed, and perhaps she really felt that way. But he saw pride and happiness in her expression as well.

"I shall have to give my coachman a raise in pay for his role in ensuring we were brought together."

"Now, Henry, that's just silly." Her mouth widened to a sly grin. "It's also exactly what I was thinking."

He laughed and would happily have kissed her again, but a disturbance in the hallway gave him pause.

"I want to see her!" Amelia's command was loud enough to hear through the door.

"Miss Amelia, you ought not to be out of bed," Mrs. Lowell admonished.

Henry walked to the door and opened it. "It's all right. Come in, Amelia."

She was dressed in the frock she'd worn yesterday. It was dry now, although wrinkled and dirty. Even though she'd gained her point and been invited to enter, she paused, looking doubtfully at Henry. Perhaps now that last night's emergencies were over, she'd begun to worry about her future. He thought of Cara's first reaction upon hearing that Amelia wasn't a Burke: fear the child would be sent away. To his knowledge, no one had told Amelia outright who Delia was, and yet she had to wonder why she'd been brought here.

He stepped back, opening the door wider. "Miss Bernay wants to see you."

Amelia entered the room, skirting Henry as though she were still not sure of him.

Cara gave the child a welcoming smile as she approached the bed. "You look well, Amelia. You were very brave last night." She reached out to take Amelia's hand. "When I fell in the water, you did your best to save me, and I'm grateful."

"Who was that woman?"

This brusque, direct question was normal for Amelia, and yet Cara looked taken aback. She glanced at Henry, clearly unsure how to answer.

"She took care of you when you were a baby," Henry said.

340

Amelia was still looking at Cara. "She was the one who sang to me, wasn't she?"

"It appears so," Cara answered.

Amelia seemed to accept this. Considering her desire to always know the whole truth about a situation, it was telling that she didn't ask the follow-up question Henry was dreading: *Is she my mother?* Perhaps she really didn't want to know the answer.

Henry supposed they ought to reprimand the girl for running away. Her foolish actions had endangered Cara's life as well as her own. Yet Henry sensed this was not the time. He took his cues from Cara, who had chosen to stress Amelia's bravery, not her foolishness.

"Why did we come here?" Amelia asked, suspicion and belligerence creeping back into her voice.

Henry sat on the chair so he could be closer to eye level with her. "As I told you last night, we will go home together."

"I don't have to stay here?" For all her bravado, there was a shadow of terror in her eyes.

"No," Henry said fervently. "Miss Bernay has to go away for a while, but in the meantime, Miss Leahy is already at Morestowe, ready to be your governess again. Maisie is waiting for you, too. I know you must be looking forward to riding her again."

Amelia's lower lip began to tremble. "I'm sorry I ran away. I'm sorry I pulled Miss Bernay in the lake. I thought you didn't want me anymore."

Cara took in a sharp breath, placing a hand to her heart. "Langham and I deeply regret bringing you here. It was not the right thing to do. Sometimes adults can do foolish things, just like children can." She looked earnestly into the girl's eyes. "Can you forgive us?"

Amelia nodded. A tiny tear breached her lower lid and slipped down one cheek.

Henry reached out, tentatively offering the girl a hug. After the briefest of pauses, she accepted it. He wrapped his arms around her, holding her tightly, and Amelia clung to him fiercely in return. She did not shed any more tears. She'd spent a lifetime learning to hold them in, it seemed. Henry understood now why parents wanted to shield their children from heartache and harm. He wanted nothing more than to make this girl feel safe and happy and loved.

It was several minutes before Amelia finally relaxed her grip and stepped back. She turned her attention to Cara. "Where are you going?"

"Well, I . . ." Cara faltered.

"That's something we haven't discussed yet," Henry broke in cheerfully. "Miss Bernay's sister, Mrs. Stephenson, says Miss Bernay would be welcome to stay with her and her husband. On the other hand, Miss Bernay's *other* sister, Mrs. Moran, absolutely insists that Miss Bernay stay with her. So it's a bit of a quandary."

Cara turned shocked eyes to Henry. "How do you know these things?"

"I spoke to them when I was in London. Very nice people. They seem eminently sensible, too." He couldn't resist a cheeky grin. "Different from you."

Cara reached out to swat him, but he leaned back, out of reach.

"Henry, tell me," Cara ordered. "How did you meet them? Does this mean Julia is back in England?"

"She's back, safe and sound, and eager to see you again. It appears you have a lot of things to catch up on."

"But how did you find them?"

"That night you told us the story about hiding from the police in a washing kettle, you mentioned Stephenson's name. So I decided to look him up. After all, if you are going to—"

He paused to glance at Amelia. It seemed that by common consent, neither he nor Cara were going to reveal their intentions just yet. Amelia stared at Cara, openmouthed. Apparently she wasn't familiar with the story of the washing kettle.

"If you are going to, er, stay with us again," Henry continued, "I thought it would be nice to get to know your family."

Her brows rose. "You were checking up on me."

"Do you mind?"

She gave up her pretense of indignation. "No. I'm glad you found them. To be honest, I've been longing to see them again."

"It was fortunate that I wrote to Stephenson when I did. He and

Julia had just returned a few days before. They knew you had left your previous employer but didn't know where you'd gone. They were desperate to learn what had become of you. Langham tells me you've been deliberately avoiding them."

"We have some issues to sort out." Turning toward the bedside table, she picked up a small pocket watch lying there and began to caress it thoughtfully. "I suppose I should do that soon."

"An excellent idea."

Henry didn't see the need to mention that he'd sent Stephenson a telegram today and already received one in return. There were a lot of happy surprises in store for Cara; her family's arrival here tomorrow would be one more.

CHAPTER

38

T HE NEXT DAY, Cara felt well enough to get out of bed. The doctor had recommended she take a few days to recover before traveling, so Henry had reserved the inn's small private sitting room for their use during the day.

At one point she found herself alone in the room, relaxing in a large chair. Langham and Amelia had taken a walk, and Henry had gone out, saying he had to attend to a few things. A book lay open in her lap, but Cara wasn't reading. She was lost in thought, marveling over all that had happened and dreaming of the days ahead. Imagining life with Henry, living at Morestowe and raising Amelia. Praying she would find some way to soften the countess's heart. Imagining how wonderful it would be when she was once more reunited with her sisters.

She must have dozed off, because in her dream she heard Julia's voice.

"We have found you at last."

Cara bolted upright when she realized the voice was real. She could scarcely believe her eyes when Julia and Rosalyn entered the room. Cara hastily set the book aside and stood up. She must have risen too quickly, because she felt light-headed. It didn't matter. She could not have fallen if she'd tried, because in an instant, the three sisters were locked together in an embrace.

She clung to them, and they to her. Cara had missed them so terribly. It was true she was still angry about the things they'd done, but they were her sisters, and for now, she was glad they were here.

When at last they released their hold on each other, wiping away their tears, Cara said, "Henry told me about meeting you in London. The doctor said I should stay here for a while, so I thought it would be days before I saw you."

"Well, we weren't going to wait," Julia said. "Michael received a telegram from Lord Morestowe, saying you'd been in an accident. Even though it said you were recovering, we had to come see for ourselves." She scrutinized Cara. "You seem to have come out of it all right."

"Did you come by yourselves?"

"Not exactly." Julia pointed toward the door.

Michael stood there. He smiled and waved but did not enter the room. He seemed to be holding back.

"I really should be giving you a piece of my mind," Cara said to Julia. "I didn't know you'd left England until I arrived in London and your former landlady told me."

Julia attempted a contrite expression. "I'm sorry you had to hear about it that way. I did write you a letter—"

"Which you deliberately planned for me to receive after you'd gone."

"I got a similar letter," Rosalyn confirmed, although Cara was surprised that she didn't seem put out by it.

"I knew you would both be upset with me, but I believed it was a risk worth taking."

"Why did you go to South America?" Cara asked. "I may have been terrible at geography in school, but even I know that is nowhere close to your beloved Africa that you talked about for so many years."

Julia gave a self-satisfied smile. "I went to South America on an entirely different kind of mission." She paused, exchanging glances with Rosalyn. What they were communicating was a mystery to Cara. Julia continued, "Michael met a man with information on the whereabouts of our father."

"Our *father?*"

Julia was smiling. The kind of smile she never wore when the subject was their father. Cara's heart began a slow, steady pounding. The hope that had kept her comforted all these years—the special hope she'd always refused to let go—pulsed through her soul. She tried to breathe, suspecting her difficulty had nothing to do with her still-sore lungs.

Rosalyn returned to the doorway and beckoned to someone just out of sight. The person's hand reached out to take Rosalyn's. Even as the rest of him came into view, Cara knew.

She *knew*.

Tears spilled over his cheeks, although he was smiling. "You are beautiful, Cara. Just as I knew you'd be. I hope you have a hug for your papa."

Cara emitted a gulping cry, bringing her hand to her mouth. She looked around to assure herself this was real and not a dream. Everyone was smiling. Henry was there, too. He must have been waiting in the hallway with her father.

When her eyes met her father's again, he opened his arms, and with another cry of wonderment, Cara fell into them.

Papa was home at last.

"It was a big surprise to me, too, as you can imagine," Rosalyn said.

Julia had just finished telling the story of going to Venezuela, locating their father, and persuading him to come back to England. She finished by describing how she'd arranged for Rosalyn to meet them at the dock in Plymouth, although Rosalyn hadn't yet known about their father.

"She nearly fainted dead away when she saw Papa," Julia said.

"From happiness, as well as surprise," Rosalyn pointed out with a smile. "I'm sure I looked as shocked as Cara did a short while ago."

Once Cara had gotten over the breathtaking thrill of seeing her father again, they had all sat down, and he had shared his harrowing story with her —how he had been coerced into gunrunning, escaped from the ship but nearly died in a hurricane, and then was rescued and given kind care by Diego's family. The saddest part was how, even after he had recovered his senses, he had spent years afraid to tell anyone the truth about who he was and where he'd been, for fear he would bring disgrace or even harm to his family. He'd felt compelled to continue the ruse that he was not altogether sound of mind.

"So many years," Papa murmured, shaking his head. "So many years."

"But we are going to make up for it now, aren't we, Papa?" Cara said. "Oceans did separate us once, but no longer." She pulled her mother's watch from her pocket. It no longer ran, because it had gone into the lake with her and been ruined by the water, but the latch still worked.

Rosalyn and Julia gasped when they saw what was in her hand.

"Cara, where did you get that?" Rosalyn said.

"I found it in a jeweler's shop. I'm still angry with you about it. Why did you pawn it?"

There was an uncomfortable pause. Cara hated that this had dampened their happy reunion, but she wasn't going to shy away from the truth. This was a day for total honesty.

From the way Rosalyn and Julia looked at one another, Cara realized they'd both known the watch was gone. And neither one had told her. "Why did you do it?" she insisted.

"I didn't pawn the watch," Rosalyn said. "Believe me, I was devastated to lose it."

"You lost it? How? When?"

"It was when I was tricked into going to that brothel my first night in London two years ago. Even though I escaped, the watch ended up in the hands of the woman who owned that terrible place. I tried to recover it but was never able to."

"Why didn't you tell me?"

"I suppose I was trying to save your feelings. You were so alarmed when you learned what happened to me. I thought if you knew the watch was lost, you would be even more distressed. It meant so much to all of us, but you've always been especially sensitive. . . ." Rosalyn's voice trailed off, and she looked unwilling to finish her sentence.

"And yet if you had told me, you would have saved me from worse anguish. I've spent weeks thinking you'd callously pawned it. In the future, please don't think you're doing me a favor by hiding things from me. I am quite grown up now."

"We can see that," Julia agreed. She looked at Henry as she said this.

Henry sent Cara a loving glance and one of his special smiles that seemed reserved only for her. The kind that melted her insides. She would never, ever grow tired of them.

"May I see the watch?" her father said.

Cara set it gently in his outstretched hand. He opened the latch and ran a finger over the engraving inside the cover. "'Oceans can never separate us,'" he read softly. He gave a long sigh. "My dear, sweet Marie. How I wish you were still here." He lifted his gaze, taking in his three daughters with misty eyes. "But I have you, my daughters, and I am grateful."

Cara, who was seated next to him on the sofa, threw her arms around him. In a moment, her sisters joined in. They hugged each other all at once, crying, but also laughing at the humor of trying to crowd onto the sofa and the joy of being together again. Seated on Cara's other side, Henry did his best to keep out of the fray.

The door to the parlor swung open. Langham and Amelia walked in, and Langham said brightly, "It looks like the party is already underway! What did we miss?"

Still laughing, they untangled themselves from the sofa.

"You've missed a lot, as it happens. However, we have lots of time to catch up," Cara said.

She slipped her hand into Henry's. He gave it a kiss that was filled with promise.

348

Epilogue

July 1882

CARA COULD NOT HAVE ASKED for a more beautiful day. The sky was a brilliant blue, providing the perfect contrast to the green landscape of summer. An ideal setting for the two figures on horseback she could see in the distance. Amelia had grown into such a confident horsewoman, able to follow Henry through fields, across streams, and along wooded trails.

Seated on the lawn chair next to Cara, her father also watched the pair. "That is one lucky child," he observed.

After Cara and Henry had returned from their honeymoon in Scotland, Papa had come to live with them. Amelia had taken to him right away. He'd assumed the role of a kindly grandfather and taught her to call him *Abuelo*. Thanks to him, the girl had become an expert at draughts—a game Papa still referred to by the American name of checkers.

"She is blessed." Cara squeezed his hand. "As am I."

Since her father's return, Cara had seen so many of her most cherished dreams come to pass. Her wedding. Her honeymoon. Bringing her father home to live with her and Henry. Her presentation at court—it still gave her heart palpitations when she thought back to that momentous occasion when she had curtsied to the Queen, and how Her Gracious Majesty had given her a kind smile. It would always be one of her most treasured memories.

Cara had never been good at waiting, and yet somehow she had survived the long months until her wedding day. Every minute had been worth it, eclipsed by the joy of walking with her father into the church so he could give her away to the man she loved.

Before her marriage, Cara and her father had stayed at the Morans' home. They'd spent countless hours together, talking over many things, healing the pain of loneliness and loss that had lodged in their hearts for so many years.

There had also been letters from Diego, describing his family's joy at Paul's happy reunion with his daughters. Paul hoped to do something more for Diego one day—perhaps send money to allow him to become an apprentice in a good trade.

Also during those months, Henry's diligent efforts regarding his business ventures were bearing fruit. Thanks to Langham's contact with Mr. Everson, the industrialist had become an eager investor in the mine. He'd brought several other men into the partnership as well. Cara's heart swelled with pride whenever she thought of this, because she had been the one to suggest contacting him.

A delightful surprise was that Mr. Everson was not only aware of George Müller's orphanage but had been a frequent contributor. He had been overjoyed to learn of Henry's fiancée's connection to the orphanage. He told them, *"I discovered that the more money I gave to Müller, the more my business prospered. I went to hear him speak and heard his message of God's love and forgiveness. All powerful lessons that I continue to benefit from today."*

Mariana, now Mr. Everson's wife, had pretended to roll her eyes at this blatant sentimentality, but Cara could tell she was touched by it as well. They were a happy couple, if wildly different from one another.

There were still challenges to face, but the situation was not as precarious as it had once been. One contributing factor was Langham himself. His showing at the Grosvenor Gallery had been a modest success, and his reputation was growing. He'd sold several paintings and been commissioned for more.

Langham had also accepted an invitation to join the board of the international shipping company run by Mr. Kinnard. Impressed by the new, positive trajectory of Langham's life, Mr. Kinnard had at last consented to become his future father-in-law. The directorship, plus the generous dowry Louise would bring with her, would keep the pair solidly afloat and enable Langham to keep painting.

Off in the distance, Henry and Amelia reached the stable yard and disappeared from sight. This only heightened Cara's anticipation. Soon the house would be filled with people. Julia and Rosalyn and their husbands were due to arrive from the railway station at any minute. Jacob Reese and his wife were coming as well. Langham and Louise were already here, along with the Eversons, who were acting as Louise's chaperones.

The only people who had not accepted Cara's invitation were Lord Nigel Hayward and Sarah, who was now his wife. Cara felt a touch of sadness as she thought about them. Henry had done his best to try to mend the situation. He'd made overtures toward them and the Needenhams, but it was going to be difficult to win their trust and friendship—if it could be done at all. God was abundant in mercy, but people's forgiveness was often harder to obtain. Henry had reminded her that this problem was in God's hands. She would keep praying that the answer would come in its proper time.

There was plenty of room for everyone, now that the east wing was complete and the family had taken up residence there. Cara had spent the last two months overseeing the redecorating of the west wing, to be used primarily by guests. She wanted the rooms to offer beauty and comfort, so that all who stayed in them would feel welcome. Morestowe Manor was impressive, but in Cara's heart, the most important thing was that it be a home.

Once everyone had gathered, Cara was going to unveil a secret that she hoped would please everyone—even, and perhaps especially, the dowager countess. It was a painting of Amelia, Henry, and Lady Morestowe. She had finally put on canvas the idea she'd first had all those months ago after Amelia's riding lesson, when the three of them had looked so happy together. That image had never left Cara's mind.

The dowager countess had eventually resigned herself to having an unconventional daughter-in-law, but her interactions with Cara were still cool. The thawing process was ongoing, and one that Cara advanced any way she could. Lady Morestowe's manner did seem to be growing less abrasive. Perhaps Langham's successes, as well as Henry's, had begun to assuage her fears and would one day allow her to fully embrace Cara as a member of the family.

Only Henry and Langham knew about the painting. Both had seen it and praised it heartily. Cara had wanted their approval before showing it publicly. Since the relationship between her and the countess was not yet on solid ground, Cara did not want to risk setting back her efforts by offending her mother-in-law.

Both brothers had agreed the portrait was flattering to all, especially to the dowager countess. Cara's goal had been to capture the beauty she'd seen in her face at that moment: an image of the woman's younger self. Her bright expression had melted the years from her face, and Cara had seen the positive aspect of her pride as a reflection of inner strength. To a lesser extent, Cara hoped she'd captured that same quality in Amelia. The two were very much alike, though Amelia was not a Burke by bloodline. Cara hoped she might get them to see what they had in common, and to build on it.

"The painting is aspirational," Henry had said. "It shows the three of us enjoying one another's company and celebrating our victories together. It looks so appealing that we'll all naturally strive for more of the same."

Langham's appraisal had been more succinct: "The old lady can't help but be pleased despite herself!"

Cara fervently hoped they were right. What if her mother-in-law hated it? Perhaps it wasn't wise to present it in such a public setting after all. It was possible Henry and Langham could have misjudged her reaction.

There wasn't time to brood over it, however. Soon everyone would gather, and she would have to follow through with her plan.

Henry and Amelia approached, walking together across the lawn. They both had mud spattered on their clothes and boots, as the woods had not yet dried out from a recent rain.

Seeing Papa seated next to Cara, Amelia broke into a run, not stopping until she had reached him and submitted to his hug. She said cheerfully, "Are we going to play checkers this afternoon, Abuelo?"

"That depends on what Miss Leahy has planned for you."

Amelia looked around, then smiled when she saw the governess was not present. "She won't mind a game or two."

"You need to get cleaned up and change your clothes," Cara said. "You're having tea with the grown-ups today, remember?"

Amelia made a face. "Do I have to?"

"I promise you'll find it interesting." Cara didn't offer further explanation, as she wanted the painting to be a surprise for Amelia, too.

Amelia heaved a sigh. "All right."

"You need to change, too," Cara said to Henry.

"Yes, my love," he said meekly, but not before pulling her close and planting a fervent kiss on her cheek. He was dirty and sunbrowned and looked immensely happy. She stepped back, but only because his nearness made her pulse race, and she was aware that Amelia was watching them, as she always did, with alert curiosity.

"Go on, then," she ordered. Henry answered her attempt at severity with a wink.

The next few hours passed in a flurry of activity as the guests arrived and Cara oversaw countless hostess tasks. The new arrivals settled into their rooms and eventually began filtering back down to the terrace. Cara was glad when, in the midst of everything, she was able to pull Julia aside.

"Were you able to get to the sanitarium?" Cara asked.

"Yes. Last week." Julia had taken an interest in Delia's illness and had gone to see her several times. "They are doing all they can for her. I wish we had a cure, but that is some time in the future. Delia is weak but cognizant of all that is going on. She asked me to send her thanks to you and Henry. She is happy and relieved to know you are keeping Amelia. I think she feels terrible for what she did and guilty for not being a good mother."

"Amelia will always have a home with us. I don't think my love for her could be any greater."

Julia nodded. "I can see that whenever you are with her." She touched her chin thoughtfully. "It reminds me of a verse in Psalms that says, 'God setteth the solitary in families.'"

"You have a Scripture for every occasion," Cara teased. "But who knows better than we do the pain of being without parents?"

"Cara, we've had our disagreements over the years, but I'm glad you were right about Papa."

"And I'm grateful you found him."

They looked at one another, relishing the new understanding they'd gained that bridged all past differences.

It was a lovely moment, if quickly interrupted by Langham coming to inform them that everyone was on the terrace, famished and ready for tea.

Cara's thoughts returned to that conversation several times during the meal. She watched Amelia interact with Henry and Papa and felt deeply grateful that she'd been able to help this child. She believed God had allowed these good things to show Cara she was forgiven for her mistake with Robbie and released from her vow never to oversee children again.

She was glad Jacob was here, along with his wife and son. Jacob had once exhorted her to seek out God's plan for her life. On her wedding day, Jacob had told her with tears in his eyes that no one could be as happy as he was that she had found it.

As tea was nearly finished, Henry stood. "Your attention, please, everyone. I believe my wife has a few announcements."

"Hear, hear!" Langham said merrily.

Henry helped Cara rise from her chair, presenting her with a flourish. "Ladies and gentlemen, Lady Morestowe."

A delightful sensation went through Cara whenever someone referred to her by her title. She was Lady Morestowe! It made her proud, and yet it was humbling, too, when she thought of how far she'd come. She looked at the many faces smiling up at her. Even her mother-in-law was doing her best to appear at ease, although there was no one here except her sons whom she might once have considered worthy of her company.

"Today we celebrate a number of happy milestones," Cara said. "The first is Langham's recent success during the spring show at the Royal Academy." She picked up a newspaper. "If I may quote one eminent art critic: 'We see in Mr. Burke's work great promise. His paintings exhibit a compelling blend of artistic influences, which he uses to create a signature style. The finely rendered details in every painting have the breath of life in them.'"

"Bravo!" Louise enthused as Langham puffed out his chest. Together, the group lifted glasses of lemonade to toast Langham.

Cara set the paper aside and extended a hand toward Julia to draw everyone's attention to her. "Another happy milestone I would like to acknowledge is Julia's successful completion of her first year at the London School of Medicine for Women. She has passed every course with honors."

This brought a round of applause, which Julia acknowledged with an appreciative smile.

"Does this mean she might get her nose out of her books—at least until classes resume in October?" Papa said, sending a wink her way.

"I hope so," Michael replied with a laugh. "Sometimes I lose her for hours at a time."

Julia had the grace to look abashed. She laid a hand on her husband's arm. "But I always make it up to you later."

A spark of love passed between them. It made Cara happy every time she saw it. Julia, who had once been determined to remain a spinster, was now happily married. She was also fulfilling her calling to the medical profession. Best of all from Cara's point of view, Julia would remain in England. Cara marveled at how wonderfully God had answered each of their prayers.

Cara cleared her throat. "I have one more piece of good news to share, and I have Rosalyn's permission to do it." She looked at her oldest sister, whose face was aglow with joy. Rosalyn glanced at Nate, who sat next to her. He wore a smile of immense satisfaction.

"As you all know," Cara began, "Rosalyn is in the chorus of the current production of *Patience* at the Savoy Theatre. However, in November she will take on a new role. It won't be on the stage. I cannot wait to meet my future niece or nephew."

This brought on a bigger round of applause, and much backslapping for Nate.

Papa looked overcome. "My beautiful daughters," he murmured, smiling through tears. He pulled out a handkerchief and blew his nose.

"And now for your news, my love," Henry prompted.

Now that the moment was here, Cara found herself tongue-tied. She could see Jensen waiting at the door for her signal to bring out the painting. Everyone looked expectantly at her, clearly wondering what was coming next.

"Perhaps I might say something," Henry offered. "I would like to reiterate how honored we are to have you all here as our guests." He waved an arm to indicate Morestowe Manor. "This place has seen a lot of changes over the past year and a half, as you all know. There were not only the structural alterations but refurbishments for the interior as well. Those changes would not have been accomplished half so well without my lovely wife. Her talent for decorating, as well as her love for this house, have made this place what it is today. A home for our family."

He laid a gentle hand on Amelia's shoulder, and she beamed up at him.

"Cara's artistic talents are not to be overlooked, either," he continued. "Today, we unveil the newest addition to our vast collection of family portraits."

He gave a nod to Jensen. The butler brought out the easel the painting was set on, covered with a cloth.

This was the moment Cara had been waiting for—in all its thrilling and yet terrifying glory. Now she understood the nervousness that had nearly overwhelmed Langham before his first public showing last fall.

Henry unveiled the painting. There was a moment of silence, and then a collective gasp of delight.

Cara watched the countess, hoping to discern her thoughts. She forgot about Amelia until the girl jumped up from her chair and rushed to the painting for a better look.

"Ooh, it's so pretty!" Amelia exclaimed. She turned an excited gaze toward Henry. "Look! It's Maisie!"

"There are people in that picture, too," Henry pointed out. "What do you think?"

Amelia took a few moments to scrutinize the painting. Her mouth dropped open. "Countess is smiling." She sounded surprised, as though she'd never seen that expression on the dowager's face before.

Cara braced for an onslaught, expecting Lady Morestowe to reprimand the girl. But she said nothing, only continued to stare at the painting, her expression inscrutable.

"Well, Mother, what do you think?" Henry asked.

After what seemed an eternity, Cara thought she detected a hint of approval on the countess's face, even if it seemed contradicted by her words. "My riding habit isn't quite that shade of blue."

"She loves it!" Langham exclaimed. "Send a telegraph to *The Times* right away!"

Everyone laughed. Even the dowager countess. They all rose from the table to gather around the painting, admiring it. Cara hung back, reveling not in their praise but simply in the happiness of having them all here.

Henry put his arm through hers. "What are you thinking, my love?"

"Your mother has a surprisingly pleasant laugh."

He grinned. "Somehow, I think we'll be hearing more of it in the future."

Langham called over to them, "We shall have to figure out how to paint a family portrait that has you in it as well."

"I'd like that," Cara said.

Henry smiled. "Perhaps we might leave Maisie out of the next portrait, though."

Amelia looked at him aghast, her hands on her hips. "What?"

"Perhaps I'll paint one that has just the two of you together," Cara offered, whereupon the child shouted with glee.

God setteth the solitary in families. It was such an apt verse. God surely had brought them all together. They had formed a family from the bonds that mattered most—those of the heart.

Author's Note

*T*HE *ARTFUL MATCH* presents a glimpse into the world of Victorian artists. As mentioned in the book, it was a highly productive time and a boon for artists. Many enjoyed both critical and financial success. Much of their art has withstood the test of time.

The Aesthetic Movement was highly popular for a time, influencing paintings, poetry, and dress. It was also a lot of fun to poke fun at. Many cartoons of the day, as well as the enduring Gilbert and Sullivan operetta *Patience*, did just that.

Some of the characters in this book, such as Lady Blanche Lindsay, Arthur Hughes, and a few other artists mentioned in passing, were real people. Other characters, such as Adrian and to a lesser extent Georgiana and Langham, were based on real artists and events in their lives that I came across in the course of my research.

Economic factors that were the basis for Henry's financial challenges were very real, too. By the late nineteenth century, many big landowners were grappling with the increasing need to find other means of generating wealth besides land rents. For the most part, those who were able to diversify into other forms of income thrived, while those who were less successful eventually became part of a growing impoverished aristocracy.

Another phenomenon of the late nineteenth and early twentieth centuries was the influx of rich American heiresses who came to England to exchange a big dowry for a title, bolstering those aristocrats whose fortunes were ailing. I found an interesting book on this subject by Gail MacColl and Carol McD. Wallace called *To Marry an English Lord*.

The dinosaur park at the Crystal Palace was set up in the 1850s. Although the Crystal Palace burned down in 1936, the dinosaur statues are still on display in the same park today. These representations of prehistoric creatures are not considered accurate by modern paleontologists, but they are still fascinating and fun to visit. It was, in a sense, the first theme park.

George Müller's famous orphanage, where Cara was raised, was a vivid testament to the power of prayer and God's loving provision for His people. This background informs Cara's thinking and many of her actions. If you are not familiar with Müller's story, I recommend the book *Delighted in God!* by Roger Steer.

I hope you've enjoyed the sojourn into Victorian London provided in the LONDON BEGINNINGS series.

Acknowledgments

MANY THANKS to Maud Eno for always being willing to answer my questions about horses, and for the many entertaining horse stories and insights, some of which made it into this book.

Heartfelt thanks to Lori Hayes for providing input on the horseback riding scenes, and most especially for your generous moral support as a fellow author. You inspired me to keep writing when I was sure the well was dry.

Big, big thanks to Elaine Klonicki, beta reader extraordinaire. Your insights for this book were, as always, spot-on and invaluable.

Special thanks to my fantastic and long-suffering editor, Jessica Barnes, who has made my books so much better. My thanks also to David Long, Noelle Chew, and Amy Green. It's wonderful to work with all of you!

Endless thanks and love to my husband, Jim, for constant support and encouragement and for all the ways, large and small, that you've supported my writing. I am truly blessed.

Jennifer Delamere writes tales of the past . . . and new beginnings. Her novels set in Victorian England have won numerous accolades, including a starred review from *Publishers Weekly* and a nomination for the Romance Writers of America's RITA Award. Jennifer holds a BA in English from McGill University in Montreal, Canada, and has been an editor of educational materials for two decades. She loves reading classics and histories, which she mines for vivid details that bring to life the people and places in her books. Jennifer lives in North Carolina with her husband, and when not writing, she is usually scouting out good day hikes or planning their next travel adventure. Learn more at jenniferdelamere.com.

You May Also Like . . .

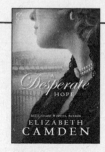

A female accountant in 1908, Eloise Drake thought she'd put her past behind her. Then her new job lands her in the path of the man who broke her heart. Alex Duval, mayor of a doomed town, can't believe his eyes when he sees Eloise as part of the entourage that's come to wipe his town off the map. Can he convince her to help him—and give him another chance?

A Desperate Hope by Elizabeth Camden
elizabethcamden.com

In 1900s Montana, Lizzy Brookstone's role as star of an all-female Wild West show is rewarding but difficult. However, trials of the heart and a mystery to be solved prove more daunting. As Lizzy and her two friends, runaway Ella and sharpshooter Mary, try to discover how Mary's brother died, all three seek freedom in a world run by men.

When You Are Near by Tracie Peterson
Brookstone Brides #1
traciepeterson.com

Ⓑ BethanyHouse

More Captivating Historical Fiction from Bethany House Publishers!

Englishwoman Verity Banning decides to start a business importing horses and other goods the residents of the West Indies need. This trade brings her to New York, where she meets revolutionary Ian McKintrick. As a friend to many Loyalists, Verity has always favored a peaceful resolution. But when a Patriot lays claim to her heart, she'll have to decide for what—and whom—she will fight.

Verity by Lisa T. Bergren, THE SUGAR BARON'S DAUGHTER #2
lisatbergren.com

With a Mohawk mother and a French father in 1759 Montreal, Catherine Duval finds it easiest to remain neutral among warring sides. But when her British ex-fiancé, Samuel, is taken prisoner by her father, he claims to have information that could end the war. At last, she must choose whom to fight for. Is she willing to commit treason for the greater good?

Between Two Shores by Jocelyn Green
jocelyngreen.com

Daphne Blakemoor was happy living in seclusion. But when ownership of the estate where she works passes to William, Marquis of Chemsford, her quiet life is threatened. William also seeks a refuge from his past, but when an undeniable family connection is revealed, can they find the courage to face their deepest wounds and forge a new path for the future?

Return of Devotion by Kristi Ann Hunter, HAVEN MANOR #2
kristiannhunter.com

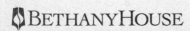
BETHANYHOUSE